OPUS 300

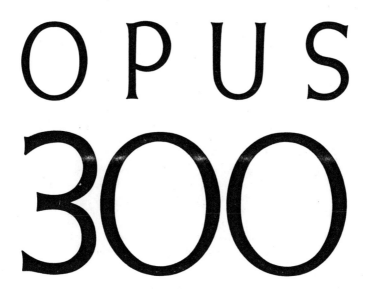

O P U S
300

ISAAC
ASIMOV

HOUGHTON MIFFLIN
COMPANY, BOSTON
1984

Library of Congress Cataloging in Publication Data

Asimov, Isaac, date
Opus 300.

I. Title.   II. Title: Opus three hundred.
PS3551.S5066   1984   813'.54   84-10753
ISBN 0-395-36108-7

Printed in the United States of America

S   10 9 8 7 6 5 4 3 2 1

The author wishes to thank the following for permission to quote selections from the works listed:

Edward Arnold (Australia) Pty Ltd: *A Grossery of Limericks.* Copyright © 1981 by Isaac Asimov and John Ciardi.

Crown Publishers Inc.: *The Annotated® Gulliver's Travels.* Copyright © 1980 by Isaac Asimov. *Extraterrestrial Civilizations.* Copyright © 1979 by Isaac Asimov. *Exploring the Earth and the Cosmos.* Copyright © 1982 by Nightfall, Inc. *In the Beginning.* Copyright © 1981 by Isaac Asimov.

Red Dembner Enterprises Corp.: *Isaac Asimov's Book of Facts.* Copyright © 1979 by Red Dembner Enterprises Corp. *Isaac Asimov Presents Superquiz II; The Fun Game of Q & A's* by Ken Fisher, published by Dembner Books, New York, 1983. Reprinted by permission of Red Dembner Enterprises Corp.

Doubleday & Company, Inc.: Excerpt from *Foundation's Edge* by Isaac Asimov, copyright © 1982 by Nightfall, Inc. Excerpt from *The Robots of Dawn* by Isaac Asimov, copyright © 1983 by Nightfall, Inc. "The Boom in Science Fiction" by Isaac Asimov, copyright © 1979 by Davis Publications, Inc., and "The Ring of Evil" by Isaac Asimov, copyright © 1980 by Triangle Communications, Inc., from *Asimov on Science Fiction;*

To Robyn

My beautiful, blond-haired, blue-eyed daughter

CONTENTS

INTRODUCTION

LET ME CALL YOUR ATTENTION to some dates.

My *Pebble in the Sky* (Book 1) was published in January 1950 by Doubleday and Company. *Opus 100* (Book 100) was published in October 1969 by Houghton Mifflin Company. *Opus 200* (Book 200) was published in March 1979 by Houghton Mifflin Company. *Opus 300* (Book 300) was published in December 1984 by Houghton Mifflin Company.

It follows that my first hundred books took me 237 months; my second hundred books took me 113 months; and my third hundred books took me 69 months.

This makes it look as though I am rapidly speeding up as I approach early middle age and that pretty soon I will be turning out a hundred books in one month and then in one day and then —

No danger. As it happens, the 69 months it took me to write my third hundred books are the result of special circumstances, which will take a bit of explanation —

One of the characteristics of the science fiction field (of which I am told I am one of the top-ranking luminaries) is the extreme richness of its anthology content.

This arises from the fact that science fiction readers have an inordinate appetite for short stories and that very few of them have been able to read all the issues of all the science fiction magazines that have been published in the last sixty years. Even if a given reader has consumed a goodly number of such issues he or she usually does not save very many, either because of lack of desire or lack of room.

After a while, readers hear descriptions of glorious stories they have missed, or remember (with nostalgia) the glorious stories they have read but no longer possess, and begin to long for a chance to relive the past. When, therefore, an anthology of science fiction short stories offers them a second chance, many fans line up to buy it. Various publishers therefore came to view such anthologies as potentially profitable ventures and, beginning in the late 1940s, anthologies began to appear — first in ones and twos, then by the dozen, and finally by the hundreds.

Naturally, an anthology is most acceptable to publishers (and to readers, I presume) when a well-known science fiction personality does the editing. His (or her) name on the cover attracts readers. And since the editor collects a portion of the earnings for himself, a large number of successful science fiction writers have, at one time or another, edited science fiction anthologies.

I have not been entirely immune to the virus, but I have certainly been resistant. The reason is that in order to turn out a good science fiction anthology, you have to read through a great many stories, choose those you think should be included in the anthology for one reason or another (quality, theme, length), obtain permissions by dealing with sometimes unreasonable authors or agents, obtain a contract from sometimes unreasonable publishers, do the bookkeeping for any money that may come in and that then must go out in appropriate shares to the various contributors, and so on.

This means *work*. It is not as much work as writing a whole book yourself, but for me writing a book is fun, and doing the kind of work involved in putting together an anthology is *not* fun. The result is that I edited few anthologies. In my first hundred books, there were three, and in my second hundred six.

At first, there was considerable uncertainty on my part as to whether I ought to count those anthologies I edited among my books, placing them on my list with an official "number" for each. After all, the major portion of these items consisted of the writings of others. To be sure, I wrote introductions, made choices, and (most important of all) spent time and labor on them, and those were legitimate points in my favor. Besides, there were so few anthologies at first that it didn't seem to matter much one way or the other, so I gave myself the benefit of the doubt and included them among my books.

By the time I passed the hundred mark in books, however, the whole question was taken out of my hands. There seemed to have grown a general proprietary interest in my prolificity. The one question everyone asked when they met me was, "How many is it now, Isaac?" If one person met me on January 15, and again on February 15, and found that the number had not increased in the interval, he felt cheated. The comment on the later occasion (this is true and I'm *not* making it up) is quite likely to be, "But that's what you told me the last time. What's wrong with you?"

In compiling the list of my second hundred books, therefore, I counted the anthologies without a qualm. It was expected of me, and besides, there were still so few that it didn't really matter.

But then, toward the end of my second hundred books, there came a turning point. I encountered Martin Harry Greenberg, and between us there grew, with remarkable rapidity, a close and affectionate friendship.

Marty, born in Florida, was a professor of political science at Florida International University when we first met through the mails (though he has since returned to Green Bay, Wisconsin, where his lovely wife, Sally, has her roots, and now teaches at the University of Wisconsin, Green Bay). A political scientist Marty may be, but his great love is science fiction. He is twenty years younger than I (also distinctly taller and entirely unspectacled) but he has read far more in the field than I. He produced some scholarly collections of science fiction and caught the anthology bug.

When Marty first got in touch with me for permission to use one of my stories in an anthology, I hesitated. I had once dealt with a Martin Greenberg in the early 1950s, and I wondered if this was the same person.

It wasn't! Marty was Martin *Harry* Greenberg, as he made clear, and I advised him to use his middle name, or initial, on any science fiction book with which he was connected in order to avoid confusion. He has done so, and I routinely address him as "Marty the Other" in our correspondence.

It is very easy to like Marty a *lot* and, as it happens, he has a personality that is like and unlike my own in just the right way. Like me, he is a meticulous hard worker who suffers when he is away from his desk. He is also an absolute straight arrow in everything that has to do with his work, financially and otherwise, so that I can rely on him *completely*.

The unlikeness is even more important. Marty loves and thrives on the task of obtaining and photocopying stories, writing for permissions, taking care of the bookkeeping, and involving himself in all the deadly minutiae that are involved in doing an anthology.

When I work with him, all I need to do is discuss with him the nature of the anthology and the type of stories to be included, then read over the stories he gathers and sends me, make the final decision on which are to be included, write the introductions and, on occasion, headnotes, and (since I live in Manhattan) trot around to the publishers with the finished manuscript or the completed contracts. A third coeditor often works with Marty and me, and in that case Marty takes care of coordinating all our labors.

My first collaboration with Marty was *One Hundred Great Science Fiction Short-Short Stories* (Book 192), which was published by Doubleday in 1978. (In this case the third coeditor was Joseph D. Olander, a fellow faculty member of Marty's at Florida International.) It began years of association between Marty and me, during which there has never once been the tiniest hint of unpleasantness.

As a result, my third hundred books include no fewer than fifty-four anthologies, almost all with Marty.

Once I began to realize, as year after year passed, that half my output was coming to consist of anthologies, I began to worry again. Was it *still* fair to count them in my list of books? Was I giving an impression of prolificity that was not entirely warranted?

I hesitated for a long time, and this is how I resolved the argument with myself.

1. People still expect prolificity of me and are annoyed if I fail them.

2. Each anthology continues to take a substantial amount of my time, effort, and expertise; enough time, all told, to cut down to a substantial extent the number of ordinary books I can produce. Therefore, if I don't count the anthologies, I would, in a sense, be penalizing myself into seeming less prolific than I am.

In the end, then, I finally decided to include the anthologies on the list of my books, but let me make it plain that such inclusions are not wholesale. Some anthologies appear with my name on them (collections of stories from my magazine, for instance), in connection with which I do not do a thing, and such anthologies are not (repeat, *not*) included in my list. At times, too, publishers put out combined volumes of books of mine, under new titles, toward which I contribute nothing new. Those are also *not* included. Every book that I *do* include on the list is one of which I am either the author or the editor, to which I have contributed significantly in time and work, and in which at least some writing of mine, done specifically for the book, is included.

What is more, in the full listing of my books in the appendix and on the back of the jacket, I indicate with asterisks those that are anthologies, so that I will not in any way sail under false colors.

PART 1

ASTRONOMY

IN THIS BOOK, I follow (as far as is possible) the order of subject matter found in Opus 100 and Opus 200. That means I start with "Astronomy," as I did in the earlier books.

In the third hundred books, the first to deal with astronomy was Extraterrestrial Civilizations (Book 203), which was published by Crown Publishers, Inc., in 1979. It was my first book with Crown, and thereby hangs a tale.

Paul Nadan, whom I had met at some gathering, was an editor at Crown. We grew quite friendly (I grow friendly easily and so, apparently, does everyone I meet), and Paul set about to persuade me to write a book for him. I was willing, of course, for I would like (if it were possible) to write all the books there are for all the publishers there are. Unfortunately, there was no use promising what I could not deliver, and it seemed I was too tied down at that time to oblige Paul.

Eventually, though, Paul suggested a book on extraterrestrial civilizations, and I was intrigued. It was something I wanted to do, and something which did not interfere at all with anything I had promised to anyone else. I said, however, that I could not give him a reasonable date of delivery.

Paul decided that didn't matter. He had a contract prepared that set no date of delivery and, at my insistence, arranged that I was not to be paid an advance until I notified Crown, in writing, that I had begun work.

That was 1974, I believe. I signed the contract, and it lay in a drawer gathering dust. Every once in a long while, Paul called to check the situation, and I was endlessly apologetic — but didn't start. Finally, in early 1978, I could bear it no longer. I promised Paul that as soon as I was finished with the book that was then occupying me, I would begin the book for him. He was delighted — but within a month, he died of a heart attack.

I was bitterly conscience-stricken. Now that it was too late, I started the book at once, dedicating it: "To the memory of Paul

Nadan (1929–1978), for whom I should have started the book sooner."

From that book I present Chapter 2 in its entirety, partly because I found it particularly interesting to write and partly because it is a complete story in itself.

from EXTRATERRESTRIAL CIVILIZATIONS (1979)

The Moon

PHASES

If we imagine ourselves looking about at our surroundings with no knowledge concerning them at all, we might be forgiven for thinking the Earth was the only world there was. What, then, made people think there were other worlds?

It was the Moon. Consider:

The predominant characteristic of the objects in the sky is their glow. The stars are little bits of sparkling light. The planets are somewhat brighter bits of sparkling light. The Sun is a round circle of blazing light. There is an occasional meteor that produces a brief line of light. There is an even more occasional comet that is an irregular hazy patch of light.

It is the light that makes the heavenly objects seem altogether different from the Earth, which in itself is dark and gives off no light.

To be sure, light can be produced on the Earth in the form of fire, but that is altogether different from the heavenly light. Earthly fires have to be fed constantly with fuel or they would flicker and go out, but the heavenly light continues forever without change.

In fact, the Greek philosopher Aristotle (384–322 B.C.) maintained that all the heavenly objects were composed of a substance called aether, separate and distinct from the elements that made up the Earth. The word "aether" is from the Greek word meaning "to blaze." The heavenly objects blazed and the Earth did not, and as long as that was thought to be true there was only one world;

one solid, dark object on which life could exist, and many blazing objects on which life could not exist.

Except that there is the Moon. The Moon is the one heavenly object that changes shape in a regular way and in a fashion that is clearly visible to the unaided eye. These different shapes of the Moon (its "phases") are ideally suited to attract attention and, except for the succession of day and night, were probably the first astronomical changes to catch the attention of primitive human beings.

The Moon goes through its complete cycle of phases in a little over twenty-nine days, which is a particularly convenient length of time. To the prehistoric farmer and hunter, the cycle of seasons (the year) was very important, but it was difficult to note that, on the average, the seasons repeated themselves every 365 or 366 days. The number was too large to be kept track of easily. To count 29 or 30 days from each new Moon to the next, and then to count 12 or 13 new Moons to each year, was much simpler and much more practical. The making of a calendar that would serve to keep track of the seasons of the year in terms of the phases of the Moon was a natural result of very early astronomical observations.

Alexander Marshak, in his book *The Roots of Civilization,* published in 1972, argues persuasively that long before the beginning of recorded history, early human beings were marking stones in a code designed to keep track of the new Moons. Gerald Hawkins, in *Stonehenge Decoded,* argues just as persuasively that Stonehenge was a prehistoric observatory also designed to keep track of the new Moon, and to predict the lunar eclipses that occasionally came at the time of the full Moon. (A lunar eclipse was a frightening "death" of the Moon upon which human beings depended for keeping track of the seasons. To be able to predict its occurrence reduced the fear.)

It was very likely the overriding practical necessity of working out a calendar based on the phases of the Moon that forced human beings into astronomy, and from that to a careful observation of natural phenomena generally, and from that to the eventual growth of science.

The fact that the phase changes were so useful could not help, it seems to me, but reinforce the notion of the existence of a benevolent deity who, out of His love of humanity, had arranged the

skies into a calendar that would guide mankind into the proper
ways of ensuring a secure food supply.

Each new Moon was celebrated as a religious festival in many
early cultures, and the care of the calendar was usually placed in
priestly hands. The very word "calendar" is from the Latin word
meaning "to proclaim," since each month only began when the
coming of the new Moon was officially proclaimed by the priests.
We could conclude, then, that a considerable portion of the religious development of mankind, of the belief in God as a benevolent parent rather than a capricious tyrant, can be traced back to
the changing face of the Moon.

In addition, the fact that close study of the Moon was so important in controlling the daily lives of human beings could not help
but give rise to the notion that the other heavenly objects might
be important in this respect, also. The face of the Moon may in
this way have contributed to the growth of astrology and, thereby,
of other forms of mysticism.

But in addition to all this (and it would scarcely seem that if the
Moon has given rise to science, religion, and mysticism, more
should be required of it) the Moon gave rise to the concept of the
plurality of worlds — the notion that the Earth was only one world
of many.

When human beings first stared at the Moon from night to night
in order to follow its phases, it was natural to suppose that the
Moon literally changed shape. It was born as a thin crescent,
waxed to a full circle of light, then waned to a crescent and died.
Each new Moon was literally a *new* Moon, a fresh creation.

Quite early on, however, it became apparent that the horns of
the lunar crescent *always* faced away from the Sun. That alone was
sufficient to indicate some connection between the Sun's and
Moon's phases. Once the notion of that connection arose, further
observation would show that the phases were connected with the
relative positions of the Sun and Moon. The Moon was full when
it and the Sun were at precisely opposite parts of the sky. The
Moon was in the half-phase when it and the Sun were separated
by ninety degrees. The Moon was in crescent shape when it was
close to the Sun, and so on.

It became apparent that if the Moon were a sphere that was as
dark as the Earth, and if the Moon shone only by the light that fell
upon it from the Sun and was reflected by it, then it would go

through precisely the cycle of phases that were actually observed. The idea arose and grew to be more and more accepted that the Moon, at least, was a dark body like Earth and was not composed of blazing "aether."

ANOTHER WORLD

If the Moon were like the Earth in being dark, might it not be like the Earth in other ways? Might it not be a second world?

As early as the fifth century B.C., the Greek philosopher Anaxagoras (500–428 B.C.) expressed his opinion that the Moon was an Earth-like world.

To imagine the Universe as consisting of one world plus bits of light is intellectually acceptable. To imagine it to consist of two worlds plus bits of light is difficult. If one of the objects in the sky is a world, why not some or all the rest? Gradually, the notion of the plurality of worlds spread. Increasing numbers of people began to think of the Universe as containing many worlds.

But not *empty* worlds. That thought apparently filled people with revulsion — if it occurred to them at all.

The one world we knew — Earth — is full of life, and it is only natural to think that life is as inevitable a characteristic of worlds generally as solidity is. Again, if one thinks of the Earth as having been created by some deity or deities, then it is logical to suppose the other worlds to have been so created as well. It would then seem nonsensical to suppose that any world would be created and left empty. What motivation could there be in creating empty worlds? What a waste it would be!

Thus, when Anaxagoras stated his belief that the Moon was an Earth-like world, he also suggested that it might be inhabited. So did other ancient thinkers, as for instance the Greek biographer Plutarch (A.D. 46–120).

Then again, if a world is inhabited, it seems natural to suppose it to be inhabited by intelligent creatures — usually pictured as very much like human beings. To suppose a world to be inhabited only by unreasoning plants and animals would, again, seem to represent an intolerable waste.

Oddly enough, there was talk of life on the Moon even before the Moon was recognized as a world. This arose out of the fact that the Moon is again unique among heavenly bodies in not being evenly shining. There are darker smudges against the bright light of the Moon, smudges that are most clearly and dramatically visible at the time of the full Moon.

It was tempting for the average unsophisticated observer of the Moon to try to make a picture out of the smudges upon its face. (In fact, even the sophisticated and knowledgeable present-day observer may be tempted to do so.)

Given the natural anthropocentricity of human beings, it was almost inevitable that those smudges were pictured as representing a human being, and the notion of the "man in the Moon" arose.

Undoubtedly the original notion was prehistoric. In medieval times, however, attempts were often made to clothe age-old notions with a cloak of biblical respectability. Therefore, the man in the Moon was thought to represent the man mentioned in Numbers 15:32–36: "And while the children of Israel were in the wilderness they found a man that gathered sticks upon the sabbath day . . . And the Lord said unto Moses, the man shall be surely put to death . . . And all the congregation brought him without the camp, and stoned him with stones, and he died."

There is no mention of the Moon in the biblical story, but it was easy to add the tale that when the man protested that he did not want to keep "Sunday" on Earth (although to the Israelites, sabbath fell on the day we call Saturday), the judges said, "Then you shall keep an eternal Monday [Moon-day] in heaven."

The man in the Moon was pictured in medieval times as bearing a thornbush, representing the sticks he had gathered; and a lantern, for he was supposed to have been gathering them at night when he hoped no one would see; and, for some reason, a dog. The man in the Moon, with these appurtenances, is part of the play within a play presented by Bottom and the other rustics in William Shakespeare's *A Midsummer Night's Dream.*

Of course, the man in the Moon was visualized as filling his entire world, since the smudges seemed smeared over the entire face of the Moon, and since the Moon appears to be a small object.

It was the Greek astronomer Hipparchus (190–120 B.C.) who first managed to work out the size of the Moon relative to the Earth by valid mathematical methods and who got essentially the right answer. The Moon is an object about one-quarter the diameter of the Earth. It was no man-in-the-Moon-sized object. It was a world not only in the dark nature of the material making it up, but in its size.

What's more, Hipparchus had worked out the distance to the Moon. It is sixty times as far from the surface of the Earth to the Moon as from the surface of the Earth to the center of the Earth.

In modern terms, the Moon is 381,000 kilometers (237,000 miles) from Earth and has a diameter of 2470 kilometers (2160 miles).

The Greeks already knew that the Moon was the nearest of the heavenly bodies and that the other objects were all much farther away. To be so much farther away and to be visible at all, they must all be worlds in size.

The notion of the plurality of worlds descended from the rarefied heights of philosophic speculation to the literary level with the first account we know of that reads like modern science fiction stories involving interplanetary travel.

About A.D. 165, a Greek writer named Lucian of Samosata wrote *A True History*, an account of a trip to the Moon. In that book, the hero is carried to the Moon by a whirlwind. He finds the Moon luminous and shining, and in the distance he can see other luminous worlds. Down below, he sees a world that is clearly his own world, the Earth.

Lucian's universe was behind the scientific knowledge of his own time, since he had the Moon glowing and he had the heavenly bodies all close together. Lucian also assumed that air filled all of space and that "up" and "down" were the same everywhere. There was no reason as yet to think that that was not so.

Every world in Lucian's universe was inhabited, and he assumed the presence of extraterrestrial intelligence everywhere. The king of the Moon was Endymion, and he was at war with the king of the Sun, Phaethon. (These names were taken out of the Greek myths, where Endymion was a youth beloved by the Moon goddess, and Phaethon was the son of the Sun god.) The Moon beings and Sun beings were quite human in appearance, in institutions, and even in their follies, for Endymion and Phaethon were at war with each other, disputing the colonization of Jupiter.

It was not for nearly thirteen hundred years, however, that a major writer dealt with the Moon again. This came in 1532 in *Orlando Furioso*, an epic poem written by the Italian poet Ludovico

Ariosto (1474–1533). In it, one of the characters travels to the Moon in the divine chariot that carried the prophet Elijah in a whirlwind to heaven. He finds the Moon well populated by civilized people.

The notion of a plurality of worlds received still another push forward with the invention of the telescope. In 1609 the Italian scientist Galileo Galilei (1564–1642) constructed a telescope and pointed it at the Moon. For the first time in history, the Moon was seen magnified, and more clearly detailed than was possible with the unaided eye.

Galileo saw mountain ranges on the Moon, together with what looked like volcanic craters. He saw dark, smooth patches that looked like seas. Quite plainly and simply, he was seeing another world.

This stimulated the further production of fictional flights to the Moon. The first was written by Johannes Kepler (1571–1630), an astronomer of the first rank, and was published posthumously in 1633. It was entitled *Somnium* because the hero reached the Moon in a dream.*

The book was remarkable in that it was the first to take into account the actual known facts about the Moon, which until then had been treated as in no way different from any earthly piece of real estate. Kepler was aware that on the Moon the nights and days were each fourteen Earth days long. However, he had air, water, and life on the Moon; there was nothing as yet to rule that out.

In 1638 the first science fiction story in the English language that dealt with a flight to the Moon was published: *The Man in the Moone*, by an English bishop named Francis Godwin (1562–1633), was published posthumously.

Godwin's book was the most influential of the early books of this nature, for it inspired a number of imitations. The hero of the book was carried to the Moon in a chariot drawn by a flock of geese (who were pictured as regularly migrating to the Moon). As usual, the Moon was populated with quite human intelligent beings.

In the same year in which Godwin's book was published, another English bishop, John Wilkins (1614–1672), a brother-in-law of Oliver Cromwell, produced a nonfictional equivalent. In his book

---

*It was the first science fiction story to be written by a professional scientist — but not, by a long shot, the last.

The Discovery of a World in the Moone, he speculated on the habitability of that body. Whereas Godwin's hero was a Spaniard (the Spaniards having been the great explorers of the previous century), Wilkins was sure it would be an Englishman who would first reach the Moon. In a way, Wilkins proved right, for the first man on the Moon was of English descent.

Wilkins, too, assumed that air existed all the way to the Moon and indeed throughout the Universe. There was, even in 1638, no understanding that such a fact would make separate heavenly bodies impossible. If the Moon were revolving about the Earth through an infinite ocean of air, air resistance would gradually slow it and finally bring it crashing, in fragments, down on the Earth — which would similarly crash into the Sun, and so on.

WATERLESSNESS

The notion of universal air had not long to live, however. In 1643 the Italian physicist Evangelista Torricelli (1608–1647), a student of Galileo, succeeded in balancing the weight of the atmosphere against a column of mercury, inventing the barometer. It turned out, from the weight of the column of mercury that balanced the downward pressure of air, that the atmosphere would be only 8 kilometers (5 miles) high if it were of uniform density. And if the density decreased with height, as it does in fact, it could only be a little higher than that before becoming too thin to support life.

It was clear, for the first time, that air did not fill the Universe but was a purely local terrestrial phenomenon. The space between the heavenly bodies was empty, a "vacuum," and this constituted, in a way, the discovery of outer space.

Without air, human beings could not travel to the Moon by means of water spouts, or geese-drawn chariots, or by any of the usual methods that would suffice to cross a gap of air.

The only way, in fact, that the gap between Earth and Moon could be closed was by using rockets, and this was first mentioned in 1647 by none other than the French writer and duelist Savinien de Cyrano de Bergerac (1619–1655). Cyrano, in his book *Voyages to the Moon and the Sun,* listed seven different ways in which a human being might travel from the Earth to the Moon, and one of them was by means of rockets. His hero actually performed the voyage, however, by one of the other (alas, worthless) methods.

As the seventeenth century progressed and observation of the Moon continued with better and better telescopes, astronomers grew aware of certain peculiarities about our satellite.

The view of the Moon, it seemed, was always clear and unchanging. Its surface was never obscured by cloud or mist. The terminator — that is, the dividing line between the light and the dark hemispheres — was always sharp. It was never fuzzy as it would be if light were refracting through an atmosphere, thus signifying the presence on the Moon of the equivalent of an earthly twilight.

What's more, when the Moon's globe approached a star, the star remained perfectly bright until the Moon's surface reached it, and then it winked out in an instant. It did not slowly dim as it would if the Moon's atmosphere reached it before the Moon's surface did, and if the starlight had to penetrate thickening layers of air.

In short, it became clear that the Moon was an airless world. And waterless, too, for closer examination showed that the dark "seas" that Galileo had seen were speckled with craters here and there. They were, if anything, seas of sand, but certainly not of water.

Without water, there could scarcely be life on the Moon. For the first time, people had to become aware that it was possible for a dead world to exist; one that was empty of life.

Let us not, however, hasten too quickly. Given a world without air and water, can we be sure it has no life?

Let us begin by considering life on Earth. Certainly, it shows a profound variability and versatility. There is life in the ocean deeps and on the ocean surface, in fresh water and on land, underground, in the air, even in deserts and frozen wastes.

There are even microscopic forms of life that do not use oxygen and to some of which oxygen is actually deadly. For them, airlessness would have no fears. (It is because of them that food sealed in a vacuum must be well heated first. Some pretty dangerous germs, including the one that produces botulism, get along fine in a vacuum.)

Well, then, is it so difficult to imagine some forms of life getting along without water, too?

Yes, quite difficult. No form of terrestrial life can do without water. Life developed in the sea, and the fluids within the living cells of all organisms, even those who now live in fresh water or on dry land and who would die if placed in the sea, are essentially a form of ocean water.

Even the life forms in the driest desert have not evolved into independence of water. Some might never drink, but they then get their necessary water in other ways — from the fluids of the food they eat, for instance — and carefully conserve what they get.

Some bacteria can survive desiccation and, in spore form, can live on for an indefinite period without water. The spore wall, however, protects the fluid within the bacterial cell. True desiccation, through and through, would kill it as quickly as it would kill us.

Viruses can retain the potentiality of life even when crystallized and with no water present. They cannot multiply, however, until they are within a cell and can undergo changes within the milieu of the cell fluid.

Ah, but all this refers to Earth life, which has developed in the ocean. On a waterless world, might not a fundamentally different kind of life develop that *was* independent of water?

Let's reason this out as follows:

On the surface of planetary worlds (on one of which the one example of life that we know of has developed) matter can exist in any of three stages: solid, liquid, or gas.

In gases, the component molecules are separated by relatively large distances and move randomly. For that reason, gas mixtures are always homogeneous, that is, all components are well mixed. Any chemical reaction that takes place in one part can equally well take place in another part and therefore spreads from one part of the system to the other with explosive rapidity. It is difficult to see how the carefully controlled and regulated reactions, which seem essential to something that is as complicated and finely balanced as living systems would appear to be, can exist in a gas.

Then, too, the molecules making up gases tend to be very simple. The complicated molecules that we can assume would be needed (if we are expected to witness the varied, versatile, and subtle changes that must surely characterize anything as varied, versatile, and subtle as life) are, under ordinary circumstances, in the solid state.

Some solids can be converted into gases by being heated sufficiently, or by being put under very low pressure. The complicated molecules characteristic of life would break up into small fragments if heated, however, and would be useless. If placed under even zero pressure, the complicated molecules will produce only insignificant quantities of vapor.

We conclude, then, that we cannot have life in a gaseous state.

In solids, the component molecules are in virtual contact, and can exist to any degree of complication. What's more, solids can be, and usually are, heterogeneous; that is, the chemical makeup in one part can be quite different from the chemical makeup in another part. In other words, different reactions can take place in different places at different rates and under different conditions.

So far, so good, but the trouble is that the molecules in solids are more or less locked in place, and chemical reactions will take place too slowly to produce the delicate changeability we associate with life. We conclude, then, that we cannot have life in the solid state.

In the liquid state, the component molecules are in virtual contact, and the possibility of heterogeneity exists, as in the solid state. However, the component molecules move about freely, and chemical reactions can proceed quickly, as in the gaseous state. What's more, both solid and gaseous substances can dissolve in liquids to produce extraordinarily complicated systems in which there is no limit to versatility of reaction.

In short, the kind of chemistry we associate with life would seem to be possible only against a liquid background. In Earth's case that liquid is water, and we will have something to say later in the book as to whether there is a possibility of any substitute.

A world, then, that is without water (and without any other liquid that might substitute) would seem to be surely incapable of supporting life.

Or am I still being too narrow minded?

Why can't life, with chemical and physical properties completely different from terrestrial life, nevertheless develop and even evolve intelligence? Why can't there be a very slow, solid life form (too slow, perhaps, to be recognized as life by us) living on the Moon or, for that matter, here on Earth? Why not a very rapid and evanescent gaseous life form, literally exploding with thought and experiencing lifetimes in split seconds, existing on the Sun, for instance.

There have been speculations in this direction. Science fiction stories have been written that postulated enormously strange life forms. The Earth itself has been considered as a living being, as have whole galaxies, and as have clouds of dust and gas in interstellar space. Life consisting of pure energy radiation has been written about and life existing outside our Universe altogether and therefore indescribable.

There is no limit to speculation in this respect, but in the absence of any evidence, they can only remain speculations. In this book, however, I will move only in those directions in which there is at least some evidence to guide me. Fragmentary and tenuous that evidence may be, and the conclusions shaky enough — but to step across the line into the region of no evidence at all I will not do.

Therefore, *until evidence to the contrary is forthcoming,* I must conclude that, on the basis of what we know of life (admittedly limited), a world without liquid is a world without life. Insofar, then, as the Moon seems to be a world without liquid, the Moon would seem to be a world without life.

We might be more cautious and say that a world without liquid is a world without life-as-we-know-it. It would be tiresome, however, to repeat the phrase constantly, and I will say it only now and then to make sure you don't forget that that is what I mean. In between, please take it for granted that in this book I am speaking of life-as-we-know-it, whenever I speak of life. Please remember also that there is not one scrap of evidence, however faint or indirect, that speaks for the existence of life-not-as-we-know-it.

Even now, we may be rushing to a conclusion too rapidly. The astronomers at their early telescopes could see clearly that there was no water on the Moon in the sense that there were no seas, great lakes, or mighty rivers. As telescopes continued to improve, no sign of "free water" on the surface ever showed up.

Yet might there not be water present in minor quantities, in small pools or bogs in the shadows of crater walls, in underground rivers and seepages, or even just in loose chemical combination with the molecules making up the Moon's solid surface?

Such water would surely not be observable through a telescope, and yet it might be enough to support life.

Yes, it might — but if life had its origin through chemical reactions taking place randomly (and we will discuss this in a later chapter), then the larger the volume in which those random processes take place, the greater the chance that they would finally succeed in producing something as complicated as life. Furthermore, the larger the volume in which the process took place, the more room there would be for the kind of prodigal outpouring of death and replacement that serves as the power drive for the random process of evolution.

Where only small quantities of water exist, the formation of life becomes very unlikely; and if it does form, its evolution is very slow. It simply passes the bounds of likelihood that there would be time and opportunity for a complex life form to arise and flourish, certainly not one complex enough to develop intelligence and a technological civilization.

Consequently, even if we admit the presence of water in quantities not visible through the telescope, we can at best postulate only very simple life. There is no way in which we can imagine the Moon to be the home of extraterrestrial intelligence — assuming it has always been as it is now.

MOON HOAX

Again I say that it is *not* the concept of extraterrestrial intelligence that is hard to grasp. It is the reverse notion that meets with resistance. Telescopic evidence (in the Moon's case) to the contrary, it remained hard to imagine dead worlds.

In 1686, the French writer Bernard le Bovier de Fontenelle (1657–1757) wrote *Conversations on the Plurality of the Worlds*, in which he speculated charmingly on life on each of the then known planets from Mercury to Saturn.

And though the case of life on the Moon was already dubious in Fontenelle's time and grew steadily more dubious, it proved quite possible to hoodwink the general public with tales of intelligent life on the Moon as late as 1835. That was the year of the "Moon Hoax."

This took place in the columns of a newly established newspaper, the *New York Sun*, which was eager to attract attention and win readers. It hired Richard Adams Locke (1800–1871), an author who had arrived in the United States three years before from his native England, to write essays for them.

Locke was interested in the possibility of life on other worlds and had even tried his hand at science fiction in that connection.

Now it occurred to him to write a little science fiction without actually saying that that was what it was.

He chose for his subject the expedition of the English astronomer John Herschel (1792–1871). Herschel had gone to Cape Town in southern Africa to study the southern sky.

Herschel had taken good telescopes with him, but they were not the best in the world. Their value lay not in themselves but in the fact that since all astronomers and astronomical observatories were at that time located in the Northern Hemisphere, the regions near the South Celestial Pole had virtually never been studied at all. Almost any telescope would have been useful.

Locke well knew how to improve on that. Beginning with the August 25, 1835, issue of the *Sun*, Locke carefully described all sorts of impossible discoveries being made by Herschel with a telescope capable (so Locke said) of such magnification that it could see objects on the Moon's surface that were only eighteen inches across.

In the second day's installment, the surface of the Moon was described. Herschel was said to have seen flowers like poppies and trees like yews and firs. A large lake, with blue water and foaming waves, was described, as were large animals resembling bisons and unicorns.

One clever note was the description of a fleshy flap across the forehead of the bisonlike creatures, a flap that could be raised or lowered to protect the animal "from the great extremes of light and darkness to which all the inhabitants of our side of the Moon are periodically subject."

Finally, creatures with human appearance, except for the possession of wings, were described. They seemed to be engaged in conversation: "Their gesticulation, more particularly the varied action of their hands and arms, appeared impassioned and emphatic. We hence inferred that they were rational beings."

Astronomers, of course, recognized the story to be nonsense, since no telescope then built (or now, either) could see such detail from the surface of the Earth, and since what was described was utterly at odds with what was known about the surface of the Moon and its properties.

The hoax was revealed as such soon enough, but in the interval the circulation of the *Sun* soared until, for a brief moment, it was the best-selling newspaper in the world. Uncounted thousands of people believed the hoax implicitly and remained eager for more, showing how anxious people were to believe in the matter of extraterrestrial intelligence — and indeed in any dramatic discovery (or purported discovery) that seems to go against the rational but undramatic beliefs of realistic science.

As the Moon's deadness became more and more apparent, however, hope remained that this was an unusual and an isolated case and that the other worlds of the Solar System might be inhabited.

When the English mathematician William Whewell (1794–1866) in his book *Plurality of Worlds*, published in 1853, suggested that some of the planets might not bear life, this definitely represented a minority opinion at the time. In 1862 the young French astronomer Camille Flammarion (1842–1925) wrote *On the Plurality of Habitable Worlds* in refutation, and this second book proved much the more popular.

Soon after the appearance of Flammarion's book, however, a new scientific advance placed the odds heavily in Whewell's favor.

AIRLESSNESS

In the 1860s the Scottish mathematician James Clerk Maxwell (1831–1879) and the Austrian physicist Ludwig Edward Boltzmann (1844–1906), working independently, advanced what is called the kinetic theory of gases.

The theory considered gases as collections of widely spaced molecules moving in random directions and in a broad range of speeds. It showed how the observed behavior of gases under changing conditions of temperature and pressure could be deduced from this.

One of the consequences of the theory was to show that the average speed of the molecules varied directly with the absolute temperature, and inversely with the square root of the mass of the molecules.

A certain fraction of the molecules of any gas would be moving at speeds greater than the average for that temperature, and might exceed the escape velocity for the planet whose gravitational attraction held them. Anything moving at more than escape velocity, whether it is a rocket ship or a molecule, can, if it does not collide with something, move away forever from the planet.

Under ordinary circumstances, so tiny a fraction of the molecules of an atmosphere might attain escape velocity — and retain it through inevitable collisions until it reached such heights that it could move away without further collision — that the atmosphere would leak away into outer space with imperceptible slowness. Thus, Earth, for which the escape velocity is 11.3 kilometers (7.0 miles) per second, holds on to its atmosphere successfully and will not lose any significant quantity of it for billions of years.

If, however, Earth's average temperature were to be substantially increased, the average speed of the molecules in its atmosphere would also be increased and so would the fraction of those molecules traveling at more than escape velocity. The atmosphere would leak away more rapidly. If the temperature were high enough, the Earth would lose its atmosphere rather quickly and become an airless globe.

Next, consider hydrogen and helium, which are gases that are composed of particles much less massive than those making up the oxygen and nitrogen of our atmosphere. The oxygen molecule (made up of two oxygen atoms) has a mass of 32 in atomic mass units, and the nitrogen molecule (made up of two nitrogen atoms) has a mass of 28. In contrast, the hydrogen molecule (made up of two hydrogen atoms) has a mass of 2 and helium atoms (which occur singly) a mass of 4.

At a given temperature, light particles move more rapidly than massive ones. A helium atom will move about three times as quickly as the massive and therefore more sluggish molecules of our atmosphere, and a hydrogen molecule will move four times as quickly. The percentage of helium atoms and hydrogen molecules that would be moving more rapidly than escape velocity would be much greater than in the case of oxygen and nitrogen.

The result is that Earth's gravity, which suffices to hold the oxygen and nitrogen molecules of its atmosphere indefinitely, would quickly lose any hydrogen or helium in its atmosphere. That would leak away into outer space. If the Earth were forming under its present condition of temperature and were surrounded by cosmic clouds of hydrogen and helium, it would not have a sufficiently strong gravitational field to collect those small and nimble molecules and atoms.

It is for this reason that Earth's atmosphere does not contain anything more than traces of hydrogen and helium, although these two gases make up by far the bulk of the original cloud of material out of which the Solar System was formed.

The Moon has a mass only one eighty-first that of the Earth and a gravitational field only one eighty-first as intense. Because it is a smaller body than the Earth, its surface is nearer its center, so that its small gravitational field is somewhat more intense at its surface than you would expect from its overall mass. At the surface, the Moon's gravitational pull is one sixth of the Earth's gravitational pull at its surface.

This is reflected in escape velocity as well. The Moon's escape velocity is only 2.37 kilometers (1.47 miles) per second. On Earth, a vanishingly small percentage of molecules of a particular gas might surpass its escape velocity. On the Moon, a substantial percentage of molecules of that same gas would surpass the Moon's much lower escape velocity.

Then, too, because the Moon rotates on its axis so slowly as to allow the Sun to remain in the sky over some particular point on its surface for two weeks at a time, its temperature during its day rises much higher than does the Earth's temperature. That further increases the percentage of molecules with speeds surpassing the escape velocity.

The result is that the Moon is without an atmosphere. To be sure, even the Moon's low gravity can hold some gases if their atoms or molecules are massive enough. The atoms of the gas krypton, for instance, have a mass of 83.8, and the atoms of the gas xenon, a mass of 131.3. The Moon's gravitational field could hold them with ease. However, these gases are so uncommon in the Universe generally that even if they occurred on the Moon and made up its atmosphere, that atmosphere would be only a trillionth as dense as the Earth's atmosphere, if that, and could at best be described as a "trace atmosphere."

To all intents and purposes, as far as the problem of extraterrestrial life is concerned, such a trace atmosphere is of no consequence, and the Moon can still fairly be described as airless.

All this has meaning with respect to a liquid such as water. Water is "volatile," that is, it has a tendency to vaporize and turn into a gas. At a given temperature, there is a countertendency for the gaseous water vapor to recondense into liquid. At any particular temperature, liquid water is therefore liable to be in equilibrium with a certain pressure of water vapor, provided that water vapor is not removed from the vicinity as, for instance, by a wind.

If the water vapor is removed, equilibrium pressure is not built up and more of the liquid water vaporizes, and still more, till it is all gone. We are all familiar with the way in which the water left behind by a rainstorm evaporates until it is finally all gone. The higher the temperature, the faster the water evaporates.

Naturally, the water vapor is not removed from the Earth altogether. If it does not condense in one place, it condenses in another as dew, fog, rain, or snow, and thus the Earth holds on to its water.

If there were liquid water on the Moon, the vapor that would form would leak out into space, for the mass of the water molecule is but 18, and the Moon's gravitational field would not hold it. The liquid water would continue to vaporize and eventually the Moon would dry up altogether. The fact that there is no air on the Moon means there is no air pressure to slow the rate of water evaporation, and the water, if it had been present, would have been lost all the more quickly.

The Moon, therefore, *must* be without water as well as without air. What's more, any airless world would be a lifeless world — not because air is necessarily essential to life, but because an airless world is a waterless world, and water is essential.

Even the kinetic theory of gases leaves loopholes, however. The possibility remains that scraps of water, even air, can exist underground on the Moon, or in chemical combination with molecules in the soil. In that case, the small molecules would be prevented from leaving by forces other than gravity — by physical barriers or chemical bonding.

Then, too, there may have been a time early in the history of the Moon when it had an atmosphere and an ocean, *before* it lost them both to space. Perhaps in those early days, life developed, even intelligent life, and it may have adapted itself, either biologically or technologically, to the gradual loss of air and water. It might, therefore, be living on the Moon in caverns, with a supply of air and water sealed in.

As late as 1901, the English writer H. G. Wells (1866–1946) could publish *The First Men on the Moon* and have his heroes find a race of intelligent Moon beings, rather insectlike in character and highly specialized, living underground.

Even that much seems doubtful, however, since calculations show that the Moon would have lost its air and water (if any) quite rapidly. It would have retained them for many times the lifetime of a human being, of course, and if we were living on the Moon when it still had an atmosphere and ocean we could live out our lives normally. The atmosphere and ocean would not last long enough, however, to allow life to develop and intelligence to evolve from zero. It wouldn't even come close to doing that.

And we seem to be at a final answer now. On July 20, 1969, the first astronauts landed on the Moon. Samples of material from the Moon's surface were brought back on this and later trips to the Moon. Apparently the Moon rocks all seem to indicate that the Moon is bone dry — that there is no trace of water upon it, nor has there been in the past.

The Moon would seem to be, almost beyond conceivable doubt, a dead world.

My books originate in all sorts of ways. One, for instance, came about through a request from Carl Sagan.

I had met Carl in early 1963, when he was still teaching at Harvard University and was a young man of twenty-seven. He was an attractive and charismatic individual even then, and we have been friends ever since.

On October 17, 1980, Carl and I (among others) were both being honored by the Explorers' Club, and we sat at the same table. Carl was deeply engaged in his enormously successful television series "Cosmos" and was planning further projects with great ebullience. Among other things, he wanted to publish books on astronomy for the general public.

He had, for instance, come across a Japanese book consisting of a collection of gorgeous astronomical paintings by Kazuaki Iwasaki. Carl wanted to do an American version of the book, but felt he needed an accompanying text that was better suited for American readers than the one in the original edition.

He asked me to supply it, and I had no wish to refuse an old friend. The book, Visions of the Universe *(Book 232), was published by The Cosmos Store (a division of Carl Sagan Productions,*

Inc.) in 1981, and Sagan himself provided a preface. It consisted of forty-six paintings by Iwasaki, for each of which I supplied a 250-word text. Here are the texts for "Mercury" and "Volcanoes on Venus."

from VISIONS OF THE UNIVERSE (1981)

Mercury

The planet nearest the Sun is Mercury — waterless, airless, lifeless, baked in the Sun's heat as it slowly turns once every fifty-nine Earth-days.

In 1974 and 1975, a probe, Mariner 10, took photographs of Mercury's surface at close range and revealed a world that looked much like our own Moon. The differences are, first, that it is larger than the Moon, being 4850 kilometers across as compared with 3476 kilometers for the Moon. (However, Mercury has only three-eighths the width of Earth and is only one-sixteenth as massive.) Another difference between Mercury and the Moon is that Mercury seems to lack the large "maria," which are areas of dark lava flows much larger than individual craters. Mercury, for the most part, seems to possess only the craters.

Of course, Mercury, which is at less than half the distance from the Sun that the Earth and Moon are, has a sky that is dominated by the Sun. This is true more at some times than others. Mercury's orbit is quite elliptical so that it comes as close as 46 million kilometers to the Sun at one point in its orbit, and recedes as far as 70 million kilometers at the opposite point. Since it revolves about the Sun in eighty-eight Earth-days, it reaches its nearest point (or "perihelion") every eighty-eight Earth-days.

The painting shows Mercury at perihelion. The surface is Moonlike and crater-littered, and in the sky is the mighty Sun, with its sunspots and prominences clearly visible (if there were any instrument that could withstand its heat and view it). Around it, following the lines of its magnetic field is its crowning glory, its beautiful corona, all against the black sky that airlessness makes necessary.

Volcanoes on Venus   .

We can't see the surface of Venus by ordinary light, but radar beams can penetrate the cloud layer and reach the solid surface. There they can be reflected and the reflection can penetrate the cloud layer again and reach us. By such reflected radar beams we can "see" the planet's surface, just as we might by reflected light. The vision is fuzzier by radar because radar waves are much longer than light waves and therefore are not reflected as sharply.

From Earth, reflected radar beams don't show much detail. In 1979, however, a Venus probe named Pioneer Venus mapped Venus by radar at close range. As a result we now have a better view of the surface than would have been thought possible a generation ago.

Some large and high mountains, which may or may not be volcanic in origin, have been detected. We aren't sure. Venus's surface doesn't seem to be split up into plates as Earth's surface is. It is the slow movement of the plates against each other that produces earthquakes and volcanoes on Earth, and without such plate movement on Venus these phenomena may be absent.

However, Venus, like Earth and all the planets, has a long history, for it was formed about 4.6 billion years ago. It seems very likely that in the past, Venus was more "alive" than it is now, with a crust that was thinner and subject to greater activities. If there are no active volcanoes now, there may well have been many in the past. The painting shows an imaginative view of Venus's surface at a time when volcanic action existed and when the white light of the hot lava, spraying upward, enlivened and brightened the otherwise dull, cloud-covered scene in a way that made Venus still more hostile to life-as-we-know-it.

The book, ten by fourteen inches in size, made use of the very best paper, thick and glossy. The reproductions of the paintings were magnificent, and the text, if I say so myself, was entirely adequate. Unfortunately, as it turned out, it is one thing to produce a fine book and another to distribute it and persuade the public to buy

it. Carl had not solved the distribution problems and the book was
an undeserved failure.

By a natural progression of thought, mention of Venus leads me to
Venus, Near Neighbor of the Sun *(Book 228), which William Mor-*
row published as a Lothrop, Lee & Shepard Book in 1981. It was
the fifth in a series of astronomy books (heavy on line drawings
and on statistical tables) that I did for teenagers. The first four had
been published among my second hundred books.

   This book dealt not only with Venus, but also with all other ob-
jects that approached the Sun at least as closely as Venus does. This
gave me an opportunity to discuss, in some detail, the unusual as-
teroid, Icarus, and an even more unusual group of comets called
the Sun-grazers.

from VENUS, NEAR NEIGHBOR OF THE SUN (1981)

Icarus

On June 26, 1949, an Apollo-object was accidentally discovered by
the German-American astronomer Walter Baade, and this turned
out to be the most unusual asteroid of all. For one thing, its period
of revolution turned out to be only 1.12 years, or 409 days, the
smallest for any asteroid up to that time. For another, its orbital
eccentricity was 0.827, the largest up to that time for any asteroid.
   A small period of revolution means a small orbit, and a large
eccentricity involving such a small orbit must mean that the perihelion is quite close to the Sun. And so it is. At perihelion, the
new asteroid is only 28.5 million kilometers (17.7 million miles)
from the Sun. This is less than half the distance of Adonis, the
previous record holder, and is only about 60 percent of the closest
approach Mercury ever makes to the Sun.
   Naturally, Baade named the asteroid Icarus, after a young man
in the Greek myths who flew on artificial wings to which feathers
were affixed with wax. When he flew too near the Sun, the wax
melted and he fell into the sea to his death. If anything flies too
near the Sun, it is the asteroid Icarus. (Icarus's approach to Earth,

however, is no record. Its closest possible approach in its present orbit is 6.4 million kilometers, or 4 million miles.)

Since 1948 other Apollo-objects have been discovered with perihelia inside Venus's orbit (see Table 50) but of them all, Icarus is still the only one with a perihelion closer than that of Mercury.

A close perihelion does not always mean a close aphelion as well. The greater the eccentricity of the orbit, the greater the lopsidedness of the two figures. The object 1978 SB, whose perihelion approach is second only to that of Icarus, has an even greater orbital eccentricity than Icarus, so that its aphelion is farther out than that of any other object in Table 50.

Table 50
Apollo-Objects

| | | | PERIHELION APPROACH | |
| | | | VENUS'S PERI-HELION | MERCURY'S PERIHELION |
	KILOMETERS	MILES	= 1	= 1
Apollo	97,200,000	60,400,000	0.90	2.12
Midas	92,800,000	57,600,000	0.86	2.02
Hermes	86,800,000	53,900,000	0.86	2.02
Cerberus	86,800,000	53,900,000	0.80	1.89
Daedalus	83,800,000	52,100,000	0.77	1.82
1976 UA	70,300,000	43,700,000	0.65	1.53
Ra-Shalom	70,300,000	43,700,000	0.65	1.53
Adonis	65,800,000	40,900,000	0.61	1.43
1974 MA	62,800,000	39,000,000	0.58	1.37
1978 SB	52,400,000	32,500,000	0.48	1.14
Icarus	28,500,000	17,700,000	0.26	0.62

On the other hand, there is Ra-Shalom, discovered in 1978 and named for the Egyptian god of the Sun and the Hebrew word for peace — in honor of the Egyptian-Israeli peace treaty. With a perihelion somewhat farther from the Sun than that of Adonis, Ra-Shalom has an aphelion only a little over a third as far from the Sun as Adonis. Ra-Shalom and 1976 UA have periods of less than a year. They are the only objects so far known, other than Venus and Mercury, to circle the Sun in less time than the Earth does.

If we imagined ourselves on one of these Apollo-objects, we would have the opportunity to make some unusual observations. Each one crosses the orbit of Earth and Venus, all but two cross the orbit of Mars, and one (Icarus) crosses the orbit of Mercury, while two others skim by it. There are therefore occasions (not in every orbital period, but once in a while) when one planet or another is unusually close and shines brightly in the sky.

Suppose, for instance, there was an observer who happened to be on Hermes in 1937 when it made its close approach to Earth. Earth would seem a starlike object to such an observer most of the time, but on this one pass, Earth would have begun to brighten unusually. It would become more and more brilliant, then begin to show a visible shape as a small crescent.

It would continue to expand, and the crescent would thicken until at closest passage it would be more or less a half-Earth, about fifty-five minutes of arc in diameter. It would be nearly twice as wide as the half-Moon appears to us and some forty times as bright. Earth would then shrink as rapidly as it had expanded, while Hermes passed on toward perihelion, not to return to Earth's vicinity for an indefinite number of years.

Each revolution, however, the Sun would expand in Hermes's sky, and in that of any Apollo-object. It is this expanded Sun that would be the most astonishing and impressive object by far (see Table 51).

It would be for Icarus that this effect would be most astonishing and impressive. On Icarus, at aphelion, an observer would see the Sun only half as wide as it appears to us on Earth, and it would then deliver only a quarter as much light and heat as it does to us.

In the course of 204 days, however, Icarus would travel from aphelion to perihelion and, in that time, the Sun would swell, slowly at first, but then ever more rapidly as, in approaching the Sun, Icarus's orbital speed became greater. Finally, at perihelion, the Sun would appear over five times as wide in Icarus's sky as it does in our own. Icarus would receive a solar blast more than twenty-seven times as intense as we do, and two and a half times as intense as even Mercury does at its perihelion (but not quite as great as that which would have been received by the mythical Vulcan).

Table 51
Perihelia of the Apollo-Objects

	AT PERIHELION	
	DIAMETER OF SUN (MINUTES OF ARC)	LIGHT AND HEAT RECEIVED (EARTH = 1)
Apollo	49	2.34
Midas	52	2.64
Hermes	55	2.95
Cerberus	55	2.95
Daedalus	57	3.17
1976 UA	68	4.52
Ra-Shalom	68	4.52
Adonis	72	5.06
1974 MA	76	5.64
1978 SB	91	8.08
Icarus	168	27.6

Icarus rotates in 2.7 hours and has a diameter of about 1.0 kilometer (0.6 mile). This means that if we assume it to be roughly spherical in shape, the surface speed at the equator would be about 1.2 kilometers per hour (0.75 mile an hour).

If we imagined ourselves trapped on Icarus's surface near perihelion, we would be safest if we were on an area where it was just a few minutes before sunrise, because that surface would have had nearly eighty minutes since sunset to cool off. (Such cooling would be rapid in the absence of an atmosphere.)

It would then be necessary, however, to walk westward at the rate of 1.2 kilometers an hour to stay ahead of the Sun. It would be a slow walk, easily managed, but you would have to keep it up for a couple of months without stopping, until the Sun shrank to a size small enough to be relatively safe.

Sun-grazers

"Short-term comets" are used-up dregs of comets that have been to the well too often. Halley's comet is the only one of them that is still spectacular.

There are, however, comets that are fresh from the vast and distant cloud far beyond the planetary system. There are comets that have not yet had their orbits interfered with by planetary gravitational effects to the point where they have been "captured." They come into the inner Solar System, yes, but only at intervals of a million years or more, and spend most of their time in the aphelion portion of their orbits, far beyond Pluto.

When such comets are at their aphelia, the Sun is to them no more than a bright star, no brighter in appearance than Venus at its brightest is to us. The Sun remains such a star without much change for a million years or so, and then it slowly begins to brighten more and more rapidly until it expands in the sky for a brief period, then shrinks rapidly, then more slowly, and becomes nothing more than a star again for a million years or so.

If Earth had such an orbit and if life could somehow be imagined to survive the long drift in outer space and the short, blazing encounter with the Sun, there would be time for human beings to evolve, develop a civilization, and perhaps die out without ever knowing that that bright star in the sky could expand to a blazing inferno (assuming that they didn't develop an advanced astronomy).

These are "long-term comets." Kohoutek's comet, which swooped around the Sun in 1974, was a long-term comet. It was a disappointment because it unexpectedly turned out to be rocky, so it didn't shine brightly and develop an enormous tail.

Many of the long-term comets seem to exist in groups, each a splinter of an original comet that broke up at perihelion. Astronomers recognize fifteen such groups of long-term comets, usually distinguished by letters. Group M make up what are called the Sun-grazers because they make an unusually close approach to the Sun at perihelion.

These not only approach the Sun more closely than Mercury at perihelion, but they are also the only known objects that approach more closely than Icarus at perihelion. They approach even more closely than the mythical Vulcan was supposed to. Eight of the Sun-grazers are now known, and the approach at perihelion to the Sun is given in Table 54.

The approach is always given to the Sun's center, and even for Icarus the difference between the approach to the center and to

Table 54
The Sun-Grazers

| YEAR OF APPEARANCE | PERIHELION DISTANCE | | | |
| | TO SUN'S CENTER | | TO SUN'S SURFACE | |
	KILOMETERS	MILES	KILOMETERS	MILES
1668	9,600,000	6,000,000	8,900,000	5,550,000
1887	1,450,000	900,000	755,000	468,000
1965	1,200,000	740,000	505,000	308,000
1882	1,150,000	715,000	455,000	283,000
1945	940,000	585,000	245,000	153,000
1843	820,000	510,000	125,000	78,000
1880	820,000	510,000	125,000	78,000
1963	790,000	492,000	95,000	60,000

the Sun's surface isn't enough to make a fuss over. In the case of the Sun-grazers it is, and in the table both distances are given.

The figures are all but incredible. They make Mercury, and even Icarus, look like objects far distant from the Sun.

When the comet of 1963 was at its perihelion the Sun was 122 degrees in diameter, stretching more than two thirds of the way from horizon to horizon and taking up just about half the sky in area. The amount of heat and light it got from the Sun at that time was about fifty-three thousand times as much as Earth gets and about two thousand times as much as Icarus gets at perihelion.

How do the Sun-grazers withstand the heat? Why don't they just pop and vanish?

To begin with, they are moving very quickly under the lash of the intense gravity of the nearby Sun. The comet of 1965 was moving at a speed of 100 kilometers per second (62 miles per second) and completed its pass in six hours. The comet of 1963 was moving at something like 180 kilometers per second (100 miles per second) and completed its pass in less than three and a half hours.

Second, the cloud of vapor and dust formed by the evaporation of the comet blocks some of the Sun's radiation from reaching what is left of the comet, and helps it survive the relatively short interval when it is nearest the Sun.

Third, the comet *does* suffer severely as a result, and it is doubtful that it can survive more than just a few passes at Sun-grazing perihelion. The original Sun-grazer has broken into eight pieces that we know of, and there may be more. The pieces themselves break up, too. The comet of 1965 broke in two as it passed the Sun. The comet of 1843 vaporized to such an extent that it formed a tail that was visible over a stretch of more than 300 million kilometers (190 million miles), a distance equal to that from the Sun to the asteroid belt.

I have an opportunity now to point out the kind of work I do in anthologies. In 1979, Harper & Row, Publishers, published The Science Fictional Solar System *(Book 208), an anthology I edited along with Marty Greenberg and Charles G. Waugh. (Waugh, a professor of psychology, lives in Maine, is tall, scholarly, courteous, and is equipped with an encyclopedic knowledge of science fiction. He has worked with Marty and me on a great many of our anthologies.)*

This anthology contained thirteen stories placed on the various bodies of the Solar System. It was my task to introduce each Solar System setting with an essay designed to point out the latest information in each case and to show where the writers had unavoidably been made out of date. Here, then, is my introduction to the two stories ("Wait It Out" by Larry Niven and "Nikita Eisenhower Jones" by Robert F. Young) that deal with Pluto.

from THE SCIENCE FICTIONAL SOLAR SYSTEM (1979)

Pluto, like Neptune, was predicted before it was found. The discrepancies in the orbit of Uranus were not entirely corrected by taking Neptune into consideration. Could there be still another planet beyond Uranus, one that was even farther from the Sun than Neptune is? Percival Lowell was particularly assiduous in his searchings but had found nothing by the time of his death in 1916.

Others at his observatory continued to search, off and on: and finally in 1930 Clyde William Tombaugh located the planet. It was considerably farther than Neptune and considerably smaller, and it could only be seen as a spot of light.

Still, its orbit could be calculated, and it was found to be a very odd one. Pluto's orbit is the most eccentric ellipse of any of the major planets.

When Pluto is at its farthest from the Sun, it is 1.6 times as far away as Neptune. It is as much farther beyond Neptune as Neptune is beyond Uranus. But when Pluto swoops in to the near end of its orbit, it is actually some 50 million kilometers (30 million miles) *closer* to the Sun than Neptune is.

Right now Pluto is approaching perihelion and is moving in closer to the Sun than Neptune is. For some twenty years (a period repeated every two and a half centuries) Neptune, not Pluto, will be the farthest planet, something that is mentioned in "Wait It Out."

There is no danger of Pluto colliding with Neptune as it passes within Neptune's orbit, however, for Pluto's orbit is in a plane that is considerably tilted compared to Neptune's. That means that Pluto passes far below Neptune as it crosses orbits.

Still, this crossing of orbits is so strange that some astronomers have speculated that Pluto was once a satellite of Neptune and had been kicked free in some catastrophe.

This notion was strengthened by the fact that Pluto was not a gas giant. In fact, it proved to be rather small. As the decades passed after its discovery, and as small bits of information were gathered, the estimates of its size shrank. At first it seemed pretty certain that it was at least as large as Earth, but eventually it was decided that it was only as large as Mars. A Mars-sized world might easily have once been a satellite of Neptune.

Then, too, Pluto's light grew dimmer and brighter regularly, and it was decided that this represented its period of rotation, with one hemisphere being icier and brighter than the other. If so, Pluto's period of rotation equaled 6.39 days.

If we disregard Mercury and Venus as having had their rotation periods interfered with by the Sun's tidal effect, it turns out that Earth, Mars, Uranus, and Neptune all have rotation periods in the region of twenty-four hours, while Jupiter and Saturn have rotation periods in the region of ten hours. A rotation period of 6.39 days is very slow — but if Pluto had once been revolving about Neptune, it might have had a period of revolution of 6.39 days, and the tidal forces of Neptune might have slowed the rotation till it was equal to the period of revolution.

Astronomers continued to think for a while that Pluto had to have a mass large enough to affect the orbits of Neptune and Uranus; and as it shrank in size, estimates of its density came to be many times as great as that of platinum. This high density is referred to in "Wait It Out," which was first published in 1968.

However, such high densities were really unthinkable and quickly went by the board. It had to be decided that Pluto was not only no larger than Mars, but no more massive, either.

Then, on June 22, 1978, James W. Christy, examining photographs of Pluto, noticed a distinct bump on one side. He examined other photographs and finally decided that Pluto had a satellite. The satellite was only 20,000 kilometers (12,500 miles) from Pluto. Considering how close together the two objects were and how far away from us, it isn't surprising we tended to see them as a single object.

The satellite, named Charon, circles Pluto in 6.39 days, which is just the time it takes for Pluto to turn on its axis. The two bodies have apparently slowed each other by tidal action, until each faces the same side to the other. They revolve about a common center of gravity like the two halves of a dumbbell about an invisible shaft.

From the distance of separation and the time of revolution, it can be shown that both bodies together have only about one-eighth the mass of our Moon. Pluto is far smaller than anyone had thought. Pluto is now thought to be about 3000 kilometers (1850 miles) in diameter and Charon about 1200 kilometers (750 miles) in diameter.

From now on, no one can write a science fiction story about Pluto without taking its very small size into account and without mentioning its satellite, which, although small, is larger compared to the planet it circles than any other satellite in the Solar System. Pluto-Charon make up the closest approach to a double planet in the system.

One thing is now clear. Pluto cannot explain the discrepancies in the motions of Uranus and Neptune. If there is an explanation, it must involve another planet, a larger one, and one that is still undiscovered. Does it exist? Perhaps probes will eventually tell us.

*So far, my astronomical selections have been from my nonfiction,
but if one science is apt to be found in my fiction as well, it is
astronomy. My novels do tend to involve space travel, and this is
especially true of the first of the two science fiction novels that are
included among my third hundred books,* Foundation's Edge
(Book 262), which was published by Doubleday in 1982.

There's a story behind Foundation's Edge. *Back in the 1940s,
when I was a terribly young man, I wrote a group of stories usually
referred to as the Foundation series. They were popular with the
readers of* Astounding Science Fiction *and, in the early 1950s, they
were put together in three volumes by Gnome Press (a very small
publishing firm run by the first Martin Greenberg — no middle
name). These volumes,* Foundation *(Book 4),* Foundation and Empire *(Book 6), and* Second Foundation *(Book 9) have been lumped
together as "The Foundation Trilogy."*

*They have remained in print ever since, both in hard and soft
covers. Eventually, they were taken over by Doubleday and
seemed (to my considerable surprise) to grow more and more popular each year.*

*There were continuing demands on the part of my readers (and
of Doubleday, too) that I write a fourth book of the series. I resisted this firmly, even though I knew very well it would bring a
lot of money into my coffers. I was afraid I wouldn't be able to
duplicate the vigor and verve of my youth.*

*In 1981, however, Doubleday lost its patience. Three decades
was enough, they decided. They called me into the editorial sanc-
tum of Betty Prashker and read me the riot act: I was going to
write another Foundation novel and that was that. Nothing was
actually said about my being thrown out the forty-third-story window if I did not instantly agree, but there was something about the
interview that made my blood run cold.*

I was also offered ten times my usual advance.

*My feeble objections to the effect that the book might be beyond
my powers and that the advance was ridiculously high and would
force Doubleday into bankruptcy were dismissed peremptorily
with a "Go home and get to work!"*

*Eventually, I did, and the results were astonishing. I had, after
all, published 261 books in semisecrecy, with only a small but
highly intelligent cadre of loyal fans who knew of them, and I had
every reason to suppose this would continue unchanged indefi-*

nitely. However, with Foundation's Edge, *I came in out of the cold. As soon as it was published, it hit the best-seller lists and remained there for half a year. The world was almost as astonished as I was.*

It was a good feeling (I must admit) but it did make me feel that I had set myself an impossibly high standard for future novels. One way out, of course, would be to end on a high point and write no more novels, but Doubleday would have none of that. They weren't scared. As soon as I handed in the manuscript, they whipped out a contract for another novel (with a still higher advance) and stated firmly that they intended to keep it up as long as I lived — and that I might as well understand that I wasn't allowed to die.

In a novel, of course, I can't deal with astronomy as didactically as I do in nonfiction, but, on the other hand, I can deal with it imaginatively. Thus, Golan Trevize, the protagonist of the book, is off in space (nothing new for him) with a companion, Janov Pelorat, who has never before been off a planetary surface. Pelorat is a bit frightened and Trevize, who is at the console of an extremely advanced computer, undertakes to educate him a bit.

from FOUNDATION'S EDGE (1982)

Pelorat seemed to shrink a little as he stared at Trevize. His long rectangle of a face grew so blank that without showing any emotion at all, it radiated a vast uneasiness.

Then his eyes shifted right — left.

Trevize remembered how he had felt on his own first trip beyond the atmosphere.

He said, in as matter-of-fact a manner as he could, "Janov" (it was the first time he had addressed the professor familiarly, but in this case experience was addressing inexperience and it was necessary to seem the older of the two), "we are perfectly safe here. We are in the metal womb of a warship of the Foundation Navy. We are not fully armed, but there is no place in the Galaxy where the name of the Foundation will not protect us. Even if some ship went mad and attacked, we could move out of its reach in a moment. And I assure you I have discovered that I can handle the ship perfectly."

Pelorat said, "It is the thought. Go — Golan, of nothingness —"

"Why, there's nothingness all about Terminus. There's just a thin layer of very tenuous air between ourselves on the surface and the nothingness just above. All we're doing is to go past that inconsequential layer."

"It may be inconsequential, but we breathe it."

"We breathe here, too. The air on this ship is cleaner and purer, and will indefinitely remain cleaner and purer than the natural atmosphere of Terminus."

"And the meteorites?"

"What about meteorites?"

"The atmosphere protects us from meteorites. Radiation, too, for that matter."

Trevize said, "Humanity has been traveling through space for twenty millennia, I believe —"

"Twenty-two. If we go by the Hallblockian chronology, it is quite plain that, counting the —"

"Enough! Have you heard of meteorite accidents or of radiation deaths? — I mean, recently? — I mean, in the case of Foundation ships?"

"I have not really followed the news in such matters, but I am a historian, my boy, and —"

"Historically, yes, there have been such things, but technology improves. There isn't a meteorite large enough to damage us that can possibly approach us before we take the necessary evasive action. Four meteorites — coming at us simultaneously from the four directions drawn from the vertices of a tetrahedron — might conceivably pin us down, but calculate the chances of that and you'll find that you'll die of old age a trillion trillion times over before you will have a fifty-fifty chance of observing so interesting a phenomenon."

"You mean, if you were at the computer?"

"No," said Trevize in scorn. "If I were running the computer on the basis of my own senses and responses, we would be hit before I ever knew what was happening. It is the computer itself that is at work, responding millions of times faster than you or I could." He held out his hand abruptly. "Janov, come let me show you what the computer can do, and let me show you what space is like."

Pelorat stared, goggling a bit. Then he laughed briefly. "I'm not sure I wish to know, Golan."

"Of course you're not sure, Janov, because you don't know what it is that is waiting there to be known. Chance it! Come! Into my room!"

Trevize held the other's hand, half leading him, half drawing him. He said, as he sat down at the computer, "Have you ever seen the Galaxy, Janov? Have you ever looked at it?"

Pelorat said, "You mean in the sky?"

"Yes, certainly. Where else?"

"I've seen it. Everyone has seen it. If one looks up, one sees it."

"Have you ever stared at it on a dark, clear night, when the Diamonds are below the horizon?"

The "Diamonds" referred to those few stars that were luminous enough and close enough to shine with moderate brightness in the night sky of Terminus. They were a small group that spanned a width of no more than twenty degrees, and for large parts of the night they were all below the horizon. Aside from the group, there was a scattering of dim stars just barely visible to the unaided eye. There was nothing more but the faint milkiness of the Galaxy — the view one might expect when one dwelt on a world like Terminus, which was at the extreme edge of the outermost spiral of the Galaxy.

"I suppose so, but why stare? It's a common sight."

"Of course it's a common sight," said Trevize. "That's why no one sees it. Why see it if you can always see it? But now you'll *see* it, and not from Terminus, where the mist and the clouds are forever interfering. You'll see it as you'd never see it from Terminus — no matter how you stared, and no matter how clear and dark the night. How I wish *I* had never been in space before, so that — like you — I could see the Galaxy in its bare beauty for the first time."

He pushed a chair in Pelorat's direction. "Sit there, Janov. This may take a little time. I have to continue to grow accustomed to the computer. From what I've already felt, I know the viewing is holographic, so we won't need a screen of any sort. It makes direct contact with my brain, but I think I can have it produce an objective image that you will see, too. — Put out the light, will you? — No, that's foolish of me. I'll have the computer do it. Stay where you are."

Trevize made contact with the computer, holding hands warmly and intimately.

The light dimmed, then went out completely, and in the darkness, Pelorat stirred.

Trevize said, "Don't get nervous, Janov. I may have a little trouble trying to control the computer, but I'll start easy and you'll have to be patient with me. Do you see it? The crescent?"

It hung in the darkness before them. A little dim and wavering at first, but getting sharper and brighter.

Pelorat's voice sounded awed. "Is that Terminus? Are we that far from it?"

"Yes, the ship's moving quickly."

The ship was curving into the night shadow of Terminus, which appeared as a thick crescent of bright light. Trevize had a momentary urge to send the ship in a wide arc that would carry them over the daylit side of the planet to show it in all its beauty, but he held back.

Pelorat might find novelty in this, but the beauty would be tame. There were too many photographs, too many maps, too many globes. Every child knew what Terminus looked like. A water planet — more so than most — rich in water and poor in minerals, good in agriculture and poor in heavy industry, but the best in the Galaxy in high technology and in miniaturization.

If he could have the computer use microwaves and translate it into a visible model, they would see every one of Terminus's ten thousand inhabited islands, together with the only one of them large enough to be considered a continent, the one that bore Terminus City and —

Turn away!

It was just a thought, an exercise of the will, but the view shifted at once. The lighted crescent moved off toward the borders of vision and rolled off the edge. The darkness of starless space filled his eyes.

Pelorat cleared his throat. "I wish you would bring back Terminus, my boy. I feel as though I've been blinded." There was a tightness in his voice.

"You're not blind. Look!"

Into the field of vision came a filmy fog of pale translucence. It spread and became brighter, until the whole room seemed to glow.

Shrink!

Another exercise of will and the Galaxy drew off, as though seen through a diminishing telescope that was steadily growing more powerful in its ability to diminish. The Galaxy contracted and became a structure of varying luminosity.

Brighten!

It grew more luminous without changing size, and because the stellar system to which Terminus belonged was above the Galactic plane, the Galaxy was not seen exactly edge-on. It was a strongly foreshortened double spiral, with curving dark-nebula rifts streaking the glowing edge of the Terminus side. The creamy haze of the nucleus — far off and shrunken by the distance — looked unimportant.

Pelorat said in an awed whisper, "You are right. I have never seen it like this. I never dreamed it had so much detail."

"How could you? You can't see the outer half when Terminus's atmosphere is between you and it. You can hardly see the nucleus from Terminus's surface."

"What a pity we're seeing it so nearly head-on."

"We don't have to. The computer can show it in any orientation. I just have to express the wish — and not even aloud."

Shift coordinates!

This exercise of will was by no means a precise command. Yet as the image of Galaxy began to undergo a slow change, his mind guided the computer and had it do what he wished!

Slowly the Galaxy was turning so that it could be seen at right angles to the Galactic plane. It spread out like a gigantic, glowing whirlpool, with curves of darkness, and knots of brightness, and a central all-but-featureless blaze.

Pelorat asked, "How can the computer see it from a position in space that must be more than fifty thousand parsecs from this place?" Then he added, in a choked whisper, "Please forgive me that I ask. I know nothing about all this."

Trevize said, "I know almost as little about this computer as you do. Even a simple computer, however, can adjust coordinates and show the Galaxy in any position, starting with what it can sense in the natural position, the one, that is, that would appear from the computer's local position in space. Of course, it makes use only of the information it can sense to begin with, so when it changes to the broadside view we would find gaps and blurs in what it would show. In this case, though —"

"Yes?"

"We have an excellent view. I suspect that the computer is outfitted with a complete map of the Galaxy and can therefore view it from any angle with equal ease."

"How do you mean, a complete map?"

"The spatial coordinates of every star in it must be in the computer's memory banks."

"*Every* star?" Pelorat seemed awed.

"Well, perhaps not all three hundred billion. It would include the stars shining down on populated planets, certainly, and probably every star of spectral class K and brighter. That means about seventy-five billion, at least."

"*Every* star of a populated system?"

"I wouldn't want to be pinned down; perhaps not all. There were, after all, twenty-five million inhabited systems in the time of Hari Seldon — which sounds like a lot but is only one star out of every twelve thousand. And then, in the five centuries since Seldon, the general breakup of the Empire didn't prevent further colonization. I should think it would have encouraged it. There are still plenty of habitable planets to expand into, so there may be thirty million now. It's possible that not all the new ones are in the Foundation's records."

"But the old ones? Surely they must all be there without exception."

"I imagine so. I can't guarantee it, of course, but I would be surprised if any long-established inhabited system were missing from the records. Let me show you something — if my ability to control the computer will go far enough."

Trevize's hands stiffened a bit with the effort and they seemed to sink further into the clasp of the computer. That might not have been necessary; he might only have had to think quietly and casually: Terminus!

He did think that and there was, in response, a sparkling red diamond at the very edge of the whirlpool.

"There's our sun," he said with excitement. "That's the star that Terminus circles."

"Ah," said Pelorat with a low, tremulous sigh.

A bright yellow dot of light sprang into life in a rich cluster of stars deep in the heart of the Galaxy but well to one side of the central haze. It was rather closer to the Terminus edge of the Galaxy than to the other side.

"And that," said Trevize, "is Trantor's sun."

Another sigh, then Pelorat said, "Are you sure? They always speak of Trantor as being located in the center of the Galaxy."

"It is, in a way. It's as close to the center as a planet can get and still be habitable. It's closer than any other major populated system. The actual center of the Galaxy consists of a black hole with a mass of nearly a million stars, so that the center is a violent place. As far as we know, there is no life in the actual center and maybe there just can't be any life there. Trantor is in the innermost subring of the spiral arms and, believe me, if you could see its night sky, you would think it was in the center of the Galaxy. It's surrounded by an extremely rich clustering of stars."

"Have you been on Trantor, Golan?" asked Pelorat in clear envy.

"Actually no, but I've seen holographic representations of its sky."

Trevize stared at the Galaxy somberly. In the great search for the Second Foundation during the time of the Mule, how everyone had played with Galactic maps — and how many volumes had been written and filmed on the subject.

And all because Hari Seldon had said, at the beginning, that the Second Foundation would be established "at the other end of the Galaxy," calling the place Star's End.

At the other end of the Galaxy! Even as Trevize thought it, a thin blue line sprang into view, stretching from Terminus, through the Galaxy's central black hole, to the other end. Trevize nearly jumped. He had not directly ordered the line, but he had thought of it quite clearly and that had been enough for the computer.

But, of course, the straight-line route to the opposite side of the Galaxy was not necessarily an indication of the "other end" that Seldon had spoken of. It was Arkady Darell (if one could believe her autobiography) who had made use of the phrase "a circle has no end" to indicate what everyone now accepted as truth —

And though Trevize suddenly tried to suppress the thought, the computer was too quick for him. The blue line vanished and was replaced with a circle that neatly rimmed the Galaxy in blue and that passed through the deep red dot of Terminus's sun.

A circle has no end, and if the circle began at Terminus, then if we searched for the other end, it would merely return to Terminus, and there the Second Foundation had indeed been found, inhabiting the same world as the First.

But if, in reality, it had not been found — if the so-called finding of the Second Foundation had been an illusion — what then? What besides a straight line and a circle would make sense in this connection?

Pelorat said, "Are you creating illusions? Why is there a blue circle?"

"I was just testing my controls. — Would you like to locate Earth?"

There was silence for a moment or two, then Pelorat said, "Are you joking?"

"No. I'll try."

He did. Nothing happened.

"Sorry," said Trevize.

"It's not there? No Earth?"

"I suppose I might have misthought my command, but that doesn't seem likely. I suppose it's more likely that Earth isn't listed in the computer's vitals."

Pelorat said, "It may be listed under another name."

Trevize jumped at that quickly. "What other name, Janov?"

Pelorat said nothing and, in the darkness, Trevize smiled. It occurred to him that things might just possibly be falling into place. Let it go for a while. Let it ripen. He deliberately changed the subject and said, "I wonder if we can manipulate time."

"Time! How can we do that?"

"The Galaxy is rotating. It takes nearly half a billion years for Terminus to move about the grand circumference of the Galaxy once. Stars that are closer to the center complete the journey much more quickly, of course. The motion of each star, relative to the central black hole, might be recorded in the computer and, if so, it may be possible to have the computer multiply each motion by millions of times and make the rotational effect visible. I can try to have it done."

He did and he could not help his muscles tightening with the effort of will he was exerting — as though he were taking hold of the Galaxy and accelerating it, twisting it, forcing it to spin against terrible resistance.

The Galaxy was moving. Slowly, mightily, it was twisting in the direction that should be working to tighten the spiral arms.

Time was passing incredibly rapidly as they watched — a false, artificial time — and, as it did so, stars became evanescent things.

Some of the larger ones — here and there — reddened and grew brighter as they expanded into red giants. And then a star in the central clusters blew up soundlessly in a blinding blaze that, for a tiny fraction of a second, dimmed the Galaxy and then was gone. Then another in one of the spiral arms, then still another not very far away from it.

"Supernovas," said Trevize a little shakily.

Was it possible that the computer could predict exactly which stars would explode and when? Or was it just using a simplified model that served to show the starry future in general terms, rather than precisely?

Pelorat said in a husky whisper, "The Galaxy looks like a living thing, crawling through space."

"It does," said Trevize, "but I'm growing tired. Unless I learn to do this less tensely, I'm not going to be able to play this kind of game for long."

He let go. The Galaxy slowed, then halted, then tilted, until it was in the view-from-the-side from which they had seen it at the start.

PART 2

EARTH SCIENCES

IN MY PREVIOUS OPUS BOOKS, Part 2 was entitled "Robots." On reflection, however, it seems to me that "Robots" is out of place here, and (with some hesitation) I have decided that I am not going to cling to something that is wrong out of a feeling for "tradition." I'm not leaving out "Robots," you can be sure. It will appear later in a more appropriate position.

In its place, I am including the section "Earth Sciences," which I neglected altogether in the first two books. This is not because I never dealt with the subject (I did!) but merely because I somehow didn't think to make it a separate section.

This time I can't avoid it, for one of my favorite books of the third hundred is Exploring the Earth and the Cosmos (Book 252), which was published by Crown in 1982. As in the case of my earlier Crown book, Extraterrestrial Civilizations, there is a sad story to tell.

When Paul Nadan died, another Crown editor, Herbert Michelman, took me over. In no time at all, I grew to like him very much and I believe the affection was returned. (It is an amazing thing, but I am almost always fond of my editors. I don't know if this is a general condition among writers.)

We had a number of happy lunches together, and once we were finished with Extraterrestrial Civilizations, he had no trouble in persuading me to do a book on the various expanding horizons of human knowledge. Working on Exploring the Earth and the Cosmos was a lot of fun, and when it was finally in production, I invited him to attend a luncheon meeting of the Dutch Treat Club, of which I am a member.

Herb attended, enjoyed himself, and I promptly proposed him as a new member — and he was as promptly accepted. On November 11, 1980, he attended his first luncheon meeting as a member. I brought him to the table at which I usually sat with my particular cronies, introduced him all around — and four hours after we said good-bye at the conclusion of the lunch, he died of a heart attack.

For the second time, I had a sad dedication to insert when Exploring the Earth and the Cosmos *finally appeared: "Dedicated to the memory of Herbert Michelman (1913–1980)."*

In the book I take up various kinds of exploration, one after the other, and in Chapter 6 I talk about the solid ball of the globe itself (having previously considered its surface). It is not a long chapter, and I quote it here in full.

from EXPLORING THE EARTH AND THE COSMOS (1982)

Below Earth's Atmosphere

THE SOLID INTERIOR

The surface of Earth, whose horizons we have been discussing thus far, has a 20-kilometer range of unevenness from the height of Mount Everest to the depth of Challenger Deep, but this range shrinks to insignificance in comparison with the size of Earth itself.

Earth is a ball that is over 12,000 kilometers in diameter, and if it were modeled into an object the size of a billiard ball, with all its surface unevennesses reproduced exactly to scale, the model would be *smoother* than an ordinary billiard ball — and the ocean would be an all but unnoticeable mist of dampness over 70 percent of its surface.

The expansion of the human horizon through mountains and oceans is *still* essentially two-dimensional, therefore. How far, then, can one extend human knowledge beyond the surface, really beyond? Do we know anything, for instance, about the interior of the solid sphere of Earth itself?

Yes, for we know something about Earth as a whole just from our knowledge of the surface.

From the manner in which ships at sea disappear over the horizon, from the way stars appear and disappear over the horizon as one travels north and south, and from the shape of Earth's shadow on the Moon, people have realized since the time of the ancient Greeks that Earth is essentially spherical in shape. Since Earth rotates, there has to be a centrifugal effect, as Isaac Newton (1642–1727) was the first to point out in the 1680s, and the surface must bulge outward more and more as one moves away from the poles, the bulge reaching a maximum outward extension at the equator. The result is that Earth is an "oblate spheroid" rather than a sphere. However, the bulge is so small compared to the size of Earth itself that seen from space, Earth would seem to be a sphere.

Thus, the diameter of Earth is 12,714 kilometers from pole to pole, and 12,757 kilometers across the equator. The equatorial bulge, at its maximum, adds 43 kilometers to the diameter, a difference of 0.32 percent.

The volume of such an oblate spheroid is 1.083×10^{12} cubic kilometers,* or, in other words, about a trillion cubic kilometers.

Somewhat more difficult to determine is the "mass" of Earth, where we might define the mass of an object (not quite accurately, but sufficiently so for our purposes) as the quantity of matter in that object.

One way of judging the mass of an object is to measure the intensity of its gravitational field, since that is strictly proportional to its mass. In 1798 the English scientist Henry Cavendish (1731–1810) very delicately measured the tiny gravitational pull of one lead sphere of known mass upon another and compared this with Earth's pull on those masses. From the much greater pull of Earth, he could calculate Earth's much greater mass.

Cavendish's initial figure for the mass of Earth was surprisingly accurate, and it has been little improved on since. The figure accepted today is 5.976×10^{24} kilograms† (which is just about 6 trillion trillion kilograms).

If we divide Earth's mass by its volume, we obtain Earth's average "density" — the mass of a unit volume of Earth. The unit volume we will use is the cubic meter.‡ The average density of Earth comes out to 5518 kilograms per cubic meter, or (in more compact symbols) 5518 kg/m^3.

It is common to compare the density of an object with that of

---

*A cubic kilometer equals 0.24 cubic miles in common American measure, so that there are just about 4 cubic kilometers to a cubic mile.

†A kilogram is equal to just about 2.2 pounds in common American measure, so that 5 kilograms equals 11 pounds.

‡A cubic meter is equal to about 1.3 cubic yards in common American measure, so that 3 cubic meters is equal to about 4 cubic yards. Also, a cubic meter is equal to one billionth (10^{-9}) of a cubic kilometer.

water, which has a density of just 1000 kg/m³. The average density of Earth, then, is just 5.518 times that of water.

The surface rocks of Earth have an average density of about 2800 kg/m³. Therefore the deeper regions of Earth must have a density considerably higher than 5518 kg/m³ in order to produce that as the average.

If Earth were uniformly rocky throughout, we would expect the density to rise with depth as the weight of thicker and thicker layers of rock above squeezed the rock below into greater and greater densities.

The pressures that would build up even at Earth's center would not be high enough, however, judging from data gathered from laboratory experiments, to compress rock into densities sufficiently high to produce the calculated average. The conclusion, then, is that Earth is not uniformly rocky throughout; somewhere near the center there is a change in structure; some substance that is denser than rock must be involved.

As it happens, meteorites are occasionally found on Earth. These represent small pieces of planetary material that ordinarily circle the Sun and have happened to collide with Earth in the course of that circling. They come in two chief varieties. Some are rocky and are in many ways similar to the kind of rock with which we are familiar here on Earth. Some, on the other hand, are metallic, and are made up of iron and the similar metal, nickel, in a roughly 9-to-1 ratio.

One theory about meteorites (*not* the one most favored today) held that they had their origin in the disintegration of a planet. If so, perhaps these two varieties of meteorites represent the two varieties of solids that make up planets. In 1866 a French geologist, Gabriel Auguste Daubrée (1814–1896), suggested that the interiormost portion of Earth was made up of an iron-nickel mixture like that of the metal meteorites.

This seemed logical, and it has remained the favored suggestion even today. If so, the density at Earth's center should be about 11,500 kg/m³, or just about twice that of the surface rocks.

EARTHQUAKES

But what about the details concerning the change in density as one moves downward? If the structure of Earth changes, if there is a more or less sudden switch from rock to metal, there should also be a sudden change in density. How can one check the solid structure of Earth for the location and extent of this sudden change? To do so, one must find something that penetrates the deep layers, that can be detected after having done so, and that can experience changes in doing so that will yield the desired information.

As it happens, there *is* such a phenomenon.

The slowly moving plates of Earth's crust may bind and then suddenly slip as they rub against each other. These slips set up powerful vibrations we call earthquakes. The strength of the vibrations falls off with distance, and so actual damage is done only in the immediate vicinity of the slippage. The vibration can, however, be detected a great distance — virtually everywhere on Earth, if the earthquake is sufficiently violent.

The earth suffers a million quakes a year, including at least ten disastrous ones and a hundred serious ones, so this is a phenomenon that forces itself on the attention of scientists.

The English geologist John Michell (1724–1793) was the first to suggest, in 1760, that earthquakes were waves set up by the shifting of masses of rock kilometers below the surface, and in 1855 the Italian physicist Luigi Palmieri (1807–1896) devised the first "seismograph" to study these waves.

In its simplest form, the seismograph consists of a massive block suspended by a comparatively weak spring from a support firmly fixed in bedrock. When the Earth moves, the suspended block remains still because of its inertia. However, the support moves with Earth's motion. This motion is recorded on a slowly rotating drum by means of a pen attached to the stationary block. Nowadays, seismographs are apt to use a ray of light marking light-sensitive paper, in order to avoid the drag of pen on paper.

The English engineer John Milne (1850–1913), using seismographs of his own design, showed conclusively in the 1890s that Michell's description of earthquakes as waves propagated through the body of the Earth was correct. He led the way to establishing seismograph stations here and there on Earth. Well over five hundred are now spread over every continent, including Antarctica.

Seismograph studies showed that earthquake waves come in two general varieties, "surface waves" and "bodily waves." The surface waves follow the curve of Earth's surface, while the bodily waves go through the interior. The path through the interior is, so to speak, a shortcut, and so bodily waves arrive first at the seismograph. The extent to which the bodily waves beat the surface waves to a particular seismograph is an indication of how far away the source of the wave (the "epicenter" of the earthquake) is.

The bodily waves are, in turn, of two types: primary ("P waves") and secondary ("S waves"). The primary waves, like sound waves, travel by alternate compression and expansion of the medium, rather like the pushing together and pulling apart of an accordion. Such waves can pass through any medium — solid, liquid, or gas.

The secondary waves, on the other hand, have the familiar form of snakelike wiggles at right angles to the direction of travel. They can travel through solids and along the surface of liquids, but they cannot travel through the body of a liquid or through a gas.

The primary waves move faster than secondary waves, and this too gives a hint as to the distance of the epicenter of an earthquake.

The speed of both the primary and secondary waves is affected by the properties of the material through which they pass. If the material is uniform in properties, the waves travel in straight lines. If the properties change, the waves curve in their path, and from the nature and extent of the curve, and from changes in the speed of travel, deductions can be made about the change in the properties of the material passed through. Thus, earthquake waves can be used as probes to investigate conditions deep under the Earth's surface.

A primary wave near the surface travels at 8 kilometers per second (or, more concisely, 8 km/sec). At 1600 kilometers below the surface, its velocity, judging from the arrival times, must be nearly 13 km/sec. Similarly, a secondary wave has a velocity of about 4.5 km/sec near the surface and 6.5 km/sec at a depth of 1600 kilometers. Since increase in velocity is a measure of increase in density, we can estimate the density of the material far beneath the surface.

Whereas at the surface Earth's rocky layer has an average density of 2800 kg/m^3, 1600 kilometers down it amounts to 5000 kg/m^3, and 2900 kilometers down to nearly 6000 kg/m^3.

At a depth of 2900 kilometers, there is an abrupt change. Secondary waves are not transmitted at all at lower depths. This is taken to mean that Earth's substance is liquid at lower depths. The change is a sharp one and there seems an abrupt alteration in properties — so abrupt that the boundary is called a discontinuity. It is, in fact, the "Gutenberg discontinuity," named for the German geologist Beno Gutenberg (1899–1960), who in 1914 demonstrated its existence.

Below the Gutenberg discontinuity is Earth's "liquid core." At the greatest depths, within 1300 kilometers of the planetary center, the core may be solid. This was first pointed out, from the behavior of earthquake waves, by the Danish geologist Inge Lehmann in 1936.

Above the Gutenberg discontinuity is Earth's "mantle."

The density of Earth leaps from about 6000 kg/m³ above the Gutenberg discontinuity to about 9000 kg/m³ below, if we go by earthquake-wave data, and this would indicate a sharp change in the chemical structure. This would fit with the notion that at the Gutenberg discontinuity the rocky mantle suddenly changes into a liquid nickel-iron core. (There are currently arguments as to whether the core is entirely metallic or whether there is a certain admixture of sulfur or oxygen, and how much.)

Though the mantle is undeniably rocky in nature, it seems to differ from the surface rocks of Earth (if we judge by comparing the behavior of earthquake waves passing through both) in being richer in magnesium and iron, and poorer in aluminum.

The mantle, then, does not quite extend to the surface of Earth. A Croatian geologist, Andrija Mohorovičić (1857–1936), studying the waves produced by a Balkan earthquake in 1909, decided that there must be a sharp increase in wave velocity at a point about 32 kilometers beneath Earth's surface. This is now known as the Mohorovičić discontinuity, and it marks the upper surface of Earth's mantle. Above it is Earth's "crust." (Core, mantle, and crust bear, coincidentally, just about the same relative proportions in volume as do the yolk, white, and shell of a hen's egg.)

Earth's crust is not evenly thick over the entire surface of Earth. The Mohorovičić discontinuity is farther beneath the surface in the continental areas than under the ocean. And on the continents, it sinks particularly low in the mountainous areas. There is, in fact, a rough symmetry, for the higher the land surface above sea level, the lower the Mohorovičić discontinuity. Thus the crust is up to 65 kilometers thick under mountain ranges, 35 kilometers thick in low-lying continental areas, and only 13 to 16 kilometers thick under oceanic areas.

The thickness of the crust in oceanic areas includes the thickness of the water overlying the seabed. Under the ocean deeps, then, the solid portion of the crust might be no more than 5 kilometers thick.

In the 1960s there was some enthusiasm concerning the possibility of drilling through the seabed to the mantle in order to bring up material that would check the conclusions of theory. If that had taken place it would represent the deepest penetration into Earth's depths by human beings. The project fell through, however.

Nevertheless, even if the project is carried through some time in the future, it doesn't seem very likely that human beings will ever penetrate by instrument (much less by some sort of vehicle) lower than the boundary of the mantle. Nor can one honestly imagine what technological breakthrough would suffice for the purpose, considering the extreme properties of Earth's solid depths.

Of the books I do for young people, the most successful to date have been the How Did We Find Out series for Walker and Company. These are books on the history of science and there have been twenty-four of these so far.

The first, How Did We Find Out the Earth Was Round? (Book 133), was published in 1973. That and the eleven that followed were part of my second hundred books, while the next twelve were part of my third hundred. Included in the second dozen is How Did We Find Out About Volcanoes? (Book 231), which was published in 1981. From this book, I present the first chapter, which tells a story that is complete in itself, and was only uncovered less than twenty years ago.

from How Did We Find Out About Volcanoes? (1981)

Explosion at Thera

In Europe, civilization first developed on the islands of the Aegean Sea, which lies between the modern nations of Greece and Turkey.

The largest island of the area is Crete. It is 3189 square miles in size, or as large as Rhode Island and Delaware put together. As early as 3000 B.C., Crete began to use metals and to develop an important culture.

Crete may have borrowed much from nearby lands that had an even older history. One such land was Egypt, four hundred miles southeast of Crete. Other lands were what is now known as Lebanon, Syria, and Iraq, six hundred miles to the east.

The older civilizations were on continents, on great tracts of land. Crete represented the first island civilization. It was interested in the sea, therefore, and was the first land to develop a navy. The Cretan ships protected the land from invasion, and the Cretan people lived comfortable and peaceful lives. They built large palaces with indoor plumbing, created beautiful art, and played interesting athletic games.

The Cretan ships also traded with the surrounding lands. With the trade, the ships carried Cretan civilization and its way of life to other islands nearby and even to the part of the European continent we now call Greece.

About a hundred miles north of Crete are a group of islands known as the Cyclades. This comes from a Greek word meaning "circle," because the chief islands of the group are arranged in a circle, more or less. Cretan civilization reached the Cyclades and the people of those small islands also grew prosperous.

The southernmost island of the Cyclades was called Thera by the ancient Greeks, though it is spelled Thira today. Italians controlled the Aegean Sea in the Middle Ages, and they called the island Santorini, a name which is still sometimes used today.

Thera is only sixty-five miles north of Crete. Many Cretan ships came to Thera and, beginning about 2000 B.C., Thera became a rich, civilized island and stayed so for five hundred years.

If you look at the map of Thera now, you will see that it is shaped like a half-circle with the opening to the west. It is only about thirty square miles in area, not much larger than the island of Manhattan.

In the opening between the top and bottom points of the half-circle are two small islands. It is almost as though Thera was originally a complete circle, like the letter O, but somehow the sea broke in from the west, leaving that part of the circle in pieces. In the center of the broken O are two tiny islands that constantly smoke, as though there were fires under them.

Beginning in 1966, scientists, digging carefully at certain sites in

Thera, found the ruins of the ancient city that was so wealthy and civilized in Cretan times. They found beautiful pottery and wall paintings.

They also found evidence of a violent explosion that must have taken place about 1500 B.C.

Thera, it seems, was actually a large mountain at that time, rising up from the bottom of the Aegean Sea. The top part, which was above the surface of the sea, was circular, so that the island was then a solid *O*.

It was not an ordinary mountain, however. Deep within it, there was great heat that was sometimes pushed up and sometimes sank down. Occasionally in mountains of this sort, as the heat grows more intense, the rock inside the mountain melts. As more and more melting takes place, the melted rock comes closer and closer to the surface. Eventually, the heat can actually melt a hole somewhere in the mountain, and through that hole, red-hot liquid rock can overflow and pour down the mountainside.

Such molten rock is called lava, from an Italian word meaning "to wash." Originally, the people of the Italian city of Naples used the word for a downpour of rain that washed the streets clean. It came to be applied to the overflowing stream of melted rock because it washed the side of the mountain clean of grass and trees.

The overflow of lava could be dangerous, of course. If there are houses and towns on the slopes and at the foot of the mountain, they can be destroyed and people can be killed.

Sometimes, more happens than just lava overflowing and pouring downward. If water seeps deep into the mountain, the growing heat will make it boil. The steam produces more and more pressure, and finally it can blow out a piece of the mountain with great force.

This is an eruption, from Latin words meaning "to explode." Great rocks are hurled high in the air. Clouds of ash and gas are thrown to great heights. Columns of fire arise and lava pours out in great quantities.

Such a mountain is always smoking and heating. But every once in a while it gets a little worse and the lava flows. It is not usually very dangerous. As long as it keeps overflowing now and then, it is not likely to explode. Also, people know that it is uncomfortable to get close to it, and they stay away and remain safe.

On the other hand, a mountain of this sort can be quiet for many centuries. People forget it ever produced lava and think of it as just another mountain. The old lava that once poured out of it makes very fertile soil, so that plants grow on the slopes of the mountain and make it look green and pleasant. People find that crops grow well there, so they establish farms and homes on the slopes and at the foot of the mountain. Pretty soon towns grow up.

Then, someday, the mountain begins to heat up again, and if steam begins to form far in the depth, it is held in by a great weight of rock that cooled down centuries before. The pressure builds up — and builds up — and builds up —

It builds up much higher than it would have if the mountain hadn't been quiet for so long and hadn't developed such a thick layer of lava that had cooled into solid rock. Finally there's an *enormous* explosion.

In 1500 B.C. the mountain on Thera exploded. It blew up and scattered itself into the upper air in a vast cloud of rocks and dust and ash. A big hole was left where it stood. The sea rushed into the hole, and the island, instead of being a solid round circle of land, became a broken ring.

Everyone on the island was surely killed, and ash and dust showered down on eastern Crete.

The bottom of the sea shook and that set up a large wave. Some people call this a tidal wave, but it has nothing to do with tides. A better name is *tsunami*, which is Japanese for "harbor waves." When such a wave, which is quite low in the open sea, enters a harbor, all the water is forced into a narrow place and it becomes very high. It can be fifty feet high or more and when it crashes onto the shore, it can drown thousands of people.

The shores of Crete and of Greece were battered by the tsunami. Crete's capital city of Knossos was badly damaged, and the whole island suffered a great disaster.

The people of Crete tried to carry on after this dreadful blow, but they could not recover. Fifty years later, about 1450 B.C., invaders from Greece conquered the island, burned its cities, and destroyed its civilization. It might not have happened, had it not been for that exploding mountain on Thera.

The later Greeks had a dim memory of that huge explosion. They had a legend about a great flood that swept over the land, a flood from which only one couple escaped. This could be a tale about the tsunami that once had struck Greece.

About 370 B.C., the Greek philosopher Plato (427–347 B.C.) wrote of a great and beautiful city that was destroyed overnight by an earthquake and sank beneath the sea. He said it was far to the west, in the ocean beyond Spain, and he called it Atlantis after the name of the Atlantic Ocean, in which he had located it.

For over two thousand years, people have wondered if there was something to the legend. Many people actually believed that somewhere beneath the waters of the Atlantic Ocean there was a drowned continent that had once been a great civilized nation.

Possibly, though, Plato was repeating something that was a memory of an event closer to home. The story may have originated with the island of Thera, which had been highly civilized but which had exploded and sunk beneath the sea.

Among my most joyous tasks is my monthly essay for The Magazine of Fantasy and Science Fiction *(or* F & SF*). The essay is usually on some scientific subject, but not necessarily so, for I am given a totally free hand. I started in the November 1958 issue and have continued without missing an issue for over a quarter of a century.*

These essays are collected, seventeen at a time, into books that are published by Doubleday, of which thirteen were included in my first two hundred books. My third hundred includes four more. Of these, the first was The Road to Infinity *(Book 206), published in 1979. From that book I present an essay entitled "The Floating Crystal Palace," which deals with — well, what do you think a floating crystal palace might be?*

from THE ROAD TO INFINITY (1979)

The Floating Crystal Palace

Last month (as I write this) my wife, Janet, and I crossed the Atlantic on the *Queen Elizabeth 2;* then, after one day in Southampton, we crossed right back.

We did this for a number of reasons. I give a pair of talks each way, Janet is crazy about ships, and both of us found ourselves in an island of peace away from the cares of the workaday world. (Actually, I managed to write a small book while on board, but that's another story.)

In one respect, though, I was disenchanted on this particular voyage. It had always been my dim assumption that there was one word that is absolutely taboo on any liner. You might say something was "very large," "huge," "monstrous," "gigantic," but you would *never* say something was — well, the adjective begins with a *t*.

I was wrong. One evening on the ship, a standup comedian said, "I hope you'll all be joining us at the big banquet tomorrow, folks. We're celebrating the anniversary of the *Titanic*."

I was shocked! Heaven knows I've never been accused of good taste in my offhand humor, but this, I thought, was going too far. Had I known he was going to say it, I might well have tried to round up a committee for the feeding of poor, deserving sharks by throwing the comedian overboard.

Did others feel the same way?

No, sir! The remark was greeted with general laughter, and I (as far as I could tell) was the only abstainer.

Why did they laugh? I thought about it, and an essay began to build in my mind. Here it is —

♦

Let's start with Saint Brendan, an Irish monk of the sixth century.

At that time, Ireland could fairly lay claim to being the cultural leader of the Western world. The West European provinces of the Roman Empire lay sunk and broken in gathering darkness, but the light of learning burned in Ireland (which had never been part of the Empire) and the knowledge of Greek was retained there, though nowhere else in the West. Until the Irish light was extinguished by the Viking invasions of the ninth century and the English incursions thereafter, there was a three-century golden age on the island.

Part of the golden age was a set of remarkable Irish explorations that reached to Iceland and perhaps even beyond. (An Irish colony may have existed on Iceland for a century, but was gone by the time the Vikings landed there in the ninth century.) One explorer we know by name was Saint Brendan.

About 550, Saint Brendan sailed northward from the west coast of Ireland and seems to have explored the islands off the northern Scottish coast — the Hebrides, the Orkneys, the Shetlands. It is possible that he went still farther north, reaching the Faeroe Islands, about 750 kilometers (470 miles) north of the northern tip of Ireland. This was almost surely the record northward penetration by sea by any human being up to that time.

Saint Brendan's voyage was remarkable enough for its time, but in later years tradition magnified it. In 800 a fictional account of his voyages was written and proved very popular. It was, in a way, a primitive example of science fiction, in that the writer drew liberally on his imagination but made careful use of travelers' tales as the supporting framework (just as modern science fiction writers would use scientific theory for the same purpose).

In the tale, for instance, Saint Brendan is described as having sighted a "floating crystal palace."

Is there anything in oceanic exploration that could give rise to this particular fantasy?

Certainly. An iceberg. Assuming this interpretation to be correct, this is the first mention of an iceberg in world literature.

In later centuries when the northern ocean was systematically explored, icebergs came to be a common sight. Where did they come from?

To be sure, the sea tends to freeze near the poles, and the Arctic Ocean is covered with a more or less unbroken layer of ice in the winter months. This sea ice is not very thick, however. The average thickness is 1.5 meters (5 feet) and some parts may reach a thickness of as much as 4 meters (13 feet).

We can imagine pieces of that sea ice breaking off as the weather warms in the spring and then floating southward, but those pieces would scarcely be impressive. They would be flat slabs of ice, topping sea level by some 40 centimeters (15 inches) or less.

Compare this to an Arctic iceberg, the top of which can tower 30 meters (100 feet) above sea level. One iceberg has been reported as having a record height of 170 meters (560 feet) above sea level — almost half as tall as the Empire State Building. Counting the portion that was submerged, that piece of ice may have been 1.6 kilometers (1 mile) from top to bottom.

Such a huge chunk of ice could have been spawned only on land.

At sea, the liquid water below the ice layer acts as a heat sink which, even in the coldest polar winter, keeps the ice from growing too thick. On land, the solid surface, with less heat capacity than water and with no currents to bring warmer material from elsewhere, drops to low, subfreezing temperatures and exerts no melting effect. The snow simply piles up from year to year and is capable of forming great thicknesses of ice.

Long-lived ice forms and thickens on mountain heights all over the world. It also forms at sea level in polar regions. The largest piece of land in the Arctic which is wholly polar is Greenland, and it is on that vast island that the ice is most extensive and thickest.

The Greenland ice sheet fills the interior of the island and is about 2500 kilometers (1500 miles) long, north to south, and up to 1100 kilometers (700 miles) wide, east to west.

The area of the Greenland ice sheet is just over 1,800,000 square kilometers (700,000 square miles) — a single piece of ice, in other words, that is about 2.6 times the area of Texas. At its thickest point, the Greenland ice sheet is about 3.3 kilometers (2 miles) thick. Along most of the Greenland coast, however, is a fringe of bare land that, in places, is up to 300 kilometers (190 miles) wide.

(It is Greenland's southwestern fringe of bare land to which Viking colonists stubbornly clung for four centuries, from 980 to 1380.)

Each year more snow falls on the Greenland ice sheet and hardly any of it melts in the warmer months (and what does, tends to refreeze the next winter), yet the ice sheet does not get endlessly thicker. Ice, you see, is plastic under pressure.

As the ice sheet thickens, its own weight tends to flatten it and spread it out. The ice, driven by enormous pressure, is forced, in the form of glaciers, to move, like solid creeping rivers, along the valleys and into the seas. These Greenland glaciers move at rates of up to 45 meters (150 feet) per day, which is an enormous speed when compared to the rate at which ordinary mountain glaciers (driven by far smaller pressures) move.

When the Greenland glaciers reach the sea, the ice does not melt appreciably. Neither the Greenland sun nor the cold seas surrounding Greenland will deliver enough heat to do much to them. The tips of the glaciers simply break off (calve) and huge lumps of ice plop into the sea. It is these that are the icebergs. (*Berg*, by the way, is German for "mountain.")

In Arctic waters, some 16,000 icebergs are calved each year.

About 90 percent of them originate from Greenland glaciers that enter the sea in Baffin Bay, which bathes the western shore of the island.

The largest glacier in the world, the Humboldt Glacier, lies in northwestern Greenland at latitude 80° N. It is 80 kilometers (50 miles) across its coastal foot, but it is too cold to break off icebergs at a record rate. Farther south, about two thirds of the length down the western coast of Greenland, the Jakobshavn Glacier calves 1400 icebergs a year.

Since ice has a density of 0.9, most of any iceberg is below the surface. The exact quantity submerged depends on how pure the ice is. The ice usually contains a great many air bubbles, which give it a milky appearance rather than the transparency of true ice, and this lowers its density. On the other hand, in approaching the sea, the glaciers may well scrape up gravel and rock which may remain with the iceberg and which would increase its overall density. On the whole, anything from 80 to 90 percent of the iceberg is submerged.

As long as icebergs remain in Arctic waters, they persist without much change. The freezing water of the Arctic Ocean will not melt them appreciably. The icebergs that form off the western coast of Greenland linger in Baffin Bay for a long time, but eventually begin to move southward through Davis Strait into the waters south of Greenland and east of Labrador.

Many icebergs are trapped along the bleak coast of Labrador and there they break up and slowly melt, but some persist, largely intact, as far south as Newfoundland, taking up to three years to make the 3000-kilometer (1800-mile) journey.

Once an iceberg reaches Newfoundland, however, its fate is sealed. It drifts past that island into the warm waters of the Gulf Stream.

In an average year some four hundred icebergs pass Newfoundland and move into the shipping lanes of the North Atlantic. Most of them melt in two weeks in the warm embrace of the Gulf Stream, but the remnants of one giant were sighted on June 2, 1934, at the record southerly latitude of 30° N, the latitude of northern Florida.

At the start of the last stage of its journey, however, an iceberg is still massive and menacing and is even more dangerous than it looks, since the major portion of it is submerged and may jut outward considerably closer to some approaching vessel than the visible upper portion does.

◆

In the years before radio, when ships were truly isolated and there was no way of knowing what lay beyond the horizon, icebergs were dangerous indeed. Between 1870 and 1890, for instance, fourteen ships were sunk and forty damaged by collision with icebergs.

Then came the *Titanic*. The *Titanic*, when it was launched in 1911, was the largest ship in the world — 270 meters (883 feet) long with a gross tonnage of 46,000 metric tons. Its hull was divided into sixteen watertight compartments; four of them could be ripped open without sinking the ship. In fact, the ship was considered unsinkable and was proclaimed so. In April 1912 it set off on its maiden voyage from Southampton to New York, carrying a glittering load of the rich and the socially prominent.

On the night of April 14–15, it sighted an iceberg at a point some 500 kilometers (300 miles) southeast of Newfoundland. The ship had been ignoring the possibility of icebergs and was going far too fast in its eagerness to set a world record for time of crossing. Consequently, by the time the iceberg was sighted, it was too late to avoid a collision.

The collision, when it came, opened a 90-meter (300-foot) gash on the ship's starboard side. A fatal five compartments were sliced open; even so the *Titanic* held out gamely. It took nearly three hours for it to sink.

That might have been enough to save the passengers, but there had been no lifeboat drills and, even if there had been, the lifeboats available had room for fewer than half the more than twenty-two hundred people aboard.

By now, radio was in use on ships and the *Titanic* sent out a distress signal. Another ship, the *Californian*, was equipped to receive the signal and was close enough that night to speed to the rescue, but it had only one radio operator and a man has to sleep sometime. There was no one on duty when the signal came in.

More than 1500 lives were lost when the *Titanic* went down. Because of the drama of that sinking, the number of lives lost, and the social position of many of the dead, the disaster revolutionized the rules governing sea travel. After the tragedy, all passenger ships were required to carry lifeboats with enough seats for everyone on board, lifeboat drills were to take place on every passage, radio receivers were operating twenty-four hours a day, with men taking shifts at the earphones, and so on.

In addition, in 1914 an International Ice Patrol was established and has been maintained ever since, to keep watch over the positions of these inanimate giants of the deep. It is supported by nineteen nations and is operated by the United States Coast Guard. The patrol supplies continuing information on all icebergs sighted below latitude 52° N, with a prediction of the movements of each over the next twelve hours.

Eventually, air surveillance and radar were added to the patrol and in the years since it was established not one ship has been sunk by an iceberg within the area under guard. Indeed, modern liners stay so far away from icebergs that passengers never even see them on the horizon. It's no wonder, then, that the passengers on the *Queen Elizabeth 2* could afford to laugh at a tasteless reference to the *Titanic*.

◆

The glaciers of western Greenland are the most dangerous iceberg formers in the world, but not the largest. They can't very well be the largest, since the Greenland ice sheet, while the second largest in the world, is a very poor second.

The largest ice sheet is that of Antarctica. The Antarctica ice sheet is a roughly circular mass of ice with a diameter of about 4500 kilometers (2800 miles) and a shoreline of over 20,000 kilometers (12,500 miles). It has an area of about 14,000,000 square kilometers (5,500,000 square miles) and is about seven and a half times the Greenland ice sheet in area — and about one and a half times the area of the United States. The average thickness of the Antarctica ice sheet is just about 2 kilometers (1¼ miles), and at its thickest, it is 4.3 kilometers (2⅔ miles).

The total volume of the Antarctica ice sheet is about 30,000,000 cubic kilometers (7,000,000 cubic miles); this is 90 percent of all the ice in the world.

There are two deep indentations into the roughly circular continent — Ross Sea and Weddell Sea. As the Antarctica ice sheet is flattened out and spreads outward, it reaches these seas first, but it doesn't calve there as the western Greenland ice sheet does. The

Antarctica ice sheet is too thick and, instead, it moves out intact over the seas to form two ice shelves.

The ice shelves remain intact for a distance of up to 1300 kilometers (800 miles) out to sea and form slabs of ice that are some 800 meters (½ mile) thick where they leave land and are still 250 meters (⅙ mile) thick at their seaward edge. The Ross Ice Shelf, the larger of the two, has an area equal to that of France.

The ice shelves do not push northward indefinitely, of course. Eventually, slabs of ice break off the seaward edge, to form huge "tabular icebergs," flat on top, up to 100 meters (330 feet) above sea level, and with lengths that can be measured in hundreds of kilometers.

In 1956 a tabular iceberg was sighted that was 330 kilometers (200 miles) long and 100 kilometers (60 miles) wide — a single piece of free-floating ice with an area half again that of the state of Massachusetts.

For the most part, Antarctic icebergs drift in the Antarctic Ocean and are carried round and round Antarctica, edging northward and slowly melting. Although representing a much larger mass of ice in total than the 400 Greenland icebergs that slip past Newfoundland each year, the Antarctic icebergs scarcely impinge upon the consciousness of mankind, since they are well away from the chief ocean trade routes of the world. Nowhere in the Southern Hemisphere are there shipping lanes as crowded as those of the North Atlantic.

An occasional Antarctic iceberg drifts quite far northward; in 1894 the last remnant of one was sighted in the western South Atlantic at latitude 26° S, not far south of Rio de Janeiro, Brazil.

◆

Icebergs are not all bad. The vast Antarctica ice sheet and the huge icebergs it spawns serve as air conditioners for the world and, by keeping the ocean depths cold, allow sea life to flourish.

Anything else? Well, let's start at another point.

The average American, drinking eight glasses of water a day, will consume 0.7 cubic meters (180 gallons) in a year. Water is also required for bathing, washing the dishes, watering the lawn, and so on, so the average American consumes, at home, 200 cubic meters (53,000 gallons) of water per year.

But Americans also need water for domestic animals, for growing crops, and for industry. To make a kilogram of steel requires 200 kilograms of water, for instance, and to grow a kilogram of wheat requires 8000 kilograms of water.

All told, the water use of the United States comes to 2700 cubic meters (710,000 gallons) per year per person.

In those regions of the world where industry is negligible and where agricultural methods are simple, water needs can be satisfied by 900 cubic meters (240,000 gallons) per person per year. The average figure for the world as a whole might come to 1500 cubic meters (400,000 gallons) per person per year.

How does this compare with the water supply of the world?

If all the water in the world were divided equally among the four billion people on Earth right now, it would amount to 320,000,000 cubic meters (85 billion gallons) for each person. That sounds like plenty. This is enough water, if efficiently recycled, to supply the needs of two hundred ten thousand times the present world population.

But wait! Fully 97.4 percent of all the water on Earth is the salt water of the ocean, and human beings don't use salt water for drinking, washing, agriculture, or industry. That 1500 cubic meters per person per year refers to fresh water only.

If all the *fresh* water on Earth were divided equally among the four billion people on Earth right now, it would amount to 8,300,000 cubic meters (2.2 billion gallons) for each person. Still not terrible. With efficient recycling, the fresh water supply could support fifty-five hundred times the present world population.

But wait! Fully 98 percent of all the fresh water on Earth is locked up in the form of ice (mostly in the Antarctica ice sheet) and it isn't available for use by human beings. The only water that human beings can use is *liquid* fresh water, found in rivers, ponds, lakes, and ground water and replenished continually by rain and melting snow.

If all the *liquid* fresh water were divided equally among the four billion people on Earth right now, it would amount to 160,000 cubic meters (42,000,000 gallons) per person per year. That's still not fatal. With efficient recycling, that is enough to support one hundred times the present population on Earth.

But wait! The recycling isn't 100 percent efficient. We can't very well use more liquid fresh water per year than is supplied each year by rain or by that portion of the snowfall that eventually melts. If all the *precipitated* liquid fresh water is divided among the four billion people on Earth right now, each would get 30,000 cubic meters (8,000,000 gallons) each year. That is enough to support twenty times the present population on Earth

But wait! The liquid fresh water of Earth is *not* evenly spread among the world's population. Nor does the rain fall evenly, either in space or in time. The result is that some areas of the world have too much water while other areas of the world have too little. There are rain forests and there are deserts; there are times when there are disastrous floods and other times when there are disastrous droughts.

Furthermore, most of the fresh water of Earth makes its way back to the sea without a reasonable chance of being used by human beings at all; and much of the fresh water that we could use is being polluted — more all the time. The result is that, amazing to say in this water-logged planet of ours, we are heading rapidly into a disastrous worldwide water shortage.

Well, then, what do we do?

1. Obviously, we must, most of all, control population. If we multiply the world's population by twenty times — something we can do in 150 years if we put our minds to it — our needs will outrun the total rain supply.

2. We must do nothing to destroy the fresh water available to us. We must minimize pollution and we must avoid destroying the soil by unwise agricultural practices that lower its ability to store water, thus promoting the spread of deserts.

3. We must minimize waste and make use of our fresh water supply more efficiently. For instance, the Amazon River, the largest in the world, discharges into the sea in one year 7200 cubic kilometers (1700 cubic miles) of fresh water, enough to supply the needs of the present population of the world indefinitely — but virtually none of it is used by man. On the other hand, we mustn't overuse the fresh water, either. We mustn't tap ground water, for instance, at a rate faster than it can be replaced, for the dropping of the ground-water level or its invasion by salt water could be ruinous.

4. Water must be viewed as a global resource and efforts must be made to transfer it from points of excess to points of deficiency, as we routinely do for food and fuel, for instance.

So much for making do with what we have. Is there any way we can increase the supply? Well —

1. We can minimize the loss of fresh water by evaporation, by placing single-molecule films of certain solid alcohols, or layers of small plastic balls, on exposed water surfaces. Such evaporation barriers are difficult to maintain, however, since wind and wave tend to break them up. And if they *are* maintained, they may interfere with the oxygenation of the water below.

2. Any rain that falls on the ocean is completely wasted. It might better fall on the land — it will then, in any case, return to the ocean, but it can be used en route. Any method of weather control we could devise that would shift the rain from sea to land would be helpful.

3. Since the ultimate source of rain is the evaporation of sea water by solar heat, we can add our human effort in that direction and get fresh water by desalinating ocean water artificially. This is not a blue-sky project but is done routinely today. Large ships get their fresh water by desalination, and energy-rich, water-poor nations such as Kuwait and Saudi Arabia do so, too — and are planning expansions of such equipment in the future. This *does* take energy in large amounts, however, and, at the moment, we are ill equipped to commit those large amounts. Is there anything else?

Well, as I noted above, 98 percent of the fresh water supply on Earth is in the form of ice, which need only be melted, not distilled. Melting would take much less energy than desalination does.

The major trouble is that the ice is chiefly in Greenland and Antarctica and is not very accessible.

Some of the ice, however, is floating on the ocean. Can icebergs be dragged to where water is needed without increasing the cost to prohibitive levels?

The Arctic icebergs of the North Atlantic are relatively far away from most of those regions on Earth that are most in need of water. They would have to be moved around Africa, for instance, to reach the Middle East and around South America to reach the American West.

But what about the huge tabular icebergs of the Antarctic? These could be moved directly northward to desiccated areas without having to dodge continental land masses. And even a relatively small iceberg of this type would represent 100,000,000 cubic meters of fresh water, or a year's supply for 67,000 people.

Such an iceberg would have to be dragged slowly northward to the Middle East, say, right through the warm waters of the tropics. The iceberg would have to be trimmed to a shiplike form to reduce water resistance; it would have to be insulated on the sides and bottom to reduce melting; and once it reached Middle East waters, it would have to be sliced up, each slice melted, and the water stored.

Can all this be done without making the expense of iceberg water greater than that of desalination water? Some experts think so, and I look forward to seeing the attempt made.

After all, how better to avenge the *Titanic* than to put icebergs to such a vital use?

PART 3

MATHEMATICS

*IT'S A PITY that mathematics is not my strong suit, because num-
bers seem to fascinate my readers. I never do an essay on a mathematical subject for F & SF without getting a packet of letters from
readers (sometimes adding to the information, and sometimes even
correcting me). Unfortunately, it seems to me I have used up most
of those facets of mathematics I can handle, so that appropriate
essays are being written at ever longer intervals. I did manage one
that I thought a beauty, however, at the request of a reader.*

*Mind you, it took me a while. There was a lapse of several years
between the time the reader wrote to ask me to do an article on
something called the "golden section" and the time I finally worked
up the courage to try my hand at it. But I did, eventually, calling
the article "To Ungild Refined Gold." It appeared in my essay collection* X Stands for Unknown *(Book 290), published by Doubleday
in 1984.*

from X STANDS FOR UNKNOWN *(1984)*

To Ungild Refined Gold

One of my less amiable characteristics is an impatience with misquotation, especially if it is from Shakespeare.

A sure way to induce the symptoms of apoplexy in me is to have
someone who is doing a comic rendition of the passage from *Romeo
and Juliet* say: "Wherefore art thou, Romeo?" with an intonation
and action indicating that the meaning is "Where are you,
Romeo?"

Not only does this indicate that the poor illiterates who are responsible have never read the play but that they don't even know
the meaning of "wherefore," or — worse yet — assume that the
audience neither knows nor cares.

A high follower in the list of misquoters whom I disesteem are those who speak of "gilding the lily."

That is a misquotation from Shakespeare's *King John,* Act 4, Scene 2, where the Earl of Salisbury lists six actions that represent "wasteful and ridiculous excess" as a way of condemning King John's insistence on a second coronation. In each case, something is described that attempts to improve that which cannot be improved, and the first two examples are "to gild refined gold, to paint the lily."

The misquoter collapses the two and says "to gild the lily," an action which somewhat lacks the exquisite inappropriateness of the two actions as given by Shakespeare.

So as my way of fighting this annoyance I intend to demonstrate a way in which I can manage "to ungild refined gold." You'll see what I mean as I go on.

When I am trapped in an assemblage, and am restless, and am sure no one is eyeing me closely, I can sometimes rescue myself by playing with numbers: adding, subtracting, multiplying, dividing, and so on.

There is no point of my doing this, you understand, because I lack all trace of mathematical talent. What I do with numbers is to mathematics what piling one toy block on top of another is to architecture. But then, you see, I don't imagine myself to be doing mathematics; I am merely protecting my brain (a rather demanding organ) from damage through boredom.

I did this even when I was quite young, and I was about twelve, I think, when I studied the relation of numbers to their squares in the following fashion:

$$1^2 = 1; \text{ and } 1 - 1 = 0$$
$$2^2 = 4; \text{ and } 4 - 2 = 2$$
$$3^2 = 9; \text{ and } 9 - 3 = 6$$
$$4^2 = 16; \text{ and } 16 - 4 = 12$$
$$5^2 = 25; \text{ and } 25 - 5 = 20$$
$$6^2 = 36; \text{ and } 36 - 6 = 30$$

By this time, I saw the regularity. If you go up the scale of integers, subtracting each integer from its square, the first integer will give you 0. You must then add 2 to get 2 for the next integer; add 4 to get 6 for the next integer; add 6 to get 12; add 8 to get 20; add 10 to get 30.

In producing the successive numbers, you go up the scale of even integers, so that I knew that the next number would be 42, and then 56, and then 72, without having to carry out the subtractions: $49 - 7$; $64 - 8$; and $81 - 9$. I was proud of myself.

I next tried something else. I wrote down each integer, and placed next to it the figure I got by subtracting it from its square and then considered how else I could represent the figure. Thus:

$$1 \quad 0 = 1 \times 0$$
$$2 \quad 2 = 2 \times 1$$
$$3 \quad 6 = 3 \times 2$$
$$4 \quad 12 = 4 \times 3$$
$$5 \quad 20 = 5 \times 4$$
$$6 \quad 30 = 6 \times 5$$

It was clear to me that every integer subtracted from its own square gave a result that was equal to that same integer multiplied by the next smaller integer.

By now, my twelve-year-old heart was beating quickly, for I got the idea that I had discovered something very unusual that, perhaps, no one had ever noticed before. (As I told you, I have no mathematical talent. Gauss would have noticed all this at the age of three, I imagine, and dismissed it as obvious.)

At any rate, I wanted to generalize this, for I was taking algebra now. I therefore let an integer, *any* integer, be "x." The next smaller integer would be "x − 1," and the square of the integers would be "x²."

I had discovered, by massive brain power, that an integer subtracted from its square, "$x^2 - x$," was equal to that integer multiplied by the next smaller "$x(x - 1)$." In other words:

$$x^2 - x = x(x - 1)$$

With that, all my joy left me, for this equation was indeed as obvious as anything could be. You just factored out the "x" on the left side, and that gave me the right side. The value of my discovery was equal to that of finding out that two dozen equaled twenty-four.

I therefore abandoned that particular line of discovery and never returned to it. And this was a shame, for had I continued to pry, I might conceivably have discovered something more which, while not exactly new, would have been far more interesting than the equation I just worked out for you. And since I'm a little over twelve now, I can manage it — so come along.

♦

Suppose we consider the problem of subtracting an integer from its square for just the first three integers: $1 - 1 = 0$; $4 - 2 = 2$; and $9 - 3 = 6$.

The differences keep going steadily upward so that we can tell that there are no subtractions of this sort that will ever give differences of 1, 3, 4, or 5. At least, not if we stick to integers.

We might, however, switch to the use of decimal fractions.

For instance, the square of 1.1 is 1.21, and $1.21 - 1.1 = 0.11$, while the square of 1.2 is 1.44, and $1.44 - 1.2 ≒ 0.24$. If we continue going upward by tenths, we find that the square of 1.6 is 2.56, and $2.56 - 1.6 = 0.96$, which is quite close to 1. Then, too, the square of 2.3 is 5.29, and $5.29 - 2.3 = 2.99$, which is even closer to 3.

In fact, we can guess, by now, that if we choose the proper decimal fraction, we can subtract that from its square and get a number pretty close to any integer we choose. Thus, the square of 4.65 is 21.6225, and $21.6225 - 4.65 = 16.9725$, which is pretty close to 17.

None of the examples I have cited give a difference that is an exact integer; they only come close. My twelve-year-old self, if he were working this out, and were as clever as I wish he had been, might have thought that by adding more decimal places he could have hit an integer on the nose. Since $2.3^2 - 2.3 = 2.99$, it should seem reasonable to expect that a tiny upward adjustment of 2.3 would get me exactly 3. For instance, $2.303^2 - 2.303 = 3.000809$. Now I'm just a trifle high, so down I go to $2.30275^2 - 2.30275 = 2.9999075$.

When I was twelve, I would not have had a pocket calculator, so working out the above relationship would have taken me quite some time, riddled me with arithmetical errors, and worn me out. I would have quickly given up.

Suppose, however, I didn't. Suppose I had the guts and persistence to try more and more decimal places and to fill more and more pieces of paper with enormous calculations. I would have found that no matter how assiduously I tried, and how many hours (or years) I spent at it, I would never find any number with any quantity of decimal places which, when subtracted from its square, would give me exactly 3. I would get closer and closer and closer, but nothing would place me exactly on 3.

There would then be two possible conclusions I could have come to: (1) If I were an ordinary boy, I would have decided that I just lacked the persistence to reach that final decimal place; (2) If I were a boy with the soul of a mathematician, I would have leaped intuitively to the notion that the number I was after was, actually, an unending and nonrepeating decimal, and I might thus have caught my first glimpse — unaided — of irrational numbers. (Unfortunately, I was never even bright enough to get to the point where I had to make the choice, so I was subordinary.)

♦

As I went on in algebra, I discovered how to solve for "x" in equations of the following type: "$ax^2 + bx + c = 0$." In such an equation, "a," "b," and "c," the "coefficients," are integers, and "x" is unknown. It turns out that in such an equation:

$$x = (\tfrac{1}{2}a)(-b + \sqrt{b^2 - 4ac}) \text{ (Equation 1)}$$

A couple of explanations: In Equation 1, the quantity in one parenthesis is to be multiplied by the quantity in the other parenthesis. Then, too, the symbol $\sqrt{}$ stands for "square root." The "square root of x," or $\sqrt{x}$, is that number which, when multiplied by itself, gives "x." Thus, $\sqrt{25} = 5$; $\sqrt{81} = 9$, and so on. (One more point: if the plus sign in Equation 1 is replaced by a minus sign, a second possible answer would be given, but we will deal with the plus sign only.)

To give an example of how Equation 1 works, suppose we deal with an equation such as "$x^2 + 8x - 5$." In that case "c" is equal to -5, and "b" is equal to $+8$. However, the plus sign is usually omitted in such cases and is considered to be "understood," so the "b" is said to be equal simply to 8.

But what is "a," the coefficient of "x^2," in the equation "$x^2 + 8x - 5$"? It would seem that the "x^2" in that equation has no coefficient at all, but that is not so. The "x^2," standing by itself, is actually "$1x^2$," but the 1 is understood and is generally omitted. Nevertheless, "a," in this case, is set equal to 1. (Personally, I would never omit anything and would always write 8 as $+8$, and "x^2" as "$1x^2$," and for that matter "x" as "x^1," but that's not what mathematicians do. It's their amiable way of saving themselves trouble at the expense of making things a little more confusing for beginners, and you can't fight Faculty Hall.)

We are now ready to return to the matter of subtracting an integer from its square to get some desired difference. We can generalize the problem algebraically by letting "x" stand for any integer, "x^2" for its square, and "y" for the integer that is the difference. We would then write:

$$x^2 - x = y$$

To make it interesting, let's pick a specific integer for "y," so we can see how this works; and, to make it simple, let's pick the smallest integer, 1. The equation becomes:

$$x^2 - x = 1$$

It is possible to subtract 1 from each side of the equality sign without changing the nature of the equation. (That's the result of one of those good old axioms: Equals subtracted from equals are equal.)

If you subtract 1 from the left side of the equality you get "$x^2 - x - 1$." If you subtract 1 from the right side, you get $1 - 1$, which is equal to 0. So you can write the equation as:

$$x^2 - x - 1 = 0 \text{ (Equation 2)}$$

If you solve this equation for "x," you will have a number which, when subtracted from its square, will give you exactly 1.

For the purpose, we will use Equation 1. For "a," the coefficient of "x^2," we have 1, for "b," the coefficient of "x," we have -1, and for "c," the final coefficient, we have -1 again.

Since "b" is equal to -1, "$-b$" $= -(-1)$, or $+1$, which is written simply 1. Again, if "b^2" $= (-1)(-1)$, or $+1$, or 1, then "2a" is equal to 2. And since "a" $= 1$, and "c" $= -1$, "4ac" is equal to $4(1)(-1)$ or -4, and $-4ac$ is equal to $-(-4)$, or $+4$, or 4.

With all this in mind, we have all we need to know to substitute numbers for the symbols in Equation 1 (and forgive me if you didn't require this step-by-step explanation). Equation 1 therefore becomes:

$$x = \tfrac{1}{2}(1 + \sqrt{1 + 4}) = \tfrac{1}{2}(1 + \sqrt{5})$$

This is the number which, when subtracted from its square, will yield a difference of exactly 1.

To express the number as an ordinary decimal, you must take the square root of 5, add 1, and divide the sum by 2.

But what is the square root of 5? What is the number which, when multiplied by itself, will give 5? That, alas, is an irrational number, an unending and nonrepeating decimal. We can get pretty close though, if we say it is 2.23606796. . . . In fact, we'll be close enough if we pretend that the square root of 5 is 2.236068. If we multiply this number by itself, 2.236068 × 2.236068, we get 5.0000001, which is off by only a ten-millionth.

If we add 1 to the square root of 5 and divide the sum by 2, we get 1.618034. (A still more correct value would be 1.61803398 . . . but 1.618034 is quite good enough for our purposes.)

If you take the square of this number you find that 1.618034 × 1.618034 = 2.618034025156. The additional 0.000000025156 is the result of the trifling inaccuracy of the figure, 1.618034. No decimal, however long, could be anything but a trifle inaccurate. The only truly accurate figure is $\frac{1}{2}(1 + \sqrt{5})$. If you square *that* number, which can be done without much trouble, but which trouble I will spare you, you will get the quantity $\frac{1}{2}(3 + \sqrt{5})$, which is greater by *exactly* 1.

♦

Suppose we consider "reciprocals" next. If you divide 1 by any number, you get another number that is the reciprocal of the first. In other words, ½ is the reciprocal of 2; ⅓ is the reciprocal of 3; 1/17.25 is the reciprocal of 17.25; and, in general, "1/x" is the reciprocal of "x."

Instead of subtracting a number from its square, let's subtract a reciprocal from its number. Using only integers, we have:

$$1 - \tfrac{1}{1} = 0$$
$$2 - \tfrac{1}{2} = 1\tfrac{1}{2}$$
$$3 - \tfrac{1}{3} = 2\tfrac{2}{3}$$
$$4 - \tfrac{1}{4} = 3\tfrac{3}{4}, \text{ and so on}$$

Except for the case of 1, we would always get a fraction; but, again, we do not have to cling to integers. Suppose we want to find a number which, when we subtract its reciprocal, will give us a difference of exactly 1.

Clearly, it will have to be a number that lies between the integers 1 and 2, so that the difference will be somewhere between 0 and 1½. Suppose, for instance, we take the number 1.5. Its reciprocal is 1/1.5. Since 1.5 = ³⁄₂, and 1/1.5 = ²⁄₃, we have ³⁄₂ − ²⁄₃ = ⁵⁄₆, which is pretty close to 1. If we move to 1.6 and subtract 1/1.6, and subtract 1/1.6, and if you trust me with the arithmetic, the answer is 0.975, which is even closer.

If we keep experimenting, however, we will quickly assure ourselves that we're not going to find any decimal we can write down which will give us *exactly* 1 when its reciprocal is subtracted. We are going to find ourselves in the realm of irrational numbers again.

So we switch to algebra and set up an equation that will represent the general case:

$$x - 1/x = 1$$

If we multiply each side of the equation by "x," the nature of the equation is left unchanged (trust me!). Since "x" times "x" is "x²"; "1/x" times "x" is 1; and 1 times "x" is "x," we have:

$$x^2 - 1 = x$$

If we subtract "x" from each side of the equation, we have:

$$x^2 - 1 - x = 0, \text{ or, rearranging}$$
$$x^2 - x - 1 = 0$$

But this is Equation 2 again, and the solution for "x" must be the same as it was before. We already know that ½(1 + $\sqrt{5}$) is exactly 1 less than its square. Well, it is also exactly 1 more than its reciprocal.

To show this plainly, let's deal with 1.618034, that very good approximation of ½(1 + $\sqrt{5}$). It turns out that 1/1.618034 = 0.618034.

◆

Now let's try again. Imagine a rectangle that is 1 unit wide and 2 units long. (It doesn't matter what the units are: inches, meters, light-years, whatever.)

In such a rectangle, the length is 2 times the width, obviously. The length and the width together, however, is 3 units, and that is 1½ times the length.

If the rectangle were 1 unit by 3, then the length is 3 times the width, but the length and width together is 4, and that sum would be 1⅓ times the length.

If the rectangle were 1 by 4, then 1 by 5, and so on, you would get pairs of figures that were 4 and 1¼, 5 and 1⅕, and so on. The two numbers would move further and further apart in size.

Can we find a rectangle where the two numbers are equal in size?

If so, that would have to be one in which the width was 1 unit and the length less than 2 units (because at 2 units, the two numbers are already unequal).

Let's go straight to algebra. Suppose the width of the rectangle is 1 unit and the length is "x" units. To express how many times "x" is greater than 1, we divide "x" by 1, and write "x/1," or simply "x."

The sum of the width and the length of the rectangle is "x + 1." To express how many times this is greater than the length alone, we have "(x + 1)/x."

We are looking for a situation in which these two relative lengths, or "ratios," are equal, and so the equation we set up is:

$$x = (x + 1)/x$$

If we multiply both sides of the equation by "x," we don't change the nature of the equation and we have:

$$x^2 = x + 1$$

If we subtract "x + 1" from both sides, we don't change the nature of the equation and we have:

$$x^2 - (x + 1) = 0$$

We can remove the parentheses if we take the negative of "x + 1" and make it "−x − 1" so that we have:

$$x^2 - x - 1 = 0$$

and there's Equation 2 again, with its usual solution.

Suppose, then, we have a rectangle in which the width is 1 unit and the length is 1.618034 units. The width and the length taken together would therefore be 2.618034. The length is, of course, 1.618034 times the width, while the length and width together would be 2.618034/1.618034, or 1.618034 times the length alone.

The ancient Greeks discovered this. Essentially, it was a way of dividing a given line into two sections, the longer of which was to the shorter section, as the whole line was to the longer section. Mathematicians have been so ravished by the beauty of this balance of ratios that about the mid-nineteenth century, it began to be called the "golden section."

A rectangle in which the width and length represented a line divided by the golden section and bent into a right angle at the division point was called a "golden rectangle."

Many people feel that the golden rectangle represents an ideal configuration that is particularly satisfying from an aesthetic viewpoint. A longer rectangle, they feel, looks too long, and a shorter one too stubby. Therefore, people have sought (and found) examples of golden rectangles in paintings, in statues, in buildings, and in many common artifacts of our society. In books on popular mathematics, the reader is presented with illustrations showing this.

Frankly, I'm skeptical. My own feeling is that aesthetics is a very complicated study and is enormously influenced by the social environment. To try to make much of the golden section in this respect is simplistic. I have only to see films made in the 1920s and 1930s, for instance, to be struck by the extent to which our ideas of female beauty (which one might casually think of as timeless) have changed in one lifetime.

I don't deny the golden rectangle is golden because of the mathematical elegance of the relationship of the sides, but trying to convert this into matters of aesthetics is to gild refined gold, and I would like to contribute my own poor bit to ungilding it.

♦

If we cling strictly to mathematics, we find that the golden section can be found in such simple geometric configurations as the regular decagon (a symmetrical ten-sided figure) and the pentagram (the star you find in the American flag). Particularly interesting in this connection, however, is the Fibonacci series, something I dealt with in an earlier essay in this series (see "T-FORMATION," August

1963). There I merely dealt with some of the large numbers that resulted. Here I will take up another aspect.

The Fibonacci series starts with two 1's and then generates new numbers by making each new one the sum of the two preceding ones.

Thus, if we start the series with 1, 1 . . . , the third number is 1 + 1, or 2, and that gives us 1, 1, 2 . . . . The next number is 1 + 2, or 3, and now we have 1, 1, 2, 3 . . . . There follows 2 + 3, or 5, so we have 1, 1, 2, 3, 5 . . . . Then comes 3 + 5 = 8, and 5 + 8 = 13, and so on. The first twenty-one terms of the Fibonacci series are, therefore:

1, 1, 2, 3, 5, 8, 13, 21, 34, 55, 89, 144, 233, 377, 610, 987, 1597, 2584, 4181, 6765, 10946 . . . .

We can continue to add additional terms indefinitely, if we are willing to add larger and larger pairs of terms, but these twenty-one will be enough for our purposes.

When the Fibonacci series was worked out (by an Italian mathematician named Fibonacci, of course) it involved biological growth. The initial problem dealt with multiplying rabbits, in fact. And yet —

Suppose we consider the ratio of successive numbers in the Fibonacci series, dividing each number by the one before, starting with the second in the series, thus:

$$\frac{1}{1} = 1$$
$$\frac{2}{1} = 2$$
$$\frac{3}{2} = 1.5$$
$$\frac{5}{3} = 1.6666 \ldots$$
$$\frac{8}{5} = 1.6$$
$$\frac{13}{8} = 1.625$$

As you see, the ratio forms an oscillating series. The value of the ratio goes up from 1 to 2, then down to 1.5, then up to 1.6666 . . . , then down to 1.6, then up to 1.625. We can be sure that this will go on, that the ratio will continue to move up and down alternately, and, in fact, it does.

However, the ratio goes up and down in successively smaller swings. First it goes from 1 to 2, but in later swings it never gets as low as 1 again, or as high as 2, either. Then it goes down from 2 to 1.5, and all future values are between 1.5 and 2. Then it goes up to 1.6666 . . . and all future values are between 1.5 and 1.666 . . . .

The oscillation gets smaller and smaller and smaller, and with each step all future values are trapped between the smaller and smaller swings.

The oscillation never stops completely. No matter how far we follow out the series, and how immense the numbers get, the ratio will continue to swing, though by ever tinier amounts. This smaller and smaller swing will always be to one side and the other of some central value, which the ratio will get ever closer to without ever quite reaching. The central value is called the limit of the series.

What is the limit of the Fibonacci series?

Let us continue the series, starting with the last ratio we have already dealt with:

$$^{13}\!/_8 = 1.625$$
$$^{21}\!/_{13} = 1.6153846 \ldots$$
$$^{34}\!/_{21} = 1.6190476 \ldots$$
$$^{55}\!/_{34} = 1.617647$$
$$^{89}\!/_{55} = 1.6181818 \ldots$$
$$^{144}\!/_{89} = 1.6179775 \ldots$$
$$^{233}\!/_{144} = 1.6180555 \ldots$$
$$^{377}\!/_{233} = 1.6180257 \ldots$$
$$^{610}\!/_{377} = 1.6180371 \ldots$$

This is getting to look awfully suspicious. Let's switch to the two last ratios in the Fibonacci series of twenty-one members that I presented earlier:

$$^{6765}\!/_{4181} = 1.618033963 \ldots$$
$$^{10946}\!/_{6765} = 1.618033998 \ldots$$

The oscillations are getting very small indeed, and they *seem* to be oscillating about the number that represents the golden section.

Can we be sure? Perhaps they are oscillating about a value that is microscopically different from the golden section.

No, that's not so. There are mathematical methods for determining the limit of such series, and one can demonstrate quite conclusively that the limit of the ratios of successive terms of a Fibonacci series is $\frac{1}{2}(1 + \sqrt{5})$.

Why is this so? I do not know, but the fact delights me. It is an example of the beauty of the unexpected that you can find everywhere in mathematics, if you have the talent for it — as I, alas, have not.

Sometimes one book inspires another. My Exploring the Earth and the Cosmos, *which deals with the expanding horizons of man, does so in a historical fashion. It describes the steps by which additional discoveries or additional extensions of knowledge or experience were made. I worried, however, that the extensions might be just numbers to the readers; that they wouldn't get a proper feel of the vastness of some things and the minuteness of others.*

It occurred to me that perhaps I could write a book in which I would describe some property in regular steps, which would have it grow larger and larger and larger; then return to the origin and follow it in another set of regular steps, growing smaller and smaller and smaller.

The book, written for Harper and Row and published in 1983, is The Measure of the Universe *(Book 274). Naturally, I started with the property of length, which is, in a way, the simplest and most familiar of all measurements. Remember that the first measuring instrument we handle in school is, in all likelihood, the ruler.*

In starting what I call "The Ladder of Length (Upward)," I described my system of measurements and the way in which I arranged the size of the steps. This gets a little mathematical, so I feel the first few pages of the book belong here.

from THE MEASURE OF THE UNIVERSE (1983)

Upward

STEP 1

1 metre (100 m)
Suppose we begin by considering the Universe in the light of measurements of length. What is the length of a line that stretches from here to a star? What is the length of a line that stretches from one side of an atom to the other?

In order to express such lengths, we will have to use a "unit of measurement," some familiar length which we can then use in multiples and in subdivisions. For instance, any adult American would have a rough idea of what kind of length a "mile" represents, so that we can speak of lengths in terms of so many miles, or of such and such a fraction of a mile. Something might be 4 miles away, or 0.5 miles away or 2769.4 miles, or one sixteen-hundredth of a mile.

Or we can use inches, or feet, or yards, always remembering that there are 12 inches to 1 foot, 3 feet to 1 yard, and 1760 yards to 1 mile. In principle, we can use any of a number of units of length that have been used to measure distance in the past, or which may still be used, even today, in specialized cases. Examples of such units are fathoms, cubits, leagues, ells, hands, and so on.

There is no point, however, in using units that a great many people are unfamiliar with. What's the use of saying that one town is 14 leagues from another if one doesn't know how long a league might be? That limits us, here in the United States, to the use of miles for long distances and inches for short ones. We can say that a certain star is so many trillions of miles away, or that a particular atom is so many billionths of an inch across.

This book is not, however, being addressed to an American audience only. It will, I hope, be translated into many languages, and in that case I should use units of measurement that are familiar to the whole world.

As it happens, virtually the whole world, except for the United States, uses a particular system of measurement called the metric system, a system first established in France in the 1790s. What's more, the rules for using the metric system were formalized and made uniform through international agreement in the 1950s. The new rules are termed, in French, *Systeme International d'Unites*, which, it is not hard to see, is "International System of Units" in English. The new rules are usually spoken of as the "SI version."

Increasingly, scientists are using the SI version, and I will use it in this book. This will not be too unfair to the United States since we cannot hold out forever against world usage. American scientists have, for many years, been using the metric system exclusively, and in fact, little by little, the United States as a whole is accepting it. It will do American readers good to get used to the system, and I will make it as painless as possible by giving the common American equivalent wherever that would be useful.

The SI unit of measurement is the "metre," from a Latin word meaning "measure." In English, the term has been commonly spelled "meter," and I have used that spelling myself until very recently. However, the SI system rigidly sets standards for spelling, pronunciation, abbreviation, and so on, in order that the scientific use of measurements be a truly international language with no chance of misunderstanding across language barriers.

This goal is an unexceptional one, and I will try to follow the rules even when (in my heart) I would rather not. For instance, I cannot help but think that "meter" is the better spelling, but the convention is "metre," and I will suppress my rebellion over the matter.

It is pronounced *"mee-ter"* (all units in the SI system are, in English, accented on the first syllable, though there may be secondary stresses elsewhere), and it is symbolized "m" so that one can write "1 metre" or "1 m" with equal validity. (The "m" is a symbol and not an abbreviation, so you don't use a period.)

The metre is not a difficult unit for Americans to grasp, since it is not very different from the familiar yard. A metre is equal to 1.094 yards, or to just about 1$\frac{1}{10}$ yards. A yard is equal to 0.9144 metres, or to just about $\frac{9}{10}$ metre. For rough approximations, you may even use the yard and the metre interchangeably.

Since a metre is also equal to 3.281 feet, and to 39.37 inches, it can be helpful, as a rule of thumb, to treat a metre as equal to 3$\frac{1}{4}$ feet, or 40 inches.

The metre can be compared to natural phenomena; sound waves, for instance. Suppose you start at middle C on the piano and move two white notes upward to E, which is the sound we usually sing as "mi" when we intone the scale. The sound wave associated with that note is just about 1 metre long.

Sound waves consist of air (or some other substance) being alternately compressed and expanded by some sort of vibration. There are also "electromagnetic waves" produced by the oscillation of an electromagnetic field. Such waves, of the type used in broadcasting television signals, are in the neighborhood of a metre in length. Waves of this length and longer are commonly called radio waves because their first practical use was in the transmission of radio signals.

But what is a metre in terms of phenomena as familiar as our body?

An unusually tall person (6½ feet tall in American units) is 2 metres tall. If such a person were to stretch out his arm sideways, shoulder high, then the distance from his nose to the tip of his outstretched fingers would be about 1 metre. If he were walking normally, his stride (that is, the swing of each foot from a position behind the other to a position in front) would be about 1 metre.

Nevertheless, this connection between the metre and the human body is coincidental. The length of the metre, as I shall later explain, was obtained from a natural length that had nothing to do with the human body.

STEP 2

3.16 metres ($10^{0.5}$ m)
The previous section, "Step 1," was headed *1 metre (10^0 m)*, while this one is headed *3.16 metres ($10^{0.5}$ m)*.

Why have I increased the measurement from 1 metre to 3.16 metres as I moved one step up the ladder, and what is the meaning of figures such as 10^0 and $10^{0.5}$?

Let's consider: Suppose I constructed the ladder by adding some constant figure to 1 metre, over and over. We might add 1 metre each time, going from 1 metre, to 2 metres, to 3 metres, to 4 metres, and so on. This is an arithmetic progression.

The higher one goes in an arithmetic progression, the less significant the addition becomes. It would be useful to consider, separately, distances of 1, 2, 3, and 4 metres, since each would have its own points of interest. By the time we reached higher figures, however, what could we say about 76 metres that had not been said about 75 metres? This situation would be even worse when we talked about 872 metres and then went on to 873 metres. Besides, consider that before we are done, we should be talking of billions of billions of metres, and would never really have a chance to do so if we move upward by steps of 1 metre.

Even if we went by bigger steps in arithmetic progression — 1 metre, 101 metres, 201 metres, 301 metres, and so on — the interest would fade as the numbers grew larger, for the steady addition of 100-metre lengths would grow steadily less significant — and it would still take forever to reach the final stage.

We might really stretch and go up by stages of 1,000,000,000 — dealing with 1 metre; 1,000,000,001 metres; 2,000,000,001 metres; and so on. It would *still* take us too long to get to the end, even then, and by moving up 1,000,000,000 metres in the first step, we would skip a great many levels of figures that would be of extreme interest.

In short, no arithmetic progression can possibly be useful as a means of constructing a ladder of the Universe. It would be too long, and it would concentrate too much attention on the very large numbers at the farther end of the ladder and too little attention on the small numbers at the nearer end of the ladder — the end nearer to ourselves.

The alternative is to *multiply* each number by some particular figure to get the next number. This would be a geometric progression. If the number by which we multiply is 2, we would have 1, 2, 4, 8, 16, 32, 64, 128, 256, 512, and so on.

A geometric progression is the proper way of building a ladder of the Universe. Not only does a geometric progression get larger much more rapidly than an arithmetic progression does and therefore give us hope of reaching really large numbers in a reasonable time; it also takes small steps at the lower end of the scale and larger and larger steps at the upper end, something that exactly matches our interest in the matter.

But what number ought we to use as a multiplier in order to build a particularly useful geometric progression?

The accident of the form in which our number system exists makes 10 a particularly simple multiplier. Thus, if we start with 1 and multiply by 10 each time, we have the series: 1, 10, 100, 1 000, 10 000, 100 000, 1 000 000, and so on. (It is customary in the United States to divide the digits in large numbers into groups of three separated by commas. In many other countries, however, commas are used as what *we* call decimal points. To avoid confusion, the SI system recommends that such groups of three digits be separated simply by a space, and this I will do from now on.)

A geometric series based on 10 as a multiplier has an elegant simplicity about it; it is therefore very commonly used, and scientists speak of "orders of magnitude" in this connection. Two objects differ by an order of magnitude in some measured property if the value of that property in one is 10 times that of the other.

There are two orders of magnitude difference if the measure of the property of one is 10 × 10, or 100 times the other; three orders of magnitude difference if the measure of the property of one is 10 × 10 × 10, or 1 000 times the other; and so on.

If, however, we consider the series 1, 10, 100, 1 000, 10 000, 100 000, 1 000 000, and so on, the numbers, as they grow larger, take up considerable room, and it becomes difficult to be sure of the number of zeros at a glance. For that reason, mathematicians have worked out more compact systems for representing such numbers.

Instead of writing the series as we just have, we can write it as 1, 10 × 10, 10 × 10 × 10, 10 × 10 × 10 × 10, and so on. The increasing numbers of tens grow steadily more unwieldy, to be sure, and the whole is even clumsier and less readily read and understood than the original. We don't have to write down each ten though; we merely have to number them.

Thus, 10^1 is one 10, standing all by itself; 10^2 is the product of two 10s multiplied together; 10^3 is the product of three 10s multiplied together; and so on. The 10, in numbers expressed this way, is the "base," and the upper number is the "exponent." A number such as 10^3 is called an exponential number.

The usefulness of such exponential numbers is easily seen:

$$10^1 = 10$$
$$10^2 = 10 \times 10 = 100$$
$$10^3 = 10 \times 10 \times 10 = 1\ 000$$
$$10^4 = 10 \times 10 \times 10 \times 10 = 10\ 000$$
$$10^5 = 10 \times 10 \times 10 \times 10 \times 10 = 100\ 000$$

You can see the regularity in this, and, without actually writing down tens, be sure that:

$$10^6 = 1\ 000\ 000$$
$$10^7 = 10\ 000\ 000$$
$$10^8 = 100\ 000\ 000, \text{ and so on.}$$

You can see that the exponent, in an exponential figure of this type, is always equal to the number of zeros in the same number written out in full. Thus, 10^{51} would be, in full, 1 000 000 000 000 000 000 000 000 000 000 000 000 000 000 000 000 000 000. Clearly 10^{51}

is a much briefer and a much less confusing way of writing the number.

The expression 10^1 can be read "ten to the first power," 10^2 as "ten to the second power," 10^3 as "ten to the third power," 10^4 as "ten to the fourth power," and so on. Often, in rapid speech among people familiar with the system, the word "power" is omitted, and the talk is of "ten to the fourth," "ten to the fifth," and so on. They might even refer to "ten to the four," "ten to the five," and so on.

What's more, 10^2 and 10^3 are rarely referred to as "ten to the second power" and "ten to the third power," but usually as "ten squared" and "ten cubed" for reasons that go back to geometry and with which we don't have to concern ourselves.

As for 10^1, that is rarely treated as an exponential figure. Since 10^1 equals 10, the exponent is almost invariably omitted so that 10^1 is written simply as 10.

Exponential numbers are much more than merely a convenient brief way of writing large numbers. They also greatly simplify multiplication and division. Thus, 10 000 × 100 000 = 1 000 000 000, as you can see for yourself if you care to work out the multiplication in full in whatever way you choose. Put it into exponential figures and you have $10^4 \times 10^5 = 10^9$.

Notice that $4 + 5 = 9$. It would seem that, in the particular multiplication cited in the previous paragraph, we added the exponents in the two numbers being multiplied to get the exponent in the product. It turns out that this is a general rule for exponential numbers. Instead of multiplying ordinary numbers, you turn them into exponential numbers and add the exponents.

Division is multiplication in reverse. Thus, 100 000/1 000 = 100. In exponential numbers, this is $10^5/10^3 = 10^2$. As you know, $5 - 3 = 2$. The general rule for exponential numbers is that division involves the subtraction of exponents.

Well, then, consider the following division: 1 000/1 000 = 1. That is perfectly straightforward and unquestioned. Suppose, though, we put it into exponential numbers. It becomes $10^3/10^3 = 10$ to which power? By the rule of exponent subtractions, since $3 - 3 = 0$, $10^3/10^3$ should be equal to 10^0. Thus, the same problem in division gives us two answers: 1 and 10^0. The only way of keeping mathematics consistent is to suppose that these two answers are equal, and that $10^0 = 1$.

In ordinary affairs, no one ever uses 10^0 in place of 1, but mathematicians sometimes do so when the exponential number preserves symmetry, or allows an arithmetical rule to be made general. I am using 10^0 in these ladders of the Universe for the sake of symmetry.

Thus, Step 1 above was listed as "1 metre" and then, in parentheses, as "10^0 m," saying the same thing in exponential number and symbol.

But what about Step 2? Why did I not jump an order of magnitude to "10 metres (10^1 m)"?

Multiplying by 10s, and moving up an order of magnitude at a time, takes steps that are too large for my purpose, at least in this particular ladder.

I could multiply by 5s instead, but that would give me a series that is clumsy: 1, 5, 25, 125, 625, 3 125, 15 625, and so on. To avoid that, I could use a hybrid of 5s and 10s, thus: 1, 5, 10, 50, 100, 500, 1 000, 5 000, and so on.

This, however, leaves us with steps of unequal size. Beginning with 1, we are multiplying first by 5, then by 2, then by 5, then by 2, and so on.

What we really want is a way of taking two multiplications to reach 10, but having each multiplication use the same multiplying value. We would then be advancing each time by half an order of magnitude.

Thus, I would multiply 1 by some number, a, which would give me a, of course (any number multiplied by 1 has a product that is the original number, unchanged). Then I would multiply a again by a and have 10. I am therefore looking for a solution to the equation $a \times a = 10$. Whenever a small number multiplied by itself gives a larger number, the small number is said to be the "square root" of the larger number. What we are looking for is the square root of 10.

Mathematicians know how to calculate square roots. Usually, square roots are "irrational"; that is, they are neither whole numbers nor fractions, but can be expressed only as an unending decimal. In such a decimal there is no pattern, so that you can never predict what the next digit will be unless you figure it out. Still, if you want to take enough trouble, you can calculate any square root to as many decimal places as you wish.

The square root of 10 is equal to 3.1622776 . . ., and so on. We don't have to worry about the additional places under ordinary conditions since 3.1622776 × 3.1622776 = 9.9999996, which is certainly close enough to 10 for our purposes. In fact, 3.16 is close enough, since 3.16 × 3.16 = 9.9856.

Thus, we have a series: 1, 3.16, 10, 31.6, 100, 316, 1 000, 3 160, and so on. In this series, all the steps are equal, as each number is multiplied by 3.16 in order to get the next higher number. Since, in this series, there are two steps in going from 1 to 10, and from 10 to 100, and from 100 to 1 000, and so on, we are indeed moving up the ladder in steps of half an order of magnitude.

What about exponentials? Suppose we want to put the equation 3.16 × 3.16 = 10 (approximately) into exponential numbers. We don't know the exponential form of 3.16, so let's just call it 10^a. We therefore have the equation $10^a \times 10^a = 10^1$. By the rule of exponents, we know that in such an equation $a + a = 1$. In that case a must equal ½ or 0.5. Therefore, the square root of 10, which is approximately 3.16, can be expressed as $10^{0.5}$. That is why Step 2 in the ladder of length is headed "3.16 metres ($10^{0.5}$ m)."

The series 1, 3.16, 10, 31.6, 100, 316, 1 000, 3 160 . . . can be expressed exponentially as 10^0, $10^{0.5}$, 10^1, $10^{1.5}$, 10^2, $10^{2.5}$, 10^3, $10^{3.5}$ . . ., and so on.

Having explained all that (which supplies us with almost all we need to know about exponentials and orders of magnitude for the rest of the book), let's consider the significance of a measurement of 3.16 metres.

This is just about equal to 10⅜ feet, so that a Step-2 length is about the height of a story in a modern building and outranges the tallest normal human being, if we ignore fanciful tales of giants in myth and legend. The tallest human being of whom there is record was Robert P. Wadlow. He was not, alas, normal, but was afflicted with giantism, a hormonal disorder. He never stopped growing, and in 1940, when he died at the age of twenty-two, he was about 2.75 metres (9 feet) tall. Even this is well short of the Step-2 length.

There is such a thing as a near-human giant in reality, too. The largest ape that ever lived is now extinct but is known from fossil teeth, jawbones, and other scraps. It is *Gigantopithecus* (Greek for "giant ape"). It looked very much like an outsize gorilla, and when

it stood erect it was perhaps 2.75 metres tall — just the height of
Wadlow, but in the case of *Gigantopithecus*, it was a normal height
and not a disorder.

There are animals that are taller than any primate, living or extinct, and that reach the Step-2 level or beyond. The height of a
male African elephant, at the shoulders, was as high as 3.8 metres
in one recorded case.

Where sound waves are concerned, one that is 3.16 metres long
is a G, two octaves below the G of the ordinary scale. It is a majes-
tic bass note (the longer the sound wave, the deeper the pitch).

An electromagnetic wave that is 3.16 metres long is still in the
TV range, but is near the upper wavelength limit of that range.

In the incredible wilderness of measurements used by humanity, I will occasionally mention one or two in the range under discussion that are still occasionally used in the United States. A rod
(or a pole or perch — all three taken from the long stick used as a
standard for that length) is defined as 5½ yards, which comes
to 5.029 metres: somewhat beyond the Step-2 length, as you can
see, but well below the Step-3 length we are about to come to.

STEP 3

10 metres (10^1 m)
When the metric system was first devised, the units received different names for each order of magnitude, the differences being
indicated by prefix.

Thus, 10 metres was set equal to 1 dekametre (pronounced, in
English, *dek*-uh-mee-ter). The prefix is symbolized as "da" to distinguish it from another prefix we'll come to later, which uses the
simple *d* as a symbol. In that way, 1 dekametre can be written as
1 dam.

The prefix "deka" is the Greek word for "ten," so that if one is
acquainted with Greek, the meaning of "dekametre" is clear at
once. Otherwise, one must simply memorize the prefix and the
meaning. Once that is done, however, it works for any kind of metric measure. A dekapoise is 10 poises, a dekawatt is 10 watts, and
so on.

Actually, the dekametre, or any metric measure using the "deka"
prefix, is rarely used. In the SI system, prefixes are used only for
every *three* orders of magnitude, since the total spread of measures

is far greater than that envisaged by the originators of the metric system. If a separate prefix were used for *every* order of magnitude through the spread we now use, the matter would become unnecessarily and impractically complicated. However, having mentioned the "deka" prefix (as I will others of the sort), I will use it henceforth, though perhaps not invariably.

A length of 10 metres corresponds approximately to the height of a three-story building. No living animal is that tall. The giraffe is the tallest living animal, and the tallest giraffe ever measured had the tip of its horns only 5.8 metres above the ground when it was standing erect, which makes it half again as tall as an elephant. (To put that into human terms, the highest pole vault achieved by a human being is about 5.7 metres.)

If we include extinct animals, the very largest dinosaurs, such as the brachiosaur, could raise their long necks until the top of the head was nearly 12 metres above the ground.

Measurements need not be made in the vertical direction only. The largest elephants may be nearly 10 metres long, if the trunk and tail are both extended. There have been reports of snakes or alligators approaching the 10-metre mark, but those are probably exaggerated. It is likely that 10 metres in any direction is about the longest any living land animal is likely to measure.

A sound wave 10 metres long is close to the deepest sound that can be heard by human ears. Sound waves with still longer waves are too deep in pitch to affect the mechanism of the human ear. They are "infrasonic" or "subsonic" waves, and we will follow them no longer.

Electromagnetic waves of this length are in the short-wave radio region. They are so called because the waves are shorter than those used in ordinary radio. Waves in the short-wave region are also used in frequency modulation (FM) radio.

STEP 4

31.6 metres ($10^{1.5}$ m)
By moving up another step we have left the world of land animals far behind. A length of 31.6 metres is the height of a ten-story building, and even the tallest brachiosaur can reach only four stories high.

In the sea, however, are animals that are not affected by gravity, since seawater buoys them to near-weightlessness whatever their size. They do not have to face the problems of supporting their great weight on legs of ever-increasing massiveness. (Elephants must have their bodies resting on virtual tree trunks, straight up and down for extra strength, and although they can move with surprising speed, they cannot jump — not an inch. The largest dinosaurs have their legs even thicker and more massive in proportion, and it may be that flesh and bone simply cannot support anything larger.)

Whales can be far larger than elephants, and can even outdo dinosaurs, without the necessity of legs at all. The water supports them. (If, however, a whale is beached, its own weight so compresses its lungs that it is unable to breathe, and suffocates.)

Even whales of moderate size exceed the largest of the land animals. The greatest of the toothed whales, the sperm whale, is just about 20 metres long, twice as long as the longest elephant, though still well below the Step-4 mark. (The sperm whale is the only whale with a throat wide enough to swallow a man whole.)

There are, however, whalebone whales, which do not live on large prey as the sperm whale does. (The sperm whale's favorite food is the giant squid, for which it is ready to dive to enormous depths and to remain underwater for over an hour.)

Whalebone whales live on tiny shrimp and fish which they strain out of the water by means of the cartilaginous fringes of "whalebone" that extend down from the roof of their mouths. Since small organisms are far more numerous than large ones, whales that feed on smaller organisms can prosper and grow to larger size than those that feed on larger ones.

The largest of the whalebone whales is the blue whale or sulfurbottom whale of Antarctic waters. The largest blue whale ever captured and measured was 33.3 metres long.

As far as pure length is concerned, there have been occasional reports of tapeworms from whale intestines, and of jellyfish that were longer. One jellyfish was reported to have tentacles that were 36 metres long. If some tentacles were stretched out in one direction and others in the opposite direction, an extreme length of some 70 metres might be recorded.

Yet jellyfish tentacles, and tapeworms, too, are very insubstantial, almost one-dimensional in nature. It is reasonably fair to say that the blue whale is the longest and largest animal of substance that lives on Earth, or that has *ever* lived on Earth.

It seems to me that for this reason alone the blue whale ought to be cherished by human beings, who must surely appreciate it as an awesome example of the potentiality of life — and yet its numbers are decreasing rapidly, and tragically.

To bring in the human world, a trained athlete can jump about 8.9 metres at most, or roughly the length of an elephant, and he can achieve a shot-put of as much as 21.8 metres, or roughly the length of a sperm whale.

STEP 5

100 metres (10^2 m)

When the metric system was first established, 100 metres was set equal to a hectometre, which is symbolized as "hm" and is pronounced *hek*-toh-mee-ter. The prefix "hecto-" is from the Greek word *hekaton*, meaning "hundred." The prefix "hecto-" is rarely used.

A length of 100 metres leaves the animal world behind. It is equal to the height of a thirty-three-story building. My own apartment in Manhattan, on the thirty-third floor, is just about 100 metres above the ground.

Manhattan (since we've mentioned it) is for the most part divided from north to south by streets running due east and west. The distance between these streets (one city block) is just about 80 metres. A distance of 100 metres is therefore about one and a quarter city blocks.

The world of life is not to be entirely ignored at the Step-5 range, however. Animals may be out of consideration, but there remains the world of plants. Taller than the longest whale are many species of trees. The tallest of all trees are the redwood trees that grow along the California coast. The tallest of these trees is reported to have attained a height of 112 metres, so that it is over four times as tall as the longest blue whale would be if it were standing on its tail.

There have been reports of still taller trees, either Douglas firs or Australian eucalyptus trees, with some estimates of heights of 150 metres or so, but these have never been verified. Of course, if the root system of a tree is included, the total height from the topmost branch to the lowermost root of a very tall tree might well be as much as 200 metres.

Human achievements are still in competition at the Step-5 range of length. At throwing the javelin, in sports competitions, a record cast of 94 metres was achieved, which is roughly the height of a tall redwood.

Human beings can, in this respect, outdo any form of life in one way, since they can build structures with measurements longer than those that can be achieved by any other form of life, and have done it surprisingly early in the history of civilization, too.

The Great Pyramid of Egypt, built forty-five hundred years ago, is 146 metres high. It is an impressive pile of rocks that would be difficult to build today, yet it was built by sheer muscle power, making use of simple, but ingenious, devices in the hands of many thousands of human beings, who had to labor for many years at the task. (It was to remain the tallest human-made structure for three thousand years.)

Electromagnetic waves in the 100-metre range are at the upper limit of the shortwave radio band.

STEP 6

316 metres ($10^{2.5}$ m)
We have now reached a length that is four city blocks long, or the length of one of the long crosstown blocks in Manhattan, say from Fifth Avenue to the Avenue of the Americas. (I apologize for being so provincial as to use Manhattan frequently, but, first, I live in Manhattan and love it; second, it has a simple geometry; and third, of all cities it is perhaps the best known to nonresidents.)

The Step-6 range is still within the world of buildings. In the late Middle Ages, the great cathedrals of western Europe began to exceed the Great Pyramid in height. The central tower of Lincoln Cathedral in England attained a height of 160 metres.

Of course, both the pyramids and the cathedrals were long labors inspired by religious enthusiasm. The first secular structure to surpass the cathedrals in height was the Washington Monument, an obelisk that is 170 metres tall. It was completed in 1884. (Here is one case where the use of the metric system obscures an interesting fact. The Washington Monument was deliberately built to a height of 555 feet and 5 inches.)

The Washington Monument was far outdone in 1889 with the completion of the Eiffel Tower, intended to commemorate the centennial of the French Revolution. It is a narrowing tower of steel, a skeleton of a building rather than a building, and was originally intended to be a temporary structure. It aroused a storm of protest from Parisians who felt it to be out of tune with the city and surpassingly ugly in its own right. It still stands, however, and Parisians, I imagine, have long since resigned themselves to it.

The Eiffel Tower is almost exactly 300 metres tall, twice the height of the Great Pyramid; and, for the first time, a manmade structure approached the Step-6 level of length.

None of these structures I mentioned, however, are intended for human beings to live and work in. They are tombs, memorials, places of worship.

Until the middle of the nineteenth century, dwelling and office buildings were almost never higher than four or five stories because the labor of climbing stairs came to be excessive after that. The first practical elevator came into use in 1859, and such devices were rapidly improved. With that, and with the fact that metal skeletons of iron and steel, rather than solid masonry, were used to bear the weight, tall buildings became truly practical.

Buildings so tall that they were hyperbolically called skyscrapers were built in several American cities but particularly on the island of Manhattan, which, for its solid phalanxes of tall buildings, came to be one of the unique places in the world.

By the beginning of the twentieth century, the skyscrapers were crowding the Step-6 level. The Metropolitan Life Insurance Building, completed in 1909, had its tower 213.34 metres (just 700 feet) above the ground.

The Woolworth Building, completed in 1913, had a height of 241 metres and remained the tallest office building in the world for a quarter of a century. (When I was a boy, "to jump over the Woolworth Building" was a proverbial expression for an impossible feat, and I used it frequently myself, though I hadn't the slightest idea what the Woolworth Building was.)

It was not till 1930 that an office building was constructed in Manhattan that outdid the Eiffel Tower and was, therefore, not only the tallest office building in the world, but the tallest human-made structure of any kind. It was the Chrysler Building, which had a height of 319 metres and thus was the first structure to rise above the Step-6 level of length.

Within a matter of months, however, it lost its lead to the Empire State Building, which was 381 metres high.

The Empire State Building held the record for a quarter of a century in its turn, until 1973, when the twin towers of the World Trade Center in Manhattan rose to a height of 411 metres. Then, the very next year, the lead passed to the Sears Tower in Chicago, which was 443 metres high. This remains the tallest office building in the world, though there are television masts here and there which are taller, some of them attaining heights of well over 600 metres.

We can express the heights of these tall buildings in another and rather dramatic way. The Empire State Building is four and three-quarters city blocks tall. The Sears Tower is five and a half city blocks tall.

The longest ocean liners are just about as long as skyscrapers are tall. At the time the Woolworth Building was completed, the British liner *Lusitania* was as long as that building was tall. The French liner *France*, launched in 1961 and, so far, the longest ship built, was 315.5 metres long, just about as long as the Chrysler Building is high.

Electromagnetic waves that are 316 metres long are just about midway in the familiar amplitude modulation (AM) radio broadcasting band.

One fairly familiar common measure that approaches the Step-6 level is the furlong. This was originally the length of a plowed furrow in a field and was set equal to 40 rods, or 220 yards, which is equivalent to 201.17 metres. Therefore, the Step-6 length of 316 metres is equal to 1.57 furlongs. (Tracks used in horse racing are still routinely measured in furlongs.)

STEP 7

1 000 metres (10^3 m)
1 kilometre (10^0 km)
When the metric system was first established, the prefix "kilo-" was established to signify 1 000 of a basic unit. This is from the

Greek *chilioi* meaning "thousand." Thus, a "kilometre," symbolized "km" and pronounced "*kil*-oh-mee-ter" (*not* with the accent on the second syllable), is equal to 1 000 metres.

The kilometre is three orders of magnitude greater than the metre, and it is the rule that distinctive prefixes are used every three orders of magnitude, in order to avoid having to deal with figures that are too large to be convenient.

In this book, I will continue to use the basic unit — in this case the metre — in the heading of each step, for the sake of continuity. I will follow it, however, with the prefixed unit, and I will use only the prefixed unit in the body of the step.

Thus, electromagnetic waves that are 1 kilometre long (and I will not say 1 000 metres) are in the longwave region of the radio wave band. These are longer than those used in ordinary radio transmission. Longwaves have various specialized uses, and they can be indefinitely long. We will leave them behind and refer to radio waves no more after this step.

The kilometre is the preferred unit for longer distances in common life, as the metre is for shorter distances. Where the metre is the rough equivalent of the yard in common measure, the kilometre is the rough equivalent of the mile. The comparison is not as close as in the metre/yard case, however, for 1 kilometer = 0.6214 miles, and 1 mile = 1.609 kilometres.

More briefly, a kilometre is ⅝ of a mile, and a mile is 1⅗ kilometres. To put it another way, 8 kilometres = 5 miles; to put it still another way, a kilometre is 3 281 feet or 1 094 yards, whereas a mile is 5 280 feet or 1 760 yards; to put it yet another way, a kilometre is 12.5 city blocks, whereas a mile is 20 city blocks.

A kilometre in New York City would represent the distance from Fifth Avenue to halfway between Eighth and Ninth avenues going westward; or from Fifth Avenue to First Avenue going eastward. Central Park, which stretches from Fifth Avenue to Eighth Avenue, is 0.8 kilometres wide.

By the time we've reached the Step-7 level, we've outranged anything human-made in height. Nothing human beings have ever constructed stretches a kilometre from bottom to top. On the other hand, there are natural elevations that rise far higher. A mountain that reaches a height of only 1 kilometre above sea level is not in the least impressive.

Ben Nevis, in west central Scotland, is the highest peak in Great Britain (certainly not a mountainous island), and it is 1.34 kilometres high.

At the Step-7 level, we can begin to talk about astronomical bodies. They come in all sizes, from tiny motes of dust upward. If we restrict ourselves to bodies sufficiently impressive to receive names, then we can begin with small asteroids that, on occasion, skim close to Earth (as astronomical distances go) and that are therefore known, with considerable exaggeration, as Earth-grazers. Of these, the best known to the general public is Icarus. That particular asteroid is well known not only because of its periodic close approach to Earth, but because of its very close approach to the Sun at one end of its orbit.

The distance across Icarus, its diameter, is, as near as can be estimated, a trifle more than 1 kilometre. That means if it were gently brought to rest in Manhattan, it would fill the lower third of Central Park (lapping over to my apartment house, probably) and would give the island a mountain about the size of Ben Nevis.

You will notice that I stopped rather abruptly. Naturally, the ladder goes on and on till I reach a length equal to the circumference of the known Universe. If you are sorry to have been forced to halt the voyage, well — one of the hidden purposes of this book is to get you interested in a particular subject so that you will dash out of the house in a frenzy to buy one or another of my books (or perhaps all of them). Now that I've mentioned it, of course, the purpose is no longer hidden.

It's hard to work mathematics into a piece of fiction, but I do it sometimes.

In 1980 I began to write a monthly mystery for Gallery. *The magazine is devoted to eroticism in word and picture but my stories were not (something I informed the editor would be the case when he asked me to write them).*

I wrote those mysteries (quite short ones) for thirty-eight issues before the magazine decided it had had enough. By that time I had put thirty of them into a collection called The Union Club Mysteries *(Book 277), published in 1983 by Doubleday.*

The stories are told in a fixed style. Four men meet in the library of the Union Club, and the conversation leads one of them, Griswold, to tell a mystery, which the others are invited to solve. (The reader is invited to solve it along with them.) Griswold's cronies never manage (though the reader may), and Griswold then reveals the solution.

Naturally, in a story that is always about twenty-two hundred words long, the gimmick is the thing, and occasionally that gimmick involves numbers in some way. That is so in the case of the story I called "1 to 999," for instance —

from THE UNION CLUB MYSTERIES (1983)

1 to 999

One can't help getting tired of Griswold at times. At least I can't.

I like him well enough. I can't help liking the old fraud, with his infinite capacity to hear in his sleep and his everlasting sipping at his scotch and soda, and his lies, and his scowls at us from under his enormous white eyebrows. But if I could catch him at his lies only once I think I would like him a lot better.

Of course, he might be telling the truth, but surely there can't be any one person in the world to whom so many impossible problems are posed. I don't believe it! I *don't* believe it.

I sat there that night in the Union Club with windy gusts of rain battering the windows now and then, and the traffic on Park Avenue rather muted, and I suppose my thoughts must have been spoken aloud.

At least, Jennings said, "What don't you believe?"

I was caught a little by surprise, but I jerked my thumb in Griswold's direction. "Him!" I said. "Him!"

I half expected Griswold to growl back at me at that, but he seemed peacefully asleep between the wings of his tall armchair, his white mustache moving in and out to his regular breathing.

"Come on," said Baranov. "You enjoy listening to him."

"That's beside the point," I said. "Think of all those deathbed hints, for instance. Come on! How many times do people die and leave mysterious clues to their murderers? I don't think it has ever happened even once in real life, but it happens to Griswold all the time — according to Griswold. It's an insult to expect us to believe it."

It was at that point that Griswold opened one icy-blue eye, and said, "The most remarkable deathbed clue I ever encountered had nothing to do with murder at all. It was a natural death and a deliberate joke of a sort, but I don't want to irritate you with the story." He opened his other eye and lifted his glass to his lips.

"Go ahead," said Jennings. "We are interested. We two, at least."

I was also, to be truthful —

♦

What I am about to relate [said Griswold] involved no crime, no police, no spies, no secret agents. There was no reason why I should have known anything about it, but one of the senior men involved knew of my reputation. I can't imagine how such a thing comes about, since I never speak of the little things I have done, for I have better things to do than advertise my prowess. It's just that others talk, things get around, and any puzzle within a thousand miles is referred to me — which is the simple reason I encounter so many. [He glared at me.]

I was not made aware of the event till it was just about over, so I must tell you most of the story as it was told to me, with appropriate condensation, of course, for I am not one to linger unnecessarily over details.

I will not name the institute at which it all took place or tell you where it is or when it happened. That would give you a chance to check my veracity, and I consider it damned impertinent that any of you should feel it required checking or that you should go about snuffling after evidence.

In this unnamed institute there were people who dealt with the computerization of the human personality. What they wanted to do was to construct a program that would enable a computer to carry on a conversation that would be indistinguishable from that of a human being. Something like that has been done in the case of psychoanalytic double-talk, where a computer is designed to play the role of a Freudian who repeats his patient's remarks. That is trivial. What the institute was after was creative small talk, the swapping of ideas.

I was told that no one at the institute really expected to accomplish the task, but the mere attempt to do so was sure to uncover much of interest about the human mind, about human emotions and personality.

No one made much progress in this matter except for Horatio Trombone. — Obviously, I have just invented that name and there is no use your trying to track it down.

Trombone had been able to make a computer do remarkable things, to respond in a fairly human fashion for a good length of time. No one would have mistaken it for a human being, of course, but Trombone did far better than anyone else had done, so there was considerable curiosity as to the nature of his program.

Trombone, however, would not divulge any information on the matter. He kept absolutely silent. He worked alone, without assistants or secretaries. He went so far as to burn all but the most essential records and keep those in a private safe. His intention, he said, was to keep matters strictly to himself until he himself was satisfied with what he had accomplished. He would then reveal all and accumulate the full credit and adulation that he was sure he deserved. One gathered he expected the Nobel Prize to begin with and to go straight uphill from there.

This struck others at the institute, you can well imagine, as eccentricity carried to the point of insanity, which may have been what it was. If he were mad, however, he was a mad genius and his superiors were reluctant to interfere with him. Not only did they feel that, left to himself, he might produce shattering scientific breakthroughs, but none of them had any hankering to go down in the science-history books as a villain.

Trombone's immediate superior, whom I will call Herbert Bassoon, argued with his difficult underling now and then. "Trombone," he would say, "if we could have a number of people combining mind and thought on this, progress would go faster."

"Nonsense," Trombone would say irascibly. "One intelligent person doesn't go faster just because twenty fools are nipping at his heels. You only have one decently intelligent person here, other than myself, and if I die before I'm done, he can carry on. I will leave him my records, but they will go only to him, and not until I die."

Trombone usually chuckled at such times, I was told, for he had a sense of humor as eccentric as his sense of privacy, and Bassoon told me that he had a premonition of just such trouble as eventually took place — though that may very well have been only hindsight.

The chance of Trombone's dying was, unfortunately, all too good, for his heart was pumping on hope alone. There had been three heart attacks, and there was a general opinion that the fourth would kill him. Nevertheless, though he was aware of the precarious thread by which his life hung, he would never name the one person he thought a worthy successor. Nor, by his actions, was it possible to judge who it might be. Trombone seemed to be amused at keeping the world in ignorance.

The fourth heart attack came while he was at work and it did kill him. He was alone at the time so there was no one to help him. It didn't kill him at once and he had time to feed instructions to his computer. At least, the computer produced a printout, which was found at the time his body was.

Trombone also left a will in the possession of his lawyer, who made its terms perfectly clear. The lawyer had the combination to the safe that held Trombone's records, and that combination was to be released to no one but Trombone's chosen successor. The lawyer did not have the name of the successor, but the will stated that there would be an indication left behind. If people were too stupid to understand it — those were the words in the will — then, after the space of one week, all his records were to be destroyed.

Bassoon argued strenuously that the public good counted for more than Trombone's irrational orders; that his dead hand must not interfere with the advance of science. The lawyer, however, was adamant; long before the law could move, the records would be destroyed, since any legal action was to be at once met with destruction according to the terms of the will.

There was nothing to do but turn to the printout, and what it contained was a series of numerals: 1, 2, 3, 4, and so on, all the numerals up to 999. The series was carefully scanned. There was not one numeral missing, not one out of place; the full list, 1 to 999.

Bassoon pointed out that the instructions for such a printout were very simple, something Trombone might have done even at the point of death. Trombone might have intended something more complicated than a mere unbroken list of numerals, but had not had a chance to complete the instruction. Therefore, Bassoon said, the printout was not a true indication of what was in Trombone's mind and the will was invalid.

The lawyer shrugged that off. It was mere speculation, he said. In the absence of evidence to the contrary, the printout had to be taken as it appeared, as saying exactly what Trombone wanted it to say.

Bassoon gathered his staff together for a meeting of minds. There were twenty men and women, any one of whom could, conceivably, have carried on Trombone's work. Every one of them would have longed for the chance, but no one of them could advance any logical bit of evidence that he or she was the one Trombone thought to be the "one decently intelligent person" among them. At least, no one could convince any of the others that he or she was the person.

Nor could a single one see any connection between that dull list of numerals and any person in the institute. I imagine some invented theories, but none were convincing to them all generally, and certainly none were convincing to the lawyer or moved him in any way.

Bassoon was slowly going mad. On the last day of the grace period, when he was no nearer a solution than at the start, he turned to me. I received his call at a time when I was very busy, but I knew Bassoon slightly, and I have always found it difficult to refuse help — especially to someone who sounded as desperate as he did.

We met in his office and he looked wretched. He told me the whole story and said, when he had finished, "It is maddening to have what may be an enormous advance in that most difficult of subjects — the working of the human mind — come to nothing because of a half-mad eccentric, a stubborn robot of a lawyer, and a silly piece of paper. Yet I can make nothing of it."

I said, "Can it be a mistake to concentrate on the numerals? Is there anything unusual about the paper itself?"

"I swear to you, no," he said energetically. "It was ordinary paper without a mark on it except for the numerals from one to nine hundred ninety-nine. We've done everything except subject it to neutron activation analysis, and I think I'd do that if I thought it would help. If you think I ought to, I will, but surely you can do better than that. Come on, Griswold; you have the reputation of being able to solve any puzzle."

I don't know where he got that notion. I never discuss such things myself.

I said, "There isn't much time —"

"I know," he said, "but I'll show you the paper; I'll introduce you to all the people who might be involved. I'll give you any information you need, any help you want — but we only have seven hours."

"Well," I said, "we may only need seven seconds. I don't know the names of the twenty people who might qualify as Trombone's successor, but if one of them has a rather unusual first name I have in mind — though it might conceivably be a surname — then I should say that is the person you are looking for."

I told him the name I had in mind and he jumped. It was unusual and one of the people at the institute did bear it. Even the lawyer admitted that person must be the intended successor, when I explained my reasoning, so the records were passed over.

However, I don't believe anything much has come of the research after all, unfortunately. In any case, that's the story.

◆

"No, it isn't," I exploded. "What was the name you suggested and how did you get it out of a list of numerals from one to nine ninety-nine?"

Griswold, who had returned placidly to his drink, looked up sharply. "I can't believe you don't see it," he said. "The numerals went from one to nine ninety-nine without missing a numeral and then stopped. I asked myself what the numerals from one to nine ninety-nine inclusive had in common that numerals higher still, say, one thousand, do not have, and how that can have anything to do with some one particular person.

"As written, I saw nothing, but suppose all those numerals were written out as English words: one, two, three, four, and so on, all the way up to nine hundred ninety-nine. That list of numbers is constructed of letters, but not of all twenty-six letters. Some letters are not to be found in the words for the first nine hundred ninety-nine numbers; letters, such as 'a,' 'b,' 'c,' 'j,' 'k,' 'm,' 'p.'

"The most remarkable of these is 'a.' It is the third most commonly used letter in the English language, with only 'e' and 't' ahead of it, yet you may go through all the numbers — one, fifty-three, seven hundred eighty-one, and you will not find a single 'a.'

Once you pass nine ninety-nine, however, it breaks down. The number 'one thousand' has an 'a' but not any of the other missing letters. It seems quite clear, then, that the message hidden behind the list is simply the absence of 'a.' What's so difficult about that?"

I said, angrily, "That's just nonsense. Even if we were to admit that the message was the absence of 'a,' what would that mean as far as the successor was concerned? A name that lacked any 'a'?"

Griswold gave me a withering look. "I thought there would be several names like that and there were. But I also thought that some one person might have the name 'Noah,' which is pretty close to 'no a,' and one of them did. How much simpler can it be?"

PART 4

PHYSICS

IN MY THIRD HUNDRED BOOKS, none are primarily on phys-ics. However, a number of my F & SF essays are on the subject, and I have picked out my favorite example among them. That is "Let Einstein Be!", an essay in which I try to explain the essence of relativity, and why it seems to be so intransigently against com-mon sense, in a way that is (I think) totally original with me.

That is something I aim for. In every one of my F & SF essays I try to include something, however small, that is original with me. I don't always succeed, but sometimes I do, and I think "Let Ein-stein Be!" is one of my successes. It is included in my essay collec-tion Counting the Eons *(Book 266), which Doubleday published in 1983.*

from COUNTING THE EONS (1983)

Let Einstein Be!

Every once in a while I review books. I hate doing so because I hate being a critic; I hate reading with a view to making judgments or poking holes. I don't even know if I'm equipped to make judg-ments and poke holes. I just want to read for pleasure and profit, and continue the reading or stop it according to whether that p and p is there or not.

Every once in a while, though, someone asks me to do a review under conditions where I can't refuse, and in this case, I found myself with three books dealing with relativity. I did the job — but I also did some thinking.

Writing books that explain relativity to the layman is virtually big business. The theory of relativity is over seventy-five years old and it still needs explaining.

It is accepted by scientists; in fact, you can't understand modern physics without it. Yet the resistance to its concepts (never mind its mathematics) on the part of the layman never ebbs. Why are the attempts to explain relativity, while apparently endless, also apparently useless?

In this connection, consider a very famous epitaph intended for Isaac Newton, written by Alexander Pope (1688–1744):

> *Nature and Nature's laws lay hid in night:*
> *God said, "Let Newton be!" and all was light.*

Very true! And just as true, at least in popular estimation, are the two lines added in recent decades by the British journalist John C. Squire (1884–1958). These are:

> *It did not last: the Devil howling, "Ho!*
> *Let Einstein be!" restored the status quo.*

And there you are! Einstein advanced crazy ideas that violated common sense, that could not be absorbed or grasped, and the public will have none of it!

And yet, in certain ways, humanity has lived through such intellectual crises before. Einstein's relativity is not the first interpretation of the Universe to violate common sense. It's just that earlier ones have ground their way into popular acceptance while relativity hasn't and perhaps never will.

I would like to give an instance of a situation as odd as anything Einstein ever dreamed up and yet one that *was* accepted.

♦

Let us suppose that two people, Smith and Jones, are standing at point X along with you and me. Smith sets off in any direction at random, walking in a perfectly straight line at a steady 5 kilometers an hour. Jones sets off in the precisely opposite direction, also walking in a perfectly straight line at the same speed.

Let us suppose that neither Smith nor Jones requires food or drink; that neither gets tired; that neither encounters any obstacle such as mountains, deserts, or oceans; that neither deviates in any way from the straight-line travel at 5 kilometers an hour.*

Let us suppose, further, that you and I remain at point X and have the ability, at every moment, to determine the distance of

---

*This is a "thought experiment" and we are allowed to simplify matters by omitting all nonessential entanglements.

Smith and Jones from ourselves and from each other. Furthermore, though we know nothing about geography, we are well versed in ordinary arithmetic and Euclidean geometry.

At the end of one hour, Smith is 5 kilometers away in one direction, Jones is 5 kilometers away in the opposite direction, and they are 10 kilometers apart.

At the end of two hours, Smith is 10 kilometers away in one direction, Jones is 10 kilometers away in the opposite direction, and they are 20 kilometers apart.

Since we know arithmetic we feel safe in predicting that at the end of ten hours, Smith will be 50 kilometers away in one direction, Jones will be 50 kilometers away in the other direction, and they will be 100 kilometers apart. (And sure enough, if we check the situation at the end of ten hours, we will find our prediction was correct.)

Knowing Euclidean geometry, we know that a straight line can be extended indefinitely, and since Smith and Jones are walking in opposite directions on a straight line, we can extrapolate our arithmetic forever.

For instance, after eight thousand hours (that's very nearly a year), Smith will be 40,000 kilometers away in one direction, Jones will be 40,000 kilometers away in the other direction, and they will be 80,000 kilometers apart.

This can be continued indefinitely by ordinary arithmetic, ordinary geometry, and ordinary common sense. Anyone who would argue with such figures would have to be out of his or her mind.

Except that now we will set up a ridiculous assumption.

Let us suppose that 20,000 kilometers is an absolutely maximum separation.* No matter how long Smith walks away from us in a straight line in a given direction, he will never get more than 20,000 kilometers away from us. What's more, no matter how long Jones walks away from us in a straight line in the opposite direction, *he* can never get more than 20,000 kilometers away from us either. What's still more, Smith and Jones, as they firmly march off in opposite directions, can never get more than 20,000 kilometers away from each other.

Some hardheaded no-nonsense guy would surely object.

---

*A better figure would be 20,037 kilometers, but I trust you will permit me the convenient approximation.

"This is simply insane!" Hardhead would say. "Why twenty thousand kilometers?"

We shrug. That's just the way things are. It's our assumption.

"All right, then," says Hardhead, "suppose Smith has walked onward until he's twenty thousand kilometers from us, and then suppose he keeps on walking. Doesn't he *have* to get farther away from us?"

No! If he reaches that maximum distance and insists on keeping on walking in the same straight line, he *can't* get farther from us. The distance between us changes but only in the sense that he now gets *closer* to us. After all, if he can't get farther when he moves, he must get closer — and he just can't get farther.

"Well, that's the most exasperatingly stupid rule anyone has ever thought up," says Hardhead, "and you must be a prize idiot to dream it up."

Well, perhaps, but let's see what the consequences are. Smith is walking in one direction, Jones in the other. After two thousand hours, Smith is 10,000 kilometers in one direction, Jones is 10,000 kilometers in the other direction, and they are 20,000 kilometers apart. Right?

"Right," says Hardhead.

If they keep on walking, Smith continues to get farther away from us and Jones continues to get farther away from us in the other direction, *but they can't get farther away from each other,* because they have reached the 20,000-kilometer maximum separation. As they keep on walking, by the rules we have set up, though each gets steadily farther away from us, each gets as steadily closer to the other.

After three thousand hours, Smith has added 5,000 kilometers to his distance from us, and so has Jones. Each is now 15,000 kilometers away from us in opposite directions. Each, however, has *decreased* the distance from the other by 5000 kilometers, so that they are now 10,000 kilometers apart.

"Let's get this straight," says Hardhead. "Smith is fifteen thousand kilometers away from us in one direction, and Jones is fifteen thousand kilometers away from us in the other direction, but Smith is only ten thousand kilometers from Jones. You're telling me that fifteen thousand plus fifteen thousand equals ten thousand. Do you realize that if you carry on with this insanity, Smith and Jones will *meet?"*

Exactly! After four thousand hours, Smith has traveled 20,000 kilometers in one direction, and Jones has traveled 20,000 kilometers in the other direction, and they will meet at point Y.

"So that twenty thousand plus twenty thousand equals zero," says Hardhead. "That's rich, that is. And what if they keep on walking?"

Well, they started off facing and walking in opposite directions, and when they meet they are still facing and walking in opposite directions. If they keep on, they will pass each other. Smith retraces Jones's steps; Jones retraces Smith's steps. They begin to move farther from each other but, having passed the 20,000-kilometer mark, they each begin to move closer to us.

After six thousand hours, Smith and Jones have gotten halfway back to us and are each only 10,000 kilometers away from us, but they have been moving away from each other and are now 20,000 kilometers apart. After they have reached the maximum separation, they start moving toward each other again. After eight thousand hours, Smith and Jones face each other once again, and both are zero kilometers away from us. We are all together again.

"I see. I see," says Hardhead. "Smith travels steadily in a given direction for eight thousand hours, and Jones travels steadily in the opposite direction for eight thousand hours. Neither one veers from the original direction and yet they end up after all that walk right back home again."

Yes, indeed, and if they keep on walking they will meet again at Y, and then at X, and then at Y, and so on forever. And through all eternity they will never be more than 20,000 kilometers from their starting point. What's more, they can do this in any direction. Smith can move away from the original point X in a totally different direction from the one he first chose, and Jones can move in the direction opposite to that, and they will still meet at point Y. It will be the same point Y, no matter which straight line they move in opposite directions upon.

"The *same* point Y? How can you tell that?"

It follows from the original assumptions. Suppose that by going along two separate lines they meet at point Y in the first case and point Y' in the second. Both points would have to be 20,000 kilometers from us by the original assumption.

Suppose, then, we try to walk from point Y to point Y'. Since point Y is 20,000 kilometers away from us and we can't walk farther away by our original assumption, then no matter which direction we take we get closer to us than 20,000 kilometers. When we arrive at point Y' we are less than 20,000 kilometers from us, and yet point Y' is 20,000 kilometers from us. The only way we can avoid the paradox is to suppose that point Y and point Y' are identical.

In fact, if you study the situation further, it turns out that given our assumption of maximum separation, any two straight lines on the surface of the earth intersect at two different points 20,000 kilometers apart, even though Euclidean geometry tells us that two straight lines can intersect at only one point no matter how far they are extended.

Since all straight lines intersect, there are no parallel lines under the maximum-separation assumption.

Furthermore, without going into the details of the demonstrations, which would be very convoluted, it could be shown that the shortest distance between two points where one is due west of the other is *not* along a line that goes due west.

In a place like the United States, to go from one point to another, which is due west, along the shortest line, one must head off a little north of west. (If you live in Australia you have to head off a little south of west.)

The farther the two east-west points are separated, the more you must angle northward to go from one to the other by the shortest route (or southward in Australia). It is even possible that if you place two points properly east and west, you will be forced to leave from one point in a due northerly direction to get to the other in minimum distance (and due southerly in Australia).

According to Euclid, the sum of the three angles of a triangle is 180°, but in a triangle drawn on the earth, ignoring any unevennesses in its surface, the sum of the angles is always *more* than 180° if we insist on sticking to the maximum-separation assumption. In fact, you can draw a triangle on the surface of the earth under conditions where each angle is a right angle, and the total sum is then 270°.

However, Hardhead abandoned us long ago. Insanity is only funny up to a point, and then it becomes infuriating.

♦

Why set up the 20,000-kilometers separation maximum if it means that the consequences will violate straightforward geometry in so many ways? It may be the kind of game that could interest people who are fascinated with recreational mathematics, but would it not lead to a dangerous divorce from reality?

No! That's just what it does not do! When navigators make long voyages across the ocean, or airplanes fly long distances anywhere, or when you want to check the time with a friend in London, or do any of a number of things — you find that all the screwball consequences of your distance maximum must be taken into account. It it those consequences which actually describe the earth, and not Hardhead's "common sense."

Euclidean geometry is "plane" geometry; the geometry that is valid on a plane, by which is meant a perfectly flat surface. The surface of the earth, however, is not perfectly flat. It is easy to deduce from the assumption of a 20,000-kilometer maximum separation that the surface of the earth is spherical. The behavior of lines on its surface is described by the deductions of "spherical" geometry and everything I have mentioned is in accord with that, provided you consider the earth a sphere which is 6,370 kilometers in radius.*

But if the earth is a sphere and if all the rules of spherical geometry are well known, why didn't people understand the spherical nature of earth at once?

Because through most of history people were involved with very small patches of the earth's surface, across which the degree of curvature was vanishingly small. The surface was so close to flat that plane geometry was good enough, and since plane geometry is the simplest form of geometry, it came to seem "common sense" and to represent universal truth.

To be sure, some Greek philosophers worked out the sphericity of the earth on theoretical principles, but it didn't really grab hold in general until the Age of Exploration began in the fifteenth century. Since it was then impossible to navigate successfully without taking earth's sphericity into consideration, the flat earth was discarded by all. (Well, there are a few amusing cranks who uphold it even today.)

Of course, that doesn't mean that everyone uses the maximum-distance assumption and understands its consequences. I simply

---

*Actually, earth is not a perfect sphere but a slightly oblate spheroid, so the geometry is not quite as I described it, but the deviations are not significant.

chose that assumption because it can be made to sound ridiculous and yet give the right answers.

Fortunately for us all, the spherical earth can be understood directly because it can be shown by a simple model. Paint the continents on a plastic sphere, and you can quickly see what happens to Smith and Jones as they walk: their separations and approaches, the relationship of point Y to point X, the intersection of lines, the reason for a northward or southward angle in traveling from east to west, and so on.

The concept of a globe is so easily grasped that even old Hardhead capitulated.

♦

But now let's try something else, by beginning with another aspect of common sense.

We all know that if we take a short run before trying a broad jump, we jump farther than if we tried it from a standing start. The speed of the run adds to the speed imparted to the jump by your thigh muscles, so that you start with a faster motion and go a greater distance before gravity pulls you to the ground again.

If you take careful measurements you will find that a ball thrown forward at a rate of 20 kilometers per hour (relative to the ground) will travel 40 kilometers per hour (relative to the ground) if thrown at its usual speed (relative to the thrower) while the thrower is traveling forward on a vehicle moving at 20 kilometers per hour.

On the other hand, if the vehicle is moving at 20 kilometers per hour, and the thrower standing upon it throws a ball with a speed of 20 kilometers per hour in the direction opposite that in which the vehicle is moving, the ball travels 0 kilometers per hour relative to the ground and simply drops downward.

Furthermore, if two vehicles are approaching each other, each moving at 20 kilometers per hour relative to the ground, then a person on one vehicle will see the other approaching at 40 kilometers per hour relative to himself or herself.

To put it as briefly as possible, speeds add and subtract just as apples and oranges do, and since this is in accordance with Isaac Newton's laws of motion, you may think of it as part of a Newtonian universe. The Newtonian universe seems as commonsensical as Euclidean geometry, largely because it's about as simple as it can be.

Now let's pull an assumption out of left field, one that involves the addition and subtraction of speeds. Let us suppose that such manipulation of speeds does *not* work for anything moving at 300,000 kilometers per second.* Something moving at that speed relative to us does *not* change its speed relative to us when it is being carried forward or backward, in the direction of its travel or against it.

Light, as it happens, moves at that speed when traveling through a vacuum, so that when we measure the speed of light relative to ourselves, it always turns out to be 300,000 kilometers per second regardless of the motion of the source of light relative to us (or our motion relative to it).

What's more, anything that ordinarily moves at a speed less than light can't be made to move at the speed of light, let alone faster than the speed of light, because if it reaches the speed of light it will be trapped there, unable to move faster or slower. Similarly, anything that ordinarily moves faster than light (like the hypothesized tachyons) could never move as slowly as light, let alone slower.

In other words, any conceivable object in a vacuum travels either forever *at* the speed of light, forever *less than* the speed of light, or forever *more than* the speed of light. The speed of light is a barrier in both directions.

Why should that be so? What is so magical about that particular speed at which light moves?

No answer, really. That's just the way the universe is.

What are the consequences of that one assumption?

First, suppose two spaceships are moving away from each other and each is traveling 200,000 kilometers per second. Surely to each spaceship, the other spaceship seems to be receding at 200,000 + 200,000 = 400,000 kilometers per second?

No! the two figures have to be added in such a way that the key figure of 300,000 kilometers per second is not exceeded. A formula must be used which includes the ratio of the speed of the spaceship to the speed of light, and which will add any two figures, each below 300,000, in such a way that the sum is nearer 300,000 than

---

*Again, 299,792 kilometers per second would be better, but I'm using the convenient, and close, approximation.

either of the two figures being added, yet never quite reaches 300,000.

Again, imagine a spaceship flashing by you at enormous speed, and imagine further that you can observe and measure the time it takes light on the ship to travel from a source to a mirror and back. You will find that because the ship is moving so quickly, the light seems to be traveling a longer distance (relative to you) than it would if the ship were standing still (relative to you). Despite the fact that the light traveled a longer distance, the speed of light on the speeding ship is the same to you as it would be if the ship were standing still, for the speed of light in a vacuum never changes. Yet the light manages to cover the greater distance.

The only conclusion is that the rate of passage of time slows on a speeding ship. If time slows and a second grows longer, then light, without increasing its speed, can travel the greater distance.

In other words, rather than abandon our silly assumption that light never changes its speed, we have to assume that time slows with increasing speed.

Now, common sense tells us that everything can change its speed if it's properly fooled with, while *nothing* can change the time rate, and therefore this tendency of relativists to do anything at all, even introduce the concept of variable time, just to save something as silly as the constancy of the speed of light, is simply enraging. The hardheads can't endure it.

Nor is a variable time rate the only thing forced upon us by the constancy of light speed. In order to save that constancy, we have to have moving objects shorten in length in the direction of their motion as they speed up.

Then again, it turns out that the scheme of adding speeds in such a way that 300,000 kilometers per second is never exceeded makes an object more and more difficult to accelerate as that magic speed is approached. A force that is sufficient to increase its speed by 50 kilometers per second will, as the object approaches the speed of light, suffice to do so by only 20 kilometers per second, and, as it approaches the speed of light still closer, by only 5 kilometers per second, and so on. Finally, as an object moves infinitesimally close to the speed of light, all the force in the universe can only accelerate it infinitesimally.

This increasing difficulty of acceleration can be stated another way. We can say that a moving object increases its mass as it moves faster and faster, for the mass of an object is defined by the ease with which it accelerates.

The time rate, the length, and the mass of an object all vary with speed according to formulas including the ratio of the speed of the object to the speed of light. At ordinary speeds, the difference from the Newtonian situation is negligible (just as over small patches of earth's surface, the difference from flatness is negligible) while as the object approaches the speed of light, the time rate and length each approach zero and the mass approaches the infinite.

Imagine! All this screwiness just to save the constancy of the speed of light.

In fact, there's more. The energy of motion of a body — its kinetic energy — is measured as half its mass times the square of its speed.* This means that mass and speed are the only things involved in energy of motion. Ordinary speed, the addition of force in order to accelerate an object, adds to its kinetic energy by increasing its speed. It increases mass also but infinitesimally, so that the increase is never noticed at ordinary speeds and mass is assumed to be constant.

As the speed of an object gets progressively nearer the speed of light and the accelerating force has a smaller and smaller effect on the speed, it has a correspondingly greater and greater effect on the mass. More of the increase of kinetic energy is represented by the increase of mass. Thus, we have to accept the fact that energy can be converted into mass and, inevitably, vice versa. The relationship between the two is the famous $e = mc^2$, which is also necessary, then, to save the constancy of light speed.

Albert Einstein worked all this out in 1905 and went on to do much more in the succeeding decade. You make the one assumption and then have to alter a large number of other things, violating common sense to do so, just to keep the assumption going.

Is it worth it?

Yes! Physicists studying vast stretches of space, intense concentrations of energy, enormous speeds, find they cannot make head or tail out of what they observe unless they assume the correctness of the various equations of relativity. The thing is that light actually

---

*I should really be saying *velocity*. Speed and velocity are not quite the same thing in physics, but please excuse the imprecision this time because I'm making a conscious effort to use colloquial language in this essay in honor of the fact that I'm discussing relativity.

has a constant speed, and all the changes in length, mass, and time with motion, all the various relativistic modifications of the New-tonian universe, *really* exist. We live in an Einsteinian universe.

The Einsteinian universe seems against common sense only because all our ordinary experience of life deals with small regions and low speeds, where the relativistic corrections are virtually zero, and Newtonian relationships are correct to a high degree of accuracy.

Well, then, we've given up the flat earth and accepted the spherical earth. Why can't we give up the Newtonian universe and accept the Einsteinian universe?

Because there is no easily grasped model of the Einsteinian universe. We don't have the equivalent of a painted globe over which we can trace lines.

Suppose there were no such thing as a globe and no way of conceptualizing one. Suppose we had to work with a maximum separation as an assumption without ever explaining what this represented in the form of a spherical earth.

In that case, people would be demanding, to this day, *why* can't we go farther than 20,000 kilometers from home, and yelling about it and getting red in the face with rage at scientists obtusely clinging to the limitation.

They would say, "If you were twenty thousand kilometers from home and kept on walking, you would somehow break the distance barrier. After all, we broke the sound barrier and we'll break the distance barrier, too. You scientists are just stupid and dogmatic."

But they *don't* say it because we can explain the situation with a globe, and they see that the 20,000-kilometer distance is indeed a sensible maximum.

But in relativity, we have nothing easy to conceptualize: we must start with the constancy of light speed and deduce the consequences. And people can't accept it.

They say, "But *why* can't we go faster than light?"

And they say, "Suppose two spaceships are moving away from each other and each is going at two hundred thousand kilometers per second; doesn't it stand to reason that each spaceship sees the other as going faster than light?"

And they say, "We broke the sound barrier, and we'll break the light barrier. You scientists are just stupid and dogmatic."

And no amount of explaining ever seems to help.

Talking about series of items like my Griswold mystery stories and my F & SF science essays, there's another I can mention — a series of short essays I've been doing for nearly a decade in American Way, *the in-flight magazine of American Airlines.*

You may ask, "Why all these series, Isaac?" and the answer is, "I can't help it." When a magazine asks me to do an item of a particular sort for each issue, I seem to be constitutionally unable to say no if there is the least chance that I can find the time for it, and that I have the qualifications for it.

*It may be that the magazine hopes I will break down after a while and be unable to keep up the pace or think up new items and that they will then be rid of me — but somehow I always manage to keep up the pace and the thinking, and then the magazine (I suppose) hesitates to be cruel and tell me to stop. (*Gallery *did it in the case of the Griswolds, but that, I think, was the result of an editorial shakeup that had nothing to do with me.)*

In any case, back in 1974 John Minihan, who was then the editor of American Way, *asked me to do a series of 750-word essays on one aspect or another of the future that faces us. The overall title of the column was to be "Change!" I agreed, and I've been keeping it up ever since.* American Way, *I admit, has encouraged me by raising the amount they pay me, in stages, until it is nearly three times what it was to begin with, even though I have never asked for a raise. (For that matter,* F & SF *has done the same thing, and I've never asked Ed Ferman for a raise, either.)*

Eventually, I chose seventy-one of my American Way *essays and put them together in a collection called* Change! *(Book 238), which was published by Houghton Mifflin in 1981. Some of the essays are on physics-related subjects, and here's one entitled "Converting It All."*

from CHANGE! *(1981)*

Converting It All

Energy can be produced at the expense of matter and in very large quantities. If a single pound of matter were converted entirely into energy, it would produce an amount equivalent to the muscular energy expended in an entire day by the human population of all the Earth.

Let's put it another way. We know the awesome power of the hydrogen bomb — the result of converting 0.7 percent of the hydrogen used as nuclear explosive into energy. If *all* the hydrogen were converted into energy, a hydrogen bomb of a given size would be 140 times as destructive as it is.

Nuclear engineers are trying to bring the hydrogen fusion reaction under control, to learn to make it progress under controlled conditions. Controlled hydrogen fusion would give us a source of energy so rich that it would last as long as the Earth is likely to.

Yet that is only one one-hundred-fortieth of the energy that's really there. Is there any way we can suck *all* the energy out of matter?

In theory, there is. The common particles that make up matter are electrons, protons, and neutrons. Each one has an antiparticle, a kind of mirror image that has one key property opposite in nature to that of the particle itself. In other words there are antielectrons, antiprotons and antineutrons, out of which antimatter can be built up.

Whenever a particle meets its own antiparticle, the two cancel each other and undergo "mutual annihilation." Nothing but energy, equivalent to that of the amount of mass that has disappeared, is left behind.

An ounce of matter and an ounce of antimatter, brought together, would explode at once, forming a ball of intense and deadly radiation. However, if the matter and antimatter were in the form of a thin drizzle of antiparticles being joined in a very slow and steady manner, energy might be formed at a manageable rate. Such controlled matter-antimatter annihilation would be an energy source 140 times as rich as the same amount of matter undergoing controlled hydrogen fusion.

There are catches, of course. For one thing, antimatter, or even individual antiparticles, does not exist in nature except for small quantities in cosmic rays or in certain radioactive transformations. Antiparticles can be formed in the laboratory but, again, in very small quantities. What's more, the energy required to form the antiparticles is considerably greater than the energy we would get back from it if we allowed it to combine with particles.

Second, even if we could form antiparticles in quantity, where would we keep them? The world is made up entirely of ordinary particles, and any antiparticles would have to be kept safely penned up, possibly in a tight electromagnetic field, out of all contact with ordinary particles, till we wish to begin the controlled interaction. The problem of working out the technique would be formidable.

As it happens, protons and neutrons, scientists now think, are made up of still more fundamental particles called quarks and antiquarks that come in a rather large variety of forms. These quarks and antiquarks can combine only in certain combinations to form protons and neutrons — plus hundreds of other particles that don't appear in ordinary matter but can be made to appear under conditions of very high energy concentrations in the laboratory.

We are only on the edge of understanding quarks, antiquarks, and their combinations, but as we learn more and more it is possible we may learn to manipulate them, with ingenuity, in ways not found in nature. (After all, we have learned to outdo nature in our handling of atoms and of subatomic particles.)

Give us time, and we may learn to build synthetic particles from quarks, particles unlike any that occur naturally. The quark particles we know, besides protons or neutrons, last only exceedingly tiny fractions of a second, but what if we can design some that endure for minutes — long enough for them to be put to use. They may even be sufficiently different from any natural quark combination not to react with ordinary matter, so that they may be stored.

And what if we can manufacture artificial particles like those we have already formed, but with an antiquark wherever a quark should be and vice versa. These should have the same stability and inertness as their mirror images.

Then, if these two sets of artificial particles, mirror images of each other, are mixed at a slow and controlled rate, we would have the ultimate fuel, one in which *all* the matter is converted to energy at a rate slow enough to be useful to us.

Of course, it's a wild dream. It's unlikely such artificial particles are possible, or could be formed without impossible energies, or could have the appropriate properties. Yet nuclear power of any kind was an equally wild dream (if anyone could even have dreamed it) in 1880.

PART 5

CHEMISTRY

MY THIRD HUNDRED BOOKS do not include any major item devoted exclusively to chemistry but, again, I have written F & SF essays that fit into this category.

In the case of my F & SF essays, the freedom I am given sometimes allows me to carry over from month to month. After all, I'm not a fanatic about squeezing everything into the four thousand words I am allotted per essay. I just type along, chattering my head off, and if, when I reach the four-thousand-word mark, I find that I haven't quite finished, I just say "more next time." Then, a month later, I give a rapid précis of what went on up to that point and continue. I once carried the subject of left-right asymmetry in physics and chemistry through five consecutive essays.

I didn't do quite that when I began an essay on what seemed to me to be a simple goal of explaining the difference between carbon and silicon so that people would understand why it was that though the two elements are chemically similar in many ways, there can be life based on carbon atoms, but not on silicon atoms. Such was my volubility, however, that the exposition stretched itself into four essays.

All four were included in X Stands for Unknown, *an essay collection I mentioned earlier, and I include the first two essays of this series, "Big Brother" and "Bread and Stone," here.*

from X STANDS FOR UNKNOWN (1984)

Big Brother

I was engaged in casual conversation with a young man the other day, and its natural course led him to remark that the south nave of the Cathedral of Saint John the Divine was going to be constructed. (A nave, as I suppose you all know, is a long narrow hall, or corridor, that is part of a church.)

As soon as the young man said the word "nave," it occurred to
me at once that if only the architect were named Hartz, and if a
couple of ladies of the evening had managed to make it to the
church before being caught by a pursuing policeman intent on an
arrest, and if the ladies claimed sanctuary, then the policeman
would be justified in declaiming:

> *The nave of Hartz;*
> *It stole those tarts!*

in parody of the well-known nursery rhyme concerning the "knave
of hearts."

Since I am a devotee of word-play, and since I admired this conceit I had invented, I felt I had to display it to the young man with
whom I was conversing.

So I began: "Now if it should happen that the south nave were
being constructed by an architect named Hartz —"

The young man said, "Yes, David Hartz."

"David Hartz?" I said, puzzled.

"Yes. Isn't he the one you're referring to? David Hartz of Yale,
I think. Do you know him?"

"Are you serious? Is the architect really named Hartz?"

"*Yes!* You're the one who brought up his name."

What could I do? I was face to face with another Coincidence,
and it killed my piece of word-play, which would have seemed drab
by comparison. I didn't bother to trot it out.

Still, if the young man is correct about the name of the architect,
then I trust that the structure will be known as "the nave of Hartz"
through all eternity, and I will gladly bribe two young women of
the appropriate profession to seek refuge there, so as to make my
word-play come true.

But coincidences are to be found not only in everyday life, but
in science also, and thereby hangs a tale —

♦

When chemists were studying the elements during the nineteenth
century, they discovered a number of interesting similarities between one element and another. If no order existed among the
elements, then those similarities would be merely unexplained
(and, perhaps, unexplainable) coincidences, and they would make
scientists as uncomfortable as fleas make a dog.

Chemists tried to find order and, in so doing, succeeded in establishing the periodic table of the elements (see "Bridging the Gaps," *F & SF*, March 1970).

Of all the elements in the list, carbon should be the dearest to us, since it is through its unusual (and, perhaps, unique) properties that life on Earth is possible.

In fact, we might even argue, if we were in a conservative mood, that carbon is the only conceivable basis of life *anywhere* in the Universe (see "The One and Only," *F & SF*, November 1972).*

Yet how can carbon be unique? According to the periodic table, carbon does not stand alone, but is the head of a "carbon family" made up of chemically similar elements. The carbon family consists of five stable elements: carbon itself, silicon, germanium, tin, and lead.

Within a family, chemical similarities are strongest between elements adjacent to each other. This means that the element most similar to carbon in chemical properties is silicon, the next in line, and it is silicon with which this essay will deal.

Carbon has an atomic number of 6 and silicon one of 14. (By comparison, the atomic numbers of germanium, tin, and lead are 32, 50, and 82, respectively.) Silicon has an atomic weight of 28, compared to carbon's 12. The silicon atom is therefore two and a third times as massive as the carbon atom. Silicon is carbon's big brother, so to speak.

The atomic number tells us the number of electrons circling the nucleus of an intact atom. Carbon has six electrons divided into two shells — two electrons in the inner shell, four in the outer one. Silicon, on the other hand, has fourteen electrons divided into three shells — two in the innermost, eight in the intermediate one, and four in the outermost. As you see, then, carbon and silicon each have four electrons in the shell farthest from the nucleus. We could describe carbon as (2/4) and silicon as (2/8/4) in terms of the electron content of their atoms.

When a carbon atom collides with another atom of any kind, it is the four electrons on the outskirts of the carbon atoms that interact with the electrons in the other atom in one way or another. This interaction produces what we call a chemical change. When a

---

*More radical views are possible, as in *Life Beyond Earth* by Gerald Feinberg and Robert Shapiro (Morrow, 1980), which I heartily recommend to all of you.

silicon atom collides, it is again the four electrons on the outskirts that interact.

All electrons are identical down to the finest measurements scientists can make. The four outermost electrons of carbon and the four of silicon behave similarly, for that reason, and the chemical properties of the two elements are, therefore, also similar.

But in that case, if carbon, with four electrons on the outskirts of its atoms, has the kind of chemical properties that allows it to serve as the basis of life, ought not silicon, with *its* four electrons on the outskirts, also serve as a basis of life?

To answer that question, let's start at the beginning.

♦

Silicon is an extremely common element. Next to oxygen, it is the most common component of Earth's crust. Some 46.6 percent of the total mass of the Earth's crust consists of oxygen atoms, and about 27.7 percent is silicon. (The other eighty elements that occur in the crust, taken together, make up the remaining 25.7 percent.) In other words, if we leave oxygen out of account, then there is more silicon in the Earth's crust than everything else put together.

Just the same, don't expect to stumble over a piece of silicon the next time you venture out into the world. It won't happen. Silicon is not to be found on Earth in its elemental form; that is, you won't find a chunk of matter made up of silicon atoms only. In the Earth's crust, all the silicon atoms that exist are combined with other kinds of atoms, chiefly those of oxygen, and therefore exist as "compounds."

For that matter, you can't pick up a hunk of Earth's crust and squeeze pure oxygen out of it, either, since the oxygen atoms present are combined with other kinds of atoms, chiefly silicon. There is considerable elemental oxygen in the Earth's atmosphere, but there is no free silicon to speak of anywhere in our reach.

Here we come across some differences between silicon and carbon. For one thing, carbon is not as common as silicon in the Earth's crust. For every 370 silicon atoms, there is only one carbon atom. (That still leaves carbon comparatively common, however.)

This is peculiar since, in the Universe as a whole, smaller atoms are more common than larger atoms (with some exceptions, for reasons that are understood), and carbon atoms are distinctly smaller than silicon atoms. In the Universe as a whole, astronomers estimate that there are seven carbon atoms for every two silicon atoms.

Why, then, is Earth's crust comparatively carbon-poor? We'll let that go for now, but I promise I will return to this matter, eventually.

Carbon, like silicon, is usually found in combination with other atoms, chiefly oxygen, but *unlike* silicon, sizable quantities of carbon are to be found in elemental form, as chunks of matter containing carbon atoms almost entirely. Coal, for instance, is anywhere from 85 to 95 percent carbon atoms.

But, then, coal originates from decaying plant material. It is the product of life. If carbon did not have properties that allowed it to serve as a basis for life, it would not occur in the free state in Earth's crust.

We might, conversely, argue that if silicon were enough like carbon to serve as the basis for another variety of life, it, too, would be likely to occur in the free state, when silicon life broke down. Consequently, if we find out why silicon won't serve as the basis of life, we will also find out why it does not occur free as carbon does.

(As a matter of fact, the only reason oxygen occurs free in the atmosphere is because of the activity of plant life, which liberates oxygen as a side effect of photosynthesis. If life did not exist on Earth, the only elements that would occur free would be those that were particulary inert, chemically. Most of these, like helium or platinum, are very rare. The least rare of the inert elements is nitrogen and, as a result, there are sizable quantities of free nitrogen not only in the atmosphere of Earth, a planet rich in life, but also in the atmosphere of Venus, a totally barren planet!)

♦

Even though nature has not been kind enough to prepare silicon in elemental form for us, chemists have learned to do it on their own. Two French chemists, Joseph Louis Gay-Lussac (1778–1850) and Louis Jacques Thénard (1777–1857), managed, in 1809, to decompose a silicon-containing compound and to obtain a reddish-brown material out of it. They did not examine it further. It is probable that this material was a mass of elemental silicon, though containing much in the way of impurities.

In 1824 the Swedish chemist Jöns Jakob Berzelius (1779–1848) obtained a similar mass of silicon by a somewhat different chemical route. Unlike Gay-Lussac and Thénard, however, Berzelius realized what he had, and went to considerable trouble to get rid of the nonsilicon impurities.

Berzelius was the first to get reasonably pure silicon and to study what he had and report on its properties. For that reason, Berzelius is usually credited with the discovery of silicon.

Berzelius's silicon was "amorphous"; that is, the individual silicon atoms were arranged in an irregular fashion so that no visible crystals formed. (The word "amorphous" is from Greek, meaning "no shape," since crystals are distinguished by their regular geometrical form.)

In 1854 the French chemist Henri Étienne Sainte-Claire Deville (1818–1881) prepared silicon crystals for the first time. These shone with a metallic luster, and this might make it seem that silicon is different from carbon in another important way: that silicon is a metal and carbon is not.

That, however, is not so. Although silicon has some properties that are similar to those of metals generally, it has others that are not, and it is therefore a "semimetal." Carbon, in the form of graphite, also has some metallic properties (it conducts electricity moderately well, for instance). The two elements, consequently, are not startlingly different in this respect.

Carbon atoms, to be sure, are not bound to arrange themselves in the manner that produces graphite. They may also arrange themselves in a more compact and symmetrical manner in order to produce diamond, which shows no metallic properties whatever (see "The Unlikely Twins," *F & SF*, October 1972).

Diamond is particularly notable for being hard, and, in 1891, the American inventor Edward Goodrich Acheson (1856–1931) discovered that carbon, when heated with clay, yields another very hard substance. Acheson thought the substance was carbon combined with alundum (a compound of aluminum and oxygen atoms, both of which are found in clay).

He therefore called the new hard substance carborundum.

Actually, carborundum turned out to be a compound of carbon and silicon (silicon atoms are also found in clay). The compound consisted of silicon and carbon atoms in equal quantities ("silicon carbide," or, in chemical symbols, SiC). This mixture of atoms took on the compact and symmetrical arrangement that occurs in diamond.

In carborundum, the carbon and silicon atoms are placed alternately within the crystal structure. The fact that one can substitute silicon atoms for every other carbon atom and still have a very hard substance shows how similar the two elements are. (Not all properties are preserved, however. Carborundum does not have the transparency or beauty of diamond.)

Carborundum, incidentally, is not quite as hard as diamond. Why is that?

Well, silicon and carbon atoms are chemically similar, thanks to the fact that both have four electrons in the outermost shell, but they are not identical. The silicon atom has three electron shells compared to the carbon atom's two. That means the distance from the outermost shell of the silicon atom to its nucleus is greater than in the case of the carbon atom.

The electrons carry a negative electric charge and are held in place by the attraction of the positive charge on the atom's nucleus. This attractive force decreases with distance and is therefore weaker in the silicon atom than in the smaller carbon atom.

Furthermore, between the outermost electrons and the nucleus in the silicon atom are the ten electrons of the two inner shells, but in the case of carbon, only the two electrons of the lone inner shell intervene. Each negatively charged inner electron, existing between the outermost shell and the nucleus, tends to neutralize the nucleus's positive charge somewhat and weakens the nucleus's hold on the outermost electrons.

When two carbon atoms cling together, that is because of the attractive force generated by the association of two electrons (one from each atom). The more firmly those two electrons are held by the respective nuclei of the two atoms, the stronger the bond between them.

Therefore, the carbon-carbon bond is stronger than the silicon-silicon bond, and the silicon-carbon bond should be of intermediate strength.

One way of demonstrating this is by melting point. As the temperature rises, the atoms vibrate more and more strongly until, finally, they break the bonds holding them together and slide over each other freely. The solid has become a liquid. The tighter the bonds, therefore, the higher the melting point must be.

Carbon doesn't actually melt, but "sublimes"; that is, it turns from a solid into a vapor directly; but we'll call that the melting point just the same. The melting point of carbon is over 3500° C while that of silicon is only 1410° C. Carborundum (which, like carbon, sublimes) has the intermediate melting point of 2700° C.

Again, you can judge the tightness of the bond by the hardness of the substance. The stronger the bond between the atoms, the more the substance resists deformation, the more easily it inflicts deformation (in the form of scratches, for instance) upon other, softer substances.

Diamond is the hardest substance known. Carborundum is not quite as hard, but is harder than silicon.

Despite the fact that carborundum is not quite as hard as diamond, it is more useful as an "abrasive" (something hard enough to wear down, through friction, softer objects, without itself being much affected). Why?

The answer is a matter of price. We all know how rare and expensive diamonds are, even impure ones of less-than-gem quality. Carborundum, on the other hand, can be made out of ordinary carbon and clay, both of which are about as cheap as anything can reasonably be expected to be.

◆

I said earlier that silicon atoms are, in nature, most frequently found in combination with oxygen atoms. The oxygen atom is readily able to accept two electrons from another atom, combining each electron it accepts with one of its own. Two electron-pairs are formed between the two atoms, and this is called a double-bond, which we can represent in the following fashion: Si = O. The silicon atom has four outer electrons, however, and it is perfectly capable of donating two electrons to each of two different oxygen atoms.

The result is O = Si = O, which can also be represented, more simply, as SiO_2, and which can be called silicon dioxide. It is an old-fashioned habit, arising in the days when chemists did not know exactly how many atoms of each element were present in combination (or that there were atoms at all), to have the name of a compound of some element with oxygen end with a final *a*. Consequently, silicon dioxide is also called silica.

In fact, silica was the name that was used first, and the final *a* indicated that it was suspected of being a combination of oxygen with an element that had not yet been isolated. Once the other element was obtained, it was named silicon from silica, the *n* ending being conventional for a nonmetallic element, as in boron, hydrogen, and chlorine.

The purest form of silica, when it contains virtually nothing but silicon and oxygen atoms, is best-known as quartz, a word of unknown origin.

The astonishing thing about quartz, if it is pure enough, is that it is transparent. There are very few naturally-occurring solids that allow light to pass through with scarcely any absorption, and quartz is one of those few.

The first such substance that early man encountered was ice, which if it is formed slowly, and in a reasonably thin layer, is transparent. When men who had encountered ice later encountered quartz, they could only think they had found another form of ice, one which had formed in so superrigid a manner under such supercold conditions, that it was no longer capable of melting.

The Greeks, therefore, called quartz *krystallos*, which was their word for "ice." This became *crystallum* in Latin and "crystal" in English. The prefix "cry" is still used to mean "very cold" as in "cryogenics" (the production of ultralow temperatures), "cryometer" (a thermometer for registering ultralow temperatures), and so on.

"Crystal," as an English word for "ice," is, however, obsolete now. It is more often used to signify a transparent object, even when it is not made of quartz. For instance, we still talk of a fortuneteller looking into her crystal ball, which is, of course, simply glass.

Then, too, when the Greeks said that each planet was part of a sphere, and turned with its sphere, those came to be spoken of as "crystalline spheres" because of their transparency. (They were *totally* transparent, for they didn't exist.)

Quartz was usually found in straight-line, smooth-plane, sharp-angled shapes, and the word "crystal" came to mean that. Naturally-occurring solids of such shapes came to be called crystals, whether they were quartz or not.

Quartz is not necessarily transparent, because it is not necessarily sufficiently pure. If the impurity is not very great, the quartz may stay transparent but gain a color; the best and most beautiful example of that is the purple amethyst.

The ancient Greeks, noting amethyst's wine color, reasoned, by the principles of sympathetic magic, that it must counter the effects of wine. Wine drunk from an amethyst cup, they were sure, would taste great but would not intoxicate. In fact, "amethyst" is from Greek words meaning "no wine." (Don't bother to try it; it won't work.)

With greater amounts of impurity, you have silica that is chemically combined with such metals as iron, aluminum, calcium, potassium, and so on — or mixtures of several of these. Such compounds are referred to as silicates and are, for the most part, dull and opaque substances. Included among the silicates are granite, basalt, clay, and so on. Indeed, Earth's rocky crust, together with the mantle beneath, are largely silicate in nature.

Flint is a common silicate, and it was very important to early man, because it could be chipped or ground into sharp edges and points and was therefore the best thing for tools like knives, hatchets, spear points, and arrow points in any society that lacked metals. The word "flint" is from an old Teutonic term meaning a "rock chip," which was what you got when you worked flint into a tool. The rock chip itself was sometimes the tool.

The Latin word for flint is *silex*, and if one wished to speak of something that was made of flint, the genitive form of the word, *silicis*, was used. It was from flint, then, that we got first "silica" for silicon dioxide, and then "silicon" for the element.

Small bits of quartz, shattered, usually, by the action of waves on a shore, form sand; and the color of sand depends upon the purity of the quartz, and if not pure, on the nature of the impurities. Pure quartz will produce a rather white sand; the usually sandy color of sand (what else?) is due to iron content.

The oxygen atom is smaller than the silicon atom but larger than the carbon atom. Therefore, silicon dioxide ought to have a higher melting point than silicon itself does, but a lower one than carborundum.

That, indeed, is the way it works out. Silicon dioxide has a melting point of about 1700° C, which is higher than that of silicon and lower than that of carborundum.

If appropriate substances that contain sodium and calcium atoms are added to sand, and if the mixture is heated, it melts and becomes glass, which is essentially a sodium-calcium silicate. Other substances can, however, be added to gain certain desired qualities such as color, or hardness, or resistance to temperature change, or limpid transparency.

Glass is, on the whole, as transparent as quartz to visible light, but glass is much more useful in most practical ways.

For one thing, glass can be made out of sand, which is much more common than intact crystals of quartz, and so it is much cheaper than quartz. For another, glass melts at a lower temperature than quartz, so it is easier to work with.

Then, too, glass does not really solidify, but remains a liquid. That liquid, however, gets stiffer and stiffer as it cools, until it is a solid to all intents and purposes. The glass we routinely handle is, in short, a liquid because its atomic arrangement is random as in liquids, rather than orderly as in solids; yet it has the rigidity of a solid. This means that glass has no sharp melting point but remains a sort of gooey liquid over a fairly large temperature range, and this, again, makes it easier to work with.

◆

Now, then, can carbon substitute for silicon and produce carbon analogs of quartz, sand, and rock; of silica and silicates?

Carbon can make a good beginning. It, too, can donate two of its four outer electrons to each of two oxygen atoms. The result is $O = C = O$, or CO_2, which is universally known as carbon dioxide and which, from the formula, certainly seems to be an analog of silicon dioxide.

The bond between carbon and oxygen atoms, all things being equal, is stronger than the bond between silicon and oxygen, since carbon atoms are smaller than silicon atoms. Therefore, it is only fair to suppose that carbon dioxide will melt at a higher temperature than silicon dioxide.

Carbon dioxide has a melting point of $-78.5°$ C (though, in actual fact, it sublimes rather than melts), and this is 1800 degrees *lower* than the melting point of silicon dioxide.

Why is that? Well, the answer to that, and to the matter of carbon's comparatively low occurrence on Earth, and to the big question of which will lead to life, and why, must await next month's essay.

Bread and Stone

In the Sermon on the Mount, Jesus assured his listeners that God the Father would be kind to humanity. He demonstrated that by pointing out that human fathers, vastly imperfect by comparison, were kind to *their* children. He said: "— what man is there of you whom if his son ask bread, will he give him a stone?" (Matthew 7:9).

A bitter echo of this verse was heard eighteen centuries later in connection with Robert Burns, the great Scottish poet, who lived and died in grinding poverty, even while he was turning out his now world-famous lyrics.

After his death in 1796, at the age of thirty-seven, the Scots discovered that he was a great poet (it is always easier to honor someone after it is no longer necessary to support him) and decided to erect a monument to him. This was told to Burns's aging mother, who received the news with less than overwhelming gratitude.

"Rabbie, Rabbie," she was reported to have said, "ye asked for bread, and they gave ye a stone."

I love the story and it brings a tear to my eye every time I tell it, but like all the historical stories I love, it may be apocryphal.

The English satirist Samuel Butler, best known for his poem "Hudibras," died in dire want in 1680, and, in 1721, Samuel Wesley, after noting Butler's monument in Westminster Abbey, wrote:

> *A poet's fate is here in emblem shown:*
> *He asked for Bread, and he received a Stone.*

It's unlikely that Mrs. Burns, three quarters of a century later, was quoting Wesley, but it seems to me likely that whoever reported Mrs. Burns's remark was really quoting.

In any case, bread is the product of the carbon atom, and stone is the product of the silicon atom. And though carbon and silicon are similar in atomic structure, their products are so different that they form a natural and powerful antithesis.

♦

I ended last month's essay by comparing carbon dioxide and silicon dioxide: the former turning into a gas at so low a temperature that it remains a gas even in the extremest wintry weather of Antarctica; the other turning into a gas at so high a temperature that even the hottest volcanoes don't produce any significant quantities of silicon dioxide vapors.

In the molecule of carbon dioxide, each carbon atom is combined with two oxygen atoms, thus: $O = C = O$. The carbon atom (C) is attached to each oxygen atom (O) by a "double bond"; that is, by two pairs of electrons. Each atom participating in such a double bond contributes one electron to each pair or two electrons altogether. The oxygen atom has only two electrons to contribute under normal circumstances; the carbon atom, four. The carbon atom, therefore, forms a double bond with each of two oxygen atoms, as shown in the formula.

The silicon atom (Si) is very similar to the carbon atom in its electron arrangements, and it, too, has four electrons to contribute to bond formulation. It, too, can form a double bond with each of two oxygen atoms, and silicon dioxide can be represented as $O = Si = O$.

At the end of last month's essay, I pointed out that the bonds holding carbon and oxygen together are stronger than those holding silicon and oxygen together, and suggested this meant that carbon dioxide should have higher melting and boiling points than silicon dioxide. The reverse is, in actual fact, true, and I posed this as a problem.

Actually, I was oversimplifying. There are indeed times when melting points and boiling points signify the breaking of strong bonds between atoms, so that the stronger the bonds the higher the melting and boiling points. This is true when each atom in a solid is held to its neighbors by strong bonds. There is then no way of converting the solid to first a liquid and then a gas, except by breaking some or all of those bonds.

In other cases, however, two to a dozen atoms are held together strongly to form a discrete molecule of moderate size, and the individual molecules are bound to each other weakly. In that case, melting and boiling points are reached when those weak intermolecular bonds are broken, and the individual molecules are freed. In that case, the strong bonds within the molecule need not be touched, and the melting points and boiling points are then usually quite low.

In the case of a boiling point, in particular, we have a situation in which the intermolecular bonds are completely broken so that a gas is produced in which the individual molecules move about freely and independently. At a sublimation point, the intermolecular bonds in a solid are completely broken to form a gas that is made up of completely independent molecules.

The boiling point of silicon dioxide is about 2300° C, while the sublimation point of carbon dioxide is $-78.5°$ C. Clearly, in heating silicon dioxide to a gas, we must break strong bonds between atoms; while in heating carbon dioxide to a gas, we need break only weak intermolecular bonds.

Why? The formulas, $O = Si = O$ and $O = C = O$, look so similar.

◆

To begin with, we must understand that a double bond is *weaker* than a single bond. This seems to go against common sense. Surely, a grip with both hands would be stronger than a grip with only one hand. Holding something with two rubber bands, two ropes, two chains would seem a stronger situation than with only one in each case.

Nevertheless, this is not so in the case of interatomic bonds. To explain that properly requires quantum mechanics, but I will do everyone a favor* by offering a more metaphoric explanation. We can imagine that there's only so much space between atoms, and that when four electrons crowd into the space to set up a double bond, they don't have enough room to establish a good grip. Two electrons, setting up a single bond, do better. Imagine yourself squeezing both hands into a constricted space, and holding on to something with thumb and forefinger of each hand. Inserting one hand and achieving a good all-fingers grip would be far more effective.

Consequently, if there is a chance to rearrange the electrons in silicon dioxide in such a way as to replace the double bonds by single bonds, the tendency will be for that to happen.

Where there are many silicon dioxide molecules present, for instance, each oxygen atom distributes its electrons so that it holds on to each of two different silicon atoms with a single bond apiece, rather than to one silicon atom with a double bond. Instead of O

*Chiefly myself!

= Si = O, you have – O – Si – O – Si – O – Si – and so on, indefinitely, in either direction.

Each silicon atom has four electrons to contribute and can form four single bonds, but each uses only two single bonds in the chain just pictured. Each silicon atom, therefore, can start an indefinite chain in two other directions, so that you end up with —

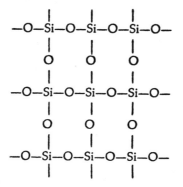

This looks two-dimensional, but it isn't really. The four bonds of silicon are distributed toward the four apices of a tetrahedron, and the result is a three-dimensional structure, rather like that in diamond or silicon carbide.

Consequently, each chunk of pure silicon dioxide (quartz) is, in effect, an enormous molecule, in which there are, on the whole, two oxygen atoms for every silicon atom. To melt and boil such a chunk requires the breaking of the strong Si – O bonds, so that we have a high boiling point, and don't encounter gaseous silicon dioxide under Earth-surface conditions.

All this remains true if other types of atoms join the silicon-oxygen lattice in numbers that are not large enough to disrupt that lattice completely, thus forming silicates. The silicates, generally, are high-melting and high-boiling.

The matter is quite different with carbon dioxide. Smaller atoms tend to form stronger bonds, so that the carbon atom, which is smaller than the silicon atom, bonds more strongly with oxygen than silicon does. In fact, even the C = O double bond, while weaker than the C – O single bond, is nevertheless sufficiently strong so that the tendency to distribute itself into single bonds is much smaller than in the case of silicon dioxide. There are certain advantages in stability of small molecules over large, and this, combined with the comparative strength of the carbon/oxygen double bond, tends to keep carbon dioxide in the form of small molecules.

If the temperature is low enough, the individual molecules of carbon dioxide cling together and form a solid, but the molecules are held together by relatively weak intermolecular bonds, and these are easily broken. Hence, the low sublimation point.

Other atoms can combine with carbon dioxide to form "carbonates," and these remain solid at Earth-surface temperatures. If heated to higher temperatures, however, they break up and give off carbon dioxide gas at considerably lower temperatures than the boiling point of silicates.

Calcium carbonate (limestone) will, for instance, give off carbon dioxide gas at about 825° C.

♦

When a planetary system forms, the process of formation produces a hot planet to begin with. If the forming planets are comparatively near the central sun, the temperature rises still higher as a result.

Under those conditions, the only solids one can have are those which consist of atoms forming large atom-lattices and which therefore have high melting and boiling points. This includes two varieties of substances that tend to separate as the planet develops: metals (chiefly iron, plus those metals that will mix with it relatively freely) and silicates.

The dense metals tend to collect at the center of the planet, with the lighter silicates surrounding that core as an outer shell.

This is the general structure of the five worlds of the inner Solar System: Mercury, Venus, Earth, Moon, and Mars. (In the case of Mars and the Moon, the metallic component is quite low.)

Those elements whose atoms fit with difficulty, or not at all, into the metallic or silicate lattice tend to be left over as individual atoms, as small molecules, or as lattices in which the atoms are but feebly held together. In all cases, they are low-melting (volatile) and, in the early days of planetary formation, existed to a large extent as vapors.

Since the metals and silicates are made up of elements that, in turn, make up a relatively small fraction of the original materials out of which planetary systems form, the worlds of the inner Solar

System are comparatively small and possess correspondingly weak gravitational fields — too weak to hold vapors.

This means the loss of most or all of some of the elements that are particularly common in the original preplanetary mixture: hydrogen, helium, carbon, nitrogen, neon, sodium, potassium, and argon.

Thus, Mercury and the Moon possess little or no hydrogen, carbon, and nitrogen, three elements without which life-as-we-know-it cannot exist. Venus and Earth are massive enough to have hung on to some of these elements, and each has a substantial atmosphere of volatiles. Mars, with a weaker gravitational field (it has only one-tenth the mass of Earth), was, because of its greater distance from the Sun, cool enough to hang on to a tiny quantity of volatile matter and has a thin atmosphere.

Beyond Mars, in the outer Solar System, the planets remained cool enough to collect substantial proportions of those volatiles which made up 99 percent of the original mixture (chiefly hydrogen and helium), so that they grew large and massive. As they grew, their gravitational fields intensified, and they were able to grow still more rapidly (the "snowball effect"). The results were the large outer planets: Jupiter, Saturn, Uranus, and Neptune. These are the so-called gas giants, made up chiefly of a mixture of hydrogen and helium, with small molecules containing carbon, nitrogen, and oxygen as substantial impurities, and with (it is presumed) relatively small cores of silicates and metals at the center.

Even the smaller worlds of the outer Solar System became cool enough, at an early stage, to collect volatiles. The molecules of these contain carbon or nitrogen or oxygen, each in combination with hydrogen. At the present very low temperatures of these worlds, these volatiles are in the solid state. They are ices, so called because of their general resemblance in properties to the best-known example here on Earth — frozen water.

The four large satellites of Jupiter, as an example, have undergone heating through Jupiter's tidal effect (which grows rapidly greater as the distance of the satellite is smaller). Ganymede and Callisto, the two farthest satellites, have undergone little heating and are essentially icy worlds, and larger than the other two. Io, the innermost, has been too warm to collect volatiles and is essentially silicate in nature, while Europa, which lies between Io and Ganymede, seems to be silicate, with an icy cover.

But let's get back to Earth, which consists of a liquid nickel-iron core, surrounded by a silicate mantle.

On the very surface are those volatiles that Earth has managed to keep. Hydrogen atoms are chiefly to be found as part of the water molecules that make up our (comparatively) vast ocean. Nitrogen atoms are to be found as two-atom molecules in the atmosphere. Carbon atoms are found as carbon dioxide in the atmosphere (in small quantities), as carbonates in the crust, and as elementary carbon in the form of coal deposits.

Earth is, however, depleted in these elements and, while they are present in sufficient quantity to allow a complete and diverse load of life, there are less of these elements on Earth by far than there is in an equal mass of matter more representative of the overall composition of the Universe (say, in an equal mass of Jupiter or the Sun).

But if the Earth's crust contains 370 silicon atoms for every carbon atom, and the two are so similar in many of their chemical properties, why should life form about the carbon atom rather than the silicon atom?

In this connection, we have to remember that life is a rather complex atomic dance. Life represents a relatively low-entropy system, maintained against an overwhelming tendency (the second law of thermodynamics) to raise the entropy. Life is made up of very complex and fragile molecules that left to themselves would break down. It contains high concentrations of certain types of atoms or molecules in some places, low concentrations in others; where, left to themselves, the concentrations would promptly begin to even out — and so on.

In order to maintain the state of low entropy, the chemistry of life keeps up an unceasing activity. It is not that molecules don't break down or that uneven concentrations don't even out; it is that the complex molecules are built up again as fast as they break down, and the concentrations made uneven as fast as they even out. It is as though we were keeping a house dry during a flood, not by stopping the flood (which we can't do) but by assiduously and tirelessly sweeping out the water as fast as it pours in.

This means that there must be a constant shuffling of atoms and molecules, and that the basic raw materials of life must exist in a form that enables them to be seized and used rapidly. The raw materials must exist as small molecules in considerable quantity under conditions that enable the bonds holding the atoms together within the molecules to be easily broken and re-formed, so that molecules of one type are forever being converted to another.

This is accomplished by use of a fluid medium in which the various molecules are dissolved. They are there present in high concentration, they move about freely, and they serve the purpose. The fluid medium used is water, which is plentiful on Earth, and which is a good solvent for a wide variety of substances. Life, in fact, is impossible without water.

The molecules that are useful for life are those that are soluble in water, therefore, or that can be made soluble. Carbon dioxide, for instance, is fairly soluble in water. Oxygen is only slightly soluble, but it attaches readily to hemoglobin so that the small quantity that does dissolve is snatched up at once, leaving room for another small quantity to dissolve, and so on.

The process of solution in water is, however, similar in some ways to the processes of melting and boiling. Interatomic or intermolecular bonds must be broken. If you have a whole lattice of atoms, the entire lattice will not enter solution as an intact mass. If the lattice can be pulled apart into smaller fragments, on the other hand, those fragments may be dissolved.

Silicates form a tightly bound lattice, and the bonds are as resistant to breakage by water as by heat. Silicates are insoluble — which is a good thing — or the oceans would dissolve much of the continental areas and produce a thick sludge, which would be neither sea nor land and in which life-as-we-know-it could not exist.

But this also means that silicon atoms do not exist in the form of small, soluble molecules and, consequently, are not incorporated into actively living tissue. Silicon therefore does not serve as the basis of life, and carbon does.

♦

That, however, is under earthly conditions. What about the other conditions?

A planet's chemical condition can be "oxidizing," or "reducing." In the former case, there is a preponderance of atoms that accept electrons, as would be the case with large quantities of free oxygen in the atmosphere. In the latter case, there is a preponderance of atoms that give up electrons, as would be the case with large quantities of free hydrogen present in the atmosphere. Earth has an oxidizing atmosphere, Jupiter a reducing one. Originally, Earth may have had a reducing atmosphere, too.

In an oxidizing atmosphere, carbon tends to exist as carbon dioxide. In a reducing atmosphere, it tends to exist as methane, the molecule of which consists of a carbon atom to which four hydrogens are attached (CH_4). In the outer Solar System, where reducing conditions are the rule, methane is extraordinarily common.

Methane is the parent of an endless number of other substances, for carbon atoms can easily attach to each other in chains or rings, with any spare bonds connected to hydrogen atoms. There are thus an enormous number of possible hydrocarbons, with molecules of various size made up of carbon and hydrogen only. Methane is merely the simplest of these.

Add an occasional atom of oxygen, nitrogen, sulfur, or phosphorus (or combinations of these) to the basic hydrocarbon skeleton, and you have the vast number and variety of compounds found in living organisms (organic compounds). These are all, after a fashion, elaborations of methane.

In short, the chemicals of life are of the type one would expect to be formed under reducing conditions, and that is one of the reasons that chemists suspect that the early Earth, at the time life came into existence, had a reducing atmosphere or, at the very least, not an oxidizing one.

Silicates are, however, characteristic of an oxidizing environment. Might not silicon form other kinds of compounds under reducing conditions? Could not silicon, like carbon, combine with four hydrogen atoms?

The answer is yes. The compound SiH_4 does exist and is called silane.

Methane has a boiling point of $-161.6°$ C, and so under Earth-surface conditions, it is always a gas. Silane is quite similar in properties, with a boiling point of $-112°$ C, so that it, too, is a gas. (The boiling point of silane is distinctly higher than that of methane, because its molecular weight is distinctly higher, 28 as compared to 16.)

Then, just as carbon can form chains with hydrogen taking up the spare bonds, so can silicon.

A two-carbon chain can add on six hydrogen atoms; a three-carbon chain, eight hydrogen atoms; and a four-carbon chain, ten hydrogen atoms. In other words, we can have C_2H_6, C_3H_8, and C_4H_{10}, which are called ethane, propane, and butane, respectively. (Each name has a rationale behind it, but that's another story for another day.)

Similarly, we have Si_2H_6, Si_3H_8, and Si_4H_{10}, which are called disilane, trisilane, and tetrasilane, respectively.

The carbon compounds have boiling points of $-88.6°$ C, $-44.5°$ C, and $-0.5°$ C, respectively, so that all three are gases under Earth-surface conditions, though butane would be a liquid under ordinary winter conditions, and propane would be a liquid under polar conditions.

The silanes have appropriately higher boiling points. Disilane has a boiling point of $-14.5°$ C, trisilane, one of $53°$ C, and tetrasilane, one of $109°$ C. Under Earth-surface conditions, disilane is a gas, while trisilane and tetrasilane are liquids.

♦

All this looks very hopeful, but there must be a catch, and there is. A single bond between carbon and oxygen has an energy content of 70 kilocalories per mole while the energy content of the bond between carbon and hydrogen is 87. There is a tendency for carbon to remain bonded to hydrogen, therefore, even in the presence of lots of oxygen. The hydrocarbons are quite stable under Earth-surface conditions.

Gasoline and paraffin are both mixtures of hydrocarbons. The former can burn in an automobile engine and the latter in a candle, but the burning has to be initiated. Left to itself, gasoline and paraffin will remain as such for extended periods of time.

The silicon-oxygen bond is, however, 89 and the silicon-hydrogen bond is 75. Silicates thus tend to remain silicates even under reducing conditions, whereas silanes are comparatively easily oxidized to silicates.

In short, the odds are weighted in favor of hydrocarbons in the case of carbon, and in favor of silicates in the case of silicon. Given the slightest excuse, carbon will be converted to hydrocarbons and life, while silicon will be converted to silicates and nonlife.

In fact, even if silanes *were* formed, the result would probably not be life. Life requires very complicated molecules, and carbon atoms can combine into very long chains and very complicated sets of rings. That is because the carbon-carbon bond is quite strong — 58.6. The silicon-silicon bond is distinctly weaker — 42.5.

This means that a chain of silicon atoms is feebler than one of carbon atoms and falls apart more readily. In fact, chemists have not been able to form anything more complicated than a hexasilane, with six silicon atoms in the molecule. Compare this with the carbon chains in ordinary fats and oils, which are commonly made up of sixteen carbon atoms linked together — and that is by no means a record.

Furthermore, carbon atoms cling together strongly enough to make possible the existence of carbon-carbon double bonds, and even triple bonds, though these are weaker than single bonds. This multiplies and remultiplies the number and variety of organic compounds that are possible.

Double and triple bonds have been thought to be not possible in the case of silicon-silicon combinations, so that whole masses of complexity were removed from potential existence.

But only *apparently.* In 1981 double bonds involving silicon atoms were, for the first time, reported. These were not in silanes, but in other types of silicon compounds that (perhaps?) might serve as the basis of life.

I admit that these essays end in the middle of the story. The third essay in the series goes on to demonstrate that silicon, even in combination with carbon, doesn't offer much hope as a basis for life; then, in the fourth essay, I make it quite clear that silicon life is not only conceivable after all, but that we seem to be on the way to it right now. It's just a matter of looking at things from a totally different standpoint.

If you want to see what I mean — well, the essay collection is available. No, no, I'm not money-mad. I'm not insisting that you buy it, although I wouldn't struggle to keep you from doing so. You can always get it at the public library — if you want to wait in line.

PART 6

BIOLOGY

AS IT HAPPENS, I *managed to be a little heavier on biology than on the physical sciences in my third hundred books. This was not a matter of deliberate choice. I choose my subjects partly on impulse, and it is partly a matter of editorial suggestion. It is never as neat and precise a plan as trying to achieve a delicate balance of subject matter.*

For instance, my How Did We Find Out? series is generally on subjects chosen by my editor, Millicent Selsam, at Walker and Company, and her own specialty is biology. No fewer than four of the ten most recent volumes in the series were biological, and three deal with evolution directly or indirectly.

Since, in recent years, I have been involved in the refutation of the nonsense that has been advanced under the title "Scientific Creationism," I have felt the increased importance of writing on evolution, and so I readily agreed to these proposals by Millie.

The three involving evolution are How Did We Find Out About Genes? *(Book 280), published in 1983;* How Did We Find Out About the Beginning of Life? *(Book 254), published in 1982; and* How Did We Find Out About Our Human Roots? *(Book 204), published in 1979. Here are selections from each.*

from HOW DID WE FIND OUT ABOUT GENES? (1983)

All living things are constantly exposed to different kinds of energy. There are highly energetic particles called cosmic rays that constantly bombard the earth. There are energetic particles and radiation that arise from tiny amounts of radioactive atoms which are always present everywhere about us. There is even sunlight, and certain chemicals that occur around us naturally. All of these things can interfere with the perfect duplication of genes, and all can work to produce different varieties of particular genes.

This means that every gene that human beings (and other living things, too) possess exists in many varieties. This makes heredity a far more complicated matter than it would be if every gene existed in one variety. Think of all the different shapes and sizes of noses; all the differences in hands, ears, height, coloring, teeth, voice, and so on. It is because of this variety that you can so easily recognize everyone you know by appearance, by voice, by manner of walking, and in many other ways.

Then, too, if there were no mutations so that all genes existed in a single variety, all members of a species would look alike.

As it is, every single living thing has its own mix of hundreds or thousands of genes and is different from every other. Among animals of a particular kind, some are faster, some are smarter, some can hide more easily, some can live better on a particular variety of food — all because each has its own complicated combination of genes.

This means that some individual animals can manage to survive more successfully than others of the same kind. Some varieties of genes, or combinations of varieties, are more useful in the long run. Other varieties are particularly useless and put their owners under such a disadvantage that they don't live long.

Useless genes tend to diminish in number as plants or animals that possess them die quickly. Those genes may never completely vanish, for new examples will turn up every once in a while as new mutations. They will not flourish, however.

Useful gene varieties that give an advantage to those living things that possess them will enable those particular creatures to live longer and better, and to have more children (many of whom will be likely to inherit that gene variety). Such a gene type will increase and become more and more common.

The way in which useful genes become more widespread, and useless genes less widespread, is called natural selection. Natural forces (the need of living things to compete with each other for food and mates and safety) select the useful gene varieties and make them common.

Most mutations that take place result in rather poor gene varieties, and even very harmful ones. That doesn't matter. It is the very few useful mutations which increase and spread.

Each different kind of plant or animal experiences mutations and natural selection and therefore comes to fit its environment more and more efficiently. Enough changes might take place over a few million years to turn one kind of animal into a slightly different (and more efficient) kind, or into two or more different kinds.

There is a slow evolution, so that birds and mammals, for instance, gradually arose by slow stages, through random mutation and natural selection, from reptiles. From simple insect-eating mammals resembling present-day tree-shrews, such animals as lemurs, monkeys, and apes gradually developed.

Several million years ago, some rather primitive apelike mammals split up into several varieties by way of random mutation and natural selection, and one of those varieties eventually developed into modern man.

from HOW DID WE FIND OUT ABOUT THE BEGINNING OF LIFE? (1982)

Scientists not only accept the notion that species have evolved from other species. They even believe they know a great many of the details of the process.

Over the long period of time that life has existed, there have been times when animals have died and been covered by mud before they could be eaten. The mud hardened in time, and the bones or shell or skin of the animal (or the wood of plants) have slowly changed into rock. Some of these rocky formations can be dug out and are then found to have just the shape of the original animal or plant parts that were buried. These rocky formations are called fossils.

Some of these fossils are tens of millions or even hundreds of millions of years old. They are of different species from those that are alive now. However, the fossil species that are now extinct (that is, no longer alive) can be fitted into the same arrangement as modern species.

There is a whole series of fossils of horselike animals, for instance. If these are arranged in order of age, we began with a small animal with four hoofs (toes) on each of its front legs. As time went on, the animal changed from one species to another, growing larger, having longer legs and fewer hoofs, until the large, horselike animals of today, with one hoof on each leg, developed.

There are also fossils of gigantic animals that lived a hundred million years ago. They are reptiles, just as modern crocodiles and lizards are reptiles, but they are much larger. These long-extinct giant reptiles are the animals that we usually speak of as dinosaurs.

There are fossils of an animal that had the tail and teeth of a lizard, but feathers like a bird. It seems to be a species that descended from reptiles and was the ancestor of birds.

Scientists learned how to judge the age of fossils more and more accurately, and the oldest fossils of plants and animals large enough to be seen without a microscope are about 600 million years old.

Back then there were no human beings. There were no cats or dogs or birds or snakes or fish. There were no animals with bones at all. In fact, there were no animals that lived on land.

The only animals that existed were those that lived in the sea, and the most complicated ones were called trilobites.

So you see, if we're going to wonder about how life started, we don't have to wonder about each of the two million species now alive. We can wonder about the fewer and simpler species that lived hundreds of millions of years ago.

Yet that's not good enough.

Even 600 million years ago there were still quite a number of different species, and the trilobites were pretty complicated animals. They were much more complicated than some of the smaller and simpler species of today.

We have to wonder how the trilobites got started.

The oldest fossils are 600 million years old but the Earth is over seven times as old as the oldest fossils, and life could have existed for much longer than the fossils indicate. If there was life long before the trilobites, however, why didn't it leave obvious fossils behind?

Actually, fossils are mostly of the parts of plants and animals that turn to rock easily. Fossils are usually formed from what were once bones and teeth and shells and wood — the hard parts of living things.

These hard parts seem to have evolved very late. When the trilobites first existed, no animal had yet developed bones, for instance, and no plants had developed much in the way of wood.

Longer than 600 million years ago, shells hadn't yet been formed either. No hard parts were formed. Plants and animals were small and soft and didn't leave fossils. In fact, to begin with, the only living things on Earth must have been microorganisms, tiny bits of life only a hundredth of an inch across or less.

Such microorganisms are formed of only a single bit of life called a cell. It was only later on, perhaps much later on, that cells grouped together in the course of evolution to form larger multicellular organisms.

With the passing of time, organisms formed that contained millions and billions of cells, and even more. (A human being contains 50 trillion cells.)

With more and more cells, it is possible for groups of them to specialize into different organs — into eyes and muscles and stomachs and shells and bones.

The first forms of life had none of this, however. They were just tiny single cells and could leave no fossils of the ordinary kind.

Just the same, in very old rocks, scientists have found microscopic markings that look as though they might be all that is left of very ancient cells.

In 1965 an American scientist, Elso S. Barghoorn, (1915–), found such microfossils in rocks that were over three billion years old.

Nowadays, scientists think that life began on Earth perhaps as long as 3.5 billion years ago, or when the Earth was only about a billion years old. Life has been developing and evolving ever since.

When we ask how life started, then, we are not asking how trilobites started. We are asking: How did those tiny microscopic bits of life start over 3.5 billion years ago?

from HOW DID WE FIND OUT ABOUT OUR HUMAN ROOTS? (1979)

Here is how we can summarize human beginnings.

About 70 million years ago, when the last dinosaurs died out, monkeylike creatures had evolved from more primitive creatures, somewhat resembling the lemurs of today.

By 40 million years ago in Africa, some of these monkeylike creatures had lost their tails, developed larger brains and better hands, and had become apelike creatures. *Aegyptopithecus* was an example.

As time went on, some of these early apelike creatures must have made their way out into southern and southeast Asia and eventually evolved into gibbons and orangutans.

Others of these early apelike creatures remained in Africa and developed into *Dryopithecus* about 25 million years ago.

Dryopithecus continued to develop in the direction of large teeth and jawbones, and strong bones, but only a moderately larger brain, and eventually evolved into both the chimpanzee and the gorilla.

About 20 million years ago, however, some *Dryopithecus* species seem to have developed in another direction. They developed smaller teeth and jaws and thinner bones. Because the teeth and jaws were smaller, these *Dryopithecus* species had to use their hands more for seizing food and bringing it to their mouths.

When the climate got drier and the forest dried out, they had to come down from the trees. Their hipbones developed in such a way that they could stand upright in the grasslands, and their hands were then free to be used all the time.

Perhaps because their hands were always free to feel things, lift things, carry things, poke things, and pull things apart, their brains were stimulated and slowly developed into a larger size.

These hand-using creatures, standing upright, were the first hominids, and they appeared about 20 million years ago.

The first recorded hominid is *Ramapithecus*, who appeared in East Africa, but who spread out into Asia perhaps 10 million years ago.

In Africa, *Ramapithecus* grew larger and brainier, and by about 4 million years ago, *Australopithecus* had developed.

Development continued in the direction of increased size of body and brain, and about 2 million years ago, the first hominids appeared who were sufficiently close in structure to the human being to be placed into genus *Homo*. Thus we have *Homo habilis*. By that time the hominid brain had developed to the point where it was larger than that of any ape that ever lived past or present. It was still considerably smaller than the brain of present-day human beings, however.

About 1.5 million years ago, *Homo erectus* had developed. He seems to have wandered into Asia as far as China and Indonesia, thus producing the relics of Peking man and Java man.

For about a million years, *Homo erectus* continued to evolve in the direction of a larger brain, and discovered the use of fire. By about 150,000 years ago, the brain was large enough for us to consider the developing creature to be an example of *Homo sapiens*.

The oldest known example of *Homo sapiens* was Neanderthal man, but by about 50,000 years ago, we had Cro-Magnon man, and after that progress became more rapid than ever.

About 10,000 years ago, *Homo sapiens* learned to grow crops, herd animals, build cities, and civilization began. About 5000 years ago, writing was invented. About 400 years ago, modern science began, and about 200 years ago, an industrial society began.

Now here we are, still trying to work out the details of our human roots.

Two of the anthologies included in my third hundred books were published by Farrar, Straus & Giroux in 1983. Both of these, in which Marty Greenberg and Charles Waugh were my coeditors, dealt with the life sciences — one on biological themes, and one on psychological ones.

The biological one is Caught in the Organ Draft *(Book 271), the title of which is borrowed from that of a very good story by Robert Silverberg, which is included in the anthology.*

I wrote headnotes for each of the dozen stories (as well as an introduction for the book as a whole), and here is my headnote to John R. Pierce's short and chilling story "Invariant," which deals with a human being who could undergo no biological change whatever.

from CAUGHT IN THE ORGAN DRAFT (1983)

Invariant

Part of life is death.

In one sense, life is immortal. Every molecule of nucleic acid in the body of any organism now alive was replicated from another which was replicated from still another which was replicated from yet another and so on back to the very origin of life. All nucleic acids now in existence form part of an unbroken chain that has endured for at least 3 billion years. In theory, particular nucleic acid molecules may have survived for eons, even though the odds against that are astronomical.

If, however, we leave single molecules aside and consider organisms made up of many cells, in turn made up of many molecules, all forms of life, however long-lived, eventually die.

Human beings are better off than most. The average mammal has a heart that beats a billion times or so before death comes. The larger the mammal, the slower the heartbeat, and the longer the life. A shrew scarcely lives longer than a year, while an elephant may live up to seventy years, and some large whales possibly up to ninety. Yet human beings, far smaller than elephants and whales, can live up to as much as 115 years, and have hearts that can beat up to *four* billion times before giving out.

Remarkable! And we don't know why!

But even human beings die eventually, and we must recognize such deaths as necessary for the greater good of the species.

For one thing, there is only so much room on Earth and, for that matter, in the Universe. If no one died, while new births continued, the Earth would rapidly be filled; and, in a remarkably few thousand years, so would the Universe (assuming we could devise means for transferring human beings freely to planets surrounding other stars).

Nevertheless, people dream of immortality, and we might suspect that if the price of immortality were an end to children, many people might accept that. They might opt for life for one generation at the cost of nonlife for all future generations.

That is not just selfishness; it is death for the species. Children have not only young brains, they have new brains: brains and bodies containing new combinations of nucleic acids. They have the power to produce new things, to reason, to create, to solve, as the old were not able to. They introduce new mutations that may lead to further evolution.

In short, death for the individual implies change — plus new and better life — for the species. In reverse, immortality for the individual means changelessness for the species, the same minds, running in the same ruts; and stultification and death for the species.

In a way, you can bring this home to the individual by putting it on a personal basis. We change constantly as we live, and with age we deteriorate. If we avoid accident and disease and approach the ultimate decay of old age, the deterioration reaches a point where we find it a relief to die and rest.

The alternative? No deterioration! No change! But is that better?

Finally, I must include my favorite biological F & SF essay from among my third hundred books. This is "Clone, Clone of My Own," which appears in the essay collection The Sun Shines Bright *(Book 237), published by Doubleday in 1981.*

My reasons for liking one or another of my pieces do not always have anything directly to do with how well they are written, how cogent the subject, or how subtly I introduce an original thought. Sometimes there is something a little earthier than that. "Clone, Clone of My Own" contains a bit of comic verse (for which I am not entirely responsible, as I explain in the essay), which I like so much I can't resist including it here.

from THE SUN SHINES BRIGHT *(1981)*

Clone, Clone of My Own

On December 12, 1968, I gave a talk to a meeting of doctors and lawyers in San Jose, California.* Naturally, I was asked to speak on a subject that would interest both groups. Some instinct told me that medical malpractice suits might interest both but would nevertheless not be a useful topic. I spoke on genetic engineering instead, therefore, and, toward the end, discussed the matter of cloning.

In the audience was my good friend of three decades, the well-

*Those of my Gentle Readers who know that under no circumstances will I take a plane need not register shock. I traveled to California and back by train. Yes, they still run.

known science fiction writer, bon vivant, and wit Randall Garrett. Out of the corner of my eye I noticed a piece of paper placed on the podium as I talked about cloning. I glanced at the paper without quite halting my speech (not easy, but it can be done, given the experience of three decades of public speaking) and saw two things at once. First, it was one of Randall's superlative pieces of satiric verse, and second, it was clearly intended to be sung to the tune of "Home on the Range."

Needed to understand the verse is merely the fact that, genetically, the distinction between human male and female is that every male cell has an X- and a Y-chromosome and that every female cell has two X-chromosomes. Therefore, if, at the moment of conception or shortly thereafter, a Y-chromosome can somehow be changed to an X-chromosome, a male will *ipso facto* be changed into a female.

Here, then, is Randall's Song, to which I took the liberty of adding four more verses myself:

(*1st verse*)

Oh, give me a clone
Of my own flesh and bone
With its Y-chromosome changed to X;
And when it is grown
Then my own little clone
Will be of the opposite sex.

(*chorus*)

Clone, clone of my own,
With its Y-chromosome changed to X;
And when I'm alone
With my own little clone
We will both think of nothing but sex.

(*2nd verse*)

Oh, give me a clone,
Hear my sorrowful moan,
Just a clone that is wholly my own;
And if it's an X
Of the feminine sex
Oh, what fun we will have when we're prone.

(3rd verse)

My heart's not of stone
As I've frequently shown
When alone with my dear little X;
And after we've dined,
I am sure we will find
Better incest than Oedipus Rex.

(4th verse)

Why should such sex vex
Or disturb or perplex
Or induce a disparaging tone?
After all, don't you see,
Since we're both of us me,
When we're making love I'm alone.

(5th verse)

And after I'm done
She will still have her fun,
For I'll clone myself twice ere I die.
And this time, without fail,
They'll be both of them male,
And they'll each ravish her by-and-by.

When I was through with my talk and with the question-and-answer session, I sang Randall's Song in my most resonant baritone and absolutely brought the house down.

Three and a half weeks later I sang it again at the annual banquet of the Baker Street Irregulars, that fine group of Sherlock Holmes fanciers, adjusting it slightly to its new task *(O give me some clones / Of the great Sherlock Holmes / With their Y-chromosomes . . .)* and brought the house down again.

But you may, by now, be asking yourself, "What's a clone?"

It's been in the news a great deal lately, but recognizing a word, and knowing what it represents, can be two different things. So let's go into the matter . . . .

♦

The word *clone* is Greek, exactly as it stands, provided you spell it in Greek letters, and it means "twig."

A clone is any organism or group of organisms that arises out of a cell or group of cells by means other than sexual reproduction. Put another way, it is an organism that is the product of asexual reproduction. Put still another way, it is an organism with a single parent, whereas an organism that arises from sexual reproduction (except where self-fertilization is possible) has two parents.

Asexual reproduction is a matter of course among one-celled organisms (though sexual reproduction can also take place), and it is also very common in the plant world.

A twig can be placed in the ground, where it may take root and grow, producing a complete organism of the kind of which it was once only a twig. Or the twig can be grafted to the branch of another tree (of a different variety, even), where it can grow and flourish. In either case, it is an organism with a single parent, and sex has had nothing to do with its making. It is because human beings first encountered this asexual form of reproduction, in connection with fruit trees probably, that such a one-parent organism of nonsexual origin is called a twig — that is, clone.

◆

And what of multicellular animals?

Asexual reproduction can take place among them as well. The more primitive the animal, that is, the less diversified and specialized its cells are, the more likely it is that asexual reproduction can take place.

A sponge, or a freshwater hydra, or a flatworm, or a starfish, can, any of them, be torn into parts and these parts, if kept in their usual environment, will each grow into a complete organism. The new organisms are clones.

Even organisms as complex as insects can in some cases give birth to parthenogenetic young, and, in the case of aphids, for instance, do so as a matter of course. In these cases, an egg cell, containing only a half set of chromosomes, does not require union with a sperm cell to supply the other half set. Instead, the egg cell's half set merely duplicates itself, producing a full set, all from the female parent, and the egg then proceeds to divide and become an independent organism, again a kind of clone.

In general, though, complex animals and, in particular, vertebrates, do not clone but engage in sexual reproduction exclusively.

Why? Two reasons.

In the first place, as an organism becomes more complex and specialized, its organs, tissues, and cells become more complex and specialized as well. The cells are so well adapted to perform their highly specialized functions that they can no longer divide and differentiate as the original egg cells did.*

This seems a terrible disadvantage. Organisms that can clone, reproducing themselves asexually, would seem to be much better off than other organisms — who must go to the trouble of finding partners and who must engage in all the complex phenomena, both physical and chemical, involved in sexual reproduction. Think of all the human beings who, for one slight flaw or another, can't have children — a problem that would be unknown if we could just release a toe and have it grow into another individual while we grew another toe.

Here comes the second reason, then. There's an evolutionary advantage to sexual reproduction that more than makes up for all the inconveniences.† In cloning, the genetic contents of new organisms remain identical with those of the original organisms, except for occasional mutations. If the organism is very efficiently adapted to its surroundings, this is useful, but it is an extremely conservative mechanism that reduces the chance of change. Any alteration in the environment could quickly lead to the extinction of a species.

In the case of sexual reproduction, every new organism has a brand-new mix of genes, half from one parent, half from another. Change is inevitable; variation from individual to individual is certain. A species in which sexual reproduction is the norm has the capacity to adapt readily to slight alterations in environment, since some of its variants are then favored over others. Indeed, a species

---

*This is not mysterious. We see an analogy on the social plane. I am a highly specialized individual and can support myself with ease as a writer, provided I am surrounded by a functioning and highly organized society. Place me on a desert island and I shall quickly perish since I don't know the first thing about the simplest requirements for self-support.

†Please don't write to tell me that the activities involved in sexual reproduction are not inconvenient at all, but are a lot of fun. I know that better than you do, whoever you are. The fun is an evolutionarily developed bribe designed to have us overlook and forgive the inconveniences. If you are a woman, you will see the point more quickly, perhaps, than a man will.

can, through sexual reproduction, split with relative ease into two or more species that will take advantage of somewhat different niches in the environment.

In short, a sexually-reproducing species evolves much more quickly than a cloning species and such difficult-to-evolve special-izations as intelligence are not likely to arise in the entire lifetime of a habitable planet, without sexual reproduction.

◆

Yet in one specialized way cloning can take place in even the most advanced animals — even in the human being.

Consider a human egg cell, fertilized by a human sperm cell. We now have a fertilized egg cell which contains a half set of genes from its mother and a half set from its father.

This fertilized egg cell cannot become an independently living organism for some nine months, for it must divide and redivide within its mother's womb, and be nourished by way of its mother's bloodstream. It must develop, specialize, and grow larger until it has developed the necessary ability to live independently. Even after it emerges from its mother's womb, it requires constant and unremitting care for a period of time before it can be trusted to care for itself.

Nevertheless, the matter of necessary care is generally irrele-vant. The fertilized egg is already a separate organism with its ge-netic characteristics fixed and unique.

The first step in the development of the fertilized egg is that it divides into two cells, which cling together. Each of these two cells divides again, and each of the four that result divides again, and so on.

If, after the first cell division, the two offspring cells, for any reason, should happen to fall apart, each offspring cell may then go on to develop into a complete organism of its own. The result is a pair of identical twins, each with the same genetic equipment and each of the same sex, of course. In a sense, each twin is a clone of the other.

There is no reason to suppose that this separation of offspring cells can't happen over and over, so that three or four or any num-ber of organisms might develop from the original fertilized egg. As a matter of practical fact, however, a mother's womb can only hold so much, and if there are multiple organisms developing, each is sure to be smaller than a single organism. The more organisms that develop, the smaller each one, and in the end, they will be too small to survive after delivery.

There are such things as identical triplets and quadruplets, but I doubt that any higher number of infants would survive long after birth without the advantages of modern medical technique. Even then it is hard enough.

Identical twins are very like each other and often display mirror-image characteristics. (I once had a chemistry professor with his nose canted to the left. His identical-twin brother had his nose canted to the right, I was told.)

It is also possible, however, though not usual, for a woman to bring two different egg cells to fruition at the same time. If both are fertilized, two children will be born who are each possessed of genetic equipment different from the other. What results is fraternal twins, who need not be of the same sex and need not resemble each other any more than siblings usually do.

♦

Consider the fertilized egg again. Every time it divides and redivides, the new cells that form inherit the same genetic equipment possessed by the original fertilized egg.

Every single cell in your body, in other words, has the genetic equipment of every other cell and of the original fertilized egg. Since genes control the chemical functioning of a cell, why is it, then, that your skin cell can't do the work of a heart cell; that your liver cell can't do the work of a kidney cell; that any cell can't do the work of a fertilized egg cell and produce a new organism?

The answer is that though all the genes are there in every cell of your body, they aren't all working alike. The cell is an intricate assemblage of chemical reactions, chemical building blocks, chemical products, and physical structures, all of which influence one another. Some genes are inhibited, some are stimulated, in a variety of ways depending on subtle factors, with the result that different cells in your body have genetic equipment in which only characteristic parts are working at characteristic rates.

Such specialized development begins in the earliest embryo, as some cells come into being on the outside of the embryo, some on the inside; some with more of the original yolk, some with less; some with first chance at absorbing nutrients from the maternal bloodstream, some with only a later chance. The details are clearly of the greatest importance to human biology, and biologists just don't know them yet.

Naturally, the ordinary somatic cells of an adult human body, with their genetic equipment working only in highly specialized ways, cannot divide into a whole organism if left to themselves. Many body cells, such as those of the muscles or nerves, have become so specialized they can't divide at all. Only the sex cells, eggs and sperm, retain the lack of genetic specialization required to produce a new organism under the proper circumstances.

Is there any way of unspecializing the genetic structure of somatic cells so as to allow them to develop into a new organism?

Well, the genes are contained in the nucleus of the cell, which makes up a small portion of the total and is marked off by a membrane of its own. Outside the nucleus is the cytoplasm of a cell, and it is the material in the cytoplasm that provides the various chemicals that help serve to inhibit or stimulate the action of the genes.

Suppose, then, the nucleus of a somatic cell were surrounded with the cytoplasm of an egg cell. Would the genetic equipment in the nucleus unblock, and would the egg cell then proceed to divide and redivide? Would it go on to form an individual with the genetic equipment of the original somatic cell, and therefore of the person from whom the somatic cell was taken? If so, the new organism would be a clone of the person who donated the somatic cell.

The technique has been tried on different animals. You begin with an unfertilized egg cell and treat it in such a way as to remove its nucleus, either by delicately cutting it out or by using some chemical process. In the place of the removed egg cell nucleus, you insert the nucleus of a somatic cell of the same (or, possibly, an allied) species, and then let nature take its course.

This has been successfully tried with animals as complex as a tadpole.

It stops being easy after the frog, though. Frog eggs are naked and can be manipulated easily. They develop in water and can just lie there after the microoperation.

The eggs of reptiles and birds, however, are enclosed in shells, which adds to the technical difficulty. The eggs of mammals are very small, very delicate, very easily damaged. Furthermore, even if a mammalian egg has had its nucleus replaced, it would then have to be implanted into the womb of a female and allowed to come to term there.

♦

The practical problems of mammalian cloning are such that there is no chance of its happening for some time. Yet biologists are anxious to perform the feat and are trying hard. Eventually, they will no doubt succeed. What purpose will it serve?

If clones can be produced wholesale, a biologist can have a whole group of animals with identical genetic equipment — a set of ten thousand identical-twin mice, let us say. Many animal experiments could be conducted with the hope of more useful results if the question of genetic variation could be eliminated.

By the addition of other genetic-engineering techniques, it might be possible to produce a whole series of animals with identical genetic equipment, except that in each case, one gene is removed or altered — a different gene in each individual, perhaps. The science of genetics would then advance in seven-league strides.

There would be practical uses, too. A prize bull or a champion egg-laying hen could be cloned, and the genetic characteristics that make the record-breaking aspects of the animal possible would be preserved without the chance of diminution by the interplay of genes obtained from a second parent.

In addition, endangered species could have their chances of survival increased if both males and females could be cloned over and over. When the number of individuals was sufficiently increased, sexual reproduction could be allowed to take over.

We might even dream of finding a frozen mammoth with some cell nuclei not entirely dead. We might then clone one by way of an elephant's womb. If we could find a male and a female mammoth . . .

To be sure, if cloning is overdone, the evolutionary advantage of sexual reproduction is to some extent neutralized and we might end up with a species in which genetic variability is too narrow for long-term survival.

It is important to remember that the most important genetic possession of any species is not this gene or that, *but the whole mixed bag.* The greater the variety of genes available to a species, the more secure it is against the vicissitudes of fortune. The exis-

tence of congenital disorders and gene deficiencies is the price paid
for the advantage of variety and versatility.

♦

And what about cloned human beings, which is, after all, the subject matter of Randall's Song?

These may never be as important as you think. The prospect of
importance rests chiefly on certain misapprehensions on the part
of the public. Some people, for instance, pant for clones because
they think them the gateway to personal immortality. That is quite
wrong.

Your clone is not *you*. Your clone is your twin brother (or sister)
and is no more you than your ordinary identical twin would be.
Your clone does not have your consciousness, and if *you* die, you
are *dead*. You do not live on in your clone. Once that is understood, I suspect that much of the interest in clones will disappear.

Some people fear clones, on the other hand, because they imagine that morons will be cloned in order to make it possible to build
up a great army of cannon fodder that despots will use for world
conquest.

Why bother? There has never been any difficulty in finding cannon fodder anywhere in the world, even without cloning and the
ordinary process of supplying new soldiers for despots is infinitely
cheaper than cloning.

More reasonably, it could be argued that the clone of a great
human being would retain his genetic equipment and would therefore be another great human being of the same kind. In that case,
the chief use of cloning would be to reproduce genius.

That, I think, would be a waste of time. We are not necessarily
going to breed thousands of transcendent geniuses out of an Einstein, or thousands of diabolical villains out of a Hitler.

After all, a human being is more than his or her genes. Your
clone is the result of your nucleus being placed into a foreign egg
cell, and the foreign cytoplasm in that egg cell will surely have an
effect on the development of the clone. The egg will have to be
implanted into a foreign womb, and that, too, will have an influence on the development of the organism.

Even if a woman were to have one of her somatic nuclei implanted into one of her own egg cells and if she were then to have
the egg cell implanted into the womb of her own mother (who, we

will assume, is still capable of bearing a child), the new organism will be born into different circumstances, and that would have an effect on its personality, too.

For instance, suppose you wanted one hundred Isaac Asimovs so that the supply of *F & SF* essays would never run out. You would then have to ask what it was that made me the kind of writer I am — or a writer at all. Was it only my genes?

I was brought up in a candy store under a father of the old school who, although he was Jewish, was the living embodiment of the Protestant ethic. My nose was kept to the grindstone until I could no longer remove it. Furthermore, I was brought up during the Great Depression and had to find a way of making a living — or I would inherit the candy store, which I desperately didn't want to do. Furthermore, I lived in a time when science fiction magazines, and pulp magazines generally, were going strong, and when a young man could sell clumsily written stories because the demand was greater than the supply.

Put it all together, it spells M-E.

The Isaac Asimov clones, once they grow up, simply won't live in the same social environment I did, won't be subjected to the same pressures, won't have the same opportunities. What's more, when I wrote, I just wrote; no one expected anything particular from me. When my clones write, their products will always be compared to the Grand Original, and that would discourage and wipe out anyone.

The end result will be that though my clones, or some of them, might turn out to be valuable citizens of one kind or another, it would be very unlikely that any one of them would be another Isaac Asimov, and their production would not be worthwhile. Whatever good they might do would not be worth the reduction they would represent in the total gene variability of humanity.

PART 7

ROBOTS AND COMPUTERS

HERE IS THE SECTION which, in the first two Opus books, was in second place. I've got it here now, because in the natural progression of the sciences, one would expect to pass from biology to psychology and, in a way, robots, which are examples of artificial intelligence, are essentially psychological in significance. Certainly my own robot stories always have psychological overtones.

Although I have written no robot short stories since 1976, and therefore have none to include in this sampling of my third hundred books, I do not come totally empty-handed.

Back in 1954, Doubleday published my robot novel entitled The Caves of Steel (Book 11) and, in 1957, it published a sequel, The Naked Sun (Book 20). Both were not only science fiction novels but were strict murder mysteries as well. Each featured a detective (Elijah Baley) and his robot assistant (R. Daneel).

Both novels were quite successful, and it was taken for granted that I would write a third in which Baley, who had been seen on a heavily human world with few robots in the first novel, and on a heavily robotic world with few humans in the second, would, in a third book, be seen on a world in which humans and robots were in balance. In fact, I had incautiously mentioned that I planned to do this. But somehow I never did, though readers' demands grew more frequent and strident.

Once Foundation's Edge was written, however, and showed signs of being unexpectedly successful, I was emboldened to take on the task of the third robot novel. (I say "emboldened" because, in the third book, it had always been my intention to consider the possibility of human-robot sex in a realistic, serious, and nonsensational manner, and I had always doubted my ability to do so.) But now I just sat down and did it, in a book entitled The Robots of Dawn (Book 281), which Doubleday published in 1983.

I include here a passage from early in the book, where Baley once again meets his robot friend, R. Daneel, and with him discusses matters relevant to the murder mystery about which the plot is centered.

from THE ROBOTS OF DAWN (1983)

The robot left through the double door and Baley nodded grimly to himself. On his trip to Solaria, it had never occurred to him to spend the useless time crossing space in learning something useful. He had come along a bit in the last two years.

He tried the door the robot had just passed through. It was locked and utterly without give. He would have been enormously surprised at anything else.

He investigated the room. There was a hyperwave screen. He handled the controls idly, received a blast of music, managed to lower the volume eventually, and listened with disapproval. Tinkly and discordant. The instruments of the orchestra seemed vaguely distorted.

He touched other contacts and finally managed to change the view. What he saw was a space-soccer game that was played, obviously, under conditions of zero-gravity. The ball flew in straight lines and the players (too many of them on each side — with fins on backs, elbows, and knees that must serve to control movement) soared in graceful sweeps. The unusual movements made Baley feel dizzy. He leaned forward and had just found and used the off-switch when he heard the door open behind him.

Baley turned and, because he thoroughly expected to see R. Giskard, he was aware at first only of someone who was *not* R. Giskard. It took a blink or two to realize that he saw a thoroughly human shape, with a broad, high-cheekboned face and with short bronze hair lying flatly backward, someone dressed in clothing with a conservative cut and color scheme.

"Jehoshaphat!" said Baley in a nearly strangled voice.

"Partner Elijah," said the other, stepping forward, a small, grave smile on his face.

"Daneel!" cried Baley, throwing his arms around the robot and hugging tightly. "Daneel!"

♦

Baley continued to hold Daneel, the one unexpected familiar object on the ship, the one strong link to the past. He clung to Daneel in a gush of relief and affection.

And then, little by little, he collected his thoughts and knew that he was hugging not Daneel but R. Daneel — *Robot* Daneel Olivaw. He was hugging a robot and the robot was holding him lightly, allowing himself to be hugged, judging that the action gave pleasure to a human being and enduring that action because the positronic potentials of his brain made it impossible to repel the embrace and so cause disappointment and embarrassment to the human being.

The insurmountable First Law of Robotics states: "A robot may not injure a human being —" and to repel a friendly gesture would do injury.

Slowly, so as to reveal no sign of his own chagrin, Baley released his hold. He even gave each upper arm of the robot a final squeeze, so that there might seem to be no shame to the release.

"Haven't seen you, Daneel," said Baley, "since you brought that ship to Earth with the two mathematicians. Remember?"

"Of a certainty, Partner Elijah. It is a pleasure to see you."

"You feel emotion, do you?" said Baley lightly.

"I cannot say what I feel in any human sense, Partner Elijah. I can say, however, that the sight of you seems to make my thoughts flow more easily, and the gravitational pull on my body seems to assault my senses with lesser insistence, and that there are other changes I can identify. I imagine that what I sense corresponds in a rough way to what it is that you may sense when you feel pleasure."

Baley nodded. "Whatever it is you sense when you see me, old partner, that makes it seem preferable to the state in which you are when you don't see me, suits me well — if you follow my meaning. But how is it you are here?"

"Giskard Reventlov, having reported you —" R. Daneel paused.

"Purified?" asked Baley sardonically.

"Disinfected," said R. Daneel. "I felt it appropriate to enter then."

"Surely you would not fear infection otherwise?"

"Not at all, Partner Elijah, but others on the ship might then be reluctant to have me approach them. The people of Aurora are sensitive to the chance of infection, sometimes to a point beyond a rational estimate of the probabilities."

"I understand, but I wasn't asking why you were here at this moment. I meant why are you here at all?"

"Dr. Fastolfe, of whose establishment I am part, directed me to board the ship that had been sent to pick you up for several reasons. He felt it desirable that you have one immediate item of the known in what he was certain would be a difficult mission for you."

"That was a kindly thought on his part. I thank him."

R. Daneel bowed gravely in acknowledgment. "Dr. Fastolfe also felt that the meeting would give me" — the robot paused — "appropriate sensations."

"Pleasure, you mean, Daneel."

"Since I am permitted to use the term, yes. And as a third reason — and the most important —"

The door opened again at that point and R. Giskard walked in.

Baley's head turned toward it and he felt a surge of displeasure. There was no mistaking R. Giskard as a robot, and its presence emphasized, somehow, the robotism of Daneel (R. Daneel, Baley suddenly thought again), even though Daneel was far the superior of the two. Baley didn't *want* the robotism of Daneel emphasized; he didn't want himself humiliated for his inability to regard Daneel as anything but a human being with a somewhat stilted way with the language.

He said impatiently, "What is it, boy?"

R. Giskard said, "I have brought the book-films you wished to see, sir, and the viewer."

"Well, put them down. Put them down. — And you needn't stay. Daneel will be here with me."

"Yes, sir." The robot's eyes — faintly glowing, Baley noticed, as Daneel's were not — turned briefly to R. Daneel, as though seeking orders from a superior being.

R. Daneel said quietly, "It will be appropriate, friend Giskard, to remain just outside the door."

"I shall, friend Daneel," said R. Giskard.

It left and Baley said with some discontent, "Why does it have to stay just outside the door? Am I a prisoner?"

"In the sense," said R. Daneel, "that it would not be permitted for you to mingle with the ship's company in the course of this voyage, I regret to be forced to say you are indeed a prisoner. Yet that is not the reason for the presence of Giskard. — And I should tell you at this point that it might well be advisable, Partner Elijah, if you did not address Giskard — or any robot — as 'boy'."

Baley frowned. "Does it resent the expression?"

"Giskard does not resent any action of a human being. It is simply that 'boy' is not a customary term of address for robots on Aurora and it would be inadvisable to create friction with the Aurorans by unintentionally stressing your place of origin through habits of speech that are nonessential."

"How do I address it, then?"

"As you address me, by the use of his accepted identifying name. That is, after all, merely a sound indicating the particular person you are addressing — and why should one sound be preferable to another? It is merely a matter of convention. And it is also the custom on Aurora to refer to a robot as 'he' — or sometimes 'she' — rather than as 'it.' Then, too, it is not the custom on Aurora to use the initial 'R,' except under formal conditions where the entire name of the robot is appropriate — and even then the initial is nowadays often left out."

"In that case — Daneel" (Baley repressed the sudden impulse to say "R. Daneel"), "how do you distinguish between robots and human beings?"

"The distinction is usually self-evident, Partner Elijah. There would seem to be no need to emphasize it unnecessarily. At least that is the Auroran view and, since you have asked Giskard for films on Aurora, I assume you wish to familiarize yourself with things Auroran as an aid to the task you have undertaken."

"The task which has been dumped on me, yes. And what if the distinction between robot and human being is *not* self-evident, Daneel? As in your case?"

"Then why make the distinction, unless the situation is such that it is essential to make it?"

Baley took a deep breath. It was going to be difficult to adjust to this Auroran pretense that robots did not exist. He said, "But then, if Giskard is not here to keep me prisoner, why is it — he — outside the door?"

"Those are according to the instructions of Dr. Fastolfe, Partner Elijah. Giskard is to protect you."

"Protect me? Against what? — Or against whom?"

"Dr. Fastolfe was not precise on that point, Partner Elijah. Still, as human passions are running high over the matter of Jander Panell —"

"Jander Panell?"

"The robot whose usefulness was terminated."

"The robot, in other words, who was killed?"

"Killed, Partner Elijah, is a term that is usually applied to human beings."

"But on Aurora distinctions between robots and human beings are avoided, are they not?"

"So they are! Nevertheless, the possibility of distinction or lack of distinction in the particular case of the ending of functioning has never arisen — to my knowledge. I do not know what the rules are."

Baley pondered the matter. It was a point of no real importance, purely a matter of semantics. Still, he wanted to probe the manner of thinking of the Aurorans. He would get nowhere otherwise.

He said slowly, "A human being who is functioning is alive. If that life is violently ended by the deliberate action of another human being, we call that 'murder' or 'homicide.' 'Murder' is, somehow, the stronger word. To be witness, suddenly, to an attempted violent end to the life of a human being, one would shout 'Murder!' It is not at all likely that one would shout 'Homicide!' It is the more formal word, the less emotional word."

R. Daneel said, "I do not understand the distinction you are making, Partner Elijah. Since 'murder' and 'homicide' are both used to represent the violent ending of the life of a human being, the two words must be interchangeable. Where, then, is the distinction?"

"Of the two words, one screamed out will more effectively chill the blood of a human being than the other will, Daneel."

"Why is that?"

"Connotations and associations; the subtle effect, not of dictionary meaning, but of years of usage; the nature of the sentences and conditions and events in which one has experienced the use of one word as compared with that of the other."

"There is nothing of this in my programming," said Daneel, with a curious sound of helplessness hovering over the apparent lack of emotion with which he said this (the same lack of emotion with which he said everything).

Baley said, "Will you accept my word for it, Daneel?"

Quickly, Daneel said, almost as though he had just been presented with the solution to a puzzle, "Without doubt."

"Now, then, we might say that a robot that is functioning is alive," said Baley. "Many might refuse to broaden the word so far, but we are free to devise definitions to suit ourselves if it is useful. It is easy to treat a functioning robot as alive and it would be unnecessarily complicated to try to invent a new word for the condition or to avoid the use of the familiar one. *You* are alive, for instance, Daneel, aren't you?"

Daneel said, slowly and with emphasis, "I am functioning!"

"Come. If a squirrel is alive, or a bug, or a tree, or a blade of grass, why not you? I would never remember to say — or to think — that I am alive but that you are merely functioning, especially if I am to live for a while on Aurora, where I am to try not to make unnecessary distinctions between a robot and myself. Therefore, I tell you that we are both alive and I ask you to take my word for it."

"I will do so, Partner Elijah."

"And yet can we say that the ending of robotic life by the deliberate violent action of a human being is also 'murder'? We might hesitate. If the crime is the same, the punishment should be the same, but would that be right? If the punishment of the murder of a human being is death, should one actually execute a human being who puts an end to a robot?"

"The punishment of a murderer is psychic-probing, Partner Elijah, followed by the construction of a new personality. It is the personal structure of the mind that has committed the crime, not the life of the body."

"And what is the punishment on Aurora for putting a violent end to the functioning of a robot?"

"I do not know, Partner Elijah. Such an incident has never occurred on Aurora, as far as I know."

"I suspect the punishment would not be psychic-probing," said Baley. "How about 'roboticide'?"

"Roboticide?"

"As the term used to describe the killing of a robot."

Daneel said, "But what about the verb derived from the noun, Partner Elijah? One never says 'to homicide' and it would therefore not be proper to say 'to roboticide.'"

"You're right. You would have to say 'to murder' in each case."

"But murder applies specifically to human beings. One does not murder an animal, for instance."

Baley said, "True. And one does not murder even a human being

by accident, only by deliberate intent. The more general term is
'to kill.' That applies to accidental death as well as to deliberate
murder — and it applies to animals as well as human beings. Even
a tree may be killed by disease, so why may not a robot be killed,
eh, Daneel?"

"Human beings and other animals and plants as well, Partner
Elijah, are all living things," said Daneel. "A robot is a human artifact, as much as this viewer is. An artifact is 'destroyed,' 'damaged,' 'demolished,' and so on. It is never 'killed.' "

"Nevertheless, Daneel, I shall say 'killed.' Jander Panell was
killed."

Daneel said, "Why should a difference in a word make any difference to the thing described?"

" 'That which we call a rose by any other name would smell as
sweet.' Is that it, Daneel?"

Daneel paused, then said, "I am not certain what is meant by
the smell of a rose, but if a rose on Earth is the common flower
that is called a rose on Aurora, and if by its 'smell' you mean a
property that can be detected, sensed, or measured by human
beings, then surely calling a rose by another sound-combination —
and holding all else equal — would not affect the smell or any other
of its intrinsic properties."

"True. And yet changes in name do result in changes in percep-
tion where human beings are concerned."

"I do not see why, Partner Elijah."

"Because human beings are often illogical, Daneel. It is not an
admirable characteristic."

Baley sank deeper into his chair and fiddled with his viewer,
allowing his mind, for a few minutes, to retreat into private
thought. The discussion with Daneel was useful in itself, for while
Baley played with the question of words, he managed to forget that
he was in space, to forget that the ship was moving forward until
it was far enough from the mass centers of the Solar System to
make the Jump through hyperspace; to forget that he would soon
be several million kilometers from Earth and, not long after that,
several light-years from Earth.

More important, there were positive conclusions to be drawn.
It was clear that Daneel's talk about Aurorans making no distinction
between robots and human beings was misleading. The Aurorans

might virtuously remove the initial "R.," the use of "boy" as a form of address, and the use of "it" as the customary pronoun, but from Daneel's resistance to the use of the same word for the violent ends of a robot and of a human being (a resistance inherent in his programming which was, in turn, the natural consequence of Auroran assumptions about how Daneel ought to behave) one had to conclude that these were merely superficial changes. In essence, Aurorans were as firm as Earthmen in their belief that robots were machines that were infinitely inferior to human beings.

That meant that his formidable task of finding a useful resolution of the crisis (if that were possible at all) would not be hampered by a misperception of Auroran society.

Baley wondered if he ought to question Giskard, in order to confirm the conclusions he reached from his conversation with Daneel — and, without much hesitation, decided not to. Giskard's simple and rather unsubtle mind would be of no use. He would "Yes, sir" and "No, sir" to the end. It would be like questioning a recording.

Well, then, Baley decided, he would continue with Daneel, who was at least capable of responding with something approaching subtlety.

He said, "Daneel, let us consider the case of Jander Panell, which I assume, from what you have said so far, is the first case of roboticide in the history of Aurora. The human being responsible — the killer — is, I take it, not known."

"If," said Daneel, "one assumes that a human being was responsible, then his identity is not known. In that, you are right, Partner Elijah."

"What about the motive? Why was Jander Panell killed?"

"That, too, is not known."

"But Jander Panell was a humaniform robot, one like yourself and not one like, for instance, R. Gis — I mean, Giskard."

"That is so. Jander was a humaniform robot like myself."

"Might it not be, then, that no case of roboticide was intended?"

"I do not understand, Partner Elijah."

Baley said, a little impatiently, "Might not the killer have thought this Jander was a human being, that the intention was homicide, not roboticide?"

Slowly, Daneel shook his head. "Humaniform robots are quite like human beings in appearance, Partner Elijah, down to the hairs and pores in our skin. Our voices are thoroughly natural, we can go through the motions of eating, and so on. And yet, in our behavior there are noticeable differences. There may be fewer with time and with refinement of technique, but as yet they are many. You — and other Earthmen not used to humaniform robots — may not easily note these differences, but Aurorans would. No Auroran would mistake Jander — or me — for a human being, not for a moment."

"Might some Spacer, other than an Auroran, make the mistake?"

Daneel hesitated. "I do not think so. I do not speak from personal observation or from direct programmed knowledge, but I do have the programming to know that all the Spacer worlds are as intimately acquainted with robots as Aurora is — some, like Solaria, even more so — and I deduce, therefore, that no Spacer would miss the distinction between human and robot."

"Are there humaniform robots on the other Spacer worlds?"

"No, Partner Elijah, they exist only on Aurora so far."

"Then other Spacers would not be intimately acquainted with humaniform robots and might well miss the distinctions and mistake them for human beings."

"I do not think that is likely. Even humaniform robots will behave in robotic fashion in certain definite ways that any Spacer would recognize."

"And yet surely there are Spacers who are not as intelligent as most, not as experienced, not as mature. There are Spacer children, if nothing else, who would miss the distinction."

"It is quite certain, Partner Elijah, that the — roboticide — was not committed by anyone unintelligent, inexperienced, or young. Completely certain."

"We're making eliminations. Good. If no Spacer would miss the distinction, what about an Earthman? Is it possible that —"

"Partner Elijah, when you arrive in Aurora, you will be the first Earthman to set foot on the planet since the period of original settlement was over. All Aurorans now alive were born on Aurora or, in a relatively few cases, on other Spacer worlds."

"The first Earthman," muttered Baley. "I am honored. Might not an Earthman be present on Aurora without the knowledge of Aurorans?"

"No!" said Daneel with simple certainty.

"Your knowledge, Daneel, might not be absolute."

"No!" came the repetition, in tones precisely similar to the first.

"We conclude, then," said Baley with a shrug, "that the roboticide was intended to be roboticide and nothing else."

"That was the conclusion from the start."

Baley said, "Those Aurorans who concluded this at the start had all the information to begin with. I am getting it now for the first time."

"My remark, Partner Elijah, was not meant in any pejorative manner. I know better than to belittle your abilities."

"Thank you, Daneel. I know there was no intended sneer in your remark. — You said just a while ago that the roboticide was not committed by anyone unintelligent, inexperienced, or young and that this is completely certain. Let us consider your remark —"

Baley knew that he was taking the long route. He had to. Considering his lack of understanding of Auroran ways and of their manner of thought, he could not afford to make assumptions and skip steps. If he were dealing with an intelligent human being in this way, that person would be likely to grow impatient and blurt out information — and consider Baley an idiot into the bargain. Daneel, however, as a robot, would follow Baley down the winding road with total patience.

That was one type of behavior that gave away Daneel as a robot, however humaniform he might be. An Auroran might be able to judge him a robot from a single answer to a single question. Daneel was right as to the subtle distinctions.

Baley said, "One might eliminate children, perhaps also most women, and many male adults by presuming that the method of roboticide involved great strength — that Jander's head was perhaps crushed by a violent blow or that his chest was smashed inward. This would not, I imagine, be easy for anyone who was not a particularly large and strong human being." From what Demachek had said on Earth, Baley knew that this was not the manner of the roboticide, but how was he to tell that Demachek herself had not been misled?

Daneel said, "It would not be possible at all for any human being."

"Why not?"

"Surely, Partner Elijah, you are aware that the robotic skeleton is metallic in nature and much stronger than human bone. Our movements are more strongly powered, faster, and more delicately controlled. The Third Law of Robotics states: 'A robot must protect its own existence.' An assault by a human being could easily be fended off. The strongest human being could be immobilized. Nor is it likely that a robot can be caught unaware. We are always aware of human beings. We could not fulfill our functions otherwise."

Baley said, "Come, now, Daneel. The Third Law states: 'A robot must protect its own existence, as long as such protection does not conflict with the First or Second Law.' The Second Law states: 'A robot must obey the orders given it by a human being, except where such orders would conflict with the First Law.' And the First Law states: 'A robot may not injure a human being or, through inaction, allow a human being to come to harm.' A human being could order a robot to destroy himself — and the robot would then use his own strength to smash his own skull. And if a human being attacked a robot, that robot could not fend off the attack without harming the human being, which would violate the First Law."

Daneel said, "You are, I suppose, thinking of Earth's robots. On Aurora — or on any of the Spacer worlds — robots are regarded more highly than on Earth and are, in general, more complex, versatile, and valuable. The Third Law is distinctly stronger in comparison to the Second Law on Spacer worlds than it is on Earth. An order for self-destruction would be questioned and there would have to be a truly legitimate reason for it to be carried through — a clear and present danger. And in fending off an attack, the First Law would not be violated, for Auroran robots are deft enough to immobilize a human being without hurting him."

"Suppose, though, that a human being maintained that, unless a robot destroyed himself, he — the human being — would be destroyed. Would not the robot then destroy himself?"

"An Auroran robot would surely question a mere statement to that effect. There would have to be clear evidence of the possible destruction of a human being."

"Might not a human being be sufficiently subtle to so arrange matters as to make it seem to a robot that the human being was indeed in great danger? Is it the ingenuity that would be required that makes you eliminate the unintelligent, inexperienced, and young?"

And Daneel said, "No, Partner Elijah, it is not."

"Is there an error in my reasoning?"

"None."

"Then the error may lie in my assumption that he was physically damaged. He was not, in actual fact, physically damaged. Is that right?"

"Yes, Partner Elijah."

(That meant Demachek had had her facts straight, Baley thought.)

"In that case, Daneel, Jander was mentally damaged. Roblock! Total and irreversible!"

"Roblock?"

"Short for robot-block, the permanent shutdown of the functioning of the positronic pathways."

"We do not use the word 'roblock' on Aurora, Partner Elijah."

"What do you say?"

"We say 'mental freeze-out.' "

"Either way, it is the same phenomenon being described."

"It might be wise, Partner Elijah, to use our expression or the Aurorans you speak to may not understand; conversation may be impeded. You stated a short while ago that different words make a difference."

"Very well. I will say 'freeze-out.' — Could such a thing happen spontaneously?"

"Yes, but the chances are infinitesimally small, roboticists say. As a humaniform robot, I can report that I have never myself experienced any effect that could even approach mental freeze-out."

"Then one must assume that a human being deliberately set up a situation in which mental freeze-out would take place."

"That is precisely what Dr. Fastolfe's opposition contends, Partner Elijah."

"And since this would take robotic training, experience, and skill, the unintelligent, the inexperienced, and the young cannot have been responsible."

"That is the natural reasoning, Partner Elijah."

"It might even be possible to list the number of human beings on Aurora with sufficient skill and thus set up a group of suspects that might not be very large in number."

"That has, in actual fact, been done, Partner Elijah."

"And how long is the list?"

"The longest list suggested contains only one name."

It was Baley's turn to pause. His brows drew together in an angry frown and he said, quite explosively, "Only one name?"

Daneel said quietly, "Only one name, Partner Elijah. That is the judgment of Dr. Han Fastolfe, who is Aurora's greatest theoretical roboticist."

"But what is, then, the mystery in all this? Whose is the one name?"

R. Daneel said, "Why, that of Dr. Han Fastolfe, of course. I have just stated that he is Aurora's greatest theoretical roboticist and, in Dr. Fastolfe's professional opinion, he himself is the only one who could possibly have maneuvered Jander Panell into total mental freeze-out without leaving any sign of the process. However, Dr. Fastolfe also states that he did not do it."

"But that no one else could have, either?"

"Indeed, Partner Elijah. There lies the mystery."

"And what if Dr. Fastolfe —" Baley paused. There would be no point in asking Daneel if Dr. Fastolfe was lying or was somehow mistaken, either in his own judgment that no one but he could have done it or in the statement that he himself had not done it. Daneel had been programmed by Fastolfe and there would be no chance that the programming included the ability to doubt the programmer.

Baley said, therefore, with as close an approach to mildness as he could manage, "I will think about this, Daneel, and we will talk again."

"That is well, Partner Elijah. It is, in any case, time for sleep. Since it is possible that, on Aurora, the pressure of events may force an irregular schedule upon you, it would be wise to seize the opportunity for sleep now. I will show you how one produces a bed and how one manages the bedclothes."

"Thank you, Daneel," muttered Baley. He was under no illusion that sleep would come easily. He was being sent to Aurora for the specific purpose of demonstrating that Fastolfe was innocent of roboticide — and success in that was required for Earth's continued security and (much less important but equally dear to Baley's heart) for the continued prospering of Baley's own career — yet, even before reaching Aurora, he had discovered that Fastolfe had virtually confessed to the crime.

The passage I have just given you, you will have noticed, contains nothing about sex. If you are interested in seeing what I've done with the motif (perhaps because you are sure I will mess it all up) you will have to read the book.

Actually, my third hundred books includes a second robot novel, and a very unusual one in a way, for it is a collaboration. I don't like to collaborate in my fiction, and have never done so except in a couple of trivial cases early in my career. This, however, is exceptional, for the collaboration was with my dear wife, Janet, who is herself a writer when she finds time left over from being a psychiatrist.

She and I together are writing what we hope will be a series of science fiction novels for young people about a teenager and his robot — a robot which is partly superhuman and partly imperfect. In fact, the title of the first book in the series is Norby, the Mixed-Up Robot *(Book 278), and Walker published it in 1983. A second Norby book is in press and a third is in preparation.*

The way this collaboration works is as follows: Janet works out the plot and the characters and does the first draft. I then read the first draft and do a final draft, making what changes seem necessary, and only those. It then appears "by Janet and Isaac Asimov." (Janet also helps design the covers — something in which I myself couldn't be less interested.)

In any case, here is the passage in Norby, the Mixed-Up Robot *in which Jeff Wells, the young hero, meets Norby for the first time. The scene is the establishment of a dealer in secondhand robots, and Jeff feels a strange attraction for an odd robot that seems to be encased in a barrel —*

from NORBY, THE MIXED-UP ROBOT (1983)

"What's in that box?" said Jeff abruptly.

The manager craned his neck to see which box Jeff was referring to, and a look of displeasure crossed his face. "Hasn't that thing been disposed of yet? You don't want that, young man."

"It must be an awfully old robot," said Jeff. The thing in the box looked like a metal barrel about sixty centimeters high, with a metal hat on top of it. It didn't seem to have legs or arms or even a head. Just a barrel and a hat. The hat had a circular brim and a dome on top.

Jeff continued to push the other boxes out of the way. He bent down to see the object more clearly.

It really was a metal barrel, dented and battered, with a label on it. It was an old paper label that was peeling off. It said, "Norb's Nails." Jeff could now distinguish places in the barrel where arms might come out if circular plates were dilated.

"Don't bother with that," said the manager, shaking his head violently. "It's a museum piece, if any museum would take it. It's not for sale."

"But what is it? Is it really a robot?"

"It's a robot all right. One of the very ancient R-two models. There's a story to it if any one is interested. It was falling apart, and an old spacer bought it, fixed it up —"

"What old spacer?" Jeff had heard stories about the old explorers of the Solar System, the human beings who went off alone to find whatever might be strange or profitable or both. Fargo knew all the stories and complained that independent spacers were getting rare now that Ing's spies were everywhere, and that Ing's pirates stole from anyone who dared travel to little-known parts of the system without official Federation escort.

"The story is that it was someone named McGillicuddy, but I never met anyone who ever heard of him. Did *you* ever hear of him?"

"No, sir."

"He's supposed to have died half a century ago, and his robot was knocked down to my father at an auction. I inherited him, but I certainly don't want him."

"Why isn't it for sale, then?"

"Because I've tried selling it. It doesn't work right, and it's always returned. I've got to scrap it."

"How much do you want for it, sir?"

The manager looked at him thoughtfully. "Didn't you just hear me tell you that it doesn't work right?"

"Yes, sir. I understand that."

"Would you be willing to sign a paper saying you understand that, and that you cannot return it even if it doesn't work right?"

Jeff felt a cold hand clutching at his chest as he thought of the admiral's money being thrown away, but he *wanted* that robot with its spacer heritage and its odd appearance. Certainly it would be a robot such as no one else had. He said, with teeth that had begun to chatter a bit, "Sure, I'll sign if you take the money I have in full payment and give me a receipt saying 'paid in full.' I also want a certificate of ownership entered into the city computer records."

"Huh!" the manager said. "You're underage."

"I look eighteen. Don't ask to see my papers, and you can say you thought I was of age."

"All right. I'll get the papers filled out."

He turned away, and Jeff squatted. He leaned forward and peered into the stasis box. This McGillicuddy must have put the workings of a robot into an empty barrel used for Norb's Nails.

Jeff looked more closely, putting his face against the dusty plastic and lifting one hand to block off light reflections. He decided that the hat was not all the way down. A band of darkness underneath showed that the robot had been put in stasis with its head not completely inside the barrel.

And there was a strange thin wire stretching from inside the darkness to the side of the stasis box.

"Don't touch that!" shouted the manager, who had happened to look up from his records.

It was too late. Jeff's outstretched finger touched the stasis box.

The manager had hopped over, mopping his forehead with a large handkerchief. "I said don't touch it. Are you all right?"

"Of course," said Jeff, stepping back.

"You didn't get a shock or anything?"

"I didn't feel a thing." But I did feel an emotion, thought Jeff. Awful loneliness. Not mine.

The manager looked at him suspiciously. "I warned you. You can't claim damage or anything like that."

"I don't want to," said Jeff. "What I want is for you to open that stasis box so I can have my robot."

"First you'll sign this paper, which says you're eighteen. I don't want you *ever* bringing it back." He kept grumbling to himself as he put it through the computoprint device that scanned the writing and turned it into neat print in triplicate.

Jeff read the paper rapidly. "You look eighteen," the manager said. "Anyone would say so. Now let me see your identification."

"It will tell you my birthdate."

"Well, cover it with your thumb. I'm not bright and won't notice you've done that. I just want to check your name and signature." He looked at the signature on the card Jeff presented. "All right," he said, "there's your copy. Now, credit voucher, please."

He looked at it, placed it in his credit slot, and returned it to Jeff, who winced, for it meant that virtually everything the admiral had given him had been transferred, quite permanently, from his account into the store's. It left him with practically nothing.

The manager waddled through the mess of boxes and touched the raised number on the dial box of the one that held the robot in the barrel. The top opened. With that, the thin wire slowly withdrew into the barrel, and the hatlike lid seemed to settle down firmly so that the band of darkness disappeared. The manager didn't seem to notice. He was too busy trying to shift the stasis box into better position.

"Careful! Careful!" said Jeff. "Don't hurt the robot."

With its hat up and its wire out, Jeff wondered if the robot had really been in a position to *think*. He felt again a stab of sympathy. If that had been so, it must have been awful to be trapped inside a box, able to think but unable to get out. How long had it been there? It must have felt so helpless.

"Please," he said to the manager. "You're being too rough. Let me help you lift it out."

"Too rough?" said the manager with a sneer. "Nothing can hurt it. For one thing, it's too far gone."

He looked up at Jeff with an unpleasant expression on his face. "You signed that paper, you know. I told you it doesn't work right, so you can't back out. I don't think you can use it for teaching purposes because it doesn't have the attachments that will allow it to tie into the Education System. It doesn't even talk. It just makes sounds that I can't make sense of."

Now, for the first time, something happened inside the barrel. The hatlike lid shot up and hit the shopkeeper in the shoulder as he was leaning over the box.

Underneath the lid was half a face. At least that's what it looked like. There were two big eyes — no! Jeff leaned across and saw that there were also two big eyes at the back — or maybe that was the front.

"Ouch," said the manager. He lifted a fist.

Jeff said, "You'll just hurt yourself if you try to hit it, sir. Besides, it's my robot now, and I'll have the law on you if you damage it."

The robot said in a perfectly clear voice that was a high and almost musical tenor, "That vicious man insulted me. He's been insulting me a *lot*. Every time he mentions me, he insults me. I can speak perfectly well, as you can hear. I can speak better than he can. Just because I have no desire to speak to my inferiors, such as that so-called manager, doesn't mean I can't speak."

The manager kept puffing out his cheeks and seemed to be trying to say something, but nothing came out.

Jeff said, quite reasonably, "That robot can certainly speak better than you can right now."

"What's more," said the robot, "I am a perfectly adequate teaching robot, as I will now demonstrate. What is your name, young man?"

"Jeff Wells."

"And what is it you would care to learn?"

"Swahili. The Martian Colony dialect — uh — sir." It suddenly occurred to Jeff that he ought to show a decent respect to a robot that clearly displayed a certain tendency to irascibility and shortness of temper.

"Good. Take my hand and concentrate. Don't let anything distract you."

The little robot's left — or possibly right — side dilated to a small opening, out of which shot an arm with a swivel elbow and two-way palms, so that it was still impossible to tell which was its front and which its back. Jeff took the hand, which had a pleasantly smooth, but not slippery, metallic texture.

"You will now learn how to say 'Good morning, how are you?' in Martian Swahili," said the robot.

Jeff concentrated. His eyebrows shot up, and he said something that clearly made no sense to the manager.

"That's just gibberish," said the manager, shrugging.

"No, it isn't," said Jeff. "I know a *little* Swahili, and what I said was Martian Swahili for 'Good morning, how are you?'; only this is the first time I've been able to pronounce it correctly."

"In that case," said the manager hastily, "you can't expect to get a teaching robot that's in working order for a miserable eighty-five credits."

"No, I can't," said Jeff, "but that's what I got it for. I have the

paper and you have the money, and that ends it, unless you want
me to tell the police you tried to sell an inoperable robot to a four-
teen-year-old. I'm sure this robot can act inoperable if I ask him
to."

The manager was puffing again.

The robot seemed to be getting taller. In fact, it *was* getting
taller. Telescoping legs were pushing out of the bottom of the barrel, with feet that faced in both directions. The robot's eyes were
now closer to the level of the little shopkeeper, who was a good
head shorter than Jeff.

The robot said, "I would suggest, inferior person, that you return the eighty-five credits to this young man, and let him have
me for nothing. An inoperable robot is worth nothing."

The manager shrieked and stepped back, falling over a stasis box
containing a set of robot weeders. "That thing is dangerous! It
doesn't obey the laws of robotics! It threatened me!" He began to
shout. "Help! Help!"

"Don't be silly, mister," Jeff said. "He was just making a suggestion. And you can keep the eighty-five credits. I don't want them."

The manager mopped his brow again. "All right, then. Get it out
of here. It's your responsibility. I don't ever want to see that robot
again. Or you, either."

Jeff walked out, holding the hand of a barrel that had once contained Norb's Nails and had now sprouted two legs, two arms, and
half a head.

"You've got a big mouth," said Jeff.

"How can you tell?" said the robot. "I talk through my hat."

"You sure do. What's your name?"

"Well, Mac — that was McGillicuddy — called me Macko, but
I didn't like that. Mac and Macko sounds like a hyperwave comedy
team. But at least he referred to me as 'he' instead of 'it.' That was
something, anyway. It showed respect. What would you like to call
me, Jeff?"

Jeff should have corrected the robot. All robots were supposed
to put a title before a human name, but it was clear that the robot
he had didn't follow customs too well, and Jeff decided he didn't
mind that. Besides, he would get tired of being called Master Jeff.

He said, "Have you always been inside a barrel of Norb's Nails?"

"No, only since McGillicuddy found me; that is, since he *re-
paired* me. He was a genius at robotics, you know." Then, with

obvious pride, the robot added, "The barrel is part of me, and I won't wear out. Not ever!"

"Oh, I don't know," said Jeff coolly. "Your label just fell off."

"That's because I don't need a label. This old but serviceable barrel doesn't contain nails any longer. It contains me. I like this barrel. It's good, strong stainless steel."

"All right," said Jeff. "In that case, since this wonderful barrel once held Norb's Nails, why don't I call you Norby?"

The robot blinked and said, "Norby . . . Norby . . . ," as though he were rolling the sound round on his tongue and tasting it — except that he didn't have a tongue and probably couldn't taste. Then he said, "I like it. I like it very much."

"Good," said Jeff. And he and Norby walked off, still hand in hand.

Notice that this section is not entitled "Robots" as in the first two Opus books, but "Robots and Computers." When I first began writing robot stories in 1939, what we today call computers had not yet entered the public consciousness, and certainly not mine. Even so, in my early stories I sometimes featured computers that were so large as to be immobile and existed only in order to solve enormously complex problems. They were computers, of course. I had the concept, but not the word.

By the 1950s, however, the word was handed to me by the facts of scientific advance, so that more and more of my stories dealt with computers rather than with robots. And although my third hundred books include no robot short stories, there is a computer short story in a collection of my short stories that Doubleday published in 1983 — The Winds of Change and Other Stories *(Book 267) — and the story I am referring to is "A Perfect Fit."*

from THE WINDS OF CHANGE AND OTHER STORIES (1983)

A Perfect Fit

Ian Bradstone, wandering his way sadly through one more town, was stopped by a cluster of people at the open door of an emporium. His first impulse was to turn and flee, but he couldn't make himself do so. The fascination of horror drew him reluctantly toward the cluster.

His curiosity must have turned his face into one big question mark, for someone at the outskirts explained the matter pleasantly. "Three-D chess. It's a hot game."

Bradstone knew how it worked. There would be half a dozen people conferring at each move, all trying to beat the computer. The chances were that they would lose. Six wood-pushers add up to one wood-pusher. He caught the unbearable glitter of the graphic and closed his eyes against it. He turned away bitterly and noted a makeshift setup of eight chessboards balanced on pegs, one above the other.

Ordinary chessboards. Plastic chessmen.

"Hey," he said, in explosive surprise.

The young man at the multiboard said, defensively, "We can't get close enough. I set this up myself so we can follow. Careful! Don't knock it down."

Bradstone said, "Is that the position as of now?"

"Yes. The guys have been arguing for ten minutes."

Bradstone looked eagerly at the position. He said, raptly, "If you move the rook from beta-B-six to delta-B-six, you get the upper hand."

The young man studied the boards. "Are you sure?"

"Certainly I'm sure. No matter what the computer does, it's going to end up losing a move to protect its queen."

More studying. The young man shouted, "Hey, in there. Guy here says you should bump the rook up two levels."

There was a collective sigh from the inner group. One voice said, "I was thinking that."

Another said, "I get it. It leaves the queen with the potentiality of vulnerability. I didn't see that." The owner of the second voice turned. "You! The fellow who made the suggestion. Would you do the honor? Would you punch in the move?"

Bradstone backed away, his face contorted in sheer horror. "No — No — I don't play." He turned and hastened away.

♦

He was hungry. Periodically, he was hungry.

Occasionally, he came across fruit stands of the type set up by small entrepreneurs who found a disregarded space in the interstices of a thoroughly computerized economy. If Bradstone were careful, he could walk off with an apple or an orange.

It was a frightening thing. There was always the chance he might be caught and, if he were, he would be asked to pay. He had the money, of course — they were very kind to him — but how could he pay?

Yet every day on a dozen occasions, he would have to undergo a transfer of credits, to use his cash card. It meant endless humiliation.

He found himself outside a restaurant. It might have been the smell of the food that had reminded him he was hungry.

He peered cautiously through the window. There were a number of people eating. Too many. It was bad enough with one or two. He couldn't make himself the center of hordes of staring, pitying eyes.

He turned away, his stomach growling, and saw that he was not the only one staring into the window. A boy was doing the same. He was about ten years old and he didn't look particularly hungry.

Bradstone attempted a tone of hearty good nature. "Hello there, young fellow. Hungry?"

The youngster looked at him suspiciously and edged away. "No!"

Bradstone made no move to come closer. If he did, the boy would undoubtedly run. He said, "I'll bet you're big enough to do your own ordering. You can order a hamburger or anything else, I'm sure."

Pride overcame suspicion. The boy said, "Sure! Anytime!"

"But you don't have a card of your own, right? So you can't complete the order. Right?"

The boy stared at him warily out of brown eyes. He was neatly dressed and had an alert and intelligent air about him.

Bradstone said, "Tell you what. I have a card and you can use it to order. Get yourself a hamburger or anything else you want. Tell you what else. You can get me something, too. Nice T-bone steak, and a baked potato and some squash and some coffee. And two pieces of apple pie. You have one."

"I got to go home and eat," said the boy.

"Come on! You'll save your father some assets. They know you here, I'm sure."

"We eat here lots of times."

"There you are. Eat here again. Only this time, *you* handle the card. You do the selection — like a grownup. Go ahead. You go in first."

There was a tense feeling in the pit of Bradstone's stomach. What he was doing made perfect sense to him and would not harm the child at all. Anyone who might be watching, however, might come to a horrible and quite wrong conclusion.

Bradstone could explain if given a chance, but how humiliating to have everyone see that he had to maneuver a little boy into doing something for him he could not do for himself.

The youngster hesitated, but he entered the restaurant and Bradstone followed, maintaining a careful distance. The youngster sat down at a table and Bradstone sat down opposite.

Bradstone smiled and handed him his card. It tingled his hands unpleasantly — as always, these days — and he was relieved to be able to let go of it. It had a hard, metallic glitter that made the muscles round his eyes twitch. He couldn't bear to look at it.

"Go ahead, boy. Make the selection," he said in a low voice. "Anything you want."

The boy hadn't lied. He could handle the small computer-outlet perfectly, his fingers flying over the controls.

"Steak for you, mister. Baked potato. Squash. Apple pie. Coffee. — You want salad, mister?" His voice had taken on a fussy I'm-grown-up sound. "My mom always orders salad, but I don't like it."

"I guess I'll try it, though. Mixed green salad. They got that? Vinaigrette dressing. They got that? You can handle that?"

"Don't see about the vin-something. — Maybe this is it."

Bradstone ended up with French dressing as it later turned out, but it did well enough.

The boy inserted the card with ease and a skill that roused Bradstone's bitter envy, even as his picturing the act made his stomach lurch.

The boy handed back the card. "I guess you had enough money," he said, importantly.

Bradstone said, "Did you notice the figure?"

"Oh, no. You're not supposed to look; that's what my dad says. I mean it didn't get rejected so there's enough for the food."

Bradstone crushed down the feeling of disappointment. He couldn't read the figures and he couldn't make himself ask others.

Eventually, he might have to go to a bank and try to invent some way of maneuvering them into telling him.

He tried to make conversation. "What's your name, sonny?"

"Reginald."

"What are you studying at home these days, Reggie?"

"Arithmetic mostly because Dad says I have to, and dinosaurs because I want to. Dad says if I stick to my arithmetic I can get the dinosaurs, too. I can program my computer to get the graphics of dinosaur motion. You know how a brontosaurus walks on land? It has to balance its neck so the center of gravity is in the hips. It holds its head way up like a giraffe unless it's in water. Then — Here's my hamburger. And your stuff, too."

It had all come along the moving belt and had stopped at the appropriate place.

The thought of one full meal without humiliation overcame Bradstone's wistfulness at the thought of manipulating a computer in the free search for information.

Reginald said, quite politely, "I'll eat the hamburger at the counter, mister."

Bradstone waved. "I hope it's a good hamburger, Reggie." Bradstone needed him no more and was relieved to have him go. Someone from the kitchen, undoubtedly a Computer-Maintenance technician, had emerged and engaged Reginald in friendly conversation — which was also a relief.

There was no question about the profession. You could always tell a Comp-Maint by his lazy air of importance, his exuded sense of knowledge that the world rested on his shoulder.

But Bradstone was concentrating on his dinner — the first full meal he had enjoyed normally in a month.

♦

It was only after he finished — quite finished in the most leisurely possible fashion — that he studied his surroundings again. The boy was long gone. Bradstone thought sadly that the boy, at least, had not pitied, had not condescended, had not patronized. He had not been old enough to find the event an odd one; had only concentrated on his own adulthood in being able to handle the computer outlet.

Adulthood!

The place was not very crowded now. The Comp-Maint was still behind the counter, presumably studying the wiring of the computerization.

It was, thought Bradstone with a pang, the major occupation of technologists virtually the world over; always programming, reprogramming, adjusting, checking the tiny electric currents that controlled the work of the world for everyone — for almost everyone.

The comfortably warm internal feeling produced by an excellent steak stirred the feeling of rebellion within Bradstone. Why not act? Why not do something about it?

He caught the Comp-Maint's eye and said in an attempt at lightness that didn't ring true even in his own ears, "Pal, I guess there are lawyers in this town?"

"You guess right."

"You couldn't suggest a good one not too far away, could you?"

The Comp-Maint said politely, "You'll find a town directory at the post office. Just punch in the request for lawyers."

"I mean a good one. Clever guy. Lost causes. Like that." He laughed, hoping to get at least a smile out of the other.

He didn't. The Comp-Maint said, "They're all described. List your needs, and you'll get evaluations, ages, addresses, case loads, fee levels. Anything you want you can get, if you play the keys properly. And it's working. I vetted it last week."

"That's not what I mean, buddy." The suggestion that he play the keys properly sent the usual frisson skidding up his spine. "I want your personal recommendation. You know?"

The Comp-Maint shook his head. "I'm not a directory."

Bradstone said, "Damn it. What's wrong with you? Name a lawyer. Any lawyer. Is there a law against knowing something without a computer to play with?"

"Use of the directory is a dime. If you've got more than a dime registered on your card, what's the problem? Don't you know how to use your card? Or are you — " His eyes widened in sudden thought. "Oh — Son of a — *That's* why you got Reggie to order your meal for you! Listen, I didn't know — "

Bradstone shrank away. He turned to hurry out of the place and nearly collided with a large man who had a ruddy complexion and a balding head.

The large man said softly, "One moment, please. Aren't you the person who bought my son a hamburger a while ago?"

Bradstone hesitated, then nodded dry-mouthed.

"I would like to pay you for it. It's all right. I know who you are and I'll handle your card for you."

The Comp-Maint interposed sharply, "If you want a lawyer, fella, Mr. Gold is a lawyer."

The sharpened interest in Bradstone's eyes made itself evident at once.

Gold said, "I *am* a lawyer if you're looking for one. It's how I knew you. I followed your case with painful attention, I assure you, and when Reggie came home with a tale of having eaten dinner already and of having used the computer, I guessed who you might be from his description. And I recognize you now, of course."

Bradstone said, "Can we talk privately?"

"My home is a five-minute walk from here."

♦

It was not a luxurious living room, but it was a comfortable one. Bradstone said, "Do you want a retainer? I can afford one."

"I know you have ample funds," said Gold. "Tell me first, though, what the problem is."

Bradstone leaned forward in his chair and said, intensely, "If you've followed my case, you must know I have been subjected to cruel and unusual punishment. I'm the first person who has received this kind of sentence. The combination of hypnosis and direct neuroconditioning has only been perfected recently. The nature of the punishment to which I have been sentenced could not be understood. It must be lifted."

Gold said, "You underwent due process in great detail, and there was no reasonable doubt that you were guilty —"

"Even so! Look! We live in a computerized world. I can't do a thing anywhere — I can't get information — I can't be fed — I can't amuse myself — I can't pay for anything, or check on anything, or just plain *do* anything — without using a computer. And I have been adjusted, as you surely know, so that I am incapable of looking at a computer without hurting my eyes, or touching one without blistering my fingers. I can't even handle my cash card or even *think* of using it without nausea."

Gold said, "Yes, I know all that. I also know you have been given ample funds for the duration of your punishment, and that the general public has been asked to sympathize and be helpful. I believe they do this."

"I don't *want* that. I don't *want* their help and their pity. I don't want to be a helpless child in a world of adults. I don't want to be an illiterate in a world of people who can read. Help me end the punishment. It's been almost a month of hell. I can't go through eleven more."

Gold sat in thought for a while. "Well, I will charge you a retainer so that I can become your legal representative, and I will do what I can for you. I must warn you, though, that I don't think the chances for success are great."

"Why? All I did was divert five thousand dollars —"

"You planned to divert far more, it was decided, but were caught before you could. It was an ingenious computer fraud, quite worthy of your well-known skill at chess, but it was still a crime. And, as you say, everything is computerized and no step, however small, can be taken these days without a computer. To defraud by means of a computer, then, is to break down what is now the essential framework of civilization. It is a terrible crime and it must be discouraged."

"Don't preach."

"I'm not. I'm explaining. You tried to break down a system and in punishment the system has been broken down for you alone and you are not otherwise mistreated. If you find your life unbearable, that merely shows you how unbearable it is that you tried, after a fashion, to break it down for everyone."

"But a year is too much."

"Well, perhaps less will still serve as a strong enough example to deter others from making the same attempt. I will try — but I'm afraid I can guess what the law will say."

"What?"

"It will say that if punishments should be made to fit the crime, yours is a perfect fit."

Computers also play a part in my nonfiction. In fact, I wrote an article in which I tell (in a lighthearted way) how I came to own a computer of my own, one that I use as a word processor. After its publication, I included that article, "The Word Processor and I," in an essay collection that I put together at the request of Prome-

*theus Books, a small firm that frequently publishes books by mem-
bers of the Committee for the Scientific Investigation of Claims of
the Paranormal. (I am a member of the organization, even though
I do no active investigating myself.)*

from THE ROVING MIND (1983)

The Word Processor and I

When *Byte* let it be known that, in their opinion, a word processor
would look good in Isaac Asimov's office, Ed Juge of Radio Shack,
down in Fort Worth, Texas, thought, in his warm and loving heart,
that that might be a good idea. On May 6, 1981, therefore, a word
processor arrived. Or at least, two big boxes and a small one, each
presumably filled with arcane incunabula, came.

I managed to hoist them from the lobby of the apartment house,
where the delivery men left them, up to the thirty-third-floor
apartment where I live. Fortunately, that was not as difficult as it
sounds, since I used the elevator.

I then placed the boxes in my office and practiced walking
around them until I got the route memorized. To make sure, I
practiced it in the dark, then with my eyes closed, then in the dark
and with my eyes closed.

In a few hours, I was able to walk through my office without ever
making contact with the boxes, or even looking in their direction.
In this way, I was able to pretend that they didn't exist. Unfortunately, part of my library shelves were blocked by them, but I
decided not to use those shelves. If I needed data contained in the
books there, I could always make it up.

This worked fine, and my heartbeat had come down to pretty
nearly normal, when, on May 12, Ron Schwartz of Radio Shack
arrived with the intention of emptying those boxes. With the help
of my dear wife, Janet, he set up a "computer corner" in our living
room. Within it, the word processor was unboxed, hooked together, and plugged in. I did my bit, to be sure. I kept saying, "I
don't think we have any space for a word processor anywhere," but
no one listened to me.

In no time at all, there it was — a Radio Shack TRS-80 Model
II Micro-Computer, along with a Daisy-Wheel Printer and a Scrip-
sit program. A bunch of floppy disks, some ribbons, and various
other pieces of formidable paraphernalia were also included.

Ron then proceeded to show me how it worked. To me it seemed
like a tremendously complex machine with a console reminiscent
of that on a Boeing 707; but Ron, unconcerned, approached it in
the most casual possible manner. He flicked the keys, and had me
do the same, so that different things happened on the screen.
Words and sentences appeared, and parts were then erased, sub-
stituted, transferred, inserted, started, stopped. Ron paused only
to stifle a yawn or two.

"You see how simple it is," he said. "If you have any difficulties,
here are two instruction booklets." (With an effort, he hoisted out
two volumes, each the size of a Manhattan telephone directory.)
"This one," he said, "comes with a series of cassettes so you can
hear a nice friendly voice tell you everything there is to know.
— And," he went on, "if reading and hearing the whole thing in
detail isn't enough, just phone me. I'll be glad to repeat
everything."

He left, and I spent the evening staring at the word processor.
Staring, it turned out, was not enough. No matter how hard I
stared, and with what intensity I *thought* at it, it did nothing. With
a sinking heart, I realized that there was no way out. I was going
to have to fiddle with the keys.

In my diary that night, I wrote: "I'll *never* learn how to use it."

Nevertheless, the indomitable spirit of the Asimovs shone
through. Painstakingly, I read the instructions, doing my best not
to move my lips as I did so. I listened to several of the cassettes,
trying to nod intelligently at odd moments.

It didn't help. On May 27, I wrote in my diary: "Very depressed
because of the word processor. Couldn't get it to double-space."

Hah! I also couldn't get it to make tables, or to reduce the mar-
gins to the insignificance I find comfortable. Nor, when I attempted to print one of my concoctions, could I get it to pause
between pages, even though it promised it would. It would wait
for me to prepare a page, with carbons; and, just before I could
insert it, the thing would merrily begin imprinting the bare platen
with my deathless prose.

On June 4, two young men from Radio Shack arrived, unfailingly pleasant, unfailingly helpful, unfailingly polite, and I wept on their shoulders in turn. Under their ministrations, the word processor behaved like a purring little pussycat, but my heart told me they would not have been gone for as much as one and a half seconds before pussycat would turn back into a Bengal tiger. My heart was not wrong.

I had, by now, developed the habit of flinching when I passed the computer corner, and throwing up my arm as though to ward off an attack. Occasionally, I would open one of the instruction books and read the cheerful instructions at random, but it all echoed meaninglessly in the vacant cavity I austerely refer to as my brain.

On June 12, the word processor had been sitting in my living room for a full month, and it had so far won every battle.

But was I downhearted? Did I feel beaten?

You bet I was, and you can also bet I did!

On June 14, I decided to make one last try before asking Radio Shack to remove the thing and take its beak from out my heart. I was going to attempt to write a short article on the word processor. Actually, I had already written it in first draft on my trusty Selectric III typewriter, but it was my intention to transpose it to the screen, correct it, and then print it.

I sat down and started the machine — and, suddenly, with no warning whatever, everything worked. It rubbed its head against my leg and purred.

I will never know what happened. The day before I had been as innocent of the ability to run the machine as I had been while it had still been in its original box. A night had passed — an ordinary night — but during it something in my brain must finally have rearranged itself. Now, there I was, running the machine like an old hand. In making my corrections, I could even use my right hand on both the "repeat" and the cursor arrows, without looking, and that little blinking devil jumped through every hoop in sight.

On June 17, I took the big step. I had a massive manuscript of a book in first draft. I put the entire first chapter onto the screen and then printed it.

I whistled while I worked.

Janet (my dear wife) came by to watch, and stood there transfixed. I waved my hand airily at her. "Nothing to it," I said. "All it takes is grit, determination, a sense of buoyant optimism, and good old Yankee know-how."

I've been working at it steadily ever since (with some minor problems I'll tell you about another time). In a matter of days after the transformation, in fact, I called up Radio Shack and told them to send someone over to set up the special tables that had arrived after the word processor itself had. "Put it all up," I said, "because I have decided I will keep the machine. I may even pay for it," I added, with devil-may-care insouciance.

Scott Stoegbauer of Radio Shack arrived on July 8 and did the job.

I said to him, "Very friendly machine you have here. Reliable. Easy to handle. Makes no trouble. All you need is raw courage and the kind of self-confidence that can surmount all hurdles."

"You are a great man, Dr. Asimov," said that very perceptive young fellow.

PART 8

HISTORY

IN THE PREVIOUS OPUS BOOKS, I had, at this point, a section called "Words." In my first two hundred books, I published no fewer than seven that dealt with different classes of words and their derivation. After that, though, it seemed to me I had done all I could in that direction so that there is nothing of the sort among my third hundred books. I therefore pass on to the section on "History."

In a way, I am scarcely the better off in doing so, for I have almost a repetition here of the situation with respect to "Words." In my first two hundred books are included fourteen books of history, but these have come to an end, at least for a time. This is not because I was running out of material, as in the case of "Words," or running out of enthusiasm, either. They simply didn't do quite well enough; they never sold paperback reprints, for instance.

In 1979, however, Simon and Schuster published a book of mine entitled A Choice of Catastrophes *(Book 207), in which I discussed all the different ways in which the world might come to an end — from disasters so large as to put an end to the Universe, or so small as merely to wipe out human civilization. Toward the end, I discussed the dangers of war, and in a particular passage, gave a quick history of that tragic amusement of humanity, which I quote here.*

from A CHOICE OF CATASTROPHES (1979)

All species compete among themselves for food, for sex, for security; there are always quarrels and fighting when these needs overlap among individuals. Generally, such quarrels are not to the death, since the individual being worsted generally flees, and the victor is generally satisfied with the immediate victory.

Where there is no high level of intelligence, there is no awareness of anything but the present; no clear foresight as to the value of forestalling future competition; no clear memory of past affronts or hurts. Inevitably, as intelligence increases, foresight and memory improve, and the point arrives when a victor is not satisfied with the immediate spoils but begins to see the advantage of killing the loser in order to prevent future challenge. Just as inevitably, the point arrives at which a loser who escapes will seek revenge, and if it is clear that a straight individual-to-individual combat will mean another loss, he will seek other means to victory, such as ambush or the gathering of reinforcements.

In short, human beings inevitably reach the level of making war not because our species is more violent and wicked than other species, but because it is more intelligent.

Naturally, as long as human beings were compelled to fight with nails, fists, legs, and teeth alone, little in the way of deadly results could be expected. Bruises and lacerations might be all that would be inflicted in a general way, and the fighting might even be viewed as healthful exercise.

The trouble is that by the time human beings were intelligent enough to plan conflict with the aid of memory and foresight, they had developed the capacity to use tools. As warriors began to swing clubs, wield stone axes, cast stone-tipped spears, and shoot stone-tipped arrows, battles became steadily bloodier. The development of metallurgy made things still worse by substituting for stone the harder and tougher bronze, and then the still harder and tougher iron.

As long as humanity consisted of roving bands of food-collectors and hunters, conflicts would surely have been brief, however, with one side or the other breaking off and fleeing when damage grew unacceptably high. Nor was there any thought of permanent conquest, for ground was not worth conquest. No group of human beings could long maintain themselves in any one place; there was always the necessity of wandering on in search of new and relatively untouched food sources.

A fundamental change came at least as early as 7000 B.C., when the glaciers of the most recent Ice Age were steadily retreating and when human beings were still using stone for tools. At that time in various places in the Middle East (and, eventually, elsewhere as well) human beings were learning to collect food for future use and even to provide for the future creation of food.

They did this by domesticating and caring for herds of animals such as sheep, goats, pigs, cattle, fowl, and making use of them for wool, milk, eggs, and, of course, meat. Properly handled there was no chance of running out, for the animals could be relied on to breed and replace themselves at, if necessary, a greater rate than they were consumed. In this way, food that was inedible or unpalatable to human beings could be used to support animals that were themselves, at least potentially, desirable food.

Even more important was the development of agriculture: the deliberate planting of grain, vegetables, and fruit trees. This made it possible for particular varieties of food to be grown in greater concentration than would exist in nature.

The result of the development of herding and agriculture was the ability of human beings to support a greater density of population than had been possible before. In regions where this advance was made a population explosion took place.

A second result was that society was made static. Herds could not be moved as easily as a human tribe on the prowl could move, but it was agriculture that was crucial here. Farms could not be moved at all. Property and land became important, and the importance of social status resting on the accumulation of possessions increased sharply.

A third result was the increased necessity of cooperation and the development of specialization. A hunting tribe is self-sufficient and the degree of specialization is low. A farming community may be forced to develop and maintain irrigation ditches and to stand guard to keep herds from dispersing or from being carried off by predators (either human or animal). A ditchdigger or a shepherd has little time for other activities, but he can barter his labor for food and other necessities.

Cooperation doesn't necessarily come about through sweet reason, unfortunately, and some activities are harder and less desirable than others. The easiest way of dealing with this problem is for one group of human beings to throw themselves on another and, by killing a few, force the remainder to do all the disagreeable work. Nor can the losers easily flee, tied as they are to farms and herds.

Facing attack by others as an ever-present possibility, farmers and herdsmen began to huddle close together and to wall themselves in for protection. The appearance of such walled cities marks the beginning of "civilization" — which comes from a Latin word meaning "city-dweller."

By 3500 B.C., cities had grown to be complex social organizations, containing many people who neither farmed nor herded, but who performed functions necessary for the farmers or herders — whether as professional soldiers, as artisans and artists, or as administrators. By then, the use of metals was coming in and soon after 3000 B.C., writing was developed in the Middle East. This was an organized system of symbols that would record information for longer periods and with less likelihood of distortion than memory alone could. With that the historic period began.

Once cities had developed, each of them in control of a surrounding territory given over to agriculture and herding (the "city-state") wars of conquest became better organized, more deadly, and — inevitable.

The early city-states were built up along the course of one river or another. The river offered an easy road of communication for trade and a source of water for the irrigation procedures that made agriculture secure. To have small stretches of the river under the control of separate city-states, always suspicious of each other and usually openly hostile, impaired its use both for communication and irrigation. It was clearly necessary for the common benefit to have the river under the control of a single political unit.

The question was which city-state was to dominate, for the notion of a federal union with all the parts sharing in the decisions never occurred to anyone as far as we know, and would probably not have been a practical course of procedure at that time. The decision of which city-state was to dominate was usually left to the fortunes of war.

The first individual we know of by name who ruled over a considerable stretch of river as a result of a previous history of what may have been military conquest is the Egyptian monarch Narmer (known as Menes in the later Greek accounts). Narmer founded the First Dynasty about 2850 B.C. and ruled over the entire lower Nile Valley. We do not have a circumstantial account of his conquests, though, and his unified rule might possibly have been the result of inheritance or diplomacy.

The first undoubted conqueror, the first man to come to power and then, in a succession of battles, establish his rule over a wide area was Sargon, of the Sumerian city of Agade. He came to power about 2334 B.C. and before his death in 2305 B.C., he had placed himself in control of the entire Tigris-Euphrates Valley. Since human beings seem always to have valued and admired the ability to win battles, he is sometimes known as Sargon the Great.

Civilization was well established by 2500 B.C. in four river valleys in Africa and Asia; those of the Nile in Egypt, of the Tigris-Euphrates in Iraq, of the Indus in Pakistan, and of the Huang-Ho in China.

From there, by conquest and by trade, the area of civilization spread outward steadily until, by A.D. 200, it stretched from the Atlantic Ocean to the Pacific in nearly unbroken fashion west and east across the northern and southern shores of the Mediterranean and across southern and eastern Asia. This represents an east-west length of something like 13,000 kilometers (8000 miles) and a north-south width of from 800 to 1600 kilometers (500 to 1000 miles). The total area of civilization may have been, at that time, some 10 million square kilometers (4 million square miles) or about one-twelfth the land area of the planet.

What's more, the political units, with time, tended to grow larger, as human beings advanced their technology and became more capable of transporting themselves and their material goods over larger and larger areas. In A.D. 200 the civilized portion of the world was broken up into four major units of approximately equal size.

On the far west, circling the Mediterranean Sea, was the Roman Empire. It reached its maximum physical extent in A.D. 116 and was still virtually intact as late as A.D. 400. East of it and extending over what is now Iraq, Iran, and Afghanistan was the neo-Persian Empire, which, in 226, underwent an accession of strength with the coming to power of Ardashir I, the founder of the Sassanian dynasty. Persia reached its greatest prosperity under Chosroes I about 550 and had a very brief territorial maximum about 620 under Chosroes II.

To the southeast of the Persians was India, which had been nearly united under Asoka about 250 B.C., and was strong again under the Gupta dynasty, which came to power about 320. Finally, to the east of India was China, which from about 200 B.C. to A.D. 200 was strong under the Han dynasty.

Barbarians

The ancient wars among the city-states and the empires, which arose out of their conglomeration about some one dominating region, never really threatened catastrophe. There was no question of wiping out the human species since, with the worst will in the world, humanity did not, at that time, possess the power required to do the job.

What was much more likely was that the more or less willful destruction of the painful accumulations of the fruits of civilization might end that aspect of the human adventure.

And yet, as long as the quarrel was between one civilized region and another, it was not to be expected that destruction of civilization as a whole would follow — at least, not with the power then in the hands of civilized humanity.

The purpose of war was to extend the power and prosperity of the victor, and it suited the conqueror to exact tribute. In order to obtain the tribute enough had to be left to the conquered to enable the tribute to be raised. It was unprofitable to destroy past the point where an object lesson had been given.

Naturally, where the testimony of the conquered survives, loud are the groans at the cruelty and rapacity of the conqueror, and with justice no doubt — but the conquered survived to groan and, fairly often, survived with enough strength to overthrow the conqueror eventually and become conquerors (just as cruel and rapacious) themselves.

And, on the whole, the area of civilization steadily increased, which is the best indication that the wars, however cruel and unjust to individuals, did not threaten an end to civilization. Indeed, one might argue that the marching armies, as an unintended side effect of their activities, spread civilization; and that stimulus of war-bred emergencies hastened innovation, which sped human technological progress.

There was, however, another kind of warfare that was more dangerous. Every civilized region in ancient times was surrounded by areas of lesser sophistication, and it is customary to refer to the unsophisticated peoples as "barbarians." (The word is of Greek origin, and refers only to the fact that foreigners spoke incomprehensibly with sounds that seemed like "bar-bar-bar" to Greek ears.

Even non-Greek civilizations were called barbarian by the Greeks. The word has come to be used for uncivilized people, however, with a strong connotation of bestial cruelty.) The barbarians were usually "nomads" (from a Greek word meaning "roaming"). Their possessions were few and consisted chiefly of animal herds, with which they traveled from pasture to pasture as the seasons changed. Their standards of living, by city standards, seemed primitive and poor; and, of course, they lacked the cultural amenities of civilization.

Regions of civilization were, in comparison, wealthy, with their accumulation of food and goods. Those accumulations were a standing temptation to the barbarians, who saw nothing wrong with helping themselves — if they could. Very often, they couldn't. The civilized regions were populous and organized. They had their walled cities for defense and usually understood the science of warfare better. Under strong governments, the barbarians were held at bay.

On one hand, the people of civilization were pinned to the ground by their possessions and were relatively immobile. The barbarians, on the other hand, were mobile. On their camels or horses, they could raid, and then retreat to raid another day. Victories against them were rarely telling and never (until relatively modern times) final.

Furthermore, many of the civilized population were "unwarlike," for living well, as civilized people do, often leads to the development of a certain lack of toleration for the risky and uncomfortable tasks set soldiers. This means that the greater numbers among the civilized do not count for as much as one might think. A relatively small barbarian warband would find a city population little more than helpless victims, if the civilized army should, for any reason, collapse in defeat.

When a civilized region fell under weak rulers who allowed the army to decay; or when, worse still, the region fell into civil war, a successful barbarian incursion was bound to follow.*

---

*Embarrassed civilized historians sometimes attempt to explain this by speaking of barbarian "hordes." The word "horde" comes from a Turkish word meaning "army" and refers to any loose tribal warband. It has come to carry an impression of great numbers, since it seems to excuse defeat at the hands of barbarians, if one can view one's civilized forebears as being overwhelmed by irresistible quantity. Actually, the barbarian "hordes" were almost invariably few in numbers — certainly fewer than those they conquered.

A barbarian takeover was far worse than the routine warfare of civilizations, since the barbarians, unused to the mechanics of civilization, often did not understand the value of keeping the victims alive in order that they might be milked regularly. The impulse was simply to help themselves and to destroy carelessly that which could not at the moment be used. Under such conditions, there would often be a breakdown of civilization over a limited area and for a limited time, at least. There would be a "dark age."

The first example of a barbarian incursion and a dark age followed, naturally enough, not long after our first example of a conqueror. Sargon the Great, his two sons, his grandson, and his great-grandson ruled, in succession, over a prosperous Sumero-Akkadian Empire. By 2219 B.C., however, when the great-grandson's rule came to an end, the empire had deteriorated to the point where Gutian barbarians from the northeast were a major problem. By 2180 B.C., the Gutians were in control of the Tigris-Euphrates Valley and there followed a century-long dark age.

The barbarians were particularly dangerous when they gained a war weapon that, temporarily at least, made them irresistible. Thus, about 1750 B.C., the tribes of Central Asia developed the horse-drawn chariot and with that swept down upon the settled lands of the Middle East and Egypt, dominating everything for a period of time.

Fortunately, barbarian invasions have never succeeded in totally wiping out civilization. The dark ages, even at their darkest, were never entirely black, and no barbarians ever failed to feel the attraction of the civilization — even the broken and decaying civilization — of the conquered. The conquerors would become civilized (and, in their turn, unwarlike) and, in the end, civilization would rise again, and usually reach new heights.

There were times when it was a civilized region which gained a new war weapon, and then it might become irresistible in turn. This happened when iron began to be smelted in eastern Asia Minor about 1350 B.C. Gradually, iron became more common, its quality improved, and iron weapons and armor began to be manufactured. When, by A.D. 900, the armies of Assyria became completely "ironized," so to speak, they began a three-century domination of western Asia.

To us of the West, the best-known example of a barbarian invasion and a dark age is that which put an end to the western portion of the Roman Empire. From A.D. 166 onward, the Roman Empire, having passed the expansionist age of its history, fought defensively against barbarian invasion. Time and again, Rome wavered and then regained lost ground under strong emperors. Then, in A.D. 378, the barbarian Goths won a great battle at Adrianople over the Romans, and the Roman legions were forever destroyed. Thereafter, Rome maintained itself for another century by hiring barbarians to fight in its army against other barbarians.

The western provinces came gradually to be under barbarian rule, and the amenities of civilization broke down. Italy itself was barbarized, and in 476 the last Roman emperor ruling in Italy, Romulus Augustus, was deposed. A five-century dark age set in, and it was not until the nineteenth century that life in western Europe grew to be as comfortable as it had been under the Romans.

And yet, though we speak of this post-Roman dark age in hushed tones, as though world civilization came within an ace of destruction, it remained a purely local phenomenon, confined to what is now England, France, Germany, and, to some extent, Spain and Italy.

At the low point in 850, when Charlemagne's attempted restoration of some measure of unity and civilization in western Europe had collapsed, and when the region was under the hammer blows of new barbarian raiders — the Northmen form the north, the Magyars from the east — as well as from the civilized Moslems of the south, what was the situation in the rest of the world?

1. The Byzantine Empire, which was the surviving remnant of the eastern half of the Roman Empire, was still strong, and its civilization was preserved in an unbroken line from that of ancient Greece and Rome. What's more, its civilization was actually spreading among the barbarian Slavs, and it was approaching a period of new might under the Macedonian dynasty, a line of warlike emperors.

2. The Abbasid Empire, representing the new religion of Islam, which had absorbed the Persian Empire and the Syrian and African provinces of the Roman Empire, was at its peak of prosperity and civilization. Its greatest monarch, Mamun the Great (son of the famous Harun al-Rashid of the Arabian Nights), had died only in 833. The independent Moslem realm in Spain was also at a high pitch of civilization (higher in fact than Spain was to see in all the centuries afterward).

3. India, under the Gurjara-Prathihara dynasty, was strong, and

its civilization continued unbroken.

4. China, though politically unsettled at this time, was at a high point in its culture and civilization, and had successfully spread that civilization to Korea and Japan.

In other words, the total area of civilization was still expanding and only in the far west was there a region that had substantially declined: a region that did not make up more than perhaps 7 percent of the total area of civilization.

Though the barbarian incursions of the fifth century loom so large and fateful in our Western history books, while doing so little damage to civilization as a whole, there were other barbarian incursions in later centuries that were far more threatening. That we are less well acquainted with the later barbarians is only because those regions of western Europe that suffered so badly in the fifth century suffered less in later centuries.

Throughout the course of history, the steppes of central Asia had bred hardy horsemen who virtually lived on their mounts.* In good years, with sufficient rain, the herds multiplied and so did the nomads. In the years of drought that followed, the nomads led their herds out of the steppes in every direction, thundering against the civilized ramparts from China to Europe.

A succession of tribesmen were, for instance, to be found in what is now the Ukraine in southern Russia, each being replaced by new waves from the east. In the time of the Assyrian Empire, the Cimmerians were to be found north of the Black Sea. They were pushed out by the Scythians about 700 B.C., and these by the Sarmatians about 200 B.C., and these by the Alans about 100 B.C.

About A.D. 300 the Huns approached from the east, and they were the most redoubtable of the central-Asian invaders up to that point. In fact, it was their coming that helped push the German barbarians into the Roman Empire. The Germans were not expanding; they were fleeing.

In 451, Attila, the most powerful of the Hunnic monarchs, penetrated as far west as Orléans in France and, near that city, fought a drawn battle with an allied army of Romans and Germans. That

---

*They were equivalent in some ways to the cowboys of the legendary American West, but where the cowboys flourished for a period of only twenty-five years, the central Asian nomads had been patrolling their herds on horseback virtually throughout recorded history.

was the farthest west any of the central-Asian tribes was ever to penetrate. Attila died the next year, and his empire collapsed almost immediately afterward.

There followed the Avars, the Bulgars, the Magyars, the Khazars, the Patzinaks, the Cumans, with the Cumans still dominating the Ukraine as late as 1200. Each new group of barbarians established kingdoms that looked more impressive on the map than they were in reality, because each consisted of a relatively small population dominating a larger one. Either the small dominating group was shoved aside by another small group from central Asia, or it melted into the dominated group and became civilized — usually both.

Then, in 1162, there was born in central Asia one Temujin. Very slowly, he managed to gain power over first one of the Mongol tribes of central Asia and then another until, in 1206, when he was forty-four years old, he was proclaimed Jenghiz Khan (very mighty king).

He was now supreme ruler over the Mongols, who, under the new leadership, perfected their style of fighting. Their forte was mobility. On their hardy ponies from which they scarcely ever needed to dismount, they could devour the miles, strike where and when they were not expected, deliver blows too rapidly to be countered, and whirl away before the bewildered foe could mobilize their slow and stupid strength to counterattack.

What had kept the Mongols from making themselves irresistible before then was that they had fought chiefly among themselves and that they had had no leader who knew how to use their potentiality. Under the rule of Jenghiz Khan, however, all civil broils ceased, and in him, they found their military leader. Jenghiz Khan is, in fact, among the greatest captains history records. Only Alexander the Great, Hannibal, Julius Caesar, and Napoleon may fairly be compared with him, and it is quite possible that of them all, he was the greatest. He turned the Mongols into the most remarkable military machine the world had yet seen. The terror of their name grew to the point that the very word of their coming was enough to paralyze those in their path and make resistance impossible.

Before his death in 1227, Jenghiz Khan had conquered the northern half of China and the Khwarezm Empire in what is now Soviet central Asia. More, he had trained his sons and his generals to continue the conquests, which they did. His son, Ogadei Khan,

succeeded to the rule, and under him the rest of China was sub-
jugated. Meanwhile, under Batu, a grandson of Jenghiz Khan, and
Subutai, the greatest of his generals, the Mongol armies advanced
westward.

In 1223, while Jenghiz Khan still lived, a Mongol raid westward
had defeated a combined Russian-Cuman army, but that had only
been a raid. Now, in 1237, the Mongols poured into Russia. By
1240 they had taken its capital city, Kiev, and virtually all of Russia
came under their control. They moved on into Poland and Hun-
gary and, in 1241, defeated a Polish-German army at Liegnitz.
They raided into Germany and down to the Adriatic. There was
nothing that seemed able to stand against them, and, looking back
on it, there seemed no reason to suppose they could not have
swept clear to the Atlantic Ocean. What stopped the Mongols was
that the word arrived that Ogadei Khan had died, and there had
to be a vote for a successor. The armies left, and while Russia remained under Mongol rule, the territories west of Russia were
free. They had had a bad mauling, but that was all.

In the reigns of Ogadei's successors, Hulagu, another grandson
of Jenghiz, conquered what is now Iran, Iraq, and eastern Turkey.
He took Baghad in 1258. Finally, Kublai Khan (also a grandson of
Jenghiz) came to the throne in 1257 and, for a period of thirty-
seven years, ruled over a Mongol Empire that included China,
Russia, the central Asian steppes, and the Middle East. It was the
largest continuous land empire that had ever existed up to that
time and, of the empires since, only the Russian Empire, and the
Soviet Union that followed it, can rival it.

The Mongol Empire had all been built up from nothing by three
generations of rulers over a period of half a century.

If ever civilization was shaken from top to bottom by barbarian
tribesmen, this was the occasion. (And a hundred years later, there
came the Black Death — no worse one-two punch had ever been
seen.)

And yet in the end the Mongols, too, did not represent a threat.
Their wars of conquest had been bloody and ruthless, to be sure,
and were deliberately designed to cow their enemies and victims,
for the Mongols were too few in number to be able to rule over
such a broad empire unless the inhabitants had been terrified into
submission.

It had indeed been in Jenghiz Khan's mind at the start to go further than this (or so it is reported). He played with the thought of destroying the cities and converting the conquered regions into pasture land for nomadic herds.

It is doubtful if he could actually have done this, or that he would not have seen the error of this course of proceeding very soon, even if he had started. As it was, though, he never reached the point of attempting it. Being a military genius, he quickly learned the value of civilized warfare and worked out ways of using the complicated technologies required for laying siege to cities, for scaling and battering walls, and so on. It is but a step from seeing the value of civilization in connection with the arts of war to seeing the value of civilization to the arts of peace as well.

One piece of useless destruction *was* carried out, however. Hulagu's army, having taken the Tigris-Euphrates Valley, went on to wantonly destroy the intricate network of irrigation canals that had been spared by all previous conquerors and had kept the area a prosperous center of civilization for five thousand years. The Tigris-Euphrates Valley was turned into the backward and impoverished region it still is today.*

As it happened, though, the Mongols became relatively enlightened rulers, not noticeably worse than those who had preceded them and, in some cases, better. Kublai Khan, in particular, was an enlightened and humane ruler under whom vast stretches of Asia experienced a golden age such as they had not had before and were not to have again until (if we stretch a point) the twentieth century. For the first and only time, the vast Eurasian continent came under unitary control from the Baltic Sea to the Persian Gulf, and eastward in a broad path to the Pacific.

When Marco Polo, from the petty patch of land that thought of itself as "Christendom," visited the mighty realm of Cathay, he was awed and thunderstruck, and the people back home refused to believe his descriptions when he wrote them out in all sober truth.

Gunpowder to Nuclear Bombs

It was not long after the Mongol invasions, however, that the seesaw struggle between the citizen farmers and the nomad barbari-

---

*The area has been in an advantageous position in the last few decades because of the presence of oil under its soil — but that is a temporary resource.

ans swung into an apparently permanent tilt. A military advance
came along that gave civilization an edge over the barbarians that
the latter could never overtake, so that the Mongols have been
called the last of the barbarians. The invention was gunpowder, a
mixture of potassium nitrate, sulfur, and charcoal, which, for the
first time, placed an explosive in the hands of humanity.* It required an increasingly elaborate chemical industry to make gunpowder, something barbarian tribes were without.

Gunpowder apparently originated in China, for it seems to have
been used there for fireworks as early as 1160. Indeed, it may have
been the Mongol invasions, and the clear road their wide empire
left for trade, that first brought knowledge of gunpowder to
Europe.†

In Europe, however, gunpowder passed from fireworks to a propulsive mechanism. Instead of hurling rocks by catapult, using
bent wood or twisted thongs in which to store the propulsive force,
gunpowder could be placed in a closed tube (a cannon) with one
open end. The cannonball to be hurled would be placed in the
open end, and the exploding gunpowder would do the propelling.

Very primitive examples of such weapons were used on several
occasions in the fourteenth century, most notably at the Battle of
Crécy, in which the English defeated the French in the opening
stages of the Hundred Years War. Such cannons as those used at
Crécy were relatively useless, however, and the battle was decided
by the English longbowmen whose arrows were far more deadly
than the cannon of the day. Indeed, the longbow remained lord of
the battlefield (on those occasions when it was used) for another
eighty years. It won the Battle of Agincourt for the English in 1415
against a French army far superior in numbers, and a final victory
for the English at Verneuil in 1424.

Improvements in gunpowder, however, and improvements in
the design and manufacture of cannon, gradually made it possible
to get reliable gunpowder artillery, which laid waste the enemy

---

*Five centuries before, the Byzantine Empire had disposed of a chemical weapon called
"Greek Fire," a mixture of substances (the recipe is not exactly known) which could burn
on water. It was used to repel Arab and Russian fleets and several times saved
Constantinople from capture. It was not an explosive, however, but an incendiary.

†And of other important technological innovations as well, notably of paper and of the
mariner's compass.

without slaying the gunners themselves. By the latter half of the fifteenth century, gunpowder ruled the battlefield and was to do so for four more centuries.

The French developed artillery, largely to counter the longbow, and the English, who had spent eighty years slowly beating France down with those longbows, were driven out again in twenty years by the French artillery. What's more, artillery contributed importantly to the final end of feudalism in western Europe. Not only could the cannonballs beat down the walls of castles and cities without undue trouble, but only a strong central government could afford to construct and maintain an elaborate artillery train, so that little by little the great nobles found themselves forced to knuckle under to the king.

Such artillery meant, once and for all, that the menace of the barbarian was at an end. No horses, however fleet, and no lances, however sure, could stand up against the cannon mouth.

Europe was still in danger from those it was pleased to consider barbarians, but who were as civilized as Europeans were.* The Turks, for instance, had first entered the realm of the Abbasid Empire as barbarians in 840, had helped cause its disintegration (which the Mongols completed), and had survived the Mongol Empire, which had split up into deteriorating fragments soon after the death of Kublai Khan.

In the process, they had become civilized and had captured Asia Minor and sections of the Near East. In 1345, the Osmanli Turks (whose realm came to be known as the Ottoman Empire) crossed into the Balkans and established themselves in Europe — from which they were never to be entirely evicted. In 1453, the Turks captured Constantinople and put a final end to the history of the Roman Empire, but they did so with the help of better artillery than was possessed by any European power.

The conquests of Tamerlane (who claimed descent from Jenghiz Khan) had meanwhile seemed to restore the age of the Mongols, and from 1381 to 1405, he won battles in Russia, in the Middle

---

*Of course, I here use "civilized" only in the sense of possessing cities and a reasonably advanced technology. A nation or people can be civilized in that sense and barbarian in their ruthless lack of humanity. We needn't point to the Turks as an example; the best case in history is that of Germany between 1933 and 1945.

East, and in India. Himself a nomad in spirit, he used the arms and organization of the civilized regions he ruled, and (except for the brief and bloody raid into India) he never moved outside the realms that had previously been conquered by the Mongols.

After the death of Tamerlane, it was at last the turn of Europe. With gunpowder and the mariner's compass, European navigators began to descend upon the shorelines of all the continents, to occupy and populate those that were largely barbarian; to dominate those that were largely civilized. For a period of 550 years, the world became increasingly European. And when European influence began to wane, it was because non-European nations grew more Europeanized, at least in the techniques of warfare, if in nothing else.

With the Mongols, then, there came a final end to any chance (never very great) of the destruction of civilization through barbarian invasion.

Nevertheless, while civilization was defending itself against barbarism, wars between civilized powers became increasingly savage. Even before the coming of gunpowder, there were cases when civilization seemed in danger of suicide, at least in some areas. In the Second Punic War (218–201 B.C.) the Carthaginian general Hannibal ravaged Italy for sixteen years, and Italy took a long time recovering. The Hundred Years War between England and France (1338–1453) threatened to reduce France to barbarism, and the Thirty Years War (1618–1648) finally added gunpowder to the earlier horrors and wiped out half of Germany's population. These wars, however, were restricted in area, and however much Italy or France or Germany might be damaged in this century or that, civilization, as a whole, continued to expand.

But then, as the era of exploration caused European dominion to spread around the world, European wars began to affect outlying continents, and the era of world wars began. The first war which might be considered a world war in the sense that armies were engaged on different continents and on the sea — all fighting, one way or another, around issues that were interconnected — was the Seven Years War (1756–1763). In this war, Prussia and Great Britain, on one side, fought against Austria, France, Russia, Sweden, and Saxony. The major battles of the war were fought in Germany, with Prussia facing impossible odds. Prussia, however, was governed by Frederick II (the Great), the last legitimate monarch to be a military genius, and he was the victor.*

Meanwhile, however, the British and French were fighting in North America, where the war had actually started in 1755. Battles were fought in western Pennsylvania and in Quebec.

Naval battles between Great Britain and France were fought in the Mediterranean, and off both the French coast in Europe and the Indian coast in Asia. Great Britain also fought the Spaniards in the sea off Cuba and the Philippines, while land battles with France were fought in India itself. (Great Britain won, taking Canada from France, and gained an unchallenged foothold in India.)

It was the twentieth century before wars spread at least as far, if not farther, than the Seven Years War did, and at an enormous gain in intensity. World War I saw serious land fighting from France to the Middle East and naval engagements all over the ocean (though the only serious naval battle involving massed warships was fought in the North Sea). World War II saw even more intense action over larger sections of Europe and the Middle East, and over larger sections of North Africa and the Far East as well, with naval and air engagements even more widespread and far larger in scale. Nor was it the widening in scale alone that posed a heightening threat to civilization. The advancing level of technology made war weapons steadily more destructive.

The reign of gunpowder came to an end in the late nineteenth century with the invention of high explosives such as TNT, nitroglycerine, and guncotton. Indeed, the Spanish-American War of 1898 was the last war of any consequence to be fought with gunpowder. Furthermore, ships began to be ironclad and to grow larger; and they carried more powerful guns.

World War I introduced the military use of tanks and airplanes and poison gas. World War II introduced the nuclear bomb. Since World War II, intercontinental ballistic missiles, nerve gases, laser beams, and biological warfare have been developed.

What's more, though war became more extensive, and the weapons of destruction became more powerful, the level of intelligence

---

*Even his genius could not have won out, however, without British money, and without the fortunate (for him) chance that his inveterate enemy, Empress Elizabeth of Russia, died on January 5, 1762, so that Russia made peace with him.

among generals did not increase. In fact, as the complexities and destructiveness of weapons increased, and as the number of men deployed grew larger, and the intricacy of combined operations extended over larger areas multiplied enormously, the requirements of quick and intelligent decisions became vastly harder to meet, and generals fell further and further short of the requirements. Generals might not have grown stupider, but they seemed to be stupider relative to the intelligence required.

The American Civil War saw tremendous damage done by incompetent generals, but this sank to insignificance as compared to the damage done by incompetent generals in World War I, and this again decreased by comparison with some of the deadly errors in World War II.

The rule, therefore, that civilized warfare will not destroy civilization, since victors and victims alike are concerned to save the fruits of civilization, no longer applies.

First, the destructiveness of weapons has intensified to such a degree that their full use can not only destroy civilization but even, perhaps, humanity itself; second, the normal incapacity of military leaders to do their job can now lead to mistakes so enormous as to destroy civilization, and even humanity, without that actually being anyone's intention. Finally, at last, we face the one true catastrophe of the fourth class that we can reasonably fear — that an all-out thermonuclear war may somehow start and be carried on, senselessly, to the point of human suicide.

This could happen, but will it?

Let us suppose that the world's political and military leaders are sane and that they retain firm control over the nuclear arsenals. In that case, there is no real chance of nuclear war. Two nuclear bombs have been used in anger — one over Hiroshima, Japan, on August 6, 1945, and one over Nagasaki, Japan, two days later. They were the only two bombs which at that time existed and the intention was to end World War II. In that they succeeded, and there was no possibility of a nuclear counterattack at that time.

For four years the United States held the only nuclear arsenal but had no real occasion to use it, since all crises which might provoke war, such as the Soviet blockade of Berlin in 1948, were countered or neutralized without the need to call upon it.

Then, on August 29, 1949, the Soviet Union exploded its first nuclear bomb, and thereafter the possibility of a war with nuclear weapons on each side arose — a war which neither side could win — and a war which both sides well knew that neither side could win.

Attempts to get a sufficiently commanding lead to make war a reasonable possibility failed. Both sides obtained the much more dangerous hydrogen fusion bomb in 1952, both sides developed missiles and satellites, both sides maintained a steady refinement of weaponry in general.

Consequently, war between the superpowers became unthinkable. The most threatening case of a war crisis came in 1962, when the Soviet Union placed missiles on Cuba, ninety miles off the coast of Florida, so that the United States was under the threat of close-range nuclear attack. The United States imposed a naval and air blockade on Cuba and delivered a virtual ultimatum to the Soviet Union to remove those missiles. From October 22 to 28, 1962, the world was as close to nuclear war as it has ever come.

The Soviet Union backed down and removed its missiles. In return, the United States, which had supported an attempt to overthrow Cuba's revolutionary government in 1961, accepted a hands-off policy on Cuba. Each side accepted something of a backdown, which would have been unthinkable in prenuclear days.

Again, the United States fought ten years in Vietnam and finally accepted a humiliating defeat, without attempting to use nuclear weapons which would at once have destroyed the enemy. Similarly, China and the Soviet Union did not move toward direct interference in the war, but contented themselves with supporting Vietnam in ways that were far short of war, since they did not want to provoke the United States into a nuclear move.

Finally, in repeated crises in the Middle East in which the United States and the Soviet Union have been ranged on opposite sides, neither of the two superpowers has attempted direct intervention. In fact, the wars of the client-states have not been allowed to continue to the point where one side or the other might be forced to attempt direct intervention.

In short, in the nearly four decades since nuclear weapons have arrived on the scene, they have (except for the protoexplosions over Hiroshima and Nagasaki) never been used in war, and the two superpowers have gone to extraordinary lengths to avoid such use.

If this continues, we will not be destroyed by nuclear war — but will it continue? After all, there is nuclear proliferation. In addition to the United States and the Soviet Union, Great Britain, France, China, and India have built nuclear weapons. Others might follow and perhaps inevitably will. Might not a minor power start a nuclear war?

If we assume that the leaders of the minor powers are also sane, then it is hard to see why they should. To have nuclear bombs is one thing; to have a large enough arsenal to avoid swift and sure annihilation from one or the other of the superpowers is quite another. It is likely in fact that any of the minor powers which even makes the faintest gesture toward use of a nuclear bomb will have both superpowers ranged against it at once.

How far can we trust to the assumption of sanity in the world's leaders, however? Nations have, in the past, been under the leadership of psychotic personalities, and even an ordinarily sane leader might, in the grip of rage and despair, be not entirely rational. We can easily imagine someone like Adolf Hitler ordering a nuclear holocaust if the alternative were the destruction of his power, but we might also imagine his underlings refusing to carry out his orders. In point of fact, some of the orders given by Hitler in his final months were *not* carried out by his generals and administrators.

Then, too, there are some national leaders right now who seem to be fanatical enough to push the nuclear trigger if they had one to push. The point is that they don't, and I suspect they are tolerated by the world, generally, precisely because they don't.

Even if all political and military leaders remain sane, is it possible that the nuclear arsenal may get out of their control and that a nuclear war will start through the panicky or psychotic decision of an underling? Worse yet, can it start through a series of small decisions, each one of which seems the only possible response to an enemy move until, finally, the nuclear war starts with no one wanting it and everyone desperately hoping it won't come? (It was in very much this way that World War I started.)

Worst of all, is it possible that world conditions may so deteriorate that a nuclear war may seem an alternative that is preferable to doing nothing?

Undoubtedly, the only certain way to avoid a nuclear war is to destroy all nuclear weapons, and the world may yet come to that before the nuclear war takes place.

PART 9

THE BIBLE

MY THIRD HUNDRED BOOKS includes one about the Bible that I wrote at the suggestion of Paul Fargis of the Stonesong Press. It came about this way.

The well-known astronomer Robert Jastrow had published a book called God and the Astronomers, *which seemed to argue that astronomers had been making discoveries that, to their own embarrassment, tended to support the biblical view of the creation. As I read the book, however, it seemed to me that either I was mistaking Jastrow, or Jastrow was mistaking both astronomy and the Bible.*

While I was having lunch with Fargis one day, the conversation turned to Jastrow's book, and it struck Fargis that I ought to write a book of my own in which I made a careful analysis of what the Bible said about creation, and what science said. I warned Fargis that if he was expecting a book that would reconcile the two views, he would be disappointed. He told me that he expected nothing but a book, so I went ahead.

The book is In the Beginning *(Book 225), and Fargis eventually placed it with Crown, which published it in 1981.* In the Beginning *is a verse-by-verse, and sometimes word-by-word, consideration of the first eleven chapters of the Book of Genesis, the section that deals with history before Abraham.*

I interpret each verse of the Bible literally, with the meaning it must have had to those who read the Bible in ancient times, and to those literal-minded fundamentalists who read the Bible today. I then compare and contrast that interpretation with the views on the same subject that are held by contemporary scientists.

I try not to be emotional or polemical about it and to be as objective as I can, but, not surprisingly, I roused the anger of a number of people on the religious side of the divide, people who tend to possess a comparatively primitive view of the Bible. In fact, In the Beginning *was attacked by some fundamentalists in San Diego, who tried to have it barred from the city's high schools. They failed.*

I will let the book speak for itself by presenting my commentary on the very first verse of the Bible.

from IN THE BEGINNING (1981)

THE FIRST BOOK OF MOSES,[1] CALLED

Genesis[2]

CHAPTER 1[3]

1. By ancient tradition, the first five books of the Bible were written by Moses, the folk hero who, according to the account given in the second through fifth books of the Bible, rescued the Israelites from Egyptian slavery.

Modern scholars are convinced that this theory of authorship is not tenable and that the early books of the Bible are not the single work of any man, and certainly not of Moses. Rather, they are a carefully edited compilation of material from a number of sources.

The theory of multiple authorship of the Bible dates only from the nineteenth century, however.

In 1611, when King James I of England appointed fifty-four scholars to produce an English translation of the Bible suitable for English-speaking Protestants, no one questioned the tradition of the Mosaic authorship of the five books. The Bible produced by these scholars is the "Authorized Version" (authorized by the king, that is, in his capacity as head of the Anglican Church). The Authorized Version is commonly referred to as the King James Bible. It is the one I am using in this book because, even today, it is the Bible in the minds of almost all English-speaking people. There have been better translations since, to be sure, but none can match the King James Version for sheer poetry.

In the King James, the initial book of the Bible is referred to as "The First Book of Moses."

2. The First Book of Moses begins, in the original Hebrew, with the word "bereshith." It was not uncommon in biblical times to refer to a book by its first word or words. (Papal bulls, to this day, are named for the two Latin words with which they begin.)

The Hebrew name for the First Book of Moses is therefore Bereshith. Since the word happens to mean "in the beginning," and since the First Book of Moses starts its tale with the creation of the Universe, it is an apt name. (In fact, I use the phrase as the title for the book you are holding.)

The Bible was first translated into another language, Greek, in the third century B.C. In the Greek version of the Bible, the Hebrew habit of using the first words as the name was not followed, and descriptive names were used instead. The First Book of Moses was named "Genesis," a Greek word meaning "coming into being." This is also an apt name, and the Greek Genesis is commonly used as the title of the first book of the Bible, even in English translation.

3. Early manuscripts of the Bible did not divide the various books into chapters and verses. It was only little by little that such divisions appeared. The present system of chapters and verses first appeared in an English Bible in 1560.

The divisions are not always logical, but there is no way of abandoning them or changing them, for they have been used in reference, in commentaries, and in concordances for four centuries now, and one cannot wipe out the usefulness of all these books.

1 In the beginning[4] God[5] created[6] the heaven[7] and the earth.[8]

4. The very first phrase in the Bible states that there was a beginning to things.

Why not? It seems natural. Those objects with which we are familiar have a beginning. You and I were born, and before that we did not exist, at least not in our present form. The same is true of other human beings, of plants and animals, and, in fact, of all living things, as far as we know from common observation.

We are surrounded, moreover, by all the works of humanity, and all these were, in one way or another, fashioned by human beings; before that, they did not exist, at least in their fashioned form.

It seems natural to feel that if all things alive and human-fashioned had a beginning, then the rule might be universal, and that things that are neither alive nor human-fashioned might also have had a beginning.

At any rate, primitive attempts to explain the Universe start with an explanation of its beginning. This seems so natural a thing that it is doubtful if anyone ever questioned the concept of a beginning in early times, however much disagreement there may have been over the details.

And in the scientific view, there is also considered to be a beginning, not only for Earth, but for the entire Universe.

Since the Bible and science both state that heaven and Earth had a beginning, does this represent a point of agreement between them?

Yes, of course — but it is a trivial agreement. There is an enormous difference between the biblical statement of beginning and the scientific statement of beginning, which I will explain because it illuminates all subsequent agreements between the biblical and scientific points of view; and, for that matter, all subsequent disagreements.

Biblical statements rest on authority. If they are accepted as the inspired word of God, all argument ends there. There is no room for disagreement. The statement is final and absolute for all time.

A scientist, on the other hand, is committed to accepting nothing that is not backed by acceptable evidence. Even if the matter in question seems obviously certain on the face of it, it is all the better if it is backed by such evidence.

Acceptable evidence is that which can be observed and measured in such a way that subjective opinion is minimized. In other words, different people repeating the observations and measurements with different instruments at different times and in different places should come to the same conclusion. Furthermore, the deductions made from the observations and measurements must follow certain accepted rules of logic and reason.

Such evidence is scientific evidence, and ideally, scientific evidence is compelling. That is, people who study the observations and measurements, and the deductions made therefrom, feel compelled to agree with the conclusions even if, in the beginning, they felt strong doubts in the matter.

One may argue, of course, that scientific reasoning is not the only path to truth; that there are inner revelations, or intuitive grasps, or blinding insights, or overwhelming authority that all reach the truth more firmly and more surely than scientific evidence does.

That may be so, but none of these alternate paths to truth is compelling. Whatever one's internal certainty, it remains difficult

to transfer that certainty simply by saying, "But I'm *sure* of it."
Other people very often remain unsure and skeptical.

Whatever the authority of the Bible, there has never been a time
in history when more than a minority of the human species has
accepted that authority, differences in interpretation have been
many and violent, and on every possible point, no one interpretation has ever won out over all others.

So intense have been the differences and so unable has any one
group been to impress other groups with its version of the "truth"
that force has very often been resorted to. There is no need here
to go into the history of Europe's wars of religion or of the burning
of heretics, to give examples.

Science, too, has seen its share of arguments, disputes, and polemics; scientists are human, and scientific ideals (like all other
ideals) are rarely approached in practice. An extraordinary number
of such arguments, disputes, and polemics have been settled on
one side or the other, and the general scientific opinion has then
swung to that side because of compelling evidence.

And yet, no matter how compelling the evidence, it remains
true, in science, that more and better evidence may turn up, that
hidden errors and false assumptions may be uncovered, that an
unexpected incompleteness may make itself visible, and that yesterday's "firm" conclusion may suddenly twist and change into a
deeper and better conclusion.

It follows, then, that the biblical statement that Earth and
heaven had a beginning is authoritative and absolute, but not compelling; while the scientific statement that Earth and heaven had
a beginning is compelling, but not authoritative and absolute.
There is a disagreement there that is deeper and more important
than the superficial agreement of the words themselves.

And even the superficial agreement of the words themselves dis-
appears as soon as we ask a further question.

For instance, if we grant the existence of a beginning, suppose
we ask just *when* that beginning took place.

The Bible does not tell us when, directly. Indeed, the Bible does
not date a single event in any of the books of the King James Version in any way that would help us tie those events into a specific
time in the system of chronology we use.

Nevertheless, the question of when the Creation took place has aroused curiosity, and various biblical scholars have made every effort to deduce its date by using various statements found in the Bible as indirect evidence.

They did not come to precisely the same answer. The generally accepted conclusion among Jewish scholars, for instance, was that the date of the Creation was October 7, 3761 B.C.

James Ussher, the Anglican archbishop of Armagh, Ireland, decided in 1645, on the other hand, that the Creation took place at 9:00 A.M. on October 23, 4004 B.C. (Ussher's calculations for this and for the dating of other events in the Bible are usually found in all the page headings of the King James Bible.) Other calculations put the Creation as far back as 5509 B.C.

Thus, the usual estimates for the age of the heaven and Earth from biblical data run from about fifty-seven hundred to seventy-five hundred years. It is over this point that the biblical conclusions represent an enormous disagreement with the conclusions of science.

The weight of scientific evidence is that Earth, and the Solar System generally, came into being in approximately their present form about 4.6 billion years ago. The Universe, generally, came into being, it would seem, about 15 billion years ago.

The age of Earth, then, according to science, is about six hundred thousand times the age according to the Bible, and the age of the Universe, according to science, is at least two million times the age according to the Bible.

In the light of the discrepancy, the mere agreement between the Bible and science that there was, in fact, a beginning, loses most of its value.

5. God is introduced at once as the motive force behind the Universe. His existence is taken for granted in the Bible, and one might, indeed, argue that the existence of God is self-evident.

Consider: All living things are born through the activities of previous living things. If there was, indeed, a beginning, as the Bible and science both agree, how then did the first living things come into existence?

If there was indeed a beginning, how did all the natural objects — land and sea, hills and valleys, sky and earth — come into being? All artificial objects were fashioned by human beings; who or what then fashioned natural objects?

The usual manner in which this is presented is something like,

"A watch implies a watchmaker." Since it is inconceivable that an object as intricate as a watch came into being spontaneously, it must therefore have been fashioned; how much more must something as intricate as the Universe have been fashioned!

In early times, the analogy was drawn much more tightly. Since human beings can, by blowing, create a tiny wind rushing out of their nostrils and mouths, the wind in nature must, by analogy, be the product of a much more powerful being blowing through nostrils and mouth. If a horse-and-chariot is a common way of progressing over land, then a glowing horse-and-chariot must be the means by which the Sun is carried over the sky.

In the myths, every natural phenomenon is likely to have a humanlike creature performing functions analogous to those of the human actions we know, so that *nothing* in nature takes place spontaneously.

These myriad specialized divinities were often pictured as at odds with each other and as producing a disorderly Universe. As thought grew deeper, the tendency was to suppose one divine being who is responsible for everything, who directs humanity, Earth, and the whole Universe, combining it all into a harmonious whole directed toward some specific end.

It is this sophisticated picture of a monotheistic God that the Bible presents — but one who constantly engages himself in the minutiae of his creation. Even under a monotheistic religion, popular thought imagines myriad angels and saints taking on specialized functions so that a form of polytheism (under a supreme monarch) exists.

In the last four centuries, however, scientists have built up an alternate picture of the Universe. The Sun doesn't move across the sky; its apparent motion is due to Earth's rotation. The wind doesn't have to be produced by giant lungs; its existence arises through the spontaneous action of air subjected to uneven heating by the Sun. In other words, a moving Sun does not imply a horse-and-chariot, after all; nor does the wind imply the mouth of a blower.

The natural phenomena of Earth and of the Universe have seemed to fall into place bit by bit as behavior that is random, spontaneous, unwilled, and that takes place within the constraints of the "laws of nature."

Scientists grew increasingly reluctant to suppose that the workings of the laws of nature were ever interfered with (something that would be defined as a "miracle"). Certainly, no such interference was ever observed, and the tales of such interferences in the past came to seem increasingly dubious.

In short, the scientific view sees the Universe as following its own rules blindly, without either interference or direction.

That still leaves it possible that God created the Universe to begin with and designed the laws of nature that govern its behavior. From this standpoint, the Universe might be viewed as a wind-up toy, which God has wound up once and for all and which is now winding down and working itself out in all its intricacy without having to be touched at all.

If so, that reduces God's involvement to a minimum and makes one wonder if He is needed at all.

So far, scientists have not uncovered any evidence that would hint that the workings of the Universe require the action of a divine being. On the other hand, scientists have uncovered no evidence that indicates that a divine being does *not* exist.

If scientists have not proved either that God exists or that He does not exist, then, from the scientific viewpoint, are we entitled to believe either alternative?

Not really. It is not reasonable to demand proof of a negative and to accept the positive in the absence of such a proof. After all, if science has not succeeded in proving that God does not exist, neither has it succeeded in proving that Zeus does not exist, or Marduk, or Thoth, or any of the myriads of gods postulated by all sorts of mythmakers. If the failure of proof of nonexistence is taken as proof of existence, then we must conclude that *all* exist.

Yet that leaves us with the final, nagging question: "But where did all this come from? How did the Universe come into being in the first place?"

If one tries to answer, "The Universe was always there; it is eternal," then one comes up against the uncomfortable concept of eternity and the irresistible assumption that everything had to have a beginning.

Out of sheer exhaustion one longs to solve everything by saying, "God made the Universe!" That gives us a start, at least.

But then we find that we have escaped eternity only by postulating it, for we are not even allowed to ask the question, "Who made God?" The question itself is blasphemous. God is eternal, by definition.

If, then, we are going to be stuck with eternity in any case, there seems some advantage to a science that lives by observing and measuring to choose an eternal something that can at least be observed and measured — the Universe itself, rather than God.

The notion of an eternal Universe introduces a great many difficulties, some of them apparently (at least in the present state of our scientific knowledge) insuperable, but scientists are not disturbed by difficulties — those make up the game. If all the difficulties were gone and all the questions answered, the game of science would be over. (Scientists suspect that will never happen.)

There, then, is perhaps the most fundamental disagreement between the Bible and science. The Bible describes a Universe created by God, maintained by Him, and intimately and constantly directed by Him, while science describes a Universe in which it is not necessary to postulate the existence of God at all.

This is *not* to say, by the way, that scientists are all atheists or that any of them must be atheists of necessity. Many scientists are as firmly religious as any nonscientist. Nevertheless, such scientists, if they are competent professionals, must operate on two levels. Whatever their faith in God in ordinary life, they must leave God out of account while engaged in their scientific observations. They can never explain a particular puzzling phenomenon by claiming it to be the result of God's suspension of natural law.

6. The first act of God recorded in the Bible is that of the creation of the Universe. But since God is eternal, there must have been an infinitely long period of time before He set our Universe into motion. What was He doing during that infinitely long period of time?

When Saint Augustine was asked that question, he is supposed to have roared, "Creating Hell for those who ask questions like that!"

Ignoring Saint Augustine (if we dare), we might speculate. God might, for instance, have spent the time creating an endless hierarchy of angels. For that matter, He might have created an endless number of universes, one after the other, each for its own purpose, with our own being merely the current member of the series, to be followed by an equally endless number of successors. Or God might, until the moment of the Creation, have done nothing but commune with His infinite self.

All possible answers to the question are merely suppositions, however, since there is no evidence for any one of them. There is not only no scientific evidence for them; there is not even any biblical evidence. The answers belong entirely to the world of legend.

But then if we switch to the world of science and think of an eternal Universe, we must ask what the Universe was like before it took on its present form about 15 billion years ago. There are some speculations. The Universe may have existed through eternity as an infinitely thin scattering of matter and energy that very slowly coalesced into a tiny dense object, the "cosmic egg," which exploded to form the Universe we now have, a Universe that will expand forever until it is an infinitely thin scattering of matter and energy again.

Or else there is an alternation of expansion and contraction, an endless series of cosmic eggs, each of which explodes to form a Universe. Our own present Universe is only the current member of an endless series.

Science, however, has found no way as yet of penetrating into a time earlier than that of the cosmic egg that exploded to form our Universe. The Bible and science agree in being unable to say anything certain about what happened before the beginning.

There is this difference. The Bible will never be able to tell us. It has reached its final form, and it simply doesn't say. Science, on the other hand, is still developing, and the time may come when it can answer questions that, at present, it cannot.

7. By heaven, in this verse, is meant the vault of the sky and the permanent objects within it — the Sun, Moon, planets, and stars. The Bible views this vault as the Babylonians did (and the Egyptians, the Greeks, and all the early peoples, apparently without exception); that is, as a solid, semicircular dome overspreading Earth. This is the biblical view throughout. Thus, in Revelation, the last book of the Bible, the final end of the heaven is described thus: "The heaven departed as a scroll when it is rolled together" (Revelation 6:14). This quoted a passage in the Old Testament (Isaiah 34:4) and clearly shows the heaven to have been viewed as no thicker, in proportion to its extent, than a sheet of parchment.

In the scientific view, however, the sky is not a simple vault, but is a vast outstretching of space-time into which our telescopes have probed for distances of 10 billion light-years, where each light-year is 5.88 trillion miles long.

8. The "heaven and the Earth" form a definite geometrical shape in the Bible. The Earth is a flat, probably circular, area of extent large enough to hold those kingdoms known to the biblical writers. The heaven is a semispherical vault that nestles down over the Earth. Human beings, by this picture, seem to live on the floor of a world that is inside a hollow semisphere.

It is so described in the Book of Isaiah: "It is he [God] that sitteth upon the circle of the earth . . . that stretcheth out the heavens as a curtain, and spreadeth them out as a tent to dwell in" (Isaiah 40:22.).

The vault of heaven would require support to keep it from collapsing, if we judge from earthly structures. The support might be a supernatural being (like the Greek myth of Atlas) or something more mechanical. The Bible has a passage that reads, "The pillars of heaven tremble" (Job 26:11).

All this is utterly different from the scientific view of Earth as a sphere, suspended in emptiness, that rotates on its axis, revolves about the Sun, takes part in the Sun's revolution about the center of the Galaxy, and is surrounded by a largely empty and virtually illimitable Universe.

PART 10

SHORT-SHORTS

SHORT-SHORT STORIES are not a particular favorite of mine, but there are times when I can't resist. Every once in a while I think of a play on words — a spoonerism, a twisted saying, something. Often such a thing strikes me as too clever, too deliciously outrageous, to be allowed to die, so I feverishly think up a few hundred words that will give me an excuse to put it down.

There are, for instance, three short-shorts in my collection The Winds of Change and Other Stories *(Book 267), a book I mentioned earlier, which end with distortions of an often-repeated phrase. You will recognize the undistorted phrase at once, and I suppose that one of the pleasures in reading such stories is the attempt to anticipate the distortion before it comes. If you succeed in the anticipation you are sure to sneer at the last line. If you fail, you are sure to groan.*

But I want neither reaction. I want you to laugh, do you hear me? I want you to laugh.

The first is "About Nothing," which is only 250 words long. The second, "Sure Thing," deals with extraterrestrial creatures. The third is "Death of a Foy," which made me *laugh. In fact, I kept laughing, on and off, for days after I had written it.*

I am also including a fourth short-short for the collection — "How It Happened" *— simply because it* doesn't *depend on a final kicker. It is, I think, funny all the way through.*

from THE WINDS OF CHANGE AND OTHER STORIES (1983)

About Nothing

All of Earth waited for the small black hole to bring it to its end. It had been discovered by Professor Jerome Hieronymus at the lunar telescope in 2125, and it was clearly going to make an approach close enough for total tidal destruction.

All of Earth made its wills and wept on each others' shoulders, saying, "Good-bye, good-bye, good-bye." Husbands said good-bye to their wives, brothers said good-bye to their sisters, parents said good-bye to their children, owners said good-bye to their pets, and lovers whispered good-bye to each other.

But as the black hole approached, Hieronymus noted there was no gravitational effect. He studied it more closely and announced, with a chuckle, that it was not a black hole after all.

"It's nothing," he said. "Just an ordinary asteroid someone has painted black."

He was killed by an infuriated mob, but not for that. He was killed only after he publicly announced that he would write a great and moving play about the whole episode.

He said, "I shall call it *Much Adieu About Nothing*."

All humanity applauded his death.

Sure Thing

As is well known, in this thirtieth century of ours, space travel is fearfully dull and time-consuming. In search of diversion many crew members defy the quarantine restrictions and pick up pets from the various habitable worlds they explore.

Jim Sloane had a rockette, which he called Teddy. It just sat there looking like a rock, but sometimes it lifted a lower edge and sucked in powdered sugar. That was all it ate. No one ever saw it move, but every once in a while it wasn't quite where people thought it was. There was a theory it moved when no one was looking.

Bob Laverty had a heliworm he called Dolly. It was green and carried on photosynthesis. Sometimes it moved to get into better light, and when it did so it coiled its wormlike body and inched along very slowly like a turning helix.

One day, Jim Sloane challenged Bob Laverty to a race. "My Teddy," he said, "can beat your Dolly."

"Your Teddy," scoffed Laverty, "doesn't move."

"Bet!" said Sloane.

The whole crew got into the act. Even the captain risked half a credit. Everyone bet on Dolly. At least it moved.

Jim Sloane covered it all. He had been saving his salary through three trips, and he put every millicredit of it on Teddy.

The race started at one end of the Grand Salon. At the other end, a heap of sugar had been placed for Teddy and a spotlight for Dolly. Dolly formed a coil at once and began to spiral its way very slowly toward the light. The watching crew cheered it on.

Teddy just sat there without budging.

"Sugar, Teddy. Sugar," said Sloane, pointing. Teddy did not move. It looked more like a rock than ever, but Sloane did not seem concerned.

Finally, when Dolly had spiraled halfway across the salon, Jim Sloane said casually to the rockette, "If you don't get out there, Teddy, I'm going to get a hammer and chip you into pebbles."

That was when people first discovered that rockettes could read minds. That was also when people first discovered that rockettes could teleport.

Sloane had no sooner made his threat when Teddy simply disappeared from his place and reappeared on top of the sugar.

Sloane won, of course, and counted his winnings slowly and luxuriously.

Laverty said, bitterly, "You *knew* the damn thing could teleport."

"No, I didn't," said Sloane, "but I knew he would win. It was a sure thing."

"How come?"

"It's an old saying everyone knows. Sloane's Teddy wins the race."

Death of a Foy

It was extremely unusual for a Foy to be dying on Earth. They were the highest social class on their planet (with a name which was pronounced — as nearly as earthly throats could make the sounds — Sortibackenstrete) and were virtually immortal.

Every Foy, of course, came to voluntary death eventually, and this one had given up because of an ill-starred love affair, if you can call it a love affair where five individuals, in order to reproduce, must indulge in a year-long mental contact. Apparently, he himself had not fit into the contact after several months of trying, and it had broken his heart — or hearts, for he had five.

All Foys had five large hearts, and there was speculation that it was this that made them virtually immortal.

Maude Briscoe, Earth's most renowned surgeon, wanted those hearts. "It can't be just their number and size, Dwayne," she said to her chief assistant. "It has to be something physiological or biochemical. I must have them."

"I don't know if we can manage that," said Dwayne Johnson. "I've been speaking to him earnestly, trying to overcome the Foy taboo against dismemberment after death. I've had to play on the feeling of tragedy any Foy would have over death away from home. And I've had to lie to him, Maude."

"Lie?"

"I told him that after death, there would be a dirge sung for him by the world-famous choir led by Harold J. Gassenbaum. I told him that by earthly belief this would mean that his astral essence would be instantaneously wafted back, through hyperspace, to his home planet of Sortib-what's-its-name. — Provided he would sign a release allowing you, Maude, to have his hearts for scientific investigation."

"Don't tell me he believed that horse excrement!" said Maude.

"Well, you know this modern attitude about accepting the myths and beliefs of intelligent aliens. It wouldn't have been polite for him not to believe me. Besides, the Foys have a profound admiration for terrestrial science, and I think this one is a little flattered that we should want his hearts. He promised to consider the suggestion, and I hope he decides soon because he can't live more than another day or so, and we must have his permission by interstellar law, and the hearts must be fresh, and — ah, his signal."

Dwayne Johnson moved in with smooth and noiseless speed.

"Yes?" he whispered, unobtrusively turning on the holographic recording device in case the Foy wished to grant permission.

The Foy's large, gnarled, rather treelike body lay motionless on the bed. The bulging eyes palpitated (all five of them) as they rose, each on its stalk, and turned toward Dwayne. The Foy's voice had a strange tone, and the lipless edges of his open, round mouth did not move, but the words formed perfectly. His eyes were making the Foyan gesture of assent as he said:

"Give my big hearts to Maude, Dwayne. Dismember me for Harold's choir. Tell all the Foys on Sortibackenstrete that I will soon be there —"

How It Happened

My brother began to dictate in his best oratorical style, the one which has the tribes hanging on his words.

"In the beginning," he said, "exactly fifteen point two billion years ago, there was a big bang and the Universe —"

But I had stopped writing. "Fifteen billion years ago?" I said incredulously.

"Absolutely," he said. "I'm inspired."

"I don't question your inspiration," I said. (I had better not. He's three years younger than I am, but I don't try questioning his inspiration. Neither does anyone else or there's hell to pay.) "But are you going to tell the story of the Creation over a period of fifteen billion years?"

"I have to," said my brother. "That's how long it took. I have it all in here" — he tapped his forehead — "and it's on the very highest authority."

By now I had put down my stylus. "Do you know the price of papyrus?" I said.

"What?" (He may be inspired, but I frequently noticed that the inspiration didn't include such sordid matters as the price of papyrus.)

I said, "Suppose you describe one million years of events to each roll of papyrus. That means you'll have to fill fifteen thousand rolls. You'll have to talk long enough to fill them, and you know that you begin to stammer after a while. I'll have to write enough to fill them, and my fingers will fall off. And even if we can afford all that papyrus and you have the voice and I have the strength, who's going to copy it? We've got to have a guarantee of a hundred copies before we can publish, and without that where will we get royalties from?"

My brother thought a while. He said, "You think I ought to cut it down?"

"Way down," I said, "if you expect to reach the public."

"How about a hundred years?" he said.

"How about six days?" I said.

He said, horrified, "You can't squeeze Creation into six days."

I said, "This is all the papyrus I have. What do *you* think?"

"Oh, well," he said, and began to dictate again, "In the beginning — Does it have to be six days, Aaron?"

I said, firmly, "Six days, Moses."

PART 11

HUMOR

IN MY SECOND HUNDRED BOOKS, no fewer than four volumes were devoted to bawdy limericks. In my third hundred, however, there is only one: A Grossery of Limericks *(Book 240), published by W. W. Norton & Company. John Ciardi and I collaborated on this one (as on one of the earlier ones). In it are 144 of my limericks and 144 of John Ciardi's. I shall quote five of mine: Numbers 5, 36, 43, 50, and 103.*

Of these, I quote Number 43 most often because I meet so many charming young women named Linda. After I quote it, I always say that what the girl in the limerick was doing in front of the window was combing her hair, and I always receive a disbelieving stare. I haven't the faintest idea what all those Lindas to whom I recite the verse think she was doing.

As for Number 103, I once offered it to the New York Times *at the time of the hostage episode, and they might have printed it but for fear of provoking an international crisis.*

from A Grossery of Limericks (1981)

5. *Symmetry*
To moralists, sex is a sin,
Yet nature suggests we begin.
  She arranged it, no doubt,
  That a fellow juts out
In the place where a damsel juts in.

36. *Standing Ovation*
There was a young woman named Dawes
Whose costume was made all of gauze.
  When they turned on the light
  Behind her one night,
All the fellows broke into applause.

43. *Mind Your Own Business*
There was a young woman named Linda
Who did it in front of the winda.
  The guys passing by
  Would give her the eye
But she didn't allow it to hinda.

50. *The Table Round*
There was once a great knight named Sir Lancelot
Who placed Queen Guinevere in a trance a lot.
  But what bothered the King
  Was: he managed the thing
By serenely removing his pants a lot.

103. *Scraping the Bottom of the Barrel*
There was a young woman named Janey
And no one alive is less brainy.
  In her search for a man
  She has gone to Iran
To wed Ayatollah Khomeini.

Among the anthologies included in my third hundred books, one is devoted entirely to humorous science fiction. It is a large book that contains cartoons and comic verse as well as stories. It is beautifully designed, but this is not surprising, considering that it was published by Houghton Mifflin Company. The title is Laughing Space, *and it was published in 1982.*

The most important thing about the book was that I did it in collaboration with my wife, Janet, who used her maiden name, J. O. Jeppson, for the purpose.

Janet, who is a psychiatrist, is also a science fiction writer. She has two published novels to her credit, The Second Experiment *and* The Last Immortal *(both published by Houghton Mifflin), and a number of published short stories that include fantasies and mysteries, as well as science fiction.*

Janet did most of the work in connection with the anthology, selecting and arranging the many items and going through endless editorial conferences. I was consulted now and then, and I wrote the general introduction and the headnotes.

Included in the anthology is the funniest story Janet has yet writ-
ten, "A Pestilence of Psychoanalysts," but I cannot include it here
since this book is devoted to my own writing. However, she and I
wrote in collaboration, especially for the book, its second item, a
triple-limerick on a subject that is close to each of our hearts. I
include it here, as one of only two pieces of writing in the book
that are collaborations, but both are with my own darling wife,
and I think that is permissible.

from LAUGHING SPACE (1982)

A Fuller Explanation of Original Sin

In the innocent primeval sea
Terra's cells lived quite singly — and free
　　From all risk of perdition
　　Since they used only fission
Reproducing — but suffered ennui.

Some adventurous cells said, "We'll grow —
Not alone, though, for that's status quo.
　　Let's become he and she,
　　Multicellularly —
So hold on to each other — let's go!"

Then together they clung; grew complex.
Fully half went concave, half convex;
　　And it all proved complete
　　When each came into heat
And announced the invention of sex.

I do not want you to think that my only efforts at humor involve
limericks. Many of my stories have elements of humor in them, and
some are entirely humorous (at least in intent). Chief among these
in recent years have been my George and Azazel stories, George
being a lovable ne'er-do-well and Azazel the tiny extraterrestrial

creature who helps him out now and then. The funniest of these stories (in my own opinion) is "The Smile That Loses." It is included in The Winds of Change and Other Stories *(Book 267), which I bring up now for the last time, I promise you.*

from THE WINDS OF CHANGE AND OTHER STORIES *(1983)*

The Smile That Loses

I said to my friend George over a beer recently (*his* beer; I was having a ginger ale), "How's your implet these days?"

George claims he has a two-centimeter-tall demon at his beck and call. I can never get him to admit he's lying. Neither can anyone else.

He glared at me balefully, then said, "Oh, yes, you're the one who knows about it! I hope you haven't told anyone else!"

"Not a word," I said. "It's quite sufficient that I think you're crazy. I don't need anyone thinking the same of me." (Besides, he has told at least half a dozen people about the demon, to my personal knowledge, so there's no necessity of *my* being indiscreet.)

George said, "I wouldn't have your unlovely inability to believe anything you don't understand — and you don't understand so much — for the worth of a pound of plutonium. And what would be left of you, if my demon ever found out you called him an implet, wouldn't be worth an atom of plutonium."

"Have you figured out his real name?" I asked, unperturbed by this dire warning.

"Can't! It's unpronounceable by any earthly pair of lips. The translation is, I am given to understand, something like: 'I am the King of Kings; look upon my works, ye mighty, and despair.' — It's a lie, of course," said George, staring moodily at his beer. "He's small potatoes in his world. That's why he's so cooperative here. In *our* world, with our primitive technology, he can show off."

"Has he shown off lately?"

"Yes, as a matter of fact," said George, heaving an enormous sigh and raising his bleak blue eyes to mine. His ragged, white mustache settled down only slowly from the typhoon of that forced exhalation of breath.

♦

It started with Rosie O'Donnell [said George], a friend of a niece of mine, and a fetching little thing altogether.

She had blue eyes, almost as brilliant as my own; russet hair, long and lustrous; a delightful little nose, powdered with freckles in the manner approved of by all who write romances; a graceful neck; a slender figure that wasn't opulent in any disproportionate way, but was utterly delightful in its promise of ecstasy.

Of course, all of this was of purely intellectual interest to me, since I reached the age of discretion years ago, and now engage in the consequences of physical affection only when women insist upon it, which, thank the fates, is not oftener than an occasional weekend or so.

Besides which, Rosie had recently married — and, for some reason, adored in the most aggravating manner — a large Irishman who does not attempt to hide the fact that he is a very muscular, and, possibly, bad-tempered person. While I had no doubt that I would have been able to handle him in my younger days, the sad fact was that I was no longer in my younger days — by a short margin.

It was, therefore, with a certain reluctance that I accepted Rosie's tendency to mistake me for some close friend of her own sex and her own time of life, and to make me the object of her girlish confidences.

Not that I blame her, you understand. My natural dignity, and the fact that I inevitably remind people of one or more of the nobler of the Roman emperors in appearance, automatically attracts beautiful young women to me. Nevertheless, I never allowed it to go too far. I always made sure there was plenty of space between Rosie and myself, for I wanted no fables or distortions to reach the undoubtedly large, and possibly bad-tempered, Kevin O'Donnell.

"Oh, George," said Rosie one day, clapping her little hands with glee, "you have no idea what a *darling* my Kevin is, and how happy he makes me. Do you know what he does?"

"I'm not sure," I began cautiously, naturally expecting indelicate disclosures, "that you ought to —"

She paid no attention. "He has a way of crinkling up his nose and making his eyes twinkle, and smiling brightly, till everything about him looks so happy. It's as though the whole world turns into golden sunshine. Oh, if I only had a photograph of him exactly like that. I've tried to take one, but I never catch him quite right."

I said, "Why not be satisfied with the real thing, my dear?"

"Oh, well!" She hesitated, then said, with the most charming blush, "he's not *always* like that, you know. He's got a *very* difficult job at the airport, and sometimes he comes home just worn out and exhausted, and then he becomes just a little touchy, and scowls at me a bit. If I had a photograph of him, as he really is, it would be such a comfort to me. — *Such* a comfort." And her blue eyes misted over with unshed tears.

I must admit that I had the merest trifle of an impulse to tell her of Azazel (that's what I call him, because I'm not going to call him by what he tells me the translation of his real name is) and to explain what he might do for her.

However, I'm unutterably discreet — I haven't the faintest notion how *you* managed to find out about my demon.

Besides, it was easy for me to fight off the impulse for I am a hard-shelled, realistic human being, not given to silly sentiment. I admit I have a semisoft spot in my rugged heart for sweet young women of extraordinary beauty — in a dignified and avuncular manner — mostly. And it occurred to me that, after all, I could oblige her without actually telling her about Azazel. — Not that she would have disbelieved me, of course, for I am a man whose words carry conviction with all but those who, like you, are psychotic.

I referred the matter to Azazel, who was by no means pleased. He said, "You keep asking for abstractions."

I said, "Not at all. I ask for a simple photograph. All you have to do is materialize it."

"Oh, is that all I have to do? If it's that simple, *you* do it. I trust you understand the nature of mass-energy equivalence."

"Just *one* photograph."

"Yes, and with an expression of something you can't even define or describe."

"I've never seen him look at me the way he would look at his wife, naturally. But I have infinite faith in your ability."

I rather expected that a helping of sickening praise would fetch him round. He said, sulkily, "You'll have to take the photograph."

"I couldn't get the proper —"

"You don't have to. I'll take care of that, but it would be much easier if I had a material object on which to focus the abstraction. A photograph, in other words; one of the most inadequate kind, even; the sort I would expect of you. And only *one* copy, of course. I cannot manage more than that and I will not sprain my subjunctival muscle for you or for any other pinheaded being in your world."

Oh, well, he's frequently crotchety. I expect that's simply to establish the importance of his role and impress you with the fact that you must not take him for granted.

I met the O'Donnells the next Sunday, on their way back from Mass. (I lay in wait for them, actually.) They were willing to let me snap a picture of them in their Sunday finery. She was delighted and he looked a bit grumpy about it. After that, just as unobtrusively as possible, I took a head shot of Kevin. There was no way I could get him to smile or dimple or crinkle or whatever it was that Rosie found so attractive, but I didn't feel that mattered. I wasn't even sure that the camera was focused correctly. After all, I'm not one of your great photographers.

I then visited a friend of mine who was a photography wiz. He developed both snaps and enlarged the head shot to an eight by eleven.

He did it rather grumpily, muttering something about how busy he was, though I paid no attention to that. After all, what possible value can his foolish activities have in comparison to the important matters that occupied me? I'm always surprised at the number of people who don't understand this.

When he completed the enlargement, however, he changed his attitude entirely. He stared at it and said, in what I can only describe as a completely offensive tone, "Don't tell me you managed to take a photo like this."

"Why not?" I said, and held out my hand for it, but he made no move to give it to me.

"You'll want more copies," he said.

"No, I won't," I said, looking over his shoulder. It was a remarkably clear photograph in brilliant color. Kevin O'Donnell was smiling, though I didn't remember such a smile at the time I snapped it. He seemed good-looking and cheerful, but I was rather indifferent to that. Perhaps a woman might observe more, or a man like my photographer friend — who, as it happened, did not have my firm grasp on masculinity — might do so.

He said, "Just one more — for me."

"No," I said firmly, and took the picture, grasping his wrist to make sure he would not withdraw it. "*And* the negative, please. You can keep the other one — the distance shot."

"I don't want *that*," he said, petulantly, and was looking quite woebegone as I left.

I framed the picture, put it on my mantelpiece, and stepped back to look at it. There was, indeed, a remarkable glow about it. Azazel had done a good job.

What would Rosie's reaction be, I wondered. I phoned her and asked if I could drop by. It turned out that she was going shopping but if I could be there within the hour —

I could, and I was. I had the photo gift-wrapped, and handed it to her without a word.

"My goodness!" she said, even as she cut the string and tore off the wrapping. "What is this? Is there some celebration, or —"

By then she had it out, and her voice died away. Her eyes widened and her breath became shorter and more rapid. Finally, she whispered, "Oh my!"

She looked up at me. "Did you take this photograph last Sunday?"

I nodded.

"But you caught him exactly. He's a*dor*able. That's *just* the look. Oh, may I *please* keep it?"

"I brought it for you," I said, simply.

She threw her arms about me and kissed me hard on the lips. Unpleasant, of course, for a person like myself who detests sentiment, and I had to wipe my mustache afterward, but I could understand her inability to resist the gesture.

I didn't see Rosie for about a week afterward.

Then I met her outside the butcher shop one afternoon, and it would have been impolite not to offer to carry the shopping bag home for her. Naturally, I wondered whether that would mean another kiss, and I decided it would be rude to refuse if the dear little thing insisted. She looked somewhat downcast, however.

"How's the photograph?" I asked, wondering whether, perhaps, it had not worn well.

She cheered up at once. "Perfect! I have it on my record player stand, at an angle such that I can see it when I'm at my chair at the dining room table. His eyes just look at me a little slantwise, so *roguishly* and his nose has *just* the right crinkle. Honestly, you'd swear he was alive. And some of my friends can't keep their eyes off it. I'm thinking I should hide it when they come, or they'll steal it."

"They might steal *him*," I said, jokingly.

The glumness returned. She shook her head and said, "I don't think so."

I tried another tack. "What does Kevin think of the photo?"

"He hasn't said a word. Not a word. He's not a visual person, you know. I wonder if he sees it at all."

"Why don't you point it out and ask him what he thinks?"

She was silent while I trudged along beside her for half a block, carrying that heavy shopping bag and wondering if she'd expect a kiss in addition.

"Actually," she said suddenly, "he's having a lot of tension at work so it wouldn't be a good time to ask him. He gets home late and hardly talks to me. Well, you know how men are." She tried to put a tinkle in her laughter, but failed.

We had reached her apartment house and I turned the bag over to her. She said, wistfully, "But thank you once again, and over and over, for the photograph."

Off she went. She didn't ask for a kiss, and I was so lost in thought that I didn't notice that fact till I was halfway home and it seemed silly to return merely to keep her from being disappointed.

About ten more days passed, and then she called me one morning. Could I drop in and have lunch with her? I held back and pointed out that it would be indiscreet. What would the neighbors think?

"Oh, that's silly," she said. "You're so incredibly old — I mean, you're such an incredibly old friend, that they couldn't possibly — Besides, I want your advice." It seemed to me she was suppressing a sob as she said that.

Well, one must be a gentleman, so I was in her sunny little

apartment at lunchtime. She had prepared ham and cheese sand-wiches and slivers of apple pie, and there was the photograph on the record player as she had said.

She shook hands with me and made no attempt to kiss me, which would have relieved me were it not for the fact that I was too dis-turbed at her appearance to feel any relief. She looked absolutely haggard. I ate half a sandwich, waiting for her to speak, and when she didn't, I was forced to ask outright for the reason there was such a heavy atmosphere of gloom about her.

I said, "Is it Kevin?" I was sure it was.

She nodded and burst into tears. I patted her hand and won-dered if that were enough. I stroked her shoulder abstractedly, and she finally said, "I'm afraid he's going to lose his job."

"Surely not. Why?"

"Well, he's so *savage;* even at work, apparently. He hasn't smiled for ages. He hasn't kissed me, or said a kind word, since I don't remember when. He quarrels with *everyone,* and *all* the time. He won't tell me what's wrong, and he gets furious if I ask. A friend of ours, who works at the airport with Kevin, called up yesterday. He says that Kevin is acting so sullen and unhappy at the job that the higher-ups are noticing. I'm *sure* he'll lose his job, but what can I *do?*"

I had been expecting something like this ever since our last meeting, actually, and I knew I would simply have to tell her the truth — damn that Azazel. I cleared my throat. "Rosie — the pho-tograph —"

"Yes, I know," she said, snatching it up and hugging it to her breasts. "It's what keeps me going. This is the *real* Kevin, and I'll always have him, *always,* no matter what happens." She began to sob.

I found it very hard to say what had to be said, but there was no way out. I said, "You don't understand, Rosie. It's the photograph that's the problem. I'm sure of it. All that charm and cheerfulness in the photograph had to come from somewhere. It had to be scraped off Kevin himself. Don't you understand?"

Rosie stopped sobbing. "What are you *talking* about? A photo-graph is just the light being focused, and film, and things like that."

"Ordinarily, yes, but *this* photograph —" I gave up. I knew Aza-zel's shortcomings. He couldn't create the magic of the photograph out of nothing, but I wasn't sure I could explain the science of it, the law of conservation of merriment, to Rosie.

"Let me put it this way," I said. "As long as that photograph sits there, Kevin will be unhappy, angry, and bad-tempered."

"But it certainly *will* sit there," said Rosie, putting it firmly back in its place, "and I can't see why you're saying such crazy things about the one wonderful object — Here, I'll make some coffee." She flounced off to the kitchen and I could see she was in a most offended state of mind.

I did the only thing I could possibly do. After all, I had been the one who had snapped the photograph. I was responsible — through Azazel — for its arcane properties. I snatched up the frame quickly, carefully removed the backing, then the photo itself. I tore the photograph across into two pieces — four — eight — sixteen, and placed the final scraps of paper in my pocket.

The telephone rang just as I finished, and Rosie bustled into the living room to answer. I restored the backing and set the frame back in place. It sat there, blankly empty.

I heard Rosie's voice squealing with excitement and happiness.

"Oh, Kevin," I heard her say, "how wonderful! Oh, I'm so glad! But why didn't you tell me? Don't you *ever* do that again!"

She came back, pretty face glowing. "Do you know what that terrible Kevin did? He's had a kidney stone for nearly three weeks now — seeing a doctor and all — and in terrible, nagging pain, and facing possible surgery — and he wouldn't tell me for fear it would cause me worry. The idiot! No wonder he was so miserable, and it never once occurred to him that his misery made me far more unhappy than knowing about it would have. Honestly! A man shouldn't be allowed out without a keeper."

"But why are you so happy now?"

"Because he passed the stone. He just passed it a little while ago and the first thing he did was to call me, which was very thoughtful of him — and about time. He sounded *so* happy and cheerful. It was just as though my old Kevin had come back to me. It was as though he had become exactly like the photograph that —"

Then, in half a shriek, "*Where's the photograph?*"

I was on my feet, preparing to leave. I was walking rather briskly toward the door, saying, "I destroyed it. That's why he passed the stone. Otherwise —"

"You *destroyed* it? You —"

I was outside the door. I didn't expect gratitude, of course, but what I *was* expecting was murder. I didn't wait for the elevator but hastened down the stairs as quickly as I reasonably could, the sound of her long wail penetrating the door and reaching my ears for a full two flights.

I burned the scraps of the photograph when I got home.

I have never seen her since. From what I have been told, Kevin has been a delightful and loving husband and they are most happy together, but the one letter I received from her — seven pages of small writing, and nearly incoherent — made it plain that she was of the opinion that the kidney stone was the full explanation of Kevin's ill humor, and that its arrival and departure in exact synchronization with the photograph was sheer coincidence.

She made some rather injudicious threats against my life and, quite anticlimactically, against certain portions of my body, making use of words and phrases I would have sworn she had never heard, much less employed.

And I suppose she will never kiss me again, something I find, for some odd reason, disappointing.

PART 12

SOCIAL SCIENCES

THE CATEGORIES IN OPUS 100, which dealt with my first hundred books, ended with "Humor." It did not occur to me at the time that I ever wrote anything in connection with the social sciences, but, of course, I do.

Some of my essays, even when I think they are about science, deal with society to some extent. In fact, I sometimes incautiously write essays that deal with society and the human condition almost exclusively, even though there is a scientific tinge to them. Thus, I wrote an article, "Alas, All Human," which I think falls under the heading of "Social Sciences." It appeared in my essay collection The Sun Shines Bright *(Book 237), which I referred to earlier.*

from THE SUN SHINES BRIGHT (1981)

Alas, All Human

When I was doing my doctoral research back in medieval times, I was introduced to an innovation. My research professor, Charles R. Dawson, had established a new kind of data notebook that one could obtain at the university bookstore for a sizable supply of coin of the realm.

It was made up of duplicate numbered pages. Of each pair, one was white and firmly sewn into the binding, while the other was yellow, and was perforated near the binding so that it could be neatly removed.

You placed a piece of carbon paper between the white and yellow when you recorded your experimental data and, at the end of each day, you zipped out the duplicate pages and handed them in to Dawson. Once a week or so, he went over the pages with you in detail.

This practice occasioned me periodic embarrassment, for the fact is, Gentle Reader, that in the laboratory I am simply not deft.

I lack manual dexterity. When I am around, test tubes drop and reagents refuse to perform their accustomed tasks. This was one of the several reasons that made it easy for me, in the fullness of time, to choose a career of writing over one of research.

When I began my research work, one of my first tasks was to learn the experimental techniques involved in the various investigations our group was conducting. I made a number of observations under changing conditions and then plotted the results on graph paper. In theory, those values ought to have fallen on a smooth curve. In actual fact, the values scattered over the graph paper as though they had been fired at it out of a shotgun. I drew the theoretical curve through the mess, labeled it "shotgun curve" and handed in the carbon.

My professor smiled when I handed in the sheet, and I assured him I would do better with time.

I did — somewhat. Came the war, though, and it was four years before I returned to the lab. And there was Professor Dawson, who had saved my shotgun curve to show people.

I said, "Gee, Professor Dawson, you shouldn't make fun of me like that."

And he said, very seriously, "I'm not making fun of you, Isaac. I'm boasting about your integrity."

That puzzled me but I didn't let on. I just said, "Thank you," and left.

Thereafter, I would sometimes try to puzzle out what he had meant. He had deliberately set up the duplicate-page system so that he could keep track of exactly what we did each day, and if my experimental technique turned out to be hopelessly amateurish, I had no choice but to reveal that fact to him on the carbon.

And then one day, nine years after I had obtained my Ph.D., I thought about it, and it suddenly occurred to me that there had been no necessity to record my data directly in my notebook. I could have kept the data on any scrap of paper and then *transferred* the observations, neatly and in good order, to the duplicate pages. I could, in that case, have omitted any observations that didn't look good.

In fact, once I got that far in my belated analysis of the situation, it occurred to me that it was even possible to make changes in data to have them look better, or to invent data in order to prove a thesis and *then* transfer them to the duplicate pages.

Suddenly, I realized why Professor Dawson had thought that my handing him the shotgun curve was a proof of integrity, and I felt terribly embarrassed.

I like to believe that I have integrity, but that shotgun curve was no proof of it. If it proved anything, it proved only my lack of sophistication.

I felt embarrassed for another reason. I felt embarrassed over having thought it out. For all those years since the shotgun curve, scientific hanky-panky had been literally inconceivable to me, and now I had conceived it, and I felt a little dirty that I had. In fact, I was at this point in the process of changing my career over into full-time writing, and I felt relieved that this was happening. Having now thought of hanky-panky, could I ever trust myself again?

I tried to exorcise the feeling by writing my first straight mystery novel, one in which a research student tampers with his experimental data and is murdered as a direct result. It appeared as an original paperback entitled *The Death-Dealers* (Avon, 1958) and was eventually republished in hardcover under my own title of *A Whiff of Death* (Walker, 1967).

And lately the subject has been brought to my attention again . . .

◆

Science itself, in the abstract, is a self-correcting, truth-seeking device. There can be mistakes and misconceptions due to incomplete or erroneous data, but the movement is always from the less true to the more true.*

Scientists are, however, not science. However glorious, noble, and supernaturally incorruptible science is, scientists are, alas, all human.

While it is impolite to suppose that a scientist may be dishonest, and heart-sickening to find out, every once in a while, that one of them is, it is nevertheless something that has to be taken into account.

No scientific observation is really allowed to enter the account books of science until it has been independently confirmed. The

---

*Lest someone ask me, "What is truth?" I will define the measure of "truth" as the extent to which a conception, theory, or natural law fits the observed phenomena of the universe.

reason is that every observer and every instrument has built-in imperfections and biases so that, even assuming perfect integrity, the observation may be flawed. If another observer, with another instrument, and with other imperfections and biases, makes the same observation, then that observation has a reasonable chance of possessing objective truth.

This requirement for independent confirmation also serves, however, to take into account the fact that the assumption of perfect integrity may not hold. It helps us counteract the possibility of scientific dishonesty.

◆

Scientific dishonesty comes in varying degrees of venality, some almost forgivable.

In ancient times, one variety of intellectual dishonesty was that of pretending that what you had produced was actually the product of a notable of the past.

One can see the reason for this. Where books could be produced and multiplied only by painstaking hand copying, not every piece of writing could be handled. Perhaps the only way of presenting your work to the public would be to pretend it had been written by Moses, or Aristotle, or Hippocrates.

If the pretender's work is useless and silly, claiming it as the product of a great man of the past confuses scholarship and mangles history until such time as the matter is straightened out.

Particularly tragic, though, is the case of an author who produces a great work for which he forever loses the credit.

Thus, one of the great alchemists was an Arab named Abu Musa Jabir ibn Hayyan (721–815). When his works were translated into Latin, his name was transliterated into Geber, and it is in that fashion he is usually spoken of.

Geber, among other things, prepared white lead, acetic acid, ammonium chloride, and weak nitric acid. Most important of all, he described his procedures with great care and set the fashion (not always followed) of making it possible for others to repeat his work and see for themselves that his observations were valid.

About 1300, another alchemist lived who made the most important of all alchemical discoveries. He was the first to describe the preparation of sulfuric acid, the most important single industrial chemical used today that is not found as such in nature.

This new alchemist, in order to get himself published, attributed his finding to Geber and it was published under that name. The result? We can speak only of the False Geber. The man who made this great discovery is unknown to us by name, by nationality, even by sex, for the discoverer might conceivably have been a woman.

Much worse is the opposite sin of taking credit for what is not yours.

The classic case involved the victimization of Niccolo Tartaglia (1500–1557), an Italian mathematician who was the first to work out a general method for solving cubic equations. In those days, mathematicians posed problems to each other, and upon their ability to solve these problems rested their reputations. Tartaglia could solve problems involving cubic equations and could pose problems of that sort which others found insoluble. It was natural in those days to keep such discoveries secret.

Another Italian mathematician, Girolamo Cardano (1501–1576) wheedled the method from Tartaglia under a solemn promise of secrecy — and then published it. Cardano did admit he got it from Tartaglia, but not very loudly, and the method for solving cubic equations is still called Cardano's rule to this day.

In a way, Cardano (who was a great mathematician in his own right) was justified. Scientific findings that are known, but not published, are useless to science as a whole. It is the publishing that is now considered crucial, and the credit goes, by general consent, to the first who publishes and not to the first who discovers.

The rule did not exist in Cardano's time, but reading it back in time, Cardano should get the credit anyway.

(Naturally, where publication is delayed through no fault of the discoverer, there can be a tragic loss of credit, and there have been a number of such cases in the history of science. That, however, is an unavoidable side effect of a rule that is, in general, a good one.)

You can justify Cardano's publication a lot easier than his having broken his promise. In other words, scientists might not actually do anything scientifically dishonest and yet behave in an underhanded way in matters involving science.

The English zoologist Richard Owen was, for instance, very much against the Darwinian theory of evolution, largely because Darwin postulated random changes that seemed to deny the existence of purpose in the Universe.

To disagree with Darwin was Owen's right. To argue against

Darwinian theory in speech and in writing was also his right. It is sleazy, however, to write on the subject in a number of anonymous articles and in those articles quote your own work with reverence and approval.

It is always impressive, of course, to cite authorities. It is far less impressive to cite yourself. To appear to do the former when you are really doing the latter is dishonest — even if you yourself are an accepted authority. There's a psychological difference.

Owen also fed rabble-rousers anti-Darwinian arguments and sent them into the fray to make emotional or scurrilous points that he would have been ashamed to make himself.

♦

Another type of flaw arises out of the fact that scientists are quite likely to fall in love with their own ideas. It is always an emotional wrench to have to admit one is wrong. One generally writhes, twists, and turns in an effort to save one's theory, and hangs on to it long after everyone else has given it up.

That is so human one need scarcely comment on it, but it becomes particularly important to science if the scientist in question has become old, famous, and honored.

The prize example is that of the Swede Jöns Jakob Berzelius (1779–1848), one of the greatest chemists in history, who, in his later years, became a powerful force of scientific conservatism. He had worked up a theory of organic structure from which he would not budge, and from which the rest of the chemical world dared not deviate for fear of his thunders.

The French chemist Auguste Laurent (1807–1853), in 1836, presented an alternate theory we now know to be nearer the truth. Laurent accumulated firm evidence in favor of his theory, and the French chemist Jean Baptiste Dumas (1800–1884) was among those who backed him.

Berzelius counterattacked furiously and, not daring to place himself in opposition to the great man, Dumas weaseled out of his former support. Laurent, however, held firm and continued to accumulate evidence. For this he was rewarded by being barred from the more famous laboratories. He is supposed to have contracted tuberculosis as a result of working in poorly heated provincial laboratories and therefore died in middle age.

After Berzelius died, Laurent's theories began to come into fashion and Dumas, recalling his own early backing of them, now tried to claim more than his fair share of the credit, proving himself rather dishonest after having proved himself rather a coward.

The scientific establishment is so often hard to convince of the value of new ideas that the German physicist Max Planck (1858–1947) once grumbled that the only way to get revolutionary advances in science accepted was to wait for all the old scientists to die.

♦

Then, too, there is such a thing as overeagerness to make some discovery. Even the most staunchly honest scientist may be tempted.

Take the case of diamond. Both graphite and diamond are forms of pure carbon. If graphite is compressed very intensely, its atoms will transform into the diamond configuration. The pressure need not be quite so high if the temperature is raised so that the atoms can move and slip around more easily. How, then, to get the proper combination of high pressure and high temperature?

The French chemist Ferdinand Fréderic Moissan (1852–1907) undertook the task. It occurred to him that carbon would dissolve to some extent in liquid iron. If the molten iron (at a rather high temperature, of course) were allowed to solidify, it would contract as it did so. The contracting iron might exert a high pressure on the dissolved carbon, and the combination of high temperature and high pressure might do the trick. If the iron were dissolved away, small diamonds might be found in the residue.

We now understand in detail the conditions under which graphite will change to carbon, and we know, beyond doubt, that the conditions of Moissan's experiments were insufficient for the purpose. He could not possibly have produced diamonds.

Except that he did.

In 1893 he exhibited several tiny impure diamonds and a sliver of colorless diamond, over half a millimeter in length, which he said he had manufactured out of graphite.

How was that possible? Could Moissan have been lying? Of what value would that have been to him, since no one could possibly have confirmed the experiment, and he himself would know he had lied?

Even so, he might have gone slightly mad on the subject, but most science historians prefer to guess that one of Moissan's assistants introduced the diamonds as a practical joke on the boss. Moissan fell for it, announced it, and the joker could not then back out.

More peculiar still is the case of the French physicist René Prosper Blondlot (1849–1930).

In 1895 the German physicist Wilhelm Konrad Roentgen (1845–1923) had discovered X-rays and had, in 1901, received the first Nobel Prize in physics. Other strange radiations had been discovered in that period: cathode rays, canal rays, radioactive rays. Such discoveries led on to scientific glory and Blondlot craved some — which is natural enough.

In 1903 he announced the existence of "N rays" (which he named in honor of the University of Nancy, where he worked). He produced them by placing solids such as hardened steel under strain. The rays could be detected and studied by the fact (Blondlot said) that they brightened a screen of phosphorescent paint, which was already faintly luminous. Blondlot claimed he could see the brightening, and some others said they could see it, too.

The major problem was that photographs didn't show the brightening and that no instrument more objective than the eager human eye upheld the claims of brightening. One day, an onlooker privately pocketed an indispensable part of the instrument Blondlot was using. Blondlot, unaware of this, continued to see the brightening and to "demonstrate" his phenomenon. Finally, the onlooker produced the part, and a furious Blondlot attempted to strike him.

Was Blondlot a conscious faker? Somehow I think he was not. He merely wanted to believe something desperately — and he did.

◆

Overeagerness to discover or prove something may actually lead to tampering with the data.

Consider the Austrian botanist Gregor Mendel (1822–1884), for instance. He founded the science of genetics and worked out, quite correctly, the basic laws of heredity. He did this by crossing strains of green-pea plants and counting the offspring with various characteristics. He thus discovered, for instance, the three-to-one ratio in the third generation of the cross of a dominant characteristic with a recessive one.

The numbers he got, in the light of later knowledge, seem to be a little too good, however. There should have been more scattering. Some people think, therefore, that he found excuses for correcting the values that deviated too widely from what he found the general rules to be.

That didn't affect the importance of his discoveries, but the subject matter of heredity comes close to the hearts of human beings. We are a lot more interested in the relationship between our ancestors and ourselves than we are in diamonds, invisible radiations, and the structure of organic compounds.

Thus, some people are anxious to give heredity a major portion of the credit for the characteristics of individual people and of groups of people; while others are anxious to give that credit to the environment. In general, aristocrats and conservatives lean toward heredity; democrats and radicals lean toward environment.*

Here one's emotions are very likely to be greatly engaged — to the point of believing that one or the other point of view *ought* to be so whether it is so or not. It apparently takes distressingly little, once you begin to think like that, to lean against the data a little bit.

Suppose one is extremely environmental (far more than I myself am). Heredity becomes a mere trifle. Whatever you inherit you can change through environmental influence and pass on to your children, who may again change them, and so on. This notion of extreme plasticity of organisms is referred to as the inheritance of acquired characteristics.

The Austrian biologist Paul Kammerer (1880–1926) believed in the inheritance of acquired characteristics. Working with salamanders and toads from 1918 onward, he tried to demonstrate this. For instance, there are some species of toads in which the male has darkly colored thumb-pads. The midwife toad doesn't, but Kammerer attempted to introduce environmental conditions that would cause the male midwife toad to develop those dark thumb-pads even though it had not inherited them.

He claimed to have produced such midwife toads and described them in his papers, but would not allow them to be examined

---

*Since I never pretend to godlike objectivity myself, I tell you right now that I lean toward environment.

closely by other scientists. Some of the midwife toads were finally obtained by scientists, however, and the thumb-pads proved to have been darkened with India ink. Presumably, Kammerer had been driven to do this through the extremity of his desire to "prove" his case. After the exposure, he killed himself.

There are equally strong drives to prove the reverse — to prove that one's intelligence, for instance, is set through heredity and that little can be done in the way of education and civilized treatment to brighten a dumbbell.

This would tend to establish social stability to the benefit of those in the upper rungs of the economic and social ladder. It gives the upper classes the comfortable feeling that those of their fellow humans who are in the mud are there because of their own inherited failings, and little need be done for them.

One psychologist who was very influential in this sort of view was Cyril Lodowic Burt (1883–1971). English upper class, educated at Oxford, teaching at both Oxford and Cambridge, he studied the IQs of children and correlated those IQs with the occupational status of the parents: higher professional, lower professional, clerical, skilled labor, semiskilled labor, unskilled labor.

He found that the IQs fit those occupations perfectly. The lower the parent was in the social scale, the lower the IQ of the child. It seemed a perfect demonstration that people should know their place. Since Isaac Asimov was the son of a shopkeeper, Isaac Asimov should expect (on the average) to be a shopkeeper himself, and shouldn't aspire to compete with his betters.

After Burt's death, however, doubts arose concerning his data. There were distinctly suspicious perfections about his statistics.

The suspicions grew and grew, and in the September 29, 1978, issue of *Science* an article appeared entitled, "The Cyril Burt Question: New Findings" by D. D. Dorfman, a professor of psychology at the University of Iowa. The blurb of the article reads: "The eminent Briton is shown, beyond reasonable doubt, to have fabricated data on IQ and social class."

And that's it. Burt, like Kammerer, wanted to believe something, so he invented the data to prove it. At least that's what Professor Dorfman concludes.

♦

Long before I had any suspicions of wrongdoing in connection with Burt, I had written an essay called "Thinking About Thinking" (see *The Planet That Wasn't*, Doubleday, 1976) in which I denounced IQ tests, and expressed my disapproval of those psychologists who thought IQ tests were good enough to determine such things as racial inferiority.

A British psychologist in the forefront of this IQ research was shown the essay by his son, and he was furious. On September 25, 1978, he wrote me a letter in which he insisted that IQ tests were culturally fair and that blacks fall twelve points below whites even when environments and educational opportunities are similar. He suggested I stick to things I knew about.

By the time I got the letter I had seen Dorfman's article in *Science* and noted that the psychologist who had written to me had strongly defended Burt against "McCarthyite character assassination." He also had apparently described Burt as "a deadly critic of other people's work when this departed in any way from the highest standards of accuracy and logical consistency" and that "he could tear to ribbons anything shoddy or inconsistent." It would appear, in other words, that not only was Burt dishonest, but he was a hypocrite in the very area of his dishonesty. (That's not an uncommon situation, I think.)

So, in my brief reply to X, I asked him how much of his work was based on the findings of Cyril Burt.

He wrote me a second letter on October 11. I expected another spirited defense of Burt, but apparently he had grown more cautious concerning him. He told me the question of Burt's work was irrelevant; that he had reanalyzed all the available data, leaving out entirely Burt's contribution; and that it made no difference to the final conclusion.

In my answer I explained that in my opinion Burt's work was totally relevant. It demonstrated that in the field of heredity versus environment, scientists' emotions could be so fiercely engaged that it was possible for one of them to stoop to falsifying results to prove a point.

Clearly, under such conditions, *any* self-serving results must be taken with a grain of salt.

I'm sure that my correspondent is an honest man, and I would not for the world cast any doubts upon his work. However, the whole field of human intelligence and its measurement is as yet a gray area. There is so much uncertainty in it that it is quite possible to be full of honesty and integrity and yet come up with results of questionable value.

I simply don't think it is reasonable to use IQ tests to produce results of questionable value, which may then serve to justify racists in their own minds and to help bring about the kinds of tragedies we have already witnessed earlier in this century.

Clearly, my own views are also suspect. I may well be as anxious to prove what I want to prove as ever Burt was, but if I must run the (honest) chance of erring, then I would rather do so in opposition to racism.

And that's that.

A couple of other samples of my comments on society are taken from The Roving Mind *(Book 272), a volume I also referred to earlier. These essays are shorter and more strongly expressed than those that appear in F & SF since, in these cases, I wanted to leave no doubt as to what my point of view is.*

from THE ROVING MIND *(1983)*

The Blind Who Would Lead

In the United States, an old, old phenomenon resurfaced in 1980. It is the voice of self-righteous, all-knowing, narrow-minded "religion," this time in the form of the self-styled Moral Majority, which has as its objectives the punishment of politicians who deviate from M.M. principles, and the dictation to all Americans of what they should read, think, and believe.

The Moral Majority speaks with the voice of absolute authority.

This is not to be confused with the kind of authority expressed by scientists, who can only claim to hope they are right pending further information. The greatest scientists have been wrong on this point or that — Newton on the nature of light, Einstein in his views of the uncertainty principle — and this does not lessen respect for their achievements. Scientists not only expect to be improved on and corrected; they hope to be. Science has its "authority," but it is an open and nonauthoritarian authority.

The Moral Majority, however, speaks, it would seem, with the voice of God. How do we know they do? Why, they themselves say so; and, since they speak with the voice of God, then their testimony that they do so is unshakable. Q.E.D. And since the voice of God is never wrong and cannot be wrong (the Moral Majority, speaking with that voice, says so) any spokesman of the M.M. is never wrong and cannot be wrong.

The Moral Majority is, in other words, a closed intellectual system, without possibility of change or admission of error. It insists that all the answers exist and have existed from the beginning because God wrote them all out in the Bible and we need only observe them to the letter.

Surely this puts an end forever to any hope of social or intellectual advance or to any rational adaptation to changing conditions. For what does the Bible say? "The letter killeth" (2 Corinthians 3:6).

We have had thousands of years of experience with the kind of absolute self-anointed authority that little men adopt and call religion. We have watched the Christian nations of the world fight each other for many centuries, each believing itself under the peculiar protection of a God they all insist is universal. Each prays separately for the destruction of the enemy and praises jubilantly God's assistance in helping them bring death and misery to that enemy, although both sides, presumably, are equally God's children.

(Nor is it only the Christians. We see Moslem Iraq fighting Moslem Iran, with each insisting that the universal Allah is aiding only its own side while the United States is supporting the other.)

One can only draw the conclusion that the "religionists" (to be distinguished from the wisely, ethically, and universally religious) are convinced, in each nation, that God is Himself a member of that nation and is rather proud of being so.

Certainly I suspect that the Americans of the Moral Majority take it for granted that God is an American citizen (naturalized, of course) and that He is, moreover, a member of the conservative wing of the Republican Party and voted for Ronald Reagan.

Furthermore, the Moral Majority types are convinced that God is forever intervening in human affairs in a kind of wrathful way, but that He is fortunately weak-willed. He may send a drought, for instance, to punish sinners; but if everyone prays and pleads and wails, He'll say, "Oh, all right," and let it rain.

If there is an earthquake and a thousand people die, and one person is uncovered from a ruined house, unhurt, the Moral Majority types cry, "A miracle!" and fall to their knees in gratitude. And the thousand who died — whose deaths, indeed, were necessary to convert the one survivor into a miracle, what of them?

Not to worry. If anything really puzzling happens, it is only necessary to remind everyone that merely human minds cannot expect to penetrate the deep, mysterious purposes of God. Except that the Moral Majority does it all the time, when they want to whip and harry the rest of us.

The Moral Majority feels absolutely secure in being under the protection of an American Republican conservative God. Still — just the same — they favor a strong national defense. God will certainly destroy the godless Soviets, but He'll need a lot of very advanced bombers, missiles, and nuclear bombs to do it with. (Scientists are perfectly moral people, to the Moral Majority, as long as they design sophisticated war weapons to control the population problem by raising the death rate — as opposed to any evil attempt they make to control it by lowering the birth rate.)

What's more, the Moral Majority types do not need to study science or consider its observations and conclusions to know that those observations are misleading and those conclusions are not only wrong — but deeply wicked. The M.M. has its own textbook of biology, astronomy, and cosmogony, in the form of the Bible, a collection of two-thousand-year-old writings by provincial tribesmen with little or no knowledge of biology, astronomy, and cosmogony.

To be sure, the Bible contains the direct words of God. How do we know? The Moral Majority says so. How do *they* know? They *say* they know, and to doubt it makes you an agent of the devil or, worse, a L-b-r-l D-m-cr-t.

And what does the Bible textbook say? Well, among other things it says the Earth was created in 4004 B.C. (Not actually, but a Moral Majority type figured that out three and a half centuries ago, and his word is also accepted as inspired.) The Sun was created three days later. The first male was molded out of dirt, and the first female was molded, some time later, out of his rib.

As far as the end of the Universe is concerned, the Book of Revelation (6:13–14) says: "And the stars of heaven fell unto the earth, even as a fig tree casteth her untimely figs, when she is shaken of a mighty wind. And the heaven departed as a scroll when it is rolled together."

The Bible textbook, then, says that the sky is a thin sheet of something or other that can be rolled up in the same way a scroll of parchment can be rolled up, and that the stars are little dots of light that can be shaken off that scroll and allowed to fall to the Earth.

Imagine the people who believe such things and who are not ashamed to ignore, totally, all the patient findings of thinking minds through all the centuries since the Bible was written.

And it is these ignorant people, the most uneducated, the most unimaginative, the most unthinking among us, who would make of themselves the guides and leaders of us all; who would force their feeble and childish beliefs on us; who would invade our schools and libraries and homes in order to tell us what books to read and what not, what thoughts to think and what not, what conclusions to accept and what not.

And what does the Bible say? "If the blind lead the blind, both shall fall into the ditch" (Matthew 15:14).

That Old-Time Violence

Violence is as human as thumbs and it's been with us a long, long time. Here's Herodotus (about 445 B.C.) talking in his "History" about King Gyges of Lydia: "As soon as Gyges was king he made an inroad on Miletus and Smyrna, and took the city of Colophon. Afterwards, however, though he reigned eight and thirty years, he did not perform a single noble exploit. I shall therefore make no further mention of him —"

Herodotus was certainly not going to waste time on an ignoble thing like a prosperous and peaceful thirty-eight-year reign. It was war and violence that drew the audience.

Or read Homer (about 800 B.C.), and in his *Iliad* you will have careful descriptions of exactly where the spear went in and where it came out. The great Achilles was given a choice between a long life spent ignobly (that is, as a hardworking farmer or herdsman, helping to feed humanity) or a short life full of immortal glory (as a wholesale slaughterer of those weaker than himself). Achilles chose the glory; those who tell the tale expect us to admire Achilles, and apparently we all do.

There's nothing new about violence; we've just used other words for it. We read about "glory," "gallantry," "derring-do," "knightly deeds," "noble exploits," "patriotic bravery," and it all comes down to violence whatever combination of glittering sounds you use.

And why? There may be many psychological reasons for it, but we can skip those. The fact is that the tales of violence served a practical, and even an essential, purpose.

Mankind lived by violence for uncounted thousands of years before history began. There were long ages in which human beings had to (if they could) kill animals for food, sometimes large animals who resented the attempt and resisted. The mastodons and mammoths were driven to extinction by puny people swarming after them with nothing more deadly than hand-thrown spears. Would anyone run the risk of angering tons of bone and muscle if he weren't fortified with violent tales of great huntsmen meeting glorious deaths against ravening beasts?

There came a time when human beings won out over the animal kingdom once and for all. Thanks to mankind's possession of fire and of long-range missile weapons like the bow and arrow, no animal, not even the strongest and most deadly predator, could stand against the human onslaught.

That, however, didn't end the need for tales of violence, for, having run out of other species to pit brain and weapon against, human beings fought other human beings. The skill and emotional drive developed by human beings over long ages of pitting feeble strength against tusks, fangs, claws, horns, and overreaching power was now expended in a civil war to the death, one that has continued to this day.

Through most of history, when a city was taken its inhabitants were quite likely to be killed or enslaved. The women were first raped, of course, and then killed or enslaved. Even the Bible recommends mass slaughter as a routine matter of warfare. (See Deuteronomy 20:15–17, for instance.)

Under such circumstances, it was important to fight to the death, since one was in any case going to die, or worse, if one lost. So the people, or, at the very least, the warrior class, were constantly fed tales of violence; of heroes who fought against overwhelming odds; of Hector standing against Achilles when all his fellow Trojans had fled; of Roland fighting off hordes of Saracens and disdaining to call for help; of the Knights of the Round Table taking on all challenges.

Youngsters had to get used to violence, had to have their hearts and minds hardened to it. They had to be made to feel the glory of fighting against odds and how sweet it was to give one's life for one's tribe, or one's city, or one's nation, or one's king, or one's fatherland, or one's motherland, or one's faith, or whatever other sounds are appropriate.

And now it's over! That old-time violence that's got us in its spell must stop!

Not because human beings have become good and sweet and gentle! Not because television makes violence too immediate by adding pictures to the sound!

Not at all! We've got to get rid of violence for the simple reason that it serves no purpose anymore, but points us all in a useless direction. It would appear that human enemies are no longer the prime threat to world survival.

The new enemies we have today — overpopulation, famine, pollution, scarcity — cannot be fought by violence. There is no way to crush those enemies, or slash them, or blast them, or vaporize them.

If they are to be defeated at all in their present incarnation, which threatens the whole world and all of mankind, rather than merely this tribe or that region, it must be by human cooperation and global determination. It is *that* which we had better start practicing. It is with tales of brotherhood and cooperation that we had better propagandize our children.

If we choose not to, and if we continue to amuse ourselves with violence just because that worked for thousands of years, then the enemies that can't be conquered by violence will conquer *us* — and it will all be over.

PART 13

LITERATURE

*AMONG MY THIRD HUNDRED BOOKS is one in which I con-
tinued the practice of annotating great works of literature. (There
were several examples of this among my second hundred.)*

The book is The Annotated® Gulliver's Travels *(Book 222),
which was published by Clarkson N. Potter, a division of Crown,
in 1980. Once, over lunch, Martin Gardner advised me to do an
annotation of Jonathan Swift's satire. He had done* The Annotated
Alice, *an annotation of* Alice in Wonderland, *which was the first
and most successful of the Clarkson Potter series. He may have
mentioned it to the Clarkson Potter people as well, for Jane West,
an editor at the firm, then asked me to do it. (She has since died,
alas — the third of my editors to die in the course of my third
hundred, and each one of them, by some curious fatality, from
Crown.)*

*In any case I was delighted at the chance and threw myself into
the job with enthusiasm. I include here the very first paragraph of
Gulliver's Travels, followed by the annotations I worked out for it.
Needless to say, the annotations did not continue as thickly
throughout the book, or it would have become a three-volume
work, but I did not stint.*

from THE ANNOTATED® GULLIVER'S TRAVELS (1980)

*The Author gives some account of himself and family. His first in-
ducements to travel. He is shipwrecked, and swims for his life, gets
safe on shore in the country of Lilliput, is made a prisoner, and
carried up the country.*

My Father had a small Estate in *Nottinghamshire;*[1] I was the Third
of five Sons. He sent me to *Emanuel-College* in *Cambridge,*[2] at
Fourteen Years old,[3] where I resided three Years,[4] and applied my
self close to my Studies: But the Charge of maintaining me (al-

though I had a very scanty Allowance) being too great for a narrow
Fortune; I was bound Apprentice[5] to Mr. *James Bates*, an eminent
Surgeon[6] in *London*, with whom I continued four Years; and my
Father now and then sending me small Sums of Money, I laid them
out in learning Navigation,[7] and other Parts of the Mathematicks,
useful to those who intend to travel, as I always believed it would
be some time or other my Fortune to do. When I left Mr. *Bates*,
I went down to my Father; where, by the Assistance of him and
my Uncle *John*, and some other Relations, I got Forty Pounds, and
a Promise of Thirty Pounds a Year to maintain me at *Leyden*:[8]
There I studied Physick[9] two Years and seven Months, knowing it
would be useful in long Voyages.

1. A county in north central England, about four-fifths the size
of the state of Rhode Island. Its largest town is, not surprisingly,
Nottingham, which is located 110 miles northwest of London. Nottinghamshire's greatest literary fame rests on the fact that ten miles
to the north of Nottingham is Sherwood Forest, the onetime haunt
of the legendary Robin Hood.

Gulliver was thus born in a rural section of England and grew
up in unsophisticated surroundings. Swift's every effort is to create
a Gulliver who is solid, middle-class, and endowed with an intelligent but unimaginative simplicity. Gulliver can be relied on to
see and report facts accurately, but he accepts them at face value.
(It is probably no accident that the only common English word his
name resembles is "gullible.") The reader must look beyond Gulliver for an interpretation of what he reports.

2. Cambridge University was founded in 1209, when a number
of discontented students from Oxford migrated there. It is located
fifty miles north of London and seventy-five miles southeast of
Nottingham.

Issac Newton became a professor of mathematics at Cambridge
in 1669, when he was only twenty-seven years old. In the thirty
years that followed, Newton became world famous, and Cambridge University gained a preeminence in science and mathematics that it holds to this day. Newton was still alive when *Gulliver's
Travels* was published (he was eighty-four years old and died the
next year) and was nearly godlike in reputation, though Swift dis-
liked him thoroughly.

Since Gulliver is represented as a science-minded person, it is only appropriate that he be described as attending Cambridge. Then, too, Cambridge did not have the enormous prestige of Oxford, so that Gulliver's presence there was another sign of his lack of social distinction. (Swift himself went to neither Oxford nor Cambridge but received his education at Trinity College in Dublin.)

3. Life was shorter in those days, and one made faster beginnings. It was quite common to enter college in one's mid-teens. Swift entered Trinity College when he was fourteen. Newton entered Cambridge at eighteen, but he was rather slow in his studies as a youth.

From the data given in the first couple of pages in the book, we can deduce that Gulliver was six years older than Swift. Gulliver seems to have been born in 1661 and to have entered Cambridge in 1675. He was, in other words, born soon after Charles II was restored to the throne. His father must therefore have lived through the turbulent period of the English civil wars and the dictatorship of Oliver Cromwell. No indication of this is given, however.

In fact, all through the book, Gulliver gives no indication whatever of any event that takes place in England or the world while he is on his travels. The reader's attention is firmly fixed on the fantasy world of the lands he discovers, and any intrusion of the real world would be a distraction that would weaken the satire.

4. Gulliver stayed in Cambridge, then, till 1678.

5. The notion of apprenticeship — learning a trade under a recognized experienced professional in the field — was an outgrowth of the guild system of the Middle Ages. The guilds were a kind of craft union which undertook to maintain high standards of workmanship and which did not wish anyone to practice a particular trade who was not thoroughly trained and who could not prove his ability to perform satisfactorily.

In Gulliver's time, the system of apprenticeship was still quite powerful. Even as late as 1756, James Watt, who was soon to be the inventor of the steam engine and the greatest engineer of his time, was not recognized by the guilds of Glasgow because he had not served his full term as apprentice.

The full term of apprenticeship was usually seven years, but

Gulliver served only four, so that he was apprenticed from 1678 to 1682.

6. Surgery was not yet recognized as a true branch of medicine. It involved the use of the hands, which made it a branch of mechanics. It was, in early times, associated with barbers, since cutting flesh was considered to be similar to cutting hair as far as skills and social position were concerned.

It was not till 1540 that some modicum of control over the actual skill and learning of barber-surgeons was established with the formation of the Company of Barber Surgeons of London. This guild was still in existence in Gulliver's time, and it required a seven-year apprenticeship.

7. Guiding a ship across an ocean and having it arrive at the desired destination was no easy matter in those days. To do it properly, there had to be some knowledge of descriptive astronomy and of the use of various instruments for the determination of latitude. Considerable knowledge of spherical trigonometry was required to prepare maps and to use them properly once they had been prepared. It is not surprising that Gulliver speaks of navigation as though it were a branch of mathematics. It is.

8. Also called Leiden. A town in the southwestern Netherlands about two hundred miles east of London. At the time *Gulliver's Travels* was published, Leyden was the site of the most highly regarded medical school in the world.

9. The Greek word for nature. Used to describe the study of medicine (as used here) and as a general word for medications taken internally. Today it is occasionally used for one specific kind of medical dose — a laxative.

I almost never write directly on the subject of writing. Despite my 20 million published words and my steady efforts to continue to increase that total, I do not consider myself an expert on the matter or even knowledgeable about it. I consider myself a "primitive" in that I have had no formal education in the subject, but have, instead, been writing from an early age out of some inner instinct or compulsion, without knowing, precisely, what I am doing.

I am, nevertheless, sometimes forced to think about writing and even write about it.

For instance, I have to write the introductions for the large num-

ber of anthologies for which I have become, at least in part, responsible. I like to make my introductions deal with themes that have something to do with the contents of the anthologies, and this means that I must sometimes discuss one aspect or another of the literary craft.

It frightens me to do so, but if I must, I must. For instance, I did an anthology called Who Done It? (Book 217), published by Houghton Mifflin in 1980. It was done with Alice Laurance (the pseudonym of Laura W. Haywood), a most charming and lovely woman, who is infinitely prettier than Martin Greenberg, my usual coeditor (as he would be the first to admit).

The book consists of seventeen original mystery stories whose authors' names are not given. The authors are listed at the beginning, however, and the reader is invited to guess which author wrote which story, so that the title of the anthology has a double meaning.

I found it necessary, therefore, to write an introduction that dealt with writing style, since one can make a reasonable guess at an unknown author only from considering the manner in which the story is written. Here is that introduction.

from WHO DONE IT? (1980)

On Style

I would like to tell you why Alice and I have put together this anthology, but I insist on telling you about it in my own way.

Why not? Once I am facing the typewriter, I am an all-powerful monarch. Only I can decide which keys to hit and which words to form.

Nor is this unfair to you, Gentle Reader, since in our free society there is nothing to force you to buy this book and therefore you need not subject yourself to my arbitrariness. (But please *do* buy the book. Alice is not as well off as I am and she could use the money. Besides, my introduction will last only a couple of pages, and then you will find all sorts of delightful stories following. You can even, if you are foolish, skip the introduction.)

All right, then, here goes, in my own way.

A book of mine (I forget which one) was reviewed in a fashion to which I have grown accustomed — unimpassioned praise. The reviewer, in other words, felt it was a good book and said so, but I did not detect in the course of the review any feeling of ecstasy on the reviewer's part. Instead, the reviewer seemed to be groping for something negative to say and seemed a little grumpy at my not having made it easier for him to find that something.

This particular reviewer said, "Of course, he has no style!"

This filled me with excitement. At last, I thought, here is a person who knows what style is and who can detect its absence. Here we have an intellectual bloodhound capable of snuffling out the faintest trace of style to its lair.

So I wrote a humble letter to the reviewer. "Dear Reviewer," I said. "For decades, I have tried to be as good a writer as possible, and this is a hard thing to do when no one can say, clearly, what makes writing good. For one thing, I've never known what style is and maybe that's why I don't have any. Since you have detected the absence of style, you must know what it is. I wonder, therefore, if you would be so kind as to tell me what style is so that I can sprinkle some of it over my next book and avoid displeasing you."

You cannot conceive my heartbreak when I got no answer at all.

What was there to do? I had to sit down and figure it out for myself. "What is style?" I asked myself, and after considerable thought, I came to some conclusions, which I will now share with you. They are purely personal ones and there may well be Great Literary Critics who will disagree with me. It is a measure of my tolerance that I have decided to allow them to.

First, just to get the underbrush out of the way, let me tell you what style is not. It is not, of necessity, complicated and convoluted writing.

Thus, another reviewer, writing of my book *In Memory Yet Green* (the first volume of my autobiography) says, "It is astonishing that he can do so much with simple declarative sentences."

When a person says, "It is astonishing that —" it may be that what he really means to say is, "I'm not very bright so I am astonished that —"

There is, after all, nothing wrong with simple declarative sentences, just as there is nothing wrong with a simple medium-done filet mignon. Some people like ketchup and I am happy for them, but how would you feel about someone who was, supposedly, an expert on food who said, "It is astonishing that filet mignon tastes as good as it does without ketchup."

So, then, what is style?

There are two chief aspects to any piece of writing: (1) what you say and (2) how you say it. The former is "content" and the latter is "style."

Everyone has his own way of writing something. It can be unbearably bad, or transcendently good. No one could possibly bear it in the first case, and no one could possibly cavil at it in the second. Very often the way of writing something falls in between, pleasing some people and displeasing others. (After all, tastes differ — which is fortunate since otherwise every man in the world would try to seduce the same woman.)

What you can't have is *no* way of writing something, unless you don't write at all.

In other words, you can have a bad style, a ridiculous style, an illiterate style, a style that is beneath contempt. But, with all due respect to the terribly intelligent reviewer who read my book, you cannot have *no* style.

For instance, you have just read the foregoing portion of this introduction (unless you have skipped it, in which case you are going to have seven years of bad luck), and you can tell something about the characteristics of its style.

In the first place, you have undoubtedly noticed that it is personal. I tend to talk about myself a lot. In fact, the first word of the introduction is *I*, which I was once told is a no-no in writing an essay.

This can easily grate on you, if you don't like presumption, if you find pushy people unbearable, if you like to choose your friends carefully, and if you never speak to strangers.

On the other hand, you can warm to a personal style if you happen to like to feel a cozy friendship with a writer, if you like to be welcomed into the printed page, if you like companionship.

Should I adopt a style that is going to grate on some people? I don't think I have a choice. If I adopted an impersonal style, saying, "It is astonishing that —" instead of "I am astonished that —" why, then, that will grate on some people, too. And if whatever style I choose is sure to grate on some people — then why not adopt one that at least pleases *me?*

I might as well not grate on myself, at least.

A personal style comes naturally to me because I tend to be aimlessly friendly; I have no inhibitions about speaking to strangers; and I like to talk about myself.

A penchant for talking about oneself is usually taken as a symptom of vanity, conceit, egomania, and a lot of other bad characteristics, and I am indeed accused of that frequently, but only by people who are not accustomed to a personal style. From people who like a personal style, I get a different set of characterizing terms, which I would quote if I *were* full of vanity, conceit, and egomania.

What else? Well, I have an informal style, which means I tend to use short words and simple sentence structure, to say nothing of occasional colloquialisms. This grates on people who like things that are poetic, weighty, complex, and, above all, obscure. On the other hand, the informal style pleases people who enjoy the sensation of reading an essay without being aware that they are reading and of feeling that ideas are flowing from the writer's brain into their own without mental friction.

Third, you will notice I have a discursive style. That is, I don't follow a straight line in my exposition. I like to use parentheses, and I pause for asides.

This can drive people crazy if they are the kind who want to get from A to B in a straight line, but it can please people who like to stop on their way to the post office to watch a butterfly for a few moments.

Anything else? I have (I think) a humorous style, or even (possibly) a witty one. I say things in a way that is not meant to be entirely serious but which should manage to elicit a smile. That doesn't mean I am not serious in the *content* of what I may write, but I think I can get it across more persuasively by tickling than by jabbing.

What is my style *not?*

It isn't the opposite of anything that it is, for one thing. It isn't impersonal, formal, direct, and serious.

As an example of something I haven't mentioned, my style is not epigrammatic, either.

Some writers tend to include a frequent seasoning of clever, pointed turns of phrase. You probably have read writers whose nearly every sentence has a striking simile or metaphor. Thus: "He looked at me as though I were lemonade to which someone had forgotten to add the ade."

That would please people who enjoy novel turns of phrase, but it grates on me. I dislike useless and distracting phrases. I would have said, "He looked at me sourly." By adding all that stuff about lemonade the reader is likely to get the vague idea that the character looking at me had a drink in his hand.

Now we can move on to another question. Is there such a thing as good style or bad style?

Yes, but when it is put that briefly, the "yes" gives a false impression.

Style is not, *in itself*, either good or bad. It's not that a personal style is good while an impersonal one is bad, or vice versa. For one thing, circumstances vary. A personal style is more suitable than an impersonal one in a friendly essay; an impersonal one is more suitable than a personal one in a business report.

Beyond that, there is the quality of writing. A personal style well done is better than an impersonal style ill done, and vice versa. In fact, any writing well done is better than any writing ill done, regardless of style.

Does that mean we should forget about style and just concentrate on good writing?

Not quite. Even when we concentrate on good writing, we cannot forget style. A writer always writes better if he is using a style with which he is comfortable or a style that fits the mood he is trying to get across. In other words, while *in general*, good writing outweighs consideration of style, for a specific writer good writing only comes if he adopts certain styles, generally the one that long custom has made his own.

Does this mean that a writer cannot change his style deliberately?

Of course he can. The more experienced he is and the more skillful, the more easily he can do it. There are even writers with a particularly sharp ear for style who can alter their styles smoothly and with ease — just as there are some people who can mimic other people's voices and mannerisms with remarkable facility.

Yet however experienced and skillful a writer may be and however gifted a mimic he may be, the matter of using a style he is not accustomed to is a matter of constant, deliberate effort. It is tiring.

At any time, if his attention wavers, he will drop into his own style, so that he must be perpetually on guard.

Even if he performs perfectly through an entire piece of writing, he is bound to be glad when he is finished, glad he has a chance to rest for a while.

And I am certain that the material in an alien style does not have quite the quality of the work produced by the same author in his own accustomed style. If one is forced to concentrate on the fine details that define style, then something has to be neglected to make up for that — and what but the other fine details that define quality?

The result is that writers generally don't imitate alien styles except for purposes of humorous parody, when quality is not in question. Thus, a person who imitates James Cagney, saying, "All right, you dirty rat, you gave it to my brother and I'll give it to you," neither expects nor attempts to do a great job of acting, and neither does his audience expect it of him.

Style is important to the reader, too. A particular reader will like one writer better than another, and in my opinion this preference is much more a matter of differences in style than in content. Just as there are some actors you may find a delight to watch even in bad motion pictures, so there are some writers whose styles give you pleasure even when the content of the book is poor.

The reader may not be aware of being influenced by style, or be able to define it or to itemize the components of it if asked to do so, but that doesn't affect the pleasure that's derived from it. (You may not be able to itemize the components and proportions in various sauces, as a skilled chef might, but you like some sauces better than others even so, and knowing the components wouldn't change your decision.)

Well, then, what has all this to do with the anthology you are holding (in case you thought I had forgotten about it)? Just this —

Some forty years ago, Ellery Queen put out an anthology called *Challenge to the Reader,* an excellent collection in which stories appeared under a fictitious name for the author. Furthermore, the stories contained detectives, each characteristic of the author, and the detective's name was also changed. The reader was challenged to identify both the author and the detective.

It was fun, but you had two possible directions to go. You could try to detect items characteristic of either the author *or* the detective. Thus, if a detective spoke of "little gray cells" and you decided he was Hercule Poirot, you knew at once that the writer was Agatha Christie.

After forty years, it seems reasonable to try the gimmick again. After all, a whole new generation of mystery writers has grown up since Ellery Queen's anthology.

Furthermore, this time Alice and I thought we'd make it harder. We've asked each author to write an original story for this anthology, but one that does *not* use a characteristic detective or a characteristic background. If Agatha Christie had a story in this book (and she hasn't, of course) it would not involve either Hercule Poirot or Miss Marple. If Dick Francis had a story in this book (and he hasn't, either) it would not involve horse racing in any way.

Then what is left?

Style. Each writer writes in his or her own style, and it is up to you to spot that style if you can. We don't expect miracles. A list of the authors from among whom you must choose is given, in alphabetical order, on the reverse of the contents page. The name of each author is given with the story in a simple code that is explained in the back of the book.

If, then, you are impatient with guessing games, or if you haven't read enough stories of enough of the authors to feel you stand a fair chance, you don't have to play. You can look up the code, write in the names of all the authors, and then read the stories. Or you can read the stories without concerning yourself at all over who wrote them. The stories are good enough, in our opinion, to stand on their own.

If, however, you *do* like to play games and are an aficionado of the mystery, and would like to try to spot styles — why, you still have the pleasure of good stories and the added fillip of trying to solve another mystery on your own.

I hope you enjoy yourself either way — and so does Alice.

As another example, there is the anthology The Future I *(Book 224), published by Fawcett Crest in 1980. It contains nineteen science fiction and fantasy stories written in the first person. My coeditors were Marty Greenberg and Joe Olander.*

Why the first person? I couldn't allow the reader to think it was a ploy of desperation in order to have a theme about which to build

an anthology. I therefore wrote an introduction on the matter,
pointing out the significant changes in technique involved in writ-
ing stories in the first person, second person, third person limited,
third person omniscient, and so on. (That meant I had to think
about the subject for the first time.) In any case, here is that
introduction.

from THE FUTURE I (1980)

First Person

Technically speaking, there are several different ways of writing a
story.

You may, for instance, have a number of characters and refer to
each of them by name and by the pronouns "he" or "she" or, possibly, "it." You are then telling the story in the "third person."

You may, if you wish, play no favorites, treating each character
with equal impersonality, repeating what they say and describing
what they do, indicating their facial expressions and tones of voice,
but never directly indicating their thoughts. A particular character
may *say* what he or she is thinking, but in that case that character
must take full responsibility for the truth of the statement. It may
be a lie, and the writer need not directly indicate whether it is a
lie or not.

Such impersonal third-person stories, dealing only with words
and actions, are particularly adapted to adventure stories, or to
cerebral stories such as the classic mystery. Knowing the thoughts
might very well be irrelevant in the first case and might spoil the
suspense in the second.

Total impersonality is uncommon, of course, because there is a
certain aridity about it. Usually, there is a protagonist, some one
person who is the center of the action and who is on scene most or
all of the time, and with whom the sympathy (or, at least, interest)
of the reader lies.

The visual media — stage, motion picture, television — are just
about exclusively this sort of impersonal third person, though usually with a protagonist.

In the visual media, the viewer may, of course, be allowed to deduce the thoughts of the characters. Direct information, such as the Shakespearean soliloquy, or the asides of Eugene O'Neill's *Strange Interlude*, are now either passé or considered stagy and artificial. However, a skillful writer, without ever giving his characters' thoughts directly, can make them unmistakable in the course of the speech and action.

Those who deal in the written word have more leeway. In books and stories it is permissible, even common, to describe the thinking processes of the characters directly, where that is deemed desirable.

On occasion, a writer may delve into the thoughts of all the characters indiscriminately in a kind of omniscient and godlike third person. This is not only very difficult to do, demanding enormous skill if the thoughts are to be distinguished from each other, but is very apt to confuse the reader, since in real life, you know the thoughts of only one character — yourself.

It is much more common, then, for a writer to delve into the thoughts of only one character at a time. The story may be broken up into separate scenes, each containing a number of characters, and in each you may view events through the eyes of only one character and are made aware of the thoughts of only that one character. This mimics life and is easily acceptable.

It is possible to shift from one character to another, seeing different scenes through different eyes. In a long novel, numerous characters may have their turn as protagonists without confusing the reader (given skillful writing).

It is also possible to remain with one character — to tell a long story, involving many characters and many scenes, yet keeping the reader's viewpoint fixed on one protagonist, seeing through only his eyes, thinking only his thoughts, throughout the entire story.

Such a one-viewpoint, third-person tale is comfortable for the reader, for again this is how he experiences life, for he sees only through his own eyes and thinks only his own thoughts.

Naturally, a skillful writer can make it plain what other characters are thinking through indirect information, but then, in real life, you can sometimes tell what other people are thinking (or you think you can).

The more you delve into the thoughts of your characters, and the more you confine your delving to one character per scene or even one character per story, the greater the tendency to shift from events to emotion, from doing to thinking, from action to reaction.

A one-viewpoint, third-person story tends to be slower, more thoughtful, more emotional than an impersonal third-person story. Each variety (or anything in between) can suit a particular story and not suit another. Each can suit a particular reader and not another. There is no "right" or "wrong" involved, or even any "better" or "worse."

A one-viewpoint, third-person story is so like the personal experience of an individual in real life that there is a sharp temptation to pretend that the story *does* represent an individual in real life — that an individual *is* telling a story that *really* happened to him.

In that case, there is an "I" in the story, and it is told in the "first person."

There has to be a suspension of disbelief, of course. We know, when we think about it, that unless the story is strict autobiography, it is just as fictional as a third-person story — that the narrator is not really telling a true story, and actually does not exist.

Nevertheless, if the writer is at all skillful we don't bother thinking that. We read it *as though* it were a true story being told by someone who lived through it.

It is possible to take a one-viewpoint, third-person story and change the name and pronouns of the protagonist to "I," "me," "my," and so on.

It might not then be necessary to change any other word of the story in order to convert it from third person to first person.

In that case, what's the difference between a one-viewpoint, third-person story and a first-person story?

There *is* a difference. In a one-viewpoint, third-person story, the protagonist, however permanently on-scene and however constantly exposing his thoughts, need not expose those thoughts at crucial moments. Those thoughts are under the control of the author. The reader realizes that and accepts the fact that it may be important to conceal thought.

In a first-person story, however, the protagonist is taken as having control over his own thoughts, and for him to conceal those thoughts seems to the reader to be unnatural. Thus, "private-eye detective" stories are often told in the first person with, however, the narrator's thoughts frequently concealed for the sake of suspense. That is what gives these stories a kind of unnatural hardness that some readers like and some don't.

The particular intimacy of first-person narration, the permanently lowered guard where thoughts are concerned, makes it more nearly possible to tell a story almost entirely in thoughts, in emotion, in reaction — distinctly more so than in any kind of third-person narration. First person offers the writer a particular opportunity to be more experimental, more harrowing, more powerful.

It is with that thought in mind that we have prepared an anthology of first-person science fiction, choosing for the most part (but not entirely) just those stories that enable the writer to look inward with all the power and turmoil that that entails.

PART 14

MYSTERIES

TWO OF THE BOOKS *in my second hundred were collections of my Black Widower mysteries (based on my real-life membership in the Trap Door Spiders). Each contained a dozen stories in which the waiter, Henry, solves a problem introduced by the guest at a banquet meeting of the Black Widowers.*

That, of course, did not end the series. In the third hundred books, there appeared a third volume, Casebook of the Black Widowers *(Book 212), published by Doubleday in 1980, containing a dozen more of Henry's ratiocinations.*

My Black Widower stories, although mysteries, rarely involve violence (something of which I seriously disapprove), so that often the Black Widowers are asked to do no more than locate something that is missing, or to work out the meaning of an ambiguous remark. There is always the danger, then, of lending the series a too-mild atmosphere. Occasionally, therefore, I manage to write a real murder *mystery, one in which someone is killed (off-stage, of course). One of the stories in* Casebook of the Black Widowers — *"What Time Is It?" — written especially for the book, is of this sort. All my mysteries are clever, of course, but this one, I think, is especially clever, so I am including it here, in full.*

from CASEBOOK OF THE BLACK WIDOWERS (1980)

What Time Is It?

The monthly banquet of the Black Widowers had proceeded in its usually noisy course and then, over the coffee, there had fallen an unaccustomed quiet.

Geoffrey Avalon sipped at his coffee thoughtfully and said, "It's the little things — the little things. I know a couple who might have been happily married forever. He was a lay reader at an Episcopalian church and she was an unreformed atheist, and they never gave each other a cross look over that. But he liked dinner at six and she liked it at seven, and that split them apart."

Emmanuel Rubin looked up owlishly from his part of the table, eyes unblinking behind thick lenses, and said, "What's 'big' and what's 'little,' Geoff? Every difference is a little difference if you're not involved. There's nothing like a difference in the time sense to reduce you to quivering rage."

Mario Gonzalo looked complacently at the high polish on his shoes and said, "Ogden Nash once wrote that some people like to sleep with the window closed and some with the window open and each other is whom they marry."

Since it was rather unusual that at any Black Widowers banquet three successive comments should be made without an explosive contradiction, it didn't really surprise anyone when Thomas Trumbull furrowed his brows and said, "That's a lot of horsehair. When a marriage breaks up, the trivial reason is never the reason."

Avalon said mildly, "I know the couple, Tom. It's my brother and sister-in-law — or ex-sister-in-law."

"I'm not arguing that they don't say they've split over a triviality, or even that they don't believe it," said Trumbull. "I just say there's something deeper. If a couple are sexually compatible, if there are no money problems, if there is no grave difference in beliefs or attitudes, then they'll stick together. If any of these things fail, then the marriage sours and the couple begin to chafe at trivialities. The trivialities then get blamed — but that's not so."

Roger Halsted, who had been chasing the last of the apple pie about his plate, now cleansed his mouth of its slight stickiness with a sip of black coffee and said, "How do you intend to prove your statement, Tom?"

"It doesn't require proof," said Trumbull, scowling. "It stands to reason."

"Only in your view," said Halsted, warmly, his high forehead flushing pinkly, as it always did when he was moved. "I once broke up with a young woman I was crazy about because she kept saying 'Isn't it a riot?' in and out of season. I swear she had no other flaw."

"You'd be perjuring yourself unconsciously," said Trumbull. "Listen Jim, call a vote."

James Drake, host for the evening, stubbed out his cigarette and looked amused. His small eyes, nested in finely wrinkled skin, darted around the table, and he said, "You'll lose, Tom."

"I don't care if I win or lose," said Trumbull, "I just want to see how many jackasses there are at the table."

"The usual number, I suppose," said Drake. "All those who agree with Tom raise their hands." Trumbull's arm shot up and was the only one to do so.

"I'm not surprised," he said, after a brief look, left and right. "How about you, Henry? Are you voting?"

Henry, the unparalleled waiter at all the Black Widower banquets, smiled paternally. "Actually, I was not, Mr. Trumbull, but if I had voted, I would have taken the liberty of disagreeing with you." He was passing about the table, distributing the brandy.

"You, too, Brutus?" said Trumbull.

Rubin finished his coffee and put the cup down with a clatter. "What the devil, all differences are trivial. Forms of life that are incredibly different superficially are all but identical on the biochemical level. There seems a world of difference between the worm and the earth it burrows in, but, considering the atoms that make it up, both of them . . ."

Trumbull said, "Don't wax poetical, Manny, or, if you must, wax it in your garage and not here. I suspect jackassery is universal but, just to make sure, I'll ask our guest if he is voting."

Drake said, "Let's make that part of the grilling, then. It's time. And you can do the grilling, Tom."

◆

The guest was Barry Levine, a small man, dark-haired, dark-eyed, slim, and nattily dressed. He was not exactly handsome, but he had a cheerful expression that was a good substitute. Gonzalo had already sketched his caricature, exaggerating the good cheer into inanity, and Henry had placed it on the wall to join the rest.

Trumbull said, "Mr. Levine, it is our custom at these gatherings of ours to ask our guest, to begin with, to justify his existence. I shall dispense with that since I will assume that your reason for existence at the moment is to back me up, if you can, in my statement — self-evident, to my way of thinking — that trivialities are trivial."

Levine smiled and said, in a slightly nasal voice, "Trivialities on the human level, or are we talking about earthworms?"

"We are talking about humans, if we omit Manny."

"In that case, I join the jackassery, since, in my occupation, I am concerned almost exclusively with trivia."

"And your occupation, please?"

"I'm the kind of lawyer, Mr. Trumbull, who makes his living by arguing with witnesses and with other lawyers in front of a judge and jury. And that immerses me in triviality."

Trumbull growled. "You consider justice a triviality, do you?"

"I do not," said Levine, with equanimity, "but that is not with what we are directly concerned in the courtroom. In the courtroom, we play games. We attempt to make favorable testimony admissible and unfavorable testimony inadmissible. We play with the rules of questioning and cross-examination. We try to manipulate the choosing of favorable jurors, and then we manipulate the thoughts and emotions of the jurors we do get. We try to play on the prejudices and tendencies of the judge as we know them to be at the start or as we discover them to be in the course of the trial. We try to block the opposition attorney or, if that is not possible, to maneuver him into overplaying his hand. We do all this with the trivia and minutiae of precedence and rationale."

Trumbull's tone did not soften. "And where in all this litany of judicial recreation does justice come in?"

Levine said, "Centuries of experience with our Anglo-American system of jurisprudence has convinced us that in the long run and on the whole, justice is served. In the short run, and in a given specific case, however, it may very well not be. This can't be helped. To change the rules of the game to prevent injustice in a particular case may, and probably will, insure a greater level of injustice on the whole — though once in a while an overall change for the better can be carried through."

"In other words," interposed Rubin, "you despair of universal justice even as a goal of the legal profession?"

"As an attainable goal, yes," said Levine. "In heaven, there may be perfect justice; on Earth, never."

Trumbull said, "I take it, then, that if you are engaged in a particular case, you are not the least interested in justice?"

Levine's eyebrows shot upward. "Where have I said that? Of course I am interested in justice. The immediate service to justice is seeing to it that my client gets the best and most efficient defense that I can give him, not merely because he deserves it, but also because American jurisprudence demands it, and because *he* is deprived of it at *your* peril, for you may be next.

"Nor is it relevant whether he is guilty or innocent, for he is legally innocent in every case until he is proven guilty according to law, rigorously applied. Whether the accused is morally or ethically innocent is a much more difficult question, and one with which I am not primarily concerned. I am secondarily concerned with it, of course, and try as I might, there will be times when I cannot do my full duty as a lawyer out of a feeling of revulsion toward my client. It is then my duty to advise him to obtain another lawyer.

"Still, if I were to secure the acquittal of a man I considered a scoundrel, the pain would not be as intense as that of failing to secure the acquittal of a man who, in my opinion, was wrongfully accused. Since I can rarely feel certain whether a man is wrongfully accused or is a scoundrel past redemption, it benefits both justice and my conscience to work for everyone as hard as I can, within the bounds of ethical legal behavior."

Gonzalo said, "Have you ever secured the acquittal of someone you considered a scoundrel?"

"On a few occasions. The fault there lay almost always in mistakes made by the prosecution — their illegal collection of evidence, or their slovenly preparation of the case. Nor would I waste pity on them. They have the full machinery of the law on their side and the boundless public purse. If we allow them to convict a scoundrel with less than the most legal of evidence and the tightest of cases simply because we are anxious to see a scoundrel punished, then where will you and I find safety? We, too, may seem scoundrels through force of circumstance or of prejudice."

Gonzalo said, "And have you ever failed to secure the acquittal of someone you considered wrongfully accused?"

Here Levine's face seemed to crumple. The fierce joy with which he defended his profession was gone, and his lower lip seemed to quiver for a moment. "As a matter of fact," he said, softly, "I am engaged in a case right now in which my client may well be convicted despite the fact that I consider him wrongfully accused."

Drake chuckled and said, "I told you they'd get that out of you eventually, Barry!" He raised his voice to address the others generally. "I told him not to worry about confidentiality; that everything here was sub rosa. And I also told him it was just possible we might be able to help him."

Avalon stiffened and said in his most stately baritone, "Do you know any of the details of the case, Jim?"

"No, I don't."

"Then how do you know we can help?"

"I called it a possibility."

Avalon shook his head. "I expect that from Mario's enthusiasm, but not from you, Jim."

Drake raised his hand. "Don't lecture, Geoff. It doesn't become you."

Levine interposed. "Don't quarrel, gentlemen. I'll be pleased to accept any help you can offer, and if you can't, I will be no worse off. Naturally, I want to impress on you the fact that even though confidentiality may be the rule here, it is particularly important in this case. I rely on that."

"You may," said Avalon stiffly.

Trumbull said, "All right, now. Let's stop this dance and get down to it. Would you give us the details of the case you're speaking of, Mr. Levine?"

"I will give you the relevant data. My client is named Johnson, which is a name that I would very likely have chosen if I were inventing fictitious names, but it is a real name. There is a chance that you might have heard of this case, but I rather think you haven't, for it is not a local case and, if you don't mind, I will not mention the city in which it occurred, for that is not relevant.

"Johnson, my client, was in debt to a loan shark, whom he knew — that is, with whom he had enough of a personal relationship to be able to undertake a personal plea for an extension of time.

"He went to the hotel room that the loan shark used as his office — a sleazy room in a sleazy hotel that fit his sleazy business. The shark knew Johnson well enough to be willing to see him, and even to affect a kind of spurious bonhomie, but would not grant the extension. This meant that when Johnson went into default he would, at the very least, be beaten up; that his business would be vandalized; that his family, perhaps, would be victimized.

"He was desperate — and I am, of course, telling you Johnson's story as he told it to me — but the shark explained quite coolly that if Johnson were let off, then others would expect the same leniency. On the other hand, if Johnson were made an example of, it would encourage others to pay promptly and perhaps deter some from incurring debts they could not repay. It was particularly galling to Johnson, apparently, that the loan shark waxed virtuous over the necessity of protecting would-be debtors from themselves."

Rubin said dryly, "I dare say, Mr. Levine, that if a loan shark were as articulate as you are, he could make out as good a case for his profession as you could for yours."

Levine said, after a momentary pause, "I would not be surprised. In fact, before you bother to point it out, I may as well say that given the reputation of lawyers with the public, people hearing the defenses of both professions might vote in favor of loan sharks as the more admirable of the two. I can't help that, but I still think that if you're in trouble you had better try a lawyer before you try a loan shark.

"To continue, Johnson was not at all impressed by the shark's rationale for trying to extract blood from a stone, then pulverizing the stone for failure to bleed. He broke down into a rage, screaming out threats he could not fulfill. In brief, he threatened to kill the shark."

Trumbull said, "Since you're telling us Johnson's story, I assume he admitted making the threat."

"Yes, he did," said Levine. "I told him at the start, as I tell all my clients, that I could not efficiently help him unless he told me the full truth, even to confessing to a crime. Even after such a confession, I would still be compelled to defend him, and to fight, at worst, for the least punishment to which he might be entitled and, at best, for acquittal on any of several conceivable grounds.

"He believed me, I think, and did not hesitate to tell me of the threat; nor did he attempt to palliate or qualify it. That impressed me, and I am under the strong impression that he has been telling me the truth. I am old enough in my profession and have suffered the protestations of enough liars to feel confident of the truth when I hear it. And, as it happens, there is evidence supporting this part of the story, though Johnson did not know that at the time and so did not tell the truth merely because he knew it would be useless to lie."

Trumbull said, "What was the evidence?"

Levine said, "The hotel rooms are not soundproof and Johnson was shrieking at the top of his voice. A maid heard just about every word and so did a fellow in an adjoining room who was trying to take a nap and who called down to the front desk to complain."

Trumbull said, "That just means an argument was going on. What evidence is there that it was Johnson who was shrieking?"

"Oh, ample," said Levine. "The desk clerk also knows Johnson, and Johnson had stopped at the desk and asked if the shark was in. The desk clerk called him and sent Johnson up — and he saw Johnson come down later — and the news of the death threat arrived at the desk between those two periods of time.

"Nevertheless, the threat was meaningless. It served, in fact, merely to bleed off Johnson's rage and to deflate him. He left almost immediately afterward. I am quite certain that Johnson was incapable of killing."

Rubin stirred restlessly. He said, "That's nonsense. Anyone is capable of killing, given a moment of sufficient rage or terror and a weapon at hand. I presume that after Johnson left, the loan shark was found dead with his skull battered in; with a baseball bat, with blood and hair on it, lying on the bed; and you're going to tell us that you're sure Johnson didn't do it."

Levine held up his glass for what he indicated with his fingers was to be a touch more brandy, smiled his thanks to Henry, and said, "I have read some of your murder mysteries, Mr. Rubin, and I've enjoyed them. I'm sure that in your mysteries such a situation could occur and you'd find ways of demonstrating the suspect to be innocent. This, however, is not a Rubin mystery. The loan shark was quite alive when Johnson left."

Rubin said, "According to Johnson, of course."

"And unimpeachable witnesses. The man who called down said there was someone being murdered in the next room, and the desk clerk sent up the security man at once, for he feared it was his friend being murdered. The security man was well armed, and though he is not an intellectual type, he is perfectly competent to serve as a witness. He knocked and called out his identity, whereupon the door opened and revealed the loan shark, whom the security man knew, quite alive — and alone. Johnson had already left, deflated and de-energized.

"The man at the desk, Brancusi is his name, saw Johnson leave a few seconds after the security man had taken the elevator up. They apparently passed each other in adjoining elevators. Brancusi called out, but Johnson merely lifted his hand and hurried out. He looked white and ill, Brancusi says. That was about a quarter after three, according to Brancusi — and according to Johnson, as well.

"As for the loan shark, he came down shortly after four and sat in the bar for an hour or more. The bartender, who knew him, testified to that and can satisfactorily enumerate the drinks he had. At about a quarter after five he left the bar and, presumably, went upstairs."

Avalon said, "Did he drink enough to have become intoxicated?"

"Not according to the bartender. He was well within his usual limit and showed no signs of being drunk."

"Did he talk to anyone in particular?"

"Only to the bartender. And according to the bartender, he left the bar alone."

Gonzalo said, "That doesn't mean anything. He might have met someone in the lobby. Did anyone see him go into the elevator alone?"

"Not as far as we know," said Levine. "Brancusi didn't happen to notice, and no one else has admitted to seeing him, or has come forward to volunteer the information. For that matter, he may have met someone in the elevator or in the corridor outside his room. We don't know, and have no evidence to show he wasn't alone when he went into his room shortly after a quarter after five.

"Nevertheless, this two-hour period between a quarter after three and a quarter after five is highly significant. The security guard, who encountered the loan shark immediately after Johnson had left at a quarter after three, found the shark composed and rather amused at the fuss. Just a small argument, he said; nothing important. Then, too, the barman insists that the loan shark's conversation and attitude throughout his time in the bar were normal and unremarkable. He made no reference to threats or arguments."

Halsted said, "Would you have expected him to?"

"Perhaps not," said Levine, "but it is still significant. After all, he knew Johnson. He knew the man to be both physically and emotionally a weakling. He had no fear of being attacked by him, or any doubt that he could easily handle him if he did attack.

"After all, he had agreed to see him without taking the precaution of having a bodyguard present, even though he knew Johnson would be desperate. He was not even temporarily disturbed by

Johnson's outburst and shrugged it off to the guard. During that entire two-hour interval he acted as though he considered my client harmless, and I would certainly make that point to the jury."

Avalon shook his head. "Maybe so, but if your story is going to have any point at all, the loan shark, you will tell us, met with a violent death. And if so, the man who made the threat is going to be suspected of the murder. Even if the loan shark was certain that Johnson was harmless, that means nothing. The loan shark may simply have made an egregious error."

Levine sighed. "The shark did die. He returned to his room at a quarter after five or a minute or two later and, I suspect, found a burglar in action. The loan shark had a goodish supply of cash in the room — necessary for his business — and the hotel was not immune to burglaries. The loan shark grappled with the intruder and was killed before half past five."

Trumbull said, "And the evidence?"

"The man in the adjoining room who had been trying to take a nap two hours before had seethed sufficiently to have been unable to fall asleep until about five and then, having finally dropped off, he was roused again by loud noises. He called down to the desk in a rage, and informed Brancusi that this time he had called the police directly."

Gonzalo said, "Did he hear the same voice he had heard before?"

"I doubt that any voice identification he would try to make would stand up in court," said Levine. "However, he didn't claim to have heard voices. Only the noises of furniture banging, glass breaking, and so on.

"Brancusi sent up the security guard who, getting no answer to his knock and call this time, used his passkey at just about half past five and found the loan shark strangled, the room in wild disorder, and the window open. The window opened on a neighboring roof two stories lower. An experienced cat burglar could have made it down without trouble and might well have been unobserved.

"The police arrived soon after, at about twenty to six."

Trumbull said, "The police, I take it, do not buy the theory that the murder was committed by a burglar."

"No. They could detect no signs on the wall or roof outside the window to indicate the recent passage of a burglar. Instead, having discovered upon inquiry of the earlier incident from the man who had called them, they scorn the possibility of coincidence and feel that Johnson made his way to the room a second time, attacked and strangled the loan shark, knocking the furniture about in the process, then opened the window to make it look as though an intruder had done the job, hastened out of the door, missing the security man by moments, and passing him on the elevator again."

Trumbull said, "Don't you believe that's possible?"

"Oh, anything's *possible*," said Levine, coolly, "but it is not the job of the prosecutor to show it's possible. He has to show it's actually so beyond a reasonable doubt. The fact that the police saw nothing on the walls or roof is of no significance whatever. They may not have looked hard enough. A negative never impresses either judge or jury — and shouldn't. And threats at a quarter after three have nothing to do with an act at twenty after five or so, unless the man who made the threat at the former time can be firmly placed on the scene at the later time."

Gonzalo was balancing his chair on its back legs with his hands gripping the table. "So what's the problem?"

"The problem is, Mr. Gonzalo," said Levine, "that Johnson *was* placed on the scene of the crime at about the time of the killing."

Gonzalo brought his chair forward with a clatter. "With good evidence?"

"The best," said Levine. "He admits it. Here is what happened: In the two hours after he had left the loan shark, Johnson hurriedly scraped up every bit of money he had, borrowed small sums from several friends, made a visit to a pawnshop, and had raised something like a third of what he owed. He then came back to the hotel, hoping for as long an extension as possible through payment of this part sum. He had little hope of success, but he had to try.

"He arrived at the hotel at about a quarter to six, after the murder had been committed, and he noted a police squad car at the curb outside the hotel. Except for noticing its existence, he paid it little attention. He had only one thing on his mind.

"He headed straight for the elevator, which happened to be at the lobby with its door open. As he stepped out of it at the loan shark's floor, he saw a policeman at the door of the room he was heading for. Almost instinctively, he ducked back into the elevator and pushed the lobby button. He was the only man in the elevator,

and there were no calls to higher floors. The elevator moved downward, stopping at no floors. When he reached the lobby, he hastened out, went home, and stayed there till the police came for
him."

A curl of cigarette smoke hung above Drake's head. He said, "I
suppose they learned of the earlier threat and took him in for
questioning."

"Right," said Levine.

"But they can't make Johnson testify against himself, so how do
they show he was on the spot at the time of the murder?"

"For one thing, Brancusi saw him when he was heading for the
elevator. Brancusi called out to head him off and prevent him from
running into the police. Johnson didn't hear him, and the elevator
doors closed behind him before Brancusi could do anything else.
Brancusi insists, however, that Johnson was back down again in
two minutes or so and hastened out. And he is prepared to swear
that Johnson left at precisely ten minutes to six."

Drake said, "Is Brancusi really sure of that?"

"Absolutely. His shift was over at six o'clock, and he was furious
at the fact that the murder had not taken place an hour later, when
he would have been off duty. As it was, he was sure he would be
needed for questioning and might be kept for hours. He was therefore unusually aware of the time. There was an electric clock on
the wall to one side of his desk, a nice large one with clear figures
that was new and had been recently installed. It was accurate to
the second, and he is absolutely certain it said ten to six."

Avalon cleared his throat. "In that case, Mr. Levine, Brancusi
backs up Johnson's story and places your client at the scene not at
the time of the murder but afterward."

Levine said, "Here is where the trivialities come in. Brancusi is
a bad witness. He has a small stutter, which makes him sound unsure of himself; he has one drooping eyelid, which makes him look
hangdog and suspicious; and he has distinct trouble in looking you
in the eye. The jury will be ready to believe him a liar.

"Second, Brancusi is a friend of Johnson's, has known him from
childhood, and is still a drinking buddy of the man. That gives him
a motive for lying, and the prosecution is sure to make the most of
that.

"Finally, Brancusi may not want to testify at all. He served six months in jail for a minor offense quite a number of years ago. He has lived a reasonably exemplary life since and naturally doesn't want that earlier incident to be made public. For one thing, it could cost him his job."

Rubin said, "Could the prosecution bring up the matter? It's irrelevant, isn't it?"

"Quite irrelevant, but if the prosecution takes the attitude that it serves to cast a doubt on the reliability of Brancusi as a witness, they might slip it past the judge."

Rubin said, "In that case, if you put neither Johnson nor Brancusi on the stand, the prosecution would still be stuck with the task of proving that Johnson was at the scene at the right time. They can't call Johnson themselves, and they won't call Brancusi to give his evidence because they then can't cross-examine him and bring out that jail term."

Levine sighed. "There's another witness. The man is an accountant named William Sandow. He had stopped at the hotel lobby to buy a small container of breath fresheners, and while he was at the newsstand, he saw Johnson pass him, hurrying out of the hotel. Later in the evening, he read about the murder, and called the police to volunteer the information. His description of the man he saw was a good one and, eventually, he made a positive identification out of a lineup.

"Sandow said that what drew his attention to the man who passed him was the look of horror and anguish on his face. Of course, he can't use terms like that on the witness stand, but the prosecution can get him to make factual statements to the effect that Johnson was sweating and trembling, and this would give him the air of an escaping murderer."

Rubin said, "No, it doesn't. Lots of things could make a man sweat and tremble, and Johnson had good reason to do so short of murder. Besides, Sandow just bears out the story of Brancusi and Johnson."

Levine shook his head. "No, he doesn't. Sandow says he happened to catch a glimpse of the time as Johnson passed him and swears it was exactly half past five, which is just after the murder was committed but *before* the police arrived. If true, that ruins Johnson's story and makes the assumption that he committed the murder a very tempting one."

Rubin said, "Brancusi backs Johnson. It's one man's word against another's. You can't convict on that."

"You can," said Levine, "if the jury believes one man and not the other. If Brancusi is bound to make a bad impression, Sandow is bound to make a good one. He is open-faced, clean-cut, has a pleasant voice, and exudes efficiency and honesty. The mere fact that he is an accountant gives him an impression of exactness. And whereas Brancusi is a friend of Johnson and therefore suspect, Sandow is a complete outsider with no reason to lie."

Rubin said, "How sure are you of that? He was very ready to volunteer information and get involved. Does he have some secret grudge against Johnson? Or some connection with the loan shark?"

Levine shrugged his shoulders. "There are such things as public-spirited citizens, even today. The fact that he came forward will be in his favor with the jury. Naturally, my office has investigated Sandow's background. We've turned up nothing we can use against him — at least so far."

There was a short silence around the table, and then finally Rubin said, "Honest people make mistakes, too. Sandow says he just happened to catch a glimpse of the time. Just how did that happen? He just happened to glance at his wristwatch? Why? Brancusi had a good reason to watch the clock. What was Sandow's?"

"He does not claim to have looked at his watch. He caught a glimpse of the same wall clock that Brancusi looked at. Presumably, both Brancusi and Sandow were looking at the same clock at the same moment. The same clock couldn't very well tell half past five to one person and ten to six to another at the same time. Clearly, one person is lying or mistaken, and the jury will believe Sandow."

Rubin said, "Brancusi was staring at the clock. Sandow just caught a glimpse. He may have caught the wrong glimpse."

Levine said, "I have considered stressing that point, but I am not sure I ought to. Sandow's statement that he just happened to catch a glimpse sounds honest, somehow. The mere fact that he doesn't claim to see more than he saw, that he doesn't make an undue effort to strengthen his evidence, makes him ring true. And he's an accountant. He says he's used to figures, that he can't help noticing and remembering them. The prosecution will surely have him say that on the stand, and the jury will surely accept that.

"On the other hand, Mr. Rubin, if I try to balance Sandow's cool certainty by having Brancusi become very, very definite and emotional about how certain he is it was ten to six, then he will carry all the less conviction for he will impress the jury as someone who is desperately trying to support a lie. And if it looks as though he is making a good impression, the prosecution will make a major effort to bring out his previous prison record."

Halsted broke in with sudden animation. "Say, could Sandow see the clock from where he says he was standing at the newsstand?"

Levine said, "A good point. We checked that out at once, and the answer is: Yes, he could. Easily."

There was another silence around the table, a rather long one.

Trumbull finally said, "Let's put it as briefly as we can. You are convinced that Johnson is innocent and that Brancusi is telling the truth. You are also convinced that Sandow is either lying or mistaken, but you can't think of any reason he might be or any way of showing he is. And the jury is going to believe Sandow and convict Johnson."

Levine said, "That's about it."

Rubin said, "Of course, juries are unpredictable."

"Yes, indeed," said Levine, "but if that's my only hope, it isn't much of one. I would like better."

Avalon's fingers were drumming noiselessly on the tablecloth. He said, "I'm a patent lawyer myself, and I have just about no courtroom experience. Still, all you need do is cast a reasonable doubt. Can't you point out that a man's liberty rests on a mere glimpse of a clock?"

"I can, and will try just as hard as I can short of pushing the prosecution into attempting to uncover Brancusi's prison record. I would like something better than that, too."

From the sideboard, Henry's voice sounded suddenly. "If you'll excuse me, Mr. Levine — I assume that the clock in question, the one to which both Mr. Brancusi and Mr. Sandow referred, is a digital clock."

Levine frowned. "Yes, it is. I didn't say it was, did I? How did you know?" His momentary confusion cleared, and he smiled. "Well, of course. No mystery. I said it was a new clock, and these days digital clocks are becoming so popular that it is reasonable to suppose that any new clock would be digital."

"I'm sure that is so," said Henry, "but that was not the reason for my conclusion. You said a few moments ago that Mr. Sandow was an accountant and that accountants couldn't help but notice and remember figures. Of course you don't notice and remember figures on an ordinary dial clock — you remember the position of the hands. On a dial clock it is just as easy to tell time when the hour numbers are replaced with dots or with nothing at all."

"Well, then?" said Levine.

"Almost any grown person of reasonable intelligence can tell time at a glance in that way. Accountants have no special advantage. A digital clock is different."

Levine said, "Since it was a digital clock, then accountants *do* have a special advantage. You're not helping me, Henry."

Henry said, "I think I am. You have been unconsciously misleading us, Mr. Levine, by giving the time in the old-fashioned way appropriate to a dial clock. You speak of a quarter after three and a quarter to six and so on. Digital clocks specifically show such times to be three-fifteen and five-forty-five. As digital clocks become more and more universal, times will be spoken of in this way exclusively, I imagine."

Levine seemed a little impatient. "How does this change anything, Henry?"

Henry said, "Your statement was that Brancusi was certain that the time at the crucial moment was ten to six, while Sandow was certain it was half past five. If this were so, and if a dial clock were involved, the position of the hands at the two times would be widely different and neither could make a mistake. A deliberate lie by one or the other would have to be involved.

"On the other hand, if it is a digital clock, Brancusi claims he read five-fifty and Sandow claims he read five-thirty, you see."

Levine said, "Ah, and you think that Sandow misread the figure five for a three. No good; it could be maintained with equal justice that Brancusi mistook the three for a five in his annoyance over the fact that the end of his shift was approaching."

Henry said, "It is not a question of a mistake that anyone could make. It is a mistake that an accountant particularly might make. There are fifty cents to half a dollar but thirty minutes to half an hour, and an accountant above all is apt to think of figures in terms of money. To an accountant five-fifty is most likely to mean five and a half dollars. A quick glimpse at a digital clock reading five-fifty might trigger the response five and a half in an accountant's mind, and he will later swear he had seen the time as half past five."

Avalon looked astonished. "You really think Mr. Sandow could have made that mistake, Henry?"

But it was Levine who answered jubilantly, "Of course! It's the only way of explaining how two people could read the same clock at the same time and honestly come up with two different answers. Besides, *there's* the reasonable doubt. Suppose I set up a screen on which I can flash numbers on the pretext that I have to test Sandow's eyesight and memory of numbers, and ask him to detect and identify numbers flashed only briefly on the screen. If I show him five-fifty with a dollar sign before it, he will be bound to say, 'five and a half dollars.' "

"If he does, I'll ask him if he means five hundred and fifty dollars or five and a half dollars — after all, does he or does he not see the decimal point? — and he will be sure to say five and a half dollars. He will then repeat that with five-fifty written in other printing styles and with the dollar sign left out. Finally, when I flash the image of a digital clock reading five-fifty and ask whether that is five and a half or ten to six, he won't even have to answer. The jury will get the point."

Levine rose to shake Henry's hand. "Thank you, Henry. I said that cases depend on trivialities, but I never dreamed that this one would rest on something as trivial as the difference between a digital clock and a dial clock."

"But," said Henry, "on that piece of trivia depends the freedom of a man who is presumably wrongfully accused of murder, and that is no triviality at all."

I have been working toward a fourth dozen of stories about the Black Widowers, but that collection has been delayed until my fourth hundred books. The reason for the delay is that I spent so much of my time writing the Griswold stories collected in The Union Club Mysteries *(Book 277). I included one of those stories earlier in this book under "Mathematics." I include another one here, a story titled "The Library Book."*

from THE UNION CLUB MYSTERIES (1983)

The Library Book

I looked about at the other three at the Union Club library (Griswold had smoothed his white mustache, taken up his scotch and soda, and settled back in his tall armchair) and said rather triumphantly, "I've got a word processor now and, by golly, I can use it."

Jennings said, "One of those typewriter keyboards with a television screen attached?"

"That's right," I said. "You type your material onto a screen, edit it there — adding, subtracting, changing — then print it up, letter-perfect, at the rate of four-hundred-plus words per minute."

"No question," said Baranov, "that if the computer revolution can penetrate your stick-in-the-mud way of life, it is well on the way to changing the whole world."

"And irrevocably," I said. "The odd part of it, too, is that there's no one man to whom we can assign the blame. We know all about James Watt and the steam engine, or Michael Faraday and the electric generator, or the Wright Brothers and the airplane, but to whom do we attribute this new advance?"

"There's William Shockley and the transistor," said Jennings.

"Or Vannevar Bush and the beginnings of electronic computers," I said, "but that's not satisfactory. It's the microchip that's putting the computer onto the assembly line and into the home, and who made that possible?"

It was only then that I was aware that for once Griswold had not closed his eyes but was staring at us, as clearly wide awake as if he were a human being. "I, for one," he said.

"You, for one, what?" I demanded.

"I, for one, am responsible for the microchip," he said haughtily.

◆

It was back in the early 1960s [said Griswold] when I received a rather distraught phone call from the wife of an old friend of mine, who, the morning's obituaries told me, had died the day before.

Oswald Simpson was his name. We had been college classmates and had been rather close. He was extraordinarily bright, was a mathematician, and after he graduated went on to work with Norbert Wiener at MIT. He entered computer technology at its beginnings.

I never quite lost touch with him, even though, as I need not tell you, my interests and his did not coincide at all. However, there is a kinship in basic intelligence, however differently it might express itself from individual to individual. This I *do* have to tell you three, as otherwise you would have no way of telling.

Simpson had suffered from rheumatic fever as a child and his heart was damaged. It was a shock, but no real surprise to me, therefore, when he died at the age of forty-three. His wife, however, made it clear that there was something more to his death than mere mortality, and I therefore drove upstate to the Simpson home at once. It only took two hours.

Olive Simpson was rather agitated, and there is no use in trying to tell you the story in her words. It took her a while to tell it in a sensible way, especially since, as you can well imagine, there were numerous distractions in the way of medical men, funeral directors, and even reporters, for Simpson, in a limited way, had been well known. Let me summarize, then:

Simpson was not a frank and outgoing person, I recall, even in college. He had a tendency to be secretive about his work, and suspicious of his colleagues. He has always felt people were planning to steal his ideas. That he trusted me and was relaxed with me I attribute entirely to my nonmathematical bent of mind. He was quite convinced that my basic ignorance of what he was doing made it impossible for me to know what notions of his to steal or what to do with them after I had stolen them. He was probably right, though he might have made allowance for my utter probity of character as well.

This tendency of his grew more pronounced as the years passed, and actually stood in the way of his advancement. He was inclined to quarrel with those about him and to make himself generally detestable in his insistence on maintaining secrecy over everything he was doing. There were even complaints that he was slowing company advances by preventing a free flow of ideas.

This, apparently, did not impress Simpson, who also developed a steadily intensifying impression that the company was cheating him. Like all companies, they wished to maintain ownership of any discoveries made by their employees, and one can see their point. The work done would not be possible without previous work done by other members of the company and was the product of the instruments, the ambience, the thought processes of the company generally.

Nevertheless, however much this might be true, there were occasionally advances made by particular persons which netted the company hundreds of millions of dollars, and the discoverer mere thousands. It would be a rare person who would not feel ill-used as a result, and Simpson felt more ill-used than anybody.

His wife's description of Simpson's state of mind in the last few years made it clear that he was rather over the line into a definite paranoia. There was no reasoning with him. He was convinced he was being persecuted by the company, that all its success could be attributed to his own work, but that it was intent on robbing him of all credit and financial reward. He was obsessed with that feeling.

Nor was he entirely wrong in supposing his own work to be essential to the company. The company recognized this or they would not have held on so firmly to someone who grew more impossibly difficult with each year.

The crisis came when Simpson discovered something he felt to be fundamentally revolutionary. It was something that he was certain would put his company into the absolute forefront of the international computer industry. It was also something which, he felt, was not likely to occur to anyone else for years, possibly for decades, yet it was so simple that the essence of it could be written down on a small piece of paper. I don't pretend to understand what it was, but I am certain now it was a forerunner of microchip technology.

It occurred to Simpson to hold out the information until the company agreed to compensate him amply, with a sum many times greater than was customary, and with other benefits as well. In this, one can see his motivation. He knew he was likely to die at any time, and he wanted to leave his wife and two children well provided for. He kept a record of the secret at home, so that his wife would have something to sell to the company in case he did die before the matter was settled, but it was rather typical of him that he did not tell her where it was. His mania for secrecy passed all bounds.

Then one morning, as he was getting ready to get to work, he said to her in an excited way, "Where's my library book?"

She said, "What library book?"

He said, "*Exploring the Cosmos*. I had it right here."

She said, "Oh. It was overdue. I returned a whole bunch of them to the library yesterday."

He turned so white she thought he was going to collapse then and there. He screamed, "How dare you do that? It was *my* library book. I'll return it when I please. Don't you realize that the company is quite capable of burglarizing the home and searching the whole place? But they wouldn't think of touching a library book. It wouldn't be mine."

He managed to make it clear, without actually saying so, that he had hidden his precious secret in the library book, and Mrs. Simpson, frightened to death at the way he was gasping for breath, said distractedly, "I'll go right off to the library, dear, and get it back. I'll have it here in a minute. Please quiet down. Everything will be all right."

She repeated over and over again that she ought to have stayed with him and seen to it that he was calmed, but that would have been impossible. She might have called a doctor, but that would have done no good even if he had come in time. He was convinced that someone in the library, someone taking out the book, would find his all-important secret and make the millions that should go to his family.

Mrs. Simpson dashed to the library, had no trouble in taking out the book once again, and hurried back. It was too late. He had had a heart attack — it was his second, actually — and he was dying. He died, in fact, in his wife's arms, though he did recognize that she had the book again, which may have been a final consolation. His last words were a struggling "Inside — inside —" as he pointed to the book. — And then he was gone.

I did my best to console her, to assure her that what had happened had been beyond her power to control. More to distract her attention than anything else, I asked her if she had found anything in the book.

She looked up at me with eyes that swam in tears. "No," she

said, "I didn't. I spent an hour — I thought it was one thing I could do for him — his last wish, you know — I spent an hour looking, but there's nothing in it."

"Are you sure?" I asked. "Do you know what it is you're looking for?"

She hesitated. "I *thought* it was a piece of paper with writing on it. Something he said made me think that. I don't mean that last morning, but before then. He said many times, 'I've written it down.' But I don't know what the paper would look like, whether it was large or small, white or yellow, smooth or folded — *anything!* Anyway, I looked through the book. I turned each page carefully, and there was no paper of any kind between any of them. I shook the book hard and nothing fell out. Then I looked at all the page numbers to make sure there weren't two pages stuck together. There weren't.

"Then I thought that it wasn't a paper, but that he had written something in the margin. That didn't seem to make sense, but I thought *maybe*. Or perhaps he had written between the lines or underlined something in the book. I looked through all of every page. There were one or two stains that looked accidental, but nothing was actually written or underlined."

I said, "Are you sure you took out the same book you had returned, Mrs. Simpson? The library might have had two copies of it, or more."

She seemed startled. "I didn't think of that." She picked up the book and stared at it, then said, "No, it must be the same book. There's that little ink mark just under the title. There was the same ink mark on the book I returned. There couldn't be two like that."

"Are you *sure?*" I said. "About the ink mark, I mean."

"Yes," she said flatly. "I suppose the paper fell out in the library, or someone took it out and probably threw it away. It doesn't matter. I wouldn't have the heart to start a big fight with the company with Oswald dead. — Though it would be nice not to have money troubles and to be able to send the children to college."

"Wouldn't there be a pension from the company?"

"Yes, the company's good that way, but it wouldn't be enough, not with inflation the way it is; and Oswald could never get any reasonable insurance with his history of heart trouble."

"Then let's get you that piece of paper, and we'll find you a lawyer, and we'll get you some money. How's that?"

She sniffed a little as though she were trying to laugh. "Well, that's kind of you," she said, "but I don't see how you're going to do it. You can't make the paper appear out of thin air, I suppose."

"Sure I can," I said, though I admit I was taking a chance in saying so. I opened the book (holding my breath), and it was there all right. I gave it to her and said, "Here you are!"

What followed was long, drawn out and tedious, but the negotiations with the company ended well. Mrs. Simpson did not become a trillionaire, but she achieved economic security, and both children are now college graduates. The company did well, too, for the microchip was on the way. Without me it wouldn't have gotten the start it did, and so, as I told you at the beginning, the credit is mine.

♦

And, to our annoyance, he closed his eyes.

I yelled sharply, "Hey!" and he opened one of them.

"Where did you find the slip of paper?" I said.

"Where Simpson said it was. His last words were 'Inside — inside —' "

"Inside the book. Of course," I said.

"He didn't say 'Inside the book,' " said Griswold. "He wasn't able to finish the phrase. He just said 'Inside —' and it was a library book."

"Well?"

"Well, a library book has one thing an ordinary book does not have. It has a little pocket in which a library card fits. Mrs. Simpson described all the things she did, but she never mentioned the pocket. Well, I remembered Simpson's last words and looked inside the pocket — and that's where it was!"

PART 15

AUTOBIOGRAPHY

*AS I MENTIONED at the conclusion of OPUS 200, I wrote a
640,000-word autobiography just as I was beginning my third
hundred books. It appeared in two volumes,* In Memory Yet Green
(Book 201), published by Doubleday in 1979, and In Joy Still Felt
(Book 216), published by Doubleday in 1980.

*However, I won't quote any passages from these books. I do
enough talking about myself in this volume as it is. Instead, here
is an essay that is only indirectly autobiographical.*

The magazine Esquire *asked me to do a piece on my father in
which (if I recall correctly) I was supposed to describe how my
view of him changed as I grew older.*

*I tried. I had taken my father for granted when I was a boy
(what boy doesn't?), and it was only when I was a mature man
that, thinking back on it, I realized that his life was, in a way, one
of heroism. The article I wrote was entitled "My Father," and I
sent it to Esquire, which promptly rejected it (I don't know why).*

*I took the rejection philosophically, for nothing I write can avoid
publication in one way or another. When it came time to prepare*
The Roving Mind *(Book 272), which I have mentioned twice before, I included it as the last and climactic essay in the book. It
had appeared nowhere before, but here is its second appearance.*

from THE ROVING MIND (1983)

My Father

My father's life made a sharp right-angled turn in January 1923.
Everything he had been and had had before — vanished.

My father, Judah Asimov, was born in a shtetl named Petrovichi,
in Russia, about 250 miles southwest of Moscow, on December 21,
1896. He was Jewish, but the tsarist oppression and its endemic
anti-Semitism made itself felt there only in its negative aspects.

There were places that Jews couldn't live, things they couldn't do, professions they couldn't enter. Jews in Petrovichi, however, were accustomed to such things and accepted the limits as a fact of life.

There were no active expressions of the anti-Semitism, however; at least, not in Petrovichi. There were no pogroms; there was no violence. My father played peacefully with Gentile boys.

What's more, both my father and mother were among the wealthier townspeople. My father's father owned a mill; my mother's father owned a general store. Both families were economically secure.

My father did not have an education in the ordinary European sense, of course. It was difficult indeed (though not impossible) for a Jew in tsarist Russia to receive what we ordinarily think of as an education, let alone go to a university. However, my father had no ambitions in that direction. He went to a Hebrew school, where he was thoroughly grounded in biblical studies and talmudic scholarship.

He learned to read and write not only Hebrew and Yiddish but Russian as well, and had an opportunity to become acquainted with Russian literature and to read enough secular Russian books to pick up a better education of the ordinary sort than the Gentile boys of the town had a chance to do. He also learned how to keep the books of his father's business, which meant a good acquaintance with the intricacies of arithmetic and calculation.

To be sure, World War I, the Russian Revolution, and the civil war that followed were all unsettling, but again Petrovichi was fortunate. The German army of Kaiser Wilhelm never reached quite as far east as Petrovichi, nor did the marauding White Russian bands reach quite as far north. The new Soviet government established itself quietly and firmly.

Petrovichi remained an island of relative calm and peace in the dreadful storm that was convulsing the land. In the wake of the fallen tsarist autocracy, the new leaders proclaimed that all people would be equal, that education and cultural activities would be encouraged, that cooperative ventures would be welcomed, and so on, and my father took them at their word.

He therefore helped organize a library, and set up regular sessions in which he read aloud from Russian classics to those who were not able to do so for themselves. He participated in a drama

group that produced classic works of Yiddish and Russian drama-
tists for Petrovichi and the surrounding towns. He organized a cooperative that bought and distributed food in order to stave off
hard times during a period of food shortage.

In all this, he was helped by the fact that the local Soviet functionary was a Gentile who, as a boy, had lived in Petrovichi and
had played with my father. Indeed, my father had helped the boy
with his homework.

And that was how things stood at the end of 1922.

What would have happened had things continued so? There
were hard times ahead. Looming beyond the horizon were the Sta-
linist purges of the 1930s, the devastating calamity of the Nazi German invasion, the discomforts of the Soviet anti-Zionist stance.

My father might have survived it all. All my experience of him
makes me certain that he would have acted always as a prudent
man, carefully weighing his actions and never allowing himself to
be misled by ambition into a dangerous exposure.

He was not of the stuff of storybook heroes and dreamed no impossible dreams. He judged the limits of the possible shrewdly and
operated within those limits.

But within those limits, he might have led a happy, useful, and
fruitful life — more educated than most of those about him, more
intelligent, more driving, more quick to seize an opportunity or
see a danger. He would have been an important and successful
man in the limited sphere within which he would have chosen to
operate, and he might have survived all dangers.

Except that, as 1922 came to an end, he was unexpectedly faced
with a situation he had not foreseen, an opportunity he could not
weigh, and he had to make a decision —

♦

My mother had an older half brother, Joseph Berman, who had
immigrated to the United States some time before World War I
and lived in Brooklyn. With Russia racked by foreign invasions,
revolutions, and civil war, he finally wrote to Petrovichi to inquire
as to the welfare of his little sister.

When my mother wrote to him and assured him she and hers
were well, my Uncle Joe invited her to come, with her husband
and children, to the United States. He himself would supply the

necessary sponsorship and the guarantee that the immigrants would not become a public charge. The immigration laws of the United States were still sufficiently liberal to make that possible.

There was a family council on the nature of the action to be taken.

Against emigration was the fact that my parents were comfortable and well off (by the standards of the place and time) and were living where they had lived all their lives, with their family, with their friends, with their steady happiness. Against emigration also was the fact that before they could leave the country they would have to get the permission of the government to do so, and surely the Soviet officials would be inclined to view the mere desire as evidence of disloyalty and act accordingly.

For emigration was the legend of the "golden land" of America, where Jews were free and everyone was rich — something my father was surely too cautious to accept at face value.

What agonies and uncertainties my father and mother endured I do not know. What arguments they made use of pro and con, what advice they received, what fears they entertained, what hopes they experienced, I can't say.

But the decision was made at last, however, and it was to emigrate. It was the only wild decision my father ever made, I think. They would leave their land, their home, their families and perhaps never see any of these things or people again (and they never did) and venture instead into a terra incognita, a land completely unknown.

Having made the decision, my father carried it through with determination. He began with his boyhood friend, who was the local commissar, up through a higher functionary in Gomel, and to Moscow itself.

During the month of January 1923, my father, with my mother and two children (my three-year-old self and my younger sister), made the trip overland to Danzig, by way of Riga. From there a coastal steamer took us to Liverpool, and then the liner *Baltic* took us to Ellis Island, which we reached on February 3, 1923.

◆

The consequences of the decision were drastic and in many ways for the worse. My father was no longer a man of substance and reputation, looked up to and well thought of. In New York, he was virtually penniless and a faceless member of an uncountable crowd.

He applied for citizenship at once and looked forward to becoming an American citizen in five years, with the full rights of citizenship despite his birth and religion — but that did not alter the practical truth that he was a "greenhorn" and suddenly, for the first time in his life, *uneducated.*

In Russia, he could speak both Yiddish and Russian, could converse with equal ease whether he faced a Jew or a Gentile, was as knowledgeable about either Jewish or Russian folkways and customs as any person in the town or in the surrounding region.

In the United States, he could not speak a word of the dominant language; he could not read the street signs; he did not know the ways of the people.

He could turn for help to his fellow Jews; but, if they had been in the United States long enough to be able to help, they could not hide their amusement at his ignorance, or their contempt for it, and he burned with embarrassment. He was a stranger in a strange land, a person of no consequence at all, and with nothing in the way of skills out of which he could make anything but the barest living. In a very important sense, he found himself illiterate and mute.

Yet he managed to find work; and in 1926, three years after he had come to the United States, he had managed somehow to accumulate the money to buy a small mom-and-pop candy store.

In that, and in other candy stores over the next thirty years, my father and mother (and the children) worked sixteen hours a day seven days a week and counted out the profits by the pennies. My father managed to carry us through the Great Depression without missing a meal or being forced to turn to charity. He managed to send me and my younger, American-born brother to college.

Eventually, when his children were grown and independent, my father sold the candy store and took a part-time job instead. (By part-time, he meant forty hours a week.)

He refused help at all times and would not take the money from either my brother or me when we were prosperous and could well afford to let him have all he wanted. In the last year of his life, he retired to Florida on his own money, and there he died of natural causes on August 4, 1969, leaving my mother enough money to support her for the remaining four years of her life.

♦

At no time did I ever hear him complain of his decision. He had not fled oppression or grinding poverty. He had come, I believe, because it was his considered intention to accept a lowered status for himself in order that his children end up with a heightened status. If that was his intention, it was fulfilled and — I am thankful to be able to say — he lived long enough to see it fulfilled. In particular, he lived to see his older son (me) a university professor and the author of a hundred books.

And it was not America alone that made it possible. It was my father as well. I like to think there is enough in me for me to have been successful under any reasonable conditions — but can I be sure? With another father, with other goals set for me, what might I have become?

Jews, generally (according to the stereotype), value learning and encourage their children to enter the intellectual professions. How true that stereotype is, or how general it is, I do not know. Certainly I have met many Jews who are neither as intelligent or as learned as many Gentiles I have met.

But the special case of my father is beyond doubt. Perhaps because he had himself passed from a state of being educated and learned to a state of being virtually illiterate, he valued education and learning all the more. He could not regain what he had once had, but he was determined that *I* was to have it.

He would not let me read the magazines he sold to others, because he felt they would muddy my thinking — but he let me read science fiction magazines, because he respected the word "science" and felt they would lure me into becoming a scientist — and he was right.

He had no money to buy me the things I wanted, and I knew that, and I rarely asked him for anything — but, when I was overwhelmed with desire for something that spelled "learning," he managed to find a way to let me have it. When I was eleven, he bought me a copy of the *World Almanac* for my birthday, when that was what I wanted. I might have cried myself sick for a baseball but I wouldn't have gotten it.

When I was fifteen, he managed to scrape together the funds to buy me a used typewriter when I wanted it. If I had wanted a bicycle, I might as well have asked for the moon. — And as soon as I submitted a story to a magazine, when I was eighteen, *and before I had actually sold one,* my father, on his own initiative, managed to find the money to buy me a *new* typewriter. That was an act of faith that staggered me.

Long afterward, when I was turning out book after book in steady progression, and giving a copy of each to my father as a matter of course, he looked through one of my more difficult science popularizations and finally managed to ask me something that must have long puzzled him.

"Isaac," he said, hesitantly, "where did you learn all this?"

"From you, Pappa," I said.

"From *me?*" he said. "I don't know one word about these things."

"Pappa," I said, "you taught me to value learning. That's all that counts. All these things are just details."

PART 16

SCIENCE FICTION

IN THE FIRST TWO OPUS BOOKS, I did not have a section on science fiction. It seemed superfluous. I had written a great deal of science fiction and everyone knew it, so there seemed to be no need to stress the fact.

Yet it seemed to me that I rarely wrote about science fiction. As it happens, that was an illusion. When, eventually, I tried collecting them, I was astonished to find how many such essays there were. So many, in fact, that although Opus 200 ended with the section "Autobiography," I now feel justified in adding a sixteenth section entitled "Science Fiction."

What caused me to start putting together such essays? Well, Isaac Asimov's Science Fiction Magazine has now existed and flourished for over eighty issues. In each one I have had an editorial, and the subject was usually (though not always) one facet or another of science fiction.

Realizing this, Marty Greenberg suggested that I do a book of essays on science fictional subjects, and it struck me as a good idea. I gathered such essays together and found fifty-five that I could use (only half of which were editorials from my magazine). The collection appeared as Asimov on Science Fiction (Book 227), which was published by Doubleday in 1981.

From it, I include one essay that first appeared as an editorial in my magazine, "The Boom in Science Fiction," and one that did not, "The Ring of Evil."

from ASIMOV ON SCIENCE FICTION (1981)

The Boom in Science Fiction

I am frequently asked by reporters: "How does the current boom in science fiction affect you?"

The answer is: "Not at all and in no way. The boom in science

fiction to which you refer is in the movies and television. My own
science fiction is in the magazines and books. The latter is doing
well, thank you, but it is the former which is having its boom, and
the two are of different species. They bear the same name but that
is where the similarity ends."

That always surprises the reporters, and it may even surprise
you, so let me explain. In order to do so, I must give the two
species different names to avoid confusion.

In the movies and television, science fiction deals primarily with
images, so we might call it image-science-fiction. Since the show-
business people and journalists who talk about image-science-fiction refer to it, abominably, as sci-fi, suppose we call image-science-fiction i-sci-fi or, better yet, eye-sci-fi.

The science fiction of magazines and books we can simply call
what we have always called it: science fiction, or possibly s.f.

To begin with, then, eye-sci-fi has an audience that is fundamentally different from that of science fiction. In order for eye-sci-fi to
be profitable it must be seen by tens of millions of people; in order
for science fiction to be profitable it need be read only by tens of
thousands of people. This means that some 90 percent (perhaps as
much as 99 percent) of the people who go to see eye-sci-fi are likely
never to have read science fiction.

The purveyors of eye-sci-fi cannot assume that their audience
knows anything about science, has any experience with the scientific imagination, or even has any interest in science fiction.

But, in that case, why should the purveyors of eye-sci-fi expect
anyone to see the pictures? Because they intend to supply something that has no essential connection with science fiction, but that
tens of millions of people are willing to pay money to see. What is
that? Why, scenes of destruction.

You can have spaceships destroying spaceships, monsters destroying cities, comets destroying the Earth. These are called "special effects," and it is what people go for. A piece of eye-sci-fi without destruction is, I think, almost unheard of. If such a thing were
made, no one would go to see it; or, if it were so good that it would
indeed pull a small audience, it would not be thought of as science
fiction of any kind.

The overriding necessity for having special effects to make sure
a piece of eye-sci-fi can make money means that such movies are
incredibly expensive. This puts the producers in a bind. They may

possibly make so much money that any expense is justified — but how can they know in advance the movie will make that kind of money? They don't, so there is always a tendency to cut down on expenses, and *cheap* special effects are incredibly bad.

Then, too, even if a producer decides to spend freely on special effects, he is quite likely to skimp on other aspects of the picture, and first in line for skimping is always the writing. The result is that the plot and dialogue of any piece of eye-sci-fi is generally several grades below poor. Once a character has managed to say "Oh, wow!" as a spaceship explodes, he is usually a spent force.

Still further, once people get used to special effects and destruction, they quickly get jaded. The next picture must have more and better special effects, which means more expense, and rottener everything-but-special-effects.

Finally, the producers of eye-sci-fi have the "bottom line" psychology — that is, they consider only the final bookkeeping calculation that tells whether one has made a profit or a loss and how much of either.

Naturally, we all have a bottom-line psychology. I write for money; and you do whatever you do for money. Still, the larger the sum of money you invest and the larger the profit or loss you may come out with, the more the bottom line tends to swallow up everything else. My own books, essays, and stories represent such small profits or losses, individually, that I can afford to go my own way, aim for the unusual now and then, take a chance on quality once in a while, shrug off the occasional failure. You, undoubtedly, can do the same. A movie or TV producer can't. One failure may wipe him out. One success may make him a millionaire.

With the intense bottom-line psychology that comes when one throw of the dice is the difference between pauperdom and affluence, it is impossible for a producer to deal with anything that he doesn't think is sure-fire. In eye-sci-fi only the special effects approach is sure-fire. Everything else, therefore, receives no attention. Even if some minor facet of the production can be changed in such a way as to greatly improve it without either trouble or expense to speak of, it won't be done. Why should the producer take the time or make the effort to do so when it doesn't matter to him, and when all his concentration must be on the sure-fire?

Well, then, do I see no good in eye-sci-fi? No, I am not a complete curmudgeon in this respect. Some eye-sci-fi can be amusing if it contains humor and has the grace not to take itself too seriously. That's why I enjoyed *Star Wars* and why I expect to enjoy *Superman* when I get around to seeing it. Then, too, if something is outright fantasy and if cartoon techniques take some of the pressure off the special effects, the results can be tolerable.

Besides that, a small percentage of those who are introduced to eye-sci-fi may happen to know how to read, and these may be impelled by curiosity to read science fiction, something they might not otherwise have thought of doing. Thus a boom in eye-sci-fi means our audience can grow somewhat even if it doesn't quite go along with the boom.

It may seem to you that I haven't made the difference between eye-sci-fi and science fiction clear. After all, consider the science fiction magazines.

Are some of them not primarily devoted to adventure science fiction, to scenes of action, to destruction?

Yes, they want action, and if it is necessary to destroy a spaceship, they destroy it — but destroying a spaceship in words is no more costly or difficult than doing anything else in words, so it doesn't take up all the mind and effort of all of us. Writers have time and will and active desire to add other things as well — plot, motivation, characterization, and some respect for science.

Since we who write for the magazines are all only human, we may fall short in these added qualities out of sheer lack of ability, but it is *never* out of a contempt for our audience or out of indifference to anything but the bottom line.

We are not nobler than the people in Hollywood; if we were exposed to their pressures, we might do just as they do.

But we are not in Hollywood, we are here; and so we need only please one thousandth the size of audience that they do. We like to think that our thousandth part of the audience happens to be the best thousandth. It is an audience that can read, that likes its adventure with good writing stirred in, that has a respect for science even when it doesn't have a professional understanding of it.

The Ring of Evil

The Lord of the Rings is a three-volume epic of the battle between Good and Evil. The first volume is *The Fellowship of the Ring,* the second, *The Two Towers*, and the third is *The Return of the King*.

The canvas is broad, the characters are many, and the action is endlessly suspenseful and exciting. And the central object of the epic, about which all revolves, is the One Ring.

There are twenty rings altogether, which give power, but Sauron, the "Dark Lord," the embodiment of Evil, the Satan figure, is the Lord of the Rings. He has made One Ring to be the master of the rest —

"One Ring to rule them all, One Ring to find them,
One Ring to bring them all and in the darkness bind them,
In the Land of Mordor where the Shadows lie."

As long as this One Ring exists, Evil cannot be defeated. Mordor is the blasted land in which Sauron rules and where everything is twisted and bent and perverted into his service. And Mordor will extend its poisoned atmosphere over all the world once the One Ring returns to Sauron.

For Sauron does not have it. In the long distant past, Sauron lost control of it, and through a series of events, part of which are described in *The Hobbit*, a kind of children's prologue to *The Lord of the Rings*, the One Ring had fallen into the hands of Bilbo Baggins, the Hobbit of the title.

There are numerous forces trying to fight for the Good and to defeat Sauron, but of them all the Hobbits are the smallest and weakest. They are about the size of children and are as unsophisticated and simple as children. Yet it falls upon another Hobbit, named Frodo, the nephew of Bilbo, to dispose of the One Ring and make sure that it will never again fall into the hands of Sauron.

At first as part of a small fellowship, struggling through a deadly and hostile world, and later with only the company of his faithful servant Sam, Frodo must find some way of avoiding Sauron's allies so that he might take the One Ring into Mordor itself. There, in Sauron's very lair, he must take it to Mount Doom, the seething volcano where the One Ring had been forged and in whose fires alone it could be melted and destroyed. With that destruction, if it can be carried through, Sauron's powers would end, and, for a time at any rate, Good would prevail.

What does this struggle represent? What contributed to its construction inside Tolkien's mind? We might wonder if Tolkien himself, if he were still alive, could tell us entirely. Such literary constructions take on a life of their own and there are never simple answers to "What does this mean?"

Tolkien was a student of the ancient Teutonic legends, and one gets a feeling that the One Ring may be an echo of the Ring of the Nibelungen, and that behind Sauron is the evil and beautiful face of Loki, the traitorous Norse god of fire.

Then, too, *The Hobbit* was written in the 1930s and *The Lord of the Rings* in the 1950s. In between was World War II, and Tolkien lived through the climactic year of 1940, when Great Britain stood alone before the forces of Hitler.

After all, the Hobbits are inhabitants of "the Shire," which is a transparent representation of Great Britain at its most idyllic, and behind Sauron there might be the demonic Adolf Hitler.

But then, too, there are wider symbolisms. Tom Bombadil is a mysterious character who seems to represent nature as a whole. The treelike Ents characterize the green forests, and the Dwarves represent the mountains and the mineral world. There are the Elves, too, powerful but passé, representatives of a time passing into limbo, who will not survive even though Sauron were destroyed.

Always, though, we come back to the One Ring. What does it represent?

In the epic, it controls unlimited power and inspires infinite desire even though it is infinitely corrupting. Those who wear it are weighed down by it and tortured, but they can't let it go, though it erodes them, body and soul. Gandalf, who is the best and strongest of the characters in the book who fight for the Good, won't touch it, for he fears it will corrupt even him.

In the end, it falls upon Frodo, small and weak, to handle it. It corrupts and damages him, too, for when he stands on Mount Doom at last, and it will take but the flick of a finger to cast the One Ring to destruction and ensure the end of Evil, he finds he cannot do it. He has become the One Ring's slave. (And in the end, it is Evil that destroys Evil, where Frodo the Good fails.)

What is the One Ring, then? What does it represent? What is it that is so desirable and so corrupting? What is it that can't be let go even though it is destroying us?

Well —

My wife, Janet, and I, on occasion, drive down the New Jersey Turnpike through a section of oil refineries where the tortured geometry of the structures stands against the sky, and where waste gases burn off in eternal flames, and where a stench reaches us that forces us to close the car windows. And as we approached it once, Janet rolled up the windows, sighed, and said, "Here comes Mordor."

She was right. The Mordor of *The Lord of the Rings* is the industrial world, which is slowly developing and taking over the whole planet, consuming it, poisoning it. The Elves represent the preindustrial technology that is passing from the scene. The Dwarves, the Ents, and Tom Bombadil represent the various facets of nature that are being destroyed. And the Hobbits of the Shire represent the simple, pastoral past of humanity.

And the One Ring?

It is the lure of technology; the seduction of things done more easily; of products in greater quantity; of gadgets in tempting variety. It is gunpowder, and the automobile, and television; all the things that people snatch for if they don't have them; all the things that people can't let go once they do have them.

Can we let go? The automobile kills fifty thousand Americans every year. Can we abandon the automobile because of that? Does anyone even seriously suggest we try?

Our American way of life demands the burning of vast quantities of coal and oil that foul our air, sicken our lungs, pollute our soil and water, but can we abandon that burning? To feed the needs of our society, we need more oil than we can supply ourselves, so that we must obtain fully half from abroad. We obtain it from lands that hold us in chains in consequence and whom we dare not offend. Can we diminish our needs in order to break those chains?

We hold the One Ring and it is destroying us and the world, and there is no Frodo to take the load of it upon himself, and there is no Mount Doom to take it to, and there are no events to ensure the One Ring's destruction.

Is all this inevitable? Has Sauron won? Have the Shadows of the Land of Mordor fallen over all the world?

We might think so, if we wish to look at only the worst of the industrial world and visualize an impossible best of the preindustrial world.

But then, the happy pastoral world of the Shire never existed except in the mind of Nostalgia. There might have been a thin leaven of landowners and aristocrats who lived pleasant lives, but those lives were made pleasant only through the unremitting labors of servants, peasants, serfs, and slaves whose lives were one long brutality. Those who inherit the traditions of a ruling class (as Tolkien did) are too aware of the past pleasantness of life, and too unaware of the nightmare that filled it just beyond the borders of the manor house.

With all the miseries and terrors that industrialization has brought, it has nevertheless, *for the first time,* brought literacy and leisure to hundreds of millions; given them some share of the material goods of the world, however shoddy and five-and-ten they might be; given them a chance at appreciating the arts, even if only at the level of comic book and hard rock; given them a chance at a life that has more than doubled in average length since preindustrial days.

It is easy to talk of the fifty thousand Americans (1 out of 4400) who are killed by automobiles each year. We forget the much larger fractions of the population who were killed each year by infectious epidemics, deficiency diseases, and hormone disorders that are today thoroughly preventable or curable.

If we cannot give up the One Ring, there's a good reason for that. If the One Ring is drawing us to our destruction, that is because we are misusing it in our greed and folly. Surely there are ways of using it wisely. Are we so willing to despair so entirely of humanity as to deny that we can be sane and wise if we must be?

No, the One Ring is not wholly Evil. It is what we make it, and we must rescue and extend those parts of it that are Good.

— But never mind.

One can read *The Lord of the Rings* without getting lost in the symbolism. It is a fascinating adventure that doesn't get consumed with the reading. I have myself read it four times and like it better each time. I think it is about time I read it a fifth time.

And in doing so, I will take care to look upon the One Ring as — a ring.

PART 17

MISCELLANEOUS

YOU WOULDN'T THINK that with my writing divided into sixteen categories it would be possible to decide that any of my books were "Miscellaneous." I am, however, forced to set up such a section.

To explain this odd situation, I was persuaded by Jerome Agel and Red Dembner, two delightful gentlemen, to do a book that would be a compendium of odd facts. To help, they got together over a dozen people, who then bombarded me with many thousands of odd and enticing items of all kinds.

I went over them all, eliminated many because I simply didn't believe them, or seriously suspected they might not be correct, and went on to contribute many items of my own that eventually made up about one fifth of the book (and collected only one fifth of the royalties, therefore).

Furthermore, I insisted that I be listed as the editor, not the author, and that the name of everyone who participated be included in the book, and this was done. (One of my foibles is that every book for which I do not write every word have ample indication of that fact. Hence, if you see a book that says nothing to the contrary you may rest assured that, however long and complicated the book may be, I have written every word without help — without even secretarial help.)

It appeared as Isaac Asimov's Book of Facts (Book 210), published by Grosset & Dunlap in 1979. As a small sampling of what the book was like, here are the items under the heading "Cities." (There are seventy-seven headings in the book, arranged alphabetically, and over three thousand items altogether.)

from ISAAC ASIMOV'S BOOK OF FACTS (1979)

Cities

All of Reykjavik, the capital of Iceland, is heated by underground hot springs. Reykjavik is probably the cleanest capital city in the world.

The city with the most blacks is New York, with 1,666,636, as of the 1970 census. The second largest "black city" is Kinshasa, Zaire, with a population of 1,623,760.

New York City's administrative code still requires that hitching posts be located in front of City Hall so that reporters can tie their horses.

At the time of the U.S. War of Independence, Philadelphia was second only to London as the largest English-speaking city in the world.

Before today's skyscrapers, London's skyline was largely the creation of a single genius, Sir Christopher Wren (1632–1723), who had had only six months of architectural training in Paris. Wren was a celebrated mathematician, but today is remembered as an architect. Among the fifty-two London churches he created from 1670 to 1711 was the great Saint Paul's Cathedral.

Tiny Juneau, Alaska — whose population in the most recent U.S. census was recorded as being in excess of six thousand — has the distinction of being the largest city in the United States in terms of area. In 1970, it merged with Douglas, which is situated on an island across the Gastineau Channel, and now 3108 square miles lie within the city limits.

About thirty-five thousand people work in the 110-story-tall twin towers of the World Trade Center in downtown New York, and about eighty thousand more visit on business every day.

There are more dentists in Ann Arbor, Michigan, proportionately, than in any other city in the United States. Ann Arbor also has proportionately more burglaries than any other city. No connection has been established between the two.

When Pierre L'Enfant's plans for "Federal City" were lost, Ben-

jamin Banneker, a Maryland free black, remembered in detail —
and in so may in part have created — the gridiron arrangement of
streets cut by diagonal avenues radiating from the Capitol and the
White House. The capitol then was laid out by Andrew Ellicott.

About 24 percent of the total ground area of Los Angeles is said
to be committed to automobiles.

From the tenth to the fifteenth centuries, when Paris and London were ramshackle towns, with streets of mud and hovels of
wood, there was a queen city in the East that was rich in gold,
filled with works of art, bursting with gorgeous churches, busy
with commerce, the wonder and the admiration of all who saw it.
The city was the capital of the Roman Empire of the Middle Ages
— Constantinople. (Indeed, there were many glamorous cities in
the non-Western world.)

Central Park in the heart of Manhattan, in New York City, is so
beautifully designed and its features so finely accentuated that it
would seem that nature herself had been the designer. Not so. The
840 acres were a marshy area littered with filth and shanties when
Frederick Law Olmsted and Calvert Vaux, in 1857, began shaping
a park that now serves as the model for other public areas in the
United States.

So many empty mine chambers — called voids — underlie
Scranton, Pennsylvania, that the secretary of mines for Pennsylvania suggested in 1970 it would be "more economical" to abandon
the city than to fill the voids.

Baghdad was once the greatest city of the world. It had a population of 2 million, and was larger even than Babylon in its prime.
Baghdad's most glamorous and legendary period began in 786 A.D.,
when Harun al-Rashid, or "Aaron the Just," ascended the throne.

The underground of Paris is unique. A system of pipes, 600 miles
long, furnishes compressed air to homes and businesses — it
serves many purposes, but it was built originally to operate clocks
and elevators.

La Paz, Bolivia, which is about 12,000 feet above sea level, is
nearly a fireproof city, and the fire engines — ordered out of civic
pride — gather dust in their firehouses. At that altitude, the
amount of oxygen in the atmosphere barely supports fire.

Mexico city, known as Tenochtitlán when it was invaded by Cor-
tez in 1519, was a flower-covered, whitewashed city five times as
large as London of the same period.

New York City has 570 miles of shoreline.

The largest city in the New World in 1650 was Potosí in Bolivia. Huge silver deposits were discovered there in 1546, and by 1650 Potosí had reached a population of 160,000. Potosí is also one of the highest cities of the world: 13,780 feet. Its population has dropped to about 60,000 because of various natural and manmade disasters and the discovery of competitive mines in Peru and Mexico.

Special oil lanterns for lighting public places began to appear in European cities in the last third of the seventeenth century. The King of Naples tried to introduce street lights, but succeeded only when holy shrines were set up at convenient street corners and the inhabitants were persuaded to keep lamps burning below them. This was the only regular illumination Naples had from the 1750s to 1806, when actual street lamps appeared.

It wasn't too long ago — 1977, to be exact — that Cairo, a city of 8 million people, had only 208,000 telephones and no telephone book. The phone system was said to have been practically worthless during the workday. Cairo businessmen often flew to Athens to place calls from hotels there.

I wrote two other books for Red Dembner, which he published under the imprint Dembner Books. They are quiz books with the questions and answers prepared by a meticulous Canadian polymath, Ken Fisher. Red asked me to go over the manuscript and recommend whether it ought to be published (I answered with an enthusiastic affirmative). He then asked me to check for any errors I could find (as far as that was possible), to divide the manuscript into two books, and to write an introduction for each. To all of this I agreed.

Red then suggested that my name be included in the title, and I agreed only on condition that Ken Fisher agreed to that and that his name appeared on the cover as the author. Both conditions were met, so Isaac Asimov Presents Superquiz *(Book 259) and* Isaac Asimov Presents Superquiz 2 *(Book 284) were published in 1982 and 1983, respectively.*

After some hesitation, I included these in my list, since I had worked on them and writing of mine appeared in each book. Here is the introduction from the second volume, entitled "The Delight of Uncertainty."

from ISAAC ASIMOV PRESENTS SUPERQUIZ 2 (1983)

The Delight of Uncertainty

Last year, *Isaac Asimov Presents Superquiz* by Ken Fisher was published, and we hoped it would do well. There was reason for hope, as I pointed out in the introduction; there is pleasure in vying with one another in answering questions and in exercising one's store of gathered knowledge. In fact, the subtitle of the book was *The Fun Game of Q & A's.*

Though experience and judgment told us this was a good project, could we be certain? After all, we live in a new age. The world has become electronic, and computers hem us in on all sides.

Here we present you with a simple book made up of nothing more advanced than print. There are no buttons to push, no screens on which answers can be displayed, no sights and sounds, no beeps and flashes, to signify right or wrong. Could we be certain that the public would be interested in a question-and-answer book without these modernistic additions?

Actually, we couldn't. Publishing is notoriously a field in which very little is a sure thing.

And yet, there are possible delights to uncertainty, too. If we were absolutely sure the book would be a success, there would be a certain dullness to receiving good news of sales and royalties. We might be apt to yawn and shift our attention to other things.

As it was, the book did better than our cautious anticipation led us to expect. Our feeling that people would go for the essentials of competition without unnecessary frills was justified in rather heaping measure. We were delighted, and as a measure of our delight, here is a second volume of *Superquiz.*

From *Isaac Asimov Presents Superquiz 2: The Fun Game of Q & A's* by Ken Fisher, published by Dembner Books, New York, 1983. Reprinted by permission of Red Dembner Enterprises Corp.

While we are on the subject of the delights of uncertainty, let me point out that such pleasures are not reserved for publishers and authors only. In this volume (and, indeed, in the first one as well) we grant each of you these same delights.

You must remember, in the first place, that those of us involved in the production of these books are not supermen who are incapable of error. This must be remembered even in connection with the most trivial and straightforward of answers. If you are asked to name a city in which there was a famous Leaning Tower, the answer would be Pisa; and if you were asked what English king had six wives, two of whom he had ordered to be executed, the answer would be Henry VIII.

In neither case would any other answer be possible, nor would we expect any dispute to arise over either matter. And yet, being human, we may possibly allow typographical errors to creep in, or undergo strange fits of forgetfulness. Thus Henry VIII may show up as Henry VII, and none of us may notice that little slip. Or in place of Pisa as the city of the Leaning Tower, we may inadvertently (thinking of something else) say Venice, and that may get away from us.

As an actual example of such slips, when I went over the first draft of this book (in order to find accidental misstatements) I came across the question, "Name the peninsula separated from the main body of Greece by the Isthmus of Corinth." A peninsula is *connected* to the mainland, not *separated*. I changed that. But who knows what similar faux pas I missed?

Therefore, if you come up with an answer that doesn't match the one given in the book, it may just be that you are not wrong. You can have all the excitement of engaging in a bit of research and discovering that *we* are wrong. I assure you that will rarely happen, but "rarely" is a long way from "never," and if you do catch us in error, please write and tell us. We will be very grateful.

Even more delightful is the chance that a question is ambiguous and lends itself to different interpretations.

For instance, suppose one of the questions were, "What is the most populous nation outside Asia?" The answer most people would expect would be "the United States." But hold on. The Soviet Union is more populous than the United States, and it is not entirely in Asia. To be sure most of it — about three-quarters —

is in Asia, but most of its population and power is in Europe. How would you answer the question, therefore?

It's not just that there's room for argument — it might even be impossible to come to a clear conclusion no matter how much you argue. There's fun in arguing, however, and if there are a number of people present, you might take a vote and fill an entire evening with discussion.

Of course, you might write to us and point out that the question does not allow an unambiguous answer, and that we ought to phrase it differently. (As a matter of fact, when I came across that question. I *did* rephrase it, and made it read, "What is the most populous nation outside Eurasia?" With that change the problem vanishes.)

What if a question reads: "What is the largest island off the coast of Asia?" A possible answer is Sumatra, which approaches quite close to the western shore of Malaya. Sumatra is a large island indeed. To the east of Sumatra, however, is the somewhat larger island of Borneo, but it is considerably farther from the Asian coast than Sumatra is. Then, hundreds of miles east of Borneo is the still larger island of New Guinea, which is not far from the northern coast of Australia. You might argue that Sumatra is clearly Asian and New Guinea is clearly Australian, but which is Borneo, Asian or Australian? For that matter, could you consider Australia itself as an island off the coast of Asia? To be sure, Australia is considered a continent — but should it be?

Or what if a question read: "What is the richest nation on earth?" The obvious answer is the United States, but wait — Do you mean in toto or per capita? The record per capita wealth is held by Kuwait, I believe. Or should you count the value of Saudi Arabia's oil reserves?

But you get the idea. There is more to a Q & A book such as this one than getting the "right" answer. You may have a chance to argue over whether there is such a thing as a right answer in the first place, and that can offer all sorts of intellectual pleasure, and a bit of education as well.

PART 18

BONUS

I AM DOING SOMETHING NOW I did not do in the first two Opus books: presenting something that is unpublished.

In November 1982, I was asked by a magazine to write an article on the future, assuming that medical advance would result in an extended life span for human beings. I therefore wrote an essay entitled "The Forever Generation."

Rather to my astonishment, it was rejected. I never ask the reasons for a rejection, but I rather suspect that the editor did not think the readers of his magazine would be comfortable with my conclusion, for I did not decide that immortality was a Good Thing.

Come to think of it, I am astonished at myself, since I grow old, have just had major surgery, and feel very mortal. I'm approaching the time when I am going to regret the absence of immortality, and yet I can't help it. I still think that immortality is not a Good Thing.

The more I thought about it, the more I resented the loss of a chance to explain to my readers why I think that, and so I've decided to try to slip this one last item past the nice people at Houghton Mifflin, even though it is not a selection from my third hundred.

It is, as I said, a bonus.

from THE FOREVER GENERATION (*never before published*)

It is the ambition of the medical profession to prevent disease in the first place, and to cure it if, despite all efforts, it should make its appearance. This is also the ambition of people generally.

Nor is any limit set on this ambition. Medical research has, as its ultimate goal, immortality; and people, generally, if offered immortality, would accept it. People might even feel it was their right. Death, after all, according to the dominant religion of the West, is not the natural condition of humanity, but the punishment brought on by Adam's sin.

To be sure, the certainty of immortality already exists for millions of the pious who believe in a blissful and eternal existence after death for those who have lived in true accordance with the tenets of their religion. Yet even these, it seems likely, might accept an immortal life on Earth, and thus indefinitely postpone heavenly bliss on the basis of the well-known statement concerning birds in the hand as opposed to those in the bush.

Nor is the promise of physical immortality entirely pie in the sky. There is a strong record of progress. Since the enunciation of the germ theory of disease by Louis Pasteur in the 1860s, the life expectancy of human beings has doubled.

Inoculations, antitoxins, antibiotics, proper standards of hygiene have all contributed to the elimination of infection as a major source of death, so that the average life span has increased from about thirty-six to about seventy-two years in those regions where modern medical procedures are available.

Nor does it mean there are merely a larger number of elderly people who are senile and helpless. People not only live longer, they live healthier, thanks to discoveries that have improved our diet and made possible therapies involving vitamins, trace minerals, and hormones.

However, as of now, we are only beginning to make inroads on the degenerative diseases that involve the gradual breakdown with time of the living mechanism itself. We can, as yet, neither surely prevent nor surely cure such diseases as atherosclerosis, cancer, rheumatoid arthritis, various kidney ailments, or (most of all) the accumulation of general decay that we refer to as old age.

The fact is that the increase in life expectancy has been almost entirely at the expense of *premature* death through infection, malnutrition, environmental damage, and so on. A person who attains the Social Security age of sixty-five is, however, no better off now than he would have been in ancient or medieval times, and life expectancy at that point would be no greater. A much larger percentage of the population reaches sixty-five now than in earlier times, to be sure, but the number of years of life remaining to that percentage is no greater than before.

Nor has the maximum life span been increased. It remains about 115 years. The fact that there are recurrent reports of longer life spans in out-of-the-way places in the world means nothing. The one thing that all the supposedly superold people in the Caucasus and elsewhere have in common is — no birth certificate.

Yet medical advance is continuing at breakneck speed, and it seems reasonable to suppose that we will continue to score victories in favor of life and health.

We may hope for continued improvements in the older techniques: new drugs, newer understanding of vitamins and trace minerals, new diagnostic methods. Beyond that, we may also expect radically new medical advances.

Organ transplantation already exists, but the technique may be greatly extended and improved. Better yet, mechanical prosthetic devices may be used to supplement or replace ailing hearts, lungs, kidneys, or livers. Methods for nerve regeneration may be devised; brain neurons may be strengthened and made to multiply at need. Surgical techniques for reaming out clogged arteries, smoothing arthritic joints, pinpointing and destroying tumors may be worked out. A better understanding of the fundamental biochemistry of the body may lead at last to methods for preventing the onset of cancer. Through biotechnological techniques involving recombinant DNA, defective genes may be altered or replaced.

Most important of all, gerontologists seem to be close to reaching a conclusion about the nature of the changes that bring on old age. That would give us the hope of learning how to prevent them, or to reverse them after onset. There are some indications that old age is controlled by the genes — that living species, other than the simplest, are the victims of "designed obsolescence," that the cells have the capacity to divide only so many times, and to endure without dividing for only so long. In that case, if we learn how to introduce the proper changes in the genes, the factors that produce old age may vanish at a stroke.

There is, of course, no point in supposing that all this will be easy or even difficult-but-inevitable. We can be on the verge of success without ever finding ourselves able to take the last step. Even startling success may leave its gaps. Thus, despite the steady advance in our control of infections over the last twelve decades, we remain helpless in the face of the common cold and, every once in a while, encounter a new infection that gives us trouble, such as the so-called Legionnaire's disease.

Therefore, it may turn out that we may not, after all, be able to extend life significantly or to do away with old age altogether.

But we *may* succeed. That is the important point. Immortality no longer seems an impossible goal. There seems no basic scientific reason to suppose that death is absolutely inevitable.

In that case, what if we do achieve immortality? What if everyone can live as long as he or she likes, provided only that one escapes a physical accident that would scramble the body past the practical hope of repair? In that case, we would have a "Forever Generation" — a world of people who would each retain his or her place in society indefinitely.

What, then, will life be like if the Forever Generation takes over?

♦

The first, and most obvious, consequence is that the population will increase rapidly.

If we assume that people will not only live forever, but will remain healthy, with all organs functioning after the manner of a hale maturity, then we must conclude that males will produce sperm and females ova forever and will, if they wish, be able to have an indefinite number of offspring.

In that case, it would be quite easy for Earth's population to double every five years, if catastrophe does not interfere. If Earth's population is, say, 5 billion at the time immortality is achieved and the Forever Generation is established, it would be something like 5 million billion one century later: a millionfold increase in one hundred years.

This would be quite an impractical situation. Earth could not possibly be made to support so large a number in so short a time. Nor could we expect to circumvent that impossibility by opening up the Moon, and space generally, to human migration. It would be impossible to move so many people into space in so short a time, especially as humanity would continue to increase, in absolute numbers, faster and faster. It would take only seven hundred years or so for the total mass of humanity to equal the total known mass of the Universe.

No, the first thing about the Forever Generation concerning

which we can be absolutely certain is that it would have to practice strict birth control.

Might we assume that since each person lives forever, the only safe thing to do is to give birth to no children at all? Should every immortal human being be sterilized and the problem dismissed in that fashion?

Not so easy. In the first place, humanity will undoubtedly move out into space so that there *will* be (at a reasonable pace) room for more human beings in the Universe, even many more than are presently alive. In that case, clearly, human beings, even immortal ones, must retain the ability to have children.

Then, too, not only will there be more room than now exists, but there will also be a need for replacement, for not even potentially immortal human beings can be expected to live forever.

There is, in the first place, accident. I have seen it estimated that if human beings died only by accident at the present rate and of the present causes, the average life expectancy would be two thousand years. Even if every effort is made to reduce the danger of accident, the life expectancy might increase, but not to infinity. We may expect a continuing small drizzle of accidental death, to which we might add an even smaller drizzle of murders.

Second, there might be medical misadventure. Even if we suppose that human beings are so treated that old age does not come, and can be reversed if it does, it may well happen that, for any number of unforeseen reasons, occasional human beings may prove resistant to the treatment or gradually become resistant. There may well be an appreciable number of human beings who, for one reason or another, eventually, *do* grow old and die.

Third, there is always the question of suicide. Some people, for one reason or another, grow tired of life. Misery, disappointment, frustration, depression force human beings even now to anticipate death though they need wait only a few decades at most to have it come on its own. If human beings thought death would never come, might not weariness drive every one of them to self-destruction sooner or later?

For all these reasons — the extension of the human range, and the small toll taken by accident, murder, medical misadventure, and suicide — children will have to be born, but at a much slower rate than at present. — Still, medical advance in reproductive physiology will make it possible for women to be fertile only when they wish (or are allowed) to have children, so there should be no problem as far as the birthrate is concerned.

♦

If we have an essentially immortal, very-low-birthrate society, we would inevitably have a steadily aging society. The average age will grow greater and greater with time (perhaps leveling off at, say, ten thousand years — at which point unavoidable deaths and occasional births would balance each other).

The prospect of a steadily aging society is a frightening one at first thought. A world full of older and older people, steadily weaker and more senile? Horrible! Jonathan Swift, in the third part of *Gulliver's Travels,* pictured a society of senescent immortals, and his powerful pen made it seem a nightmare indeed.

But that is not the kind of immortality we envisage or have a right to expect. It is not only death we are looking forward to stopping, but the aging process itself. We will have people developing from infancy, through childhood and youth, into a perpetual maturity. Senility is simply not part of the picture.

Might there be other disadvantages to an aging society, though, even one that remains healthily mature? Would particular individuals hold positions in various organizations on Earth and monopolize them indefinitely? How would a vice president of a firm feel serving under a president who would live forever? Would we have a world in which there would be no chance for advancement?

That does not seem likely. It seems reasonable to suppose that if even life itself eventually grows wearisome, particular jobs certainly should. Resignations would be a regular phenomenon and might even be enforced by law (as an American President today is not allowed to serve more than eight years). There would thus be advancement by rotation, rather than by death, and that might be an improvement, since people in their extended lives, by not holding on to any one position too long, would be able to sample a large variety of positions. Life would then remain interesting, and suicide would be staved off longer than would otherwise be expected.

♦

Are there no disadvantages to be seen in a Forever Generation?

I can see several. The longer the life expectancy, the greater the punishment for a gamble that does not pay off.

Consider the famous cry of Sergeant Quirt in *What Price Glory?* "Come on, you sons of bitches, do you expect to live forever?" After all, since you must die eventually, why not die for a great cause?

But what if you *do* expect to live forever? What cause would be worth dying for? What risk would you dare take if failure may mean the loss not of twenty years of life, but twenty thousand years of a life you have not yet grown tired of?

Would not the Forever Generation tend to consist of people who will take no chances, who will cling desperately only to that which they know by experience will work? Would it not make up a quintessentially conservative society?

And would it not grow worse with time?

After all, who would be subtracted from society? In part, those who fall prey to accident, and while accidents might occur to anyone, they will occur more often to those who are a bit more likely to take a risk than to those who are not.

Then again, suicides will be subtracted from society, and who will tend to make their exits sooner? Those who weary sooner, surely, and they are likely to be those who would welcome change and find themselves worn out by the conservatism and standpattism of the Forever Generation. These, it seems to me, would be the people who in the evanescent generations of today would have been the innovators, the initiators, the creators, the leaders.

Those who tend to be content with whatever is, who find themselves satisfied to repeat endlessly the dull routine, would last much longer before desperation set in, and their dullness would increasingly epitomize the Forever Generation.

Is that a small price to pay for the benefits of immortality? — A certain stodginess and dullness in society that would, after all, suit the members of that society?

It may be a larger price than we suspect, for it is not enough to think of the individuals. We must think of the whole species.

In the case of the Forever Generation, evolution would slow to a crawl. Over extended periods of time, the human beings facing the Universe would represent the same, same, same, same minds over the centuries and millennia — thinking the same thoughts, coming up with the same solutions — minds so familiar with the usual questions that all new problems would be met with total incomprehension.

Remember the importance of the new generation. It is not just that they have young brains, because we can imagine that in the Forever Generation brains will stay forever young, or, at least, forever nonsenescent. It is not even that the new generation has empty brains as yet lacking the debris of experience and mistake. The older brains of the Forever Generation might conceivably undergo, periodically, a kind of emptying or rejuvenation. And even if they don't, experience has its advantages, too.

No, what is really important about the new generation is that its members are literally *new!* The brain of a child is not merely young and uncluttered, it is entirely *new* — the product of a gene combination that has very likely not existed in its precise form at any time in the history of humanity.

Every child is a new throw of the dice, a new ticket in the genetic sweepstakes, a new chance, a new hope, a new possible step toward something fundamentally better than humanity as it now exists. In the Forever Generation, the number of children will be so few that the newness will be utterly blanketed and rendered ineffectual.

It is no accident that those living creatures among whom the generations replace each other rapidly are more successful, on the whole, than those in which replacement is slow. The long-lived elephants are magnificent creatures, but there are only two species, both on their way out. The short-lived rodents exist in hundreds of species and flourish even today. The still-shorter-lived insects exist in hundreds of thousands of species and dominate all animal life. We can wipe out so many mammalian species with scarcely an effort, and yet there is no evidence that we have ever succeeded in wiping out a single insect species, even when we've tried with all our might and with every weapon of an advanced technology.

With a large-brained species like ourselves, a comparatively long life is essential, for it takes time for our huge cerebrum to develop fully and even more time to fill it with enough data to become optimally useful. But even with us, there is a limit, and as life grows longer there comes a point where the species weakens.

Even if the Forever Generation remains too intelligent to allow other species to evolve past it, it will still be defeated by problems it cannot solve because it cannot take risks and cannot deal with the unfamiliar.

After all, the death of the individual is programmed in the genes, and any such programming is very likely included because it has survival value for the species as a whole. The species lives because the old generation of individuals, having fulfilled its function, is swept from the board to allow a new and possibly better generation to take over.

And if we interfere with that, we take the terrible risk of giving immortality to the individual at the price of mortality to the species.

A final word —

Don't think that I can avoid feeling guilty over preparing these Opus *books. It does seem an example of hubris to rub readers' noses into all these books of mine, and to include a number of dubious items such as anthologies, quiz books, and so on, in order (it might seem) to increase the numbers.*

I do apologize — but I'm going to continue preparing them, anyway.

For one thing, Austin Olney of Houghton Mifflin insists. He is the kindliest person I know, but there is iron hidden under his velvet glove. For another, I enjoy doing these books.

You have the consolation of knowing that I can't keep it up forever, since no one lives forever, but I'm going to try to hang on as long as I can and to keep on writing as long as I live — so be prepared.

APPENDIX

MY THIRD
HUNDRED BOOKS

231	How Did We Find Out About Volcanoes?	Walker	1981
232	Visions of the Universe	Cosmos Store	1981
*233	Catastrophes!	Fawcett	1981
*234	Isaac Asimov Presents the Best Science Fiction of the 19th Century	Daw Books	1981
*235	The Seven Cardinal Virtues of Science Fiction	Fawcett	1981
*236	Fantastic Creatures	Franklin Watts	1981
237	The Sun Shines Bright	Doubleday	1981
238	Change!	Houghton Mifflin	1981
*239	Raintree Reading Series 1	Raintree	1981
240	A Grossery of Limericks	Norton	1981
*241	Miniature Mysteries	Taplinger	1981
*242	The Twelve Crimes of Christmas	Avon	1981
*243	Isaac Asimov Presents the Great Science Fiction Stories: 1944	Daw Books	1981
*244	Space Mail 2	Fawcett	1981
*245	Tantalizing Locked Room Mysteries	Walker	1982
*246	TV: 2000	Fawcett	1982
*247	Laughing Space	Houghton Mifflin	1982
248	How Did We Find Out About Life in the Deep Sea?	Walker	1982
249	The Complete Robot	Doubleday	1982
*250	Speculations	Houghton Mifflin	1982
*251	Flying Saucers	Fawcett	1982
252	Exploring the Earth and the Cosmos	Crown	1982
*253	Raintree Reading Series 2	Raintree	1982
254	How Did We Find Out About the Beginning of Life?	Walker	1982
*255	Dragon Tales	Fawcett	1982
*256	The Big Apple Mysteries	Avon	1982
257	Asimov's Biographical Encyclopedia of Science and Technology (2nd revised edition)	Doubleday	1982
*258	Isaac Asimov Presents the Great Science Fiction Stories: 1945	Daw Books	1982
259	Isaac Asimov Presents Superquiz	Dembner	1982
*260	The Last Man on Earth	Fawcett	1982
*261	Science Fiction A to Z	Houghton Mifflin	1982
262	Foundation's Edge	Doubleday	1982
*263	Isaac Asimov Presents the Best Fantasy of the Nineteenth Century	Beaufort	1982
*264	Isaac Asimov Presents the Great Science Fiction Stories: 1946	Daw Books	1982
265	How Did We Find Out About the Universe?	Walker	1982

266	Counting the Eons	Doubleday	1983
267	The Winds of Change and Other Stories	Doubleday	1983
*268	Isaac Asimov Presents the Great Science Fiction Stories: 1947	Daw Books	1983
*269	Show Business Is Murder	Avon	1983
*270	Hallucination Orbit	Farrar, Straus & Giroux	1983
*271	Caught in the Organ Draft	Farrar, Straus & Giroux	1983
272	The Roving Mind	Prometheus	1983
*273	The Science Fiction Weight-Loss Book	Crown	1983
274	The Measure of the Universe	Harper & Row	1983
*275	Isaac Asimov Presents the Best Horror and Supernatural Stories of the Nineteenth Century	Beaufort	1983
*276	Starships	Fawcett	1983
277	The Union Club Mysteries	Doubleday	1983
278	Norby, the Mixed-Up Robot	Walker	1983
*279	Isaac Asimov Presents the Great Science Fiction Stories: 1948	Daw Books	1983
280	How Did We Find Out About Genes?	Walker	1983
281	The Robots of Dawn	Doubleday	1983
*282	13 Horrors of Halloween	Avon	1983
*283	Creations	Crown	1983
284	Isaac Asimov Presents Superquiz 2	Dembner	1983
*285	Wizards	New American Library	1983
*286	Those Amazing Electronic Thinking Machines	Franklin Watts	1983
*287	Computer Crimes and Capers	Academy Chicago	1983
*288	Intergalactic Empires	New American Library	1983
*289	Machines That Think	Holt, Rinehart & Winston	1983
290	X Stands for Unknown	Doubleday	1984
*291	One Hundred Great Fantasy Short-Short Stories	Doubleday	1984
*292	Raintree Reading Series 3	Raintree	1984
*293	Isaac Asimov Presents the Great Science Fiction Stories: 1949	Daw Books	1984
*294	Witches	New American Library	1984
*295	Murder on the Menu	Avon	1984
*296	Young Mutants	Harper & Row	1984
*297	Isaac Asimov Presents the Best SF Firsts	Beaufort Books	1984
298	Norby's Other Secret	Walker	1984
299	How Did We Find Out About Computers?	Walker	1984
300	Opus 300	Houghton Mifflin	

*Anthologies